NO LONGER PROPERTY OF
SEATTLE PUBLIC LIBRARY

D1042360

Her Mother's Secret

Also by Rosanna Ley

The Villa
Bay of Secrets
Return to Mandalay
The Saffron Trail
Last Dance in Havana
The Little Theatre by the Sea

ROSANNA LEY

Her Mother's Secret

Quercus

First published in Great Britain in 2018 by

Quercus Editions Ltd
Carmelite House
50 Victoria Embankment
London EC4Y 0DZ

An Hachette UK company

Copyright © 2018 Rosanna Ley

The moral right of Rosanna Ley to be
identified as the author of this work has been
asserted in accordance with the Copyright,
Designs and Patents Act, 1988.

All rights reserved. No part of this publication
may be reproduced or transmitted in any form
or by any means, electronic or mechanical,
including photocopy, recording, or any
information storage and retrieval system,
without permission in writing from the publisher.

A CIP catalogue record for this book is available
from the British Library

HB ISBN 978 1 78648 341 6
TPB ISBN 978 1 78648 342 3
EB ISBN 978 1 78648 344 7

This book is a work of fiction. Names, characters,
businesses, organizations, places and events are
either the product of the author's imagination
or used fictitiously. Any resemblance to
actual persons, living or dead, events or
locales is entirely coincidental.

10 9 8 7 6 5 4 3 2 1

Typeset by CC Book Production

Printed and bound in Great Britain by Clays Ltd, St Ives plc

To Grey who does the driving and to all
the camper vans who have ever taken us to France
(Ralph, Colin and Claude).

CHAPTER I

Colette

Colette let herself in at the front door of the house on Peverell Terrace – she'd been lodging here for a year so it felt as much like home as anywhere had lately. Before that . . . There had been other lodgings, other jobs, helping to look after her grandparents. And before that, fifteen years before that, was Belle-Île-en-Mer, the island of her birth.

She slipped her jacket on to the hook by the door, stepped on to the first stair, put a hand on the wooden banister, and saw it. A letter. Thin air-mail paper. Her name in spidery, sloping, old-fashioned writing that for a second looked like . . . But it wasn't. Colette exhaled. She grabbed the envelope and took the stairs at a gallop – just in case Adam and Louise her friendly landlords should emerge from the kitchen and fancy a chat. Because it wasn't from her mother, no, but it had a French postmark and so it had to be from Belle-Île.

Something must have happened. Colette opened the door to her studio on the second floor. The one room comprised sitting area, bedroom and kitchenette; the small bathroom was

1

next door. Usually, she walked over to the window the second she came in, because the special thing about the studio was the view. But not today. Today, she dropped her bag on to the table and held the envelope gingerly between thumb and forefinger as if it might bite or even swallow her whole. She took a deep breath and ripped it open.

Dear Colette.

No, it wasn't her mother's hand. Colette's gaze flipped to the bottom of the short letter. *Sincerely, Francine Quintin*, she read. Francine was her mother's neighbour. She read on, with more urgency now. Why would Francine Quintin be writing to her?

J'espère que tu vas bien. It was written in French of course and these days Colette hardly spoke the language of her homeland, let alone read it. The writing was difficult to decipher too. She frowned, let the words work to form their old meanings. Her British mother had always spoken English with her from as far back as she could remember – at least when no one else was around. Perhaps Thea Lenoire had known even then that one day Colette would leave Belle-Île-en-Mer and return to the place that was Thea's beginning rather than her own. Colette sighed. She had lived in Cornwall for fifteen of her thirty-two years. By now, she reckoned she thought in English too.

I hope you are well, she read again. *I am sorry to have to tell you that your mother is not.*

Her mother was not well. The unfamiliar French words danced clumsily on the page. *Your mother is very ill*, she read. *She may not have long to live. She has leukaemia.*

Colette stared at the words. *May not have long to live. Leukaemia.* But her mother was only sixty-five. These days that was still quite young. At least, it wasn't old. How could her mother have leukaemia?

2

You should come here as soon as possible, the letter went on, *before it is too late. She does not know I am writing. But as you are aware, there is only you.*

Colette stared at the words until they blurred. *There is only you . . .* Her mobile bleeped a text in. She ignored it.

She couldn't believe that everything outside still looked as it had a few minutes ago, before she'd entered the house. How was it possible? And yet . . . From the picture window, a shaft of early evening sunlight still dappled the water and slanted through on to the bleached pine floorboards of the studio. Colette crossed the room. She looked out over Porthleven harbour and the green-grey ocean; the assorted buildings on the other side of the inlet, the higgledy red-ridge tiles and grey slate roofs of the tall Victorian houses in Bay View Terrace, the wide expanse of cloudy sky. There was a ship way out at sea, no more than an inky stamp on the horizon, while in the harbour basin the brightly coloured pleasure craft and fishing boats bobbed in the yellow light.

Her mother had leukaemia. Just over a year ago, Colette's grandparents had both died – her grandfather only three weeks after the woman he adored – and Colette had been upset and furious that her mother hadn't even had the grace to attend the funeral. Colette hadn't spoken to her since. Before that there had been other issues; a long estrangement, so many things unsaid. And before that . . . Colette didn't even want to think about it now.

She looked down at Francine's letter still in her hand. She pictured Francine's dour features and thin, complaining mouth. Their neighbour in Sauzon had always had her nose to the *rideaux*, her crochet-lace curtains, desperate to catch all the action – probably because it had been years since she'd

3

experienced any herself, Colette used to think. Francine seemed to know everything that went on. She had seen fifteen-year-old Colette creeping home late with her *amour*, she had seen them kissing at the gate, and more besides. And she hadn't wasted a second before relaying every detail to Maman.

'Clearly, it is because the girl has no father.' Colette could hear the smugness in Francine's voice. 'And incidentally, Thea, I have not seen either of you in church for a while, eh?'

Her mother's murmured reply, Colette could not catch.

'You must take a firm hand with the girl, Thea,' continued Francine. 'She is your responsibility now, you know.'

Responsibility. That was Francine. And it seemed that now, nothing had changed. She still knew it all. And so, it had fallen to her to tell Colette that her mother had leukaemia.

Gulls were still circling over the harbour and people were still wandering down the long finger of the granite jetty eating ice-creams and enjoying the last of the early evening sun on this late spring day. Nothing had changed and yet everything had changed. There was an art exhibition in the old lifeboat station, it was market day and Porthleven had been heaving, crammed with families who flocked here at half-terms and holidays. Colette knew more about that than most – she worked in the holiday letting office in the harbour.

Why had her mother not told Colette herself? Why had Francine not simply picked up the phone? But Colette knew why. Francine wouldn't know her number and as for her mother . . . Colette grabbed her mobile from her bag, found the number she called so rarely, listened to the phone ring and ring.

Without realising it, she had crumpled the letter in her fist. She straightened it out. 'Maman.' *There is only you.* Colette felt

4

the emotional floodgates shift. She closed her eyes, felt herself sway. She had turned her back on her mother and the island fifteen years ago and God knows she'd had her reasons. Most of the time it was easy enough not to think about it. But now . . .

Colette's mobile rang. She glanced at the number but didn't answer it, continued looking out instead over the jumbled buildings around Porthleven harbour – the old fish-curing factory, the china clay store, the ice house, the lime kiln and the black and white Ship Inn. This town had been her mother's home – at least until she'd left Porthleven at the age of eighteen. Had her mother felt as Colette had felt when she left Belle-Île-en-Mer? They'd been almost exactly the same age after all. She realised that she had no idea; they'd never talked of it. There were so many things they hadn't talked of. And there was still so much that Colette didn't understand. But . . . Leukaemia. Her mother could be dying. And what Francine had said was true – there was only her.

The ringtone of her mobile stopped, then started up again. Mark was not the kind of man who could be ignored. She put the letter on the table and picked up her phone. 'Hello.'

'Hi, sweetie.' He sounded almost unbearably cheerful. 'I'm outside.'

'Oh.' She couldn't think. Her mind was still trying to process the contents of the letter, this awful news. 'Mark . . .' For a moment, it hovered unspoken on her tongue.

'So, can I come in?' There was laughter in his voice now.

Colette forced herself to focus. 'Course you can.' She was vaguely surprised that her voice sounded so normal. She went to the window, looked directly down to the pavement where he was standing; tall, dark, smart in his light-pink shirt, dark chinos and jacket.

5

He grinned and waved.

'I'll come down.' Colette shoved the letter into her bag. She took a deep breath and headed for the stairs. Her emotions were tangled, her feelings numb. She wasn't sure that she was ready to talk about this to anyone, not even Mark – at least not yet.

CHAPTER 2

Colette

In Koto Kai's – one of their favourite restaurants – Colette let Mark do most of the talking while Francine's letter continued to simmer quietly in her bag.

'How's your day been?' he asked her, his attention half on the menu.

'Oh, busy, you know.' Today at the letting office had been much the same as usual: managing the cleaners, a complaint from a holidaymaker, more bookings – mostly for the summer to come but also for winter when the town was at its most dramatic and chilly with high winds and even higher seas sometimes, lashing the houses of Harbour Road. 'How was yours?'

Over cocktails, he filled her in. Mark managed an estate agents; it was successful and he was on commission. Privately, Colette thought that the number of places being bought for holiday lets was shocking; it didn't seem right that house prices were far too high for the locals to afford to buy. She'd said this to Mark on more than one occasion and he was always outraged.

'Everyone has a right to move around,' he said. 'Look at you. Everyone has a right to find somewhere else they want to live.' He had a point. And Colette knew him well enough to let it go.

They ordered, and when the starter came Mark launched into a long story about a property along Loe Bar that was derelict but had great potential. '. . . And they offered a hundred and thirty thousand for the place. I mean, after all that, what a joke.'

Colette blinked at him. Her starter of squid with mango salad had tasted as delicious as ever, but she had almost eaten it without noticing.

He leaned forward. 'Colette? Are you even listening to me?'

'Sorry, yes.' She tried to recapture some of the conversation. 'With those sea views? Did they really?' She forced a little laugh, unconvincing enough for Mark to frown.

The waitress brought their mains – pork belly with pak choi for him and Massaman chicken curry with jasmine rice for her. It was decorative, highly aromatic and she had chosen it for the delicate blend of spices with coconut. But tonight she simply wasn't hungry.

Before she could even taste it, Mark reached over to put his hand on hers. She looked down at their two hands. Why did she feel the urge to pull hers from under the pressure of his? Why didn't she just tell him about the letter? He was so caring. What was the matter with her?

Colette had been feeling pretty vulnerable that first day Mark Johnson had walked into the letting office. It was only weeks after her grandfather's death and she felt so lost now that both her grandparents were gone. She wanted to work, she needed a distraction, but she couldn't help thinking of Grandpa's sad face and how her mother hadn't even come to say goodbye.

8

Mark was asking about a property they'd been letting out that was about to be marketed for sale and he'd chosen Colette to talk to.

'You're new here, aren't you?' It was a casual enough enquiry but even then, Colette had sensed that with Mark, nothing was casual. He saw something and he went for it – that was his style.

'Only a few months.' Since first arriving in Porthleven fifteen years ago, Colette had drifted; it had seemed so hard to find her way. She had worked a summer season in the town as a waitress, staying with her grandparents, finding her feet as Granny J had put it; she had lived in Truro and done more of the same. Her grandparents hadn't seemed too surprised that Colette had left Belle-Île and she hadn't wanted to confide the reasons; they had accepted that she wanted to travel, wanted to see something of the UK and that she wanted to spend time with them. Her grandparents were pleased, she knew. She had done a stint in St Ives working in a gift shop this time and had returned to Porthleven for the summer season to be near them. Only when their health had begun to fail, had she made things more permanent. She had secured a job in a business that continued all year round and she had found the little studio in Peverell Terrace.

'New in town too?'

'Not exactly.' She explained a bit about the coming and going.

'So you have family here?' He didn't seem in any hurry to get back to work. Colette caught the glance of Tracey, her boss.

'My grandparents lived here, but—' She didn't want to go on, but Mark seemed to understand.

He leaned closer. 'I'd like to talk some more – over a drink perhaps?'

'Oh. Well . . .' She hadn't been going out so much lately.

'How about The Ship at eight tonight?' Even then, Mark had smoothed his way over her hesitations as if they didn't exist. 'It's full of old codgers,' he added, 'but they're a nice enough lot if you don't mind listening to tales of smuggling and wrecking in Porthleven in days gone by.'

Colette had laughed, surprised at herself, not sure if he was joking or not. She'd already come across quite a few of the old-timers, the 'fish 'n' guts Porthleveners,' as some referred to them, though this was a town full of incomers, whether from two years ago or twenty. Even her grandparents weren't born here; they'd moved to Cornwall in the early fifties shortly before Colette's mother was born. Porthleven had been a thriving town back then, apparently – thirteen butchers' shops alone, her grandmother had told her once.

Colette had looked at Mark with his dapper dark hair, grey suit and blue tie. Why not? she'd thought. Why not admit it? She was lonely. She'd made friends, but they were hard to keep when you moved around a lot. There had been a few boyfriends too, but no one serious. She was still feeling a bit raw, but she needed to get out, she needed to shake herself up a little and get on with her life. Maybe this confident-sounding man might help her do that. 'OK, I'd like to.' And that was how she and Mark had begun.

'Is something wrong, darling?' His voice was tender now, his brown eyes kind.

He was a good man, Colette reminded herself. A nice man. He had taken her out, talked to her, comforted her when she was still grieving for the loss of her grandparents. He was always there for her, he would help her if she needed him – or even if she didn't, she thought sometimes. She gazed down at the food on her plate. So what was stopping her? She ought to be telling her boyfriend about this, not bottling it up inside.

Mark removed his hand, nodded encouragingly and started eating.

'Well . . .' Colette opened her mouth to tell him about the letter, about her mother, about the leukaemia. Then she saw a flicker in his eyes as he glanced over her shoulder.

She stopped. It was this thing he did – as if someone else might be having a more interesting conversation, as if he was slightly irritated that she was taking time to get going. She'd seen that flicker before. When she wanted to have some time to herself and he wanted to do something together. When a waiter in a restaurant didn't respond quickly enough to his requests. When an attractive woman on a nearby table was laughing a glittering laugh. Colette knew that look and she didn't much like it. She didn't want to tell Mark about the letter because he would immediately take charge, he would tell her what to do about it. And this time, for once, she wanted to make up her own mind.

'Up to our eyes at the office,' she said, 'that's all.' And she took a mouthful of caramelised sweet potato.

'Hmm.' He frowned. 'They work you too hard at that place. But now it's the weekend.' He grinned his handsome grin. 'So, how about a day out tomorrow? We could go up to Bude or Exmoor. Have a walk. A pub lunch. Some you and me time. What do you reckon?' He turned his attention back to his pork belly.

'Lovely.' Colette felt a ridiculous panic begin to rise. She was breathless though she hadn't even moved. She got to her feet. 'I just have to . . .' She grabbed her bag. 'Go to the bathroom.'

'Oh? OK, fine.' He watched her curiously as she left the

table. She had the odd feeling that sometime in the future he'd be telling this story to someone, say – *So then she dashes off to the bathroom right in the middle of dinner. I ask you. How crazy is that?*

Colette gripped the banister and made her descent down the wide wooden staircase with the wrought-iron railings, huge paintings of Porthleven's stormy waves staring down at her from the walls above. She shut the door of the Ladies' behind her and let out a breath. Mark was lovely, but he didn't always understand that sometimes she needed more space. She appreciated the way that he organised their lives. She loved his tenderness, their intimacy, the security he had given her. But just occasionally she felt as trapped as she had on the island. Trapped and somehow losing an important part of her.

It must be the letter that had brought this on . . . In the loo, she pulled it from her bag and read it again. She closed her eyes and tried to recapture something of her mother. Her voice: the pauses and the stresses; the rhythm that was her mother's rhythm, her way of talking, her way of life. Colette thought of her childhood days – the dreaminess in her mother's eyes sometimes when she looked at her, as if she was almost not there at all; as if she were forever thinking of someone else, someone she loved more perhaps, some place she would rather be. So who had always come first for Thea Lenoire? Not her husband Sébastien, not her parents in Cornwall, and certainly not her daughter.

'Maman, maman . . .' Colette remembered how she had tried to get her mother's attention, tugging on her arm and apron strings until she would push her gently away. 'Run along and play, Colette. Maman is busy.'

Always busy. Running the flower shop, tending the plants, arranging the bouquets for christenings, weddings and funerals.

There is a funeral parlour in Sauzon, so why not a flower shop? Colette had often heard her say. *Why not? It is not just for death, no, it is for remembering. For life, for colour. To bring a smile to people's faces. Why not?*

Colette swallowed hard. And now? Would she be able to get her mother's attention now? Would she find any answers to all the things she needed to know? She shoved the letter back in her bag. She'd been in here for ages – Mark would be sending in the cavalry if she was any longer.

She made her way back up the elegant staircase into the long narrow room with a high ceiling that had been used as a sail-making loft once upon a time. Now, the Asian-style restaurant had positioned all its tables in a long row next to the windows for the best harbour views and a pleasing sense of space, each one lit with a cream candle in a brass lantern. The atmosphere was buzzy. There were more candles in a metal cage on the gleaming counter of the bar and ceiling lights encased in large woven baskets. The panelled walls were cream and white, the wooden floor the colour of hazelnuts. Usually, Colette found the decor tranquil, but tonight . . .

Sure enough, Mark looked worried as she slipped back on to the bench seat by the window.

'Hey,' he said, 'are you OK?'

Colette nodded. 'But ready to go when you are.' She pushed her plate to one side.

He raised an eyebrow. 'Not feeling well?'

'I'm not very hungry.' She gave a little shrug. 'Sorry.'

He leaned towards her and once again took her hand. 'Your place or mine?' He was smiling, and Colette smiled back at him. It was hardly his fault. How could he know what was wrong when she hadn't told him?

'Mine?' It was only five minutes' walk away and Adam and Louise never minded. 'For a change,' she added quickly, seeing his expression.

He barely hesitated, though Colette knew he'd much rather go back to Highburrow. 'Course not.' He got out his wallet and waved away her offer to contribute. 'Don't be silly. I earn lots more than you and anyway, we're together, aren't we?' And then spent several long minutes frowning and scrutinising the bill. Colette didn't mind. He was generous, but also careful; there was nothing wrong with that.

They strolled back along the harbourside towards Colette's, hand in hand. 'You've been quiet tonight,' he said. Spindrifts of light from lamps and windows seemed to bounce gently against the slick surface of the water, and she could hear music and voices wafting from a bar and restaurant nearby. 'Miles away.'

She moved closer towards him as they walked. So almost in synch, she thought. And it was her fault they weren't closer. 'Sorry, darling.' She squeezed his hand. Belle-Île, she realised, was never as far away as she'd tried to make it. Here in Porth-leven there were echoes of the place everywhere she looked.

'I always wanted to have a French girlfriend,' Mark said as they turned to climb Institute Hill. It was dark up here and narrow, but the steep path would bring them right up to the house on the Terrace. 'It was my ambition.'

She laughed. 'But I'm not French, I'm half-British, remember.'

'Even better.' He turned to kiss the top of her head. 'You've still got a sexy accent and you understand me.'

They were halfway up the path already and Colette let her gaze travel over the rooftops and back towards the shiny darkness of the sea.

'It's stupid, though.' Mark bent so that he was breathing into her hair. He looked up towards the terrace past Flagstaff House, and Colette followed his gaze – and his train of thought. He was right, she thought. She did understand him. 'Me rattling around in a whole place of my own, you living in someone else's house here. When we could be together all the time.'

This conversation came up every three weeks or so, give or take. Which told her how important it was and how much he thought about it. She should be flattered. She *was* flattered. *Why do you want to live in someone else's house when we could live together in mine?*

It was a good question. Was it Mark? Was it her? Was it whatever they formed together? His house at Highburrow was modern and spacious; it had all the mod cons but . . . It didn't have the right view, she had joked to him in the past. The truth was that although Mark wanted it to happen, it was a commitment Colette wasn't ready to make.

She answered the question by reaching up to him for a kiss, then more kisses when they got inside and by the time they made love in the bed that was in her space, rented or not, the question had dissolved. It would re-form, though, like the snail trails of foam that circled the rocks on Pointe des Poulains, the northernmost point of Belle-Île-en-Mer; it would re-form and crash into the rocks outside the harbour once more. It always did.

In the middle of the night, Colette slipped out of bed, careful not to wake Mark. She sat in the chair by the window and switched on her laptop. The waxing moon was sending a pool of light on to the water in the harbour; the mismatched buildings circling the basin stood guard; the dark, curling sea was quiet, gently rolling in. Colette googled channel ferries, transport links and finally the ferry from Quiberon to Belle-Île. She scribbled notes, made calculations, got out her credit card. At last she closed down her laptop and sat staring out to sea and thinking of that other sea she'd grown up with. It had been such a long time. She closed her eyes. Felt a shiver of fear – or maybe anticipation? But she was ill and she was her mother. How could she not go?

When Mark woke up at seven-thirty, she greeted him with coffee and a croissant. Guilt breakfast, she thought. But it was a new day and things seemed clearer this morning.

'Haven't we skipped something here?' he groaned, but he sat up and ate it anyway.

Colette took a deep breath. She reached out and smoothed his dark hair from his forehead. It wouldn't be easy. 'Mark, I had a letter yesterday,' she began.

'Oh?'

'It was about my mother.'

He raised an eyebrow. 'About her?'

'It was from her neighbour, a woman called Francine.'

'What did it say?' She had all his attention now.

'My mother's ill.' Colette swallowed. Why would she cry? Her mother had never believed in her. Why would she cry for her now?

'What's wrong with her?' Mark pushed the tray aside and swung his legs out of the bed. He was naked except for black boxers.

'She has leukaemia.' Her voice trembled. It was insidious, the word as much as the disease. Colette could almost feel it growing and taking over.

'Why the hell didn't you say?' Mark grabbed hold of her and held her close. 'So that's what was bothering you last night?'

She nodded, didn't trust herself to speak.

'It's all right, darling,' he soothed. 'I'm here. I'll look after you.'

'I have to go back there.' She leaned against his shoulder. 'I have to see her.' Mark was a tall and sturdy man. His solidity had always made her feel safe.

'Yes, darling.' He was stroking her hair. 'We'll both go. I'll get some time off work, we'll—'

'No.' She drew away from him then. This was why she hadn't told him last night. 'I'm sorry, Mark.' She hated to say it. 'But I have to do this alone.'

CHAPTER 3

Étienne

Étienne sat bolt upright in bed, blinked, stared sightlessly into the darkness. *Merde.* Where the hell was he? He was bathed in a cold sweat. What in the *nom de Dieu* had he been dreaming about?

But he knew. In that same moment, he knew. He tore a hand through his hair, blinked again as if he could dispel them so easily – the Summer Gang of the old days: Denis's narrow brown face, Jules's bullish sturdiness, the gleam of triumph in Yann's dark eyes. Gabriel . . . And now, Étienne was sufficiently awake to register the skinny sliver of light creeping between the shutters, the fact that this bed was facing the window. It was a different bed in a different room. He was not at home – *naturellement*, he was not at home.

He sighed, ran his palm along the satin of the auber-gine-coloured counterpane. The fabric was so smooth and perfect that the roughness of his skin caught a thread. Not that it mattered. His mother had always insisted on good-quality bedding and towels. Only now, it no longer mattered, because

18

she was gone. He resumed a prone position, stared up at the ceiling – white, corniced, no cobwebs. Waited for the sadness of losing his mother to pass, as she had. He had already been grieving for six months, and he suspected the grieving would never stop, only fade.

But that was only a part of it. There were shadows on this white ceiling, always shadows, even if he were to fling open the wooden shutters and let in the spring morning. There would always be shadows because he was here on the island of Belle-Île, which he had not set foot on for twenty years; he was here in his mother's house, in his old bed. And this was the bed he had slept in during all those blissful, uncomplicated other summers. The summers before.

Étienne groaned. It was too early to get up – surely? He'd brought pen and paper with him, even his laptop; he was a writer, was this not so? One had to look the part; one had to be ready. Inspiration might as easily tap him on the shoulder here as in Locmariaquer. There was a chance, at least, that a half-decent idea might come.

Back home, on the other side of that deceptively narrow strait of water between the Gulf of Morbihan and Belle-Île-en-Mer, Étienne got up whenever he wanted to, he had no one else to annoy. Who would care if he rose at 4 a.m. to finish a chapter because it had burnt its way into his dreams? Who would object to him falling asleep at noon at his desk? It was far better, he had decided long ago, for a writer to be a solitary being. That writer could then be as selfish as he pleased. He could nip into that other world whenever the urge arose, returning to reality only when the necessary work was done. He could daydream around the house and be blissfully unaware of how the hours were passing. He was thinking, he was

19

working – the two were intertwined as threads in a rope. He could relax as and when he wanted to. He could . . .

Run away, some other voice replied. Étienne brushed it from him, this insect of truth. He was adept at this. And besides, he was here, was he not? He was here, tasked as befitted a son's duty with sorting out all his mother's things. Things she had collected over the years: heavy satin bedspreads – one of which was still lying like a dead creature on top of him – delicately embroidered tablecloths, thick towels warm from the airing cupboard that he longed to bury his face in. Things like her clothes . . . *Merde*, he couldn't face the clothes. Heavy wooden furniture – that was easier, it didn't feel sentimental, he didn't think his mother would object to a man from Le Palais coming in with a big white van to buy it all in one lot to sell in his second-hand shop to someone young and broke who needed to fill their new home.

But the rest of it . . . *Mon Dieu*. Étienne had taken it all in briefly when he arrived last night, paced around each small room like some half-crazed caged animal, opening cupboards and drawers to get the gist of what he had to do, how much stuff there might be, not stopping for a moment, lest it start seeping into him. The grief of losing her. This place.

Had it been a nightmare? He frowned. It was hardly surprising that he would have a nightmare in the place where the biggest nightmare of all had occurred, the place he'd imagined he'd never come back to, despite the fact that after his father's death, Étienne's mother had chosen to spend her final years here. And yet he could close his eyes now and still see their faces. Jules, Yann, Denis and Gabriel – the Summer Gang. And now that the cold sweat had evaporated, they were all grinning as they so often had back then – at least, before. Denis was

20

slapping Jules on the back and Yann was shouting something over his shoulder as he pedalled madly into the summer wind. They had all been friends, every summer. And yet they had all lost touch. Or to be more exact, Étienne had lost contact with every last one of them.

He sat up, swung his legs out of bed. The way to dispel the bad thoughts of night-time was to raise the blinds on the new day, he'd always found. So, he flung open the wooden shutters to look at that day. The light was still pale, but promising; the sun sending silvery fronds on to the surface of the water – reminiscent of the doily-like leaves of Dusty Miller, a furry plant that flourished in Étienne's garden back in Locmariaquer. He leaned on the windowsill and threaded his fingers through the decorative tracery on the wrought-iron grille. This house in Sauzon, his mother's house – his house now, he reminded himself, but only until it could be sold, that much was a sure thing – squatted above the café and spread out behind it, so that the overhanging first floor was able to house two bedrooms, a bathroom and a sitting room, while the ground floor boasted only a kitchen and utility. It was unusual, yes (Étienne imagined himself saying this to the *notaire*), but it had the undisputed advantage of looking out over the pretty port of Sauzon and the sea. It was, had always been, idyllic.

Étienne surveyed the scene in the road below. Beyond the blue metal railings, Quai Guerveur was drifting into early-morning life. The café owner, a cigarette hanging between his lips, was dragging out metal chairs and tables, a few women with shopping bags walked purposefully alongside the harbour, heading for the boulangerie perhaps, which would be open by now. Boats, so many boats, all shapes and sizes – tourist crafts

21

most of them – sat patiently waiting for their day to begin. But there was one fisherman hauling a crate on to the harbour wall. Étienne craned to see, watched him rip off his oilskin, hoist the crate on to the fish stall. Étienne sniffed. He could smell the fish – and the sea air, which was the air he always breathed at home too in Locmariaquer, but which was subtly different here. And he could smell coffee.

He needed no further prompt. He loped downstairs to the kitchen to make some. Coffee, then a shower, then down to buy a croissant from the boulangerie – hopefully without talking to anyone on the way. Back to the house, phone the *notaire* to get the ball rolling, start sorting the house. That was the plan. He straightened his shoulders. He had a job to do here. It had taken him six months to even get to the island. And so, yes, there would be cobwebs on the ceiling if, when she'd left, his mother had not had the forethought to employ a cleaning woman to come in once a fortnight to keep the place nice, as if she might one day come back to live here again. But she didn't. She stayed over on the mainland in the nursing home he had found for her – until the end. Étienne missed her. Even so. He would grieve in his own way and in his own time.

He put the tinny old percolator on to boil. Why was he so angry? There was coffee, thankfully, in the same cupboard to the left of the old stove – along with dozens of other old tins holding an assortment of once-useful items. He might go out for a walk in the afternoon, he decided – somewhere safe and pleasant (as a writer, 'pleasant' was one of his most hated words, but as a person he found uses for it) such as the harbourside. He didn't think about the other obvious option. But mostly, Étienne simply wanted to get this place sorted as soon as he could and with as little fuss or interaction with the islanders

22

as possible. And then he would be on the first ferry home, no worries. 'Just try and stop me,' he said out loud, to the day or to the house or even perhaps to the island itself.

His coffee brewed with the usual spitting and snarling that he remembered from this percolator in the past, and he took it upstairs to the desk in the living room which also overlooked the port and Rue Saint-Nicolas behind. The flower shop was still there, he noted. He switched on his laptop, located the café's WiFi and clicked on Facebook.

Like many people, Étienne had a love–hate relationship with Facebook. Mostly he hated it – he had a particular dislike of posts about food and posts from people compelled to announce they had arrived at some swanky restaurant or hotel the night before. Who cared? He didn't like posts about animals (especially kittens) and political posts made him grind his teeth. Photos of happy family groups made him resentful and suspicious – why didn't they simply enjoy each other's company instead of notifying Facebook what a splendid time they were having? He didn't want to know who was ill (it was depressing, and surely there was something inherently wrong with grieving on a social media site?) and he sure as hell didn't want to know what anyone had watched on TV last night. There should, he concluded, be a 'hate' button. And yes, there it was, at thirty-five Étienne had become a grumpy old man. Most of all, he disliked authors publicising their books on Facebook, which was the only thing he ever used it for.

Apart from today. Today, he bit his thumbnail, stared out to sea and typed in the first name: *Yann Chirac*. Yann had to come first – hadn't he always? There were several photos but only one that could be him. Étienne zoomed in. If he became

23

friends with that person, Facebook suggested, he could see all their posts. Étienne declined.

After forty-five minutes of tentative stalking, he gave up. None of them had ever tried to find him, had they? His site was public to all, hence the impersonal nature of his posts and the infrequency of them too. 'Social media is the future,' his agent and friend Didier had said to him recently. 'You've got to be on it, to win it.' Étienne played the game – but grudgingly. A man had to live, but he didn't have to sell his soul.

In the boulangerie he submitted to the mild questioning of Madame Riou even before he got to the front of the queue. 'Lucie's son, isn't it?' She peered around at him. 'So sad. *Je suis désolée.* Lucie is much missed.'

'*Merci beaucoup, Madame.*' He tried not to sound ungracious, but . . .

'*Oui.* I heard you were coming back.'

So, the Sauzon grapevine was still flourishing. In front of him and behind, people were nodding and murmuring their condolences. '*Merci.*' He smiled, nodded, sighed.

'Your mother would have been happy to see you back, you know.' Madame spoke with some certainty. Her eyes were sharp, her fingers nimble as she attended to orders, rearranging pastries in baskets, loading the shelf with more crusty baguettes.

Étienne was at the counter now. Yes, it was true that his mother had constantly wanted him to come over to visit. '*Un croissant, s'il vous plaît, Madame.*' How sad and lonely it sounded, he thought. '*Et une baguette,*' as an afterthought.

Madame nodded as if it were only to be expected. 'For how long will you stay?' She held on to the bag as if to keep him in the shop.

Étienne met her black-eyed gaze. 'I'm only here to sort her things and put the house up for sale,' he said.

She didn't reply.

Étienne felt he needed to justify his actions. 'I live in Loc-mariaquer.' He said this quite loudly as if to inform himself and anyone else who might be listening. 'I've always lived there.' And he had never wanted to come back here.

'*Oui, oui.*' Madame turned to pull another tray of pastries out of her oven. The steam and the sweet scent of them filled the air. 'You write books, *n'est-ce pas*? Lucie was so proud of you.' She popped one of the pastries in Étienne's paper bag and handed it to him with a smile.

'Oh? *Mais oui. Merci.*' Étienne wasn't sure what to say to this. What was appropriate? He shrugged – that was about the only gesture he'd left out so far. Had his mother been proud? Yes, she had. She had even tried to read his books, though the kind of bloodthirsty thrillers Étienne wrote were very far from her taste, he knew. He nodded more thanks to Madame and began working his way back towards the doorway as fast as he could.

'So you will sell the house?'

He opened his mouth to reply. There were now several people between him and Madame and they all turned to look at him.

'Why not keep it as a holiday home? *Mais oui*, why not indeed?' There was a general buzz of approval.

'Well . . .'

'Then you could come over yourself sometimes.'

'Myself?'

'You know.' She clicked her tongue. 'For a holiday. Like the old days, *non*?'

But of course. A holiday. She didn't know, then. Or she had

forgotten. Had they all forgotten? Étienne smiled. Opened the shop door. He couldn't remember the last time he had smiled and nodded so much in one morning.

'She would be glad,' Madame threw these final crumbs just as he had left the shop and was about to close the door behind him.

'Glad, Madame?'

'That at least you have come over to sort out her things.' Madame shuddered. 'Better than a stranger, *non*?'

Oui, oui. Better than a stranger . . . He heard the rest of the queue murmur their assent. Again, he nodded.

He made his escape and breathed the fresh air outside into his lungs. He shouldn't have come out so early, of course. An hour later and he might have been one of the many anonymous tourists buying their breakfast and bread for lunch. But it was true, what Madame Riou had said. His mother had been too kind to say so, in her final weeks, when she might or might not have known that her end was drawing near. She knew he didn't want to go back to Belle-Île, so she wouldn't ask that of him, not now. But she would have wanted him to sort through her things. Much, much better than a stranger. That in itself was a good reason for coming back. His mother deserved that much at least.

Étienne hot-footed it back to the house before anyone else could offer their condolences. His mother had never been able to persuade her only son to visit her here and so she had continued to return to Morbihan on the ferry to see him, once a month, carrying bread and fruit and maybe some oysters in her basket – as if, without her, that son of hers might even forget to eat. Étienne sighed. Maybe that's what she told them all. He eyed the paper bag of pastries he was carrying. He should have come here for her before now. But . . . It was a big but.

In the house, he made more coffee and ate the croissant and

the patisserie, absent-mindedly wiping buttery fingers on his jeans. He trawled through the first drawer of papers, creating three piles: to recycle, to deal with, to keep. Thankfully, pile number one was the highest; his mother had kept every document ever posted or given to her, it seemed.

In the second drawer were the photographs that hadn't made it to the neatly stacked and labelled albums in the ancient mahogany bookcase. Nothing digital for his mother – no, not until the day she died. These were the blurred memories of the happier days after his mother had given up her work 'in the oysters', after his father had been made foreman at the warehouse, after the gift of his maternal grandmother's inheritance which had enabled his mother to buy this little house in Sauzon. My dream, she had called it. She had persuaded Étienne's father to paint it pink with mint-green shutters and he had rolled his eyes but done it anyway. The family had come here every summer, his father too – when the oysters of Locmariaquer could spare him.

Étienne picked up a handful of snaps. Here he was in the sea, laughing and splashing around – sun-bronzed, carefree, ten or eleven years old maybe. Here he was on his old red bicycle, knobbly kneed, legs like spindles, only a year or two older. Here was a picture of the three of them standing outside the little pink house, here they were standing on the deck of the ferry. Étienne felt his eyes blur.

He didn't know how long he spent looking through the photographs. He didn't know how long he'd spent looking out to sea. But the photographs and the ocean had sent him back there, to that time of his life when everything had changed, and he reached for his notebook and his pen before he even knew what he would write. He only knew that somehow, he had to go back there – otherwise he would never be free.

CHAPTER 4

Colette

Colette climbed off the Belle-Île bus and began the oh-so-familiar walk into town. The curve of the road as it swept around the harbour basin, the trees on the far hill, roses and geraniums in window boxes, an old bicycle propped against an oleander tree. Each step seemed to tug at her heart.

Sauzon was beautiful as ever – the clear waters of the harbour, the pretty houses painted green and yellow, pink and blue, grey and white. So elegant, so charming. The same pine tree stood on the corner, the same tamarisks feathered the top of the granite cliff wall. Colette paused for a moment to re-absorb this place so rooted within her. So many times in the past, she had witnessed gasps from holidaymakers seeing the picture-postcard perfection of Sauzon for the first time. *You live here? How wonderful* . . . Tourists of course saw the pastel-painted houses overlooking the cool blue waters of the Atlantic, where fishing boats and pleasure craft floated in happy harmony through the haze of rose-coloured holiday spectacles. They didn't see the place in the winter, in the storms, when—

'Colette? Colette! It has been so long!'

The voice rang out from the other side of the harbour road, the Rue du Chemin Neuf. Colette recognised Anneliese who owned the crêperie in the village. 'Anneliese, *bonjour*!' she called back to her. She hurried across to where Anneliese stood, hands on ample hips.

'Look at you, *chérie* . . . You went away a girl and you have come back a woman.'

Colette smiled. It was true, she supposed, although sometimes she thought the transition had taken place so much earlier with the death of her father.

Anneliese held out her arms and Colette stepped into her warm embrace. They kissed on both cheeks then drew apart.

'*Ça va, chérie?*'

'*Très bien*, Anneliese. And you?' She was older too of course, her skin more lined, but her eyes were as warm and friendly as ever. 'How are things? How is Jean-Luc?' Immediately, Colette felt herself slip seamlessly into the French way of speaking, of being, that she had been born to.

She and Anneliese chatted for a few moments, Anneliese's soft voice full of pity, for she must have known that Colette's mother was very ill. No doubt she was curious too about what had kept Colette away for so many years – wouldn't they all be? But Colette didn't want to stay too long. She needed to breathe deeply and drink it all in. She needed to get there.

Moving on towards the tip of the harbour, she passed the white walls and decorative red shutters of the *tabac*, the grocery shop and other places that had sprung up since she'd left. Because, yes, she saw now that there had been many changes. Colette's steps slowed. There were fewer fishing boats, more yachts. Houses had been smartened up and made good. And the new shops were the kind that catered for tourists, with their fancy pottery and the type of coastal clothing in narrow stripes, hemps and linen that rather reminded her of Cornwall.

There was a gallery too, showing pictures of the jagged rocks whipped by sea-foam that formed cotton-like flecks in stormy weather, after which Les Aiguilles de Port Coton were named. Monet had famously painted them – the story was that he came here for five days and stayed for seventy-five, painting thirty-nine canvases. Colette wouldn't be surprised. The rocks looked different from every angle, and they'd since been drawn by many an admirer wanting to follow in Monet's brushstrokes. Like Cornwall, the island attracted artists, writers, sculptors. Like Cornwall, the island had a certain kind of light . . .

Colette felt a gust of longing. She would go there. She would go to all the places she loved that she'd visited with her father – the old church at Locmaria and the pretty bay beyond, the Pointe des Poulains where the actress Sarah Bernhardt had famously made her home, the little village of Bangor, the rocks at Port Coton. But first . . .

Some things were the same. There was the rather imposing Saint-Nicolas Church in Place de L'Église, there was the bou-langerie. She walked on down Quai Joseph Naudin which ran seamlessly into Guerveur. And there . . . Her breath caught. There was the quayside stall where her father had washed, gutted and sold his fish. She drew closer. She ran her fingers along the hard, pitted surface, the very same marble slabs. Above the battered stainless steel sink, coloured lights were strung gaily above the stall, as if it were part of some fairground attraction instead of a man's living.

Her father had always been busy too, out fishing all hours, filleting and preparing the catch of mullet or sea bass on this very stall, selling to Sauzon's restaurants and townspeople alike. But he still found time for Colette. She would run down to the quayside to meet him, strain her eyes squinting out to sea, searching for the sight of the familiar little blue and white boat. As it approached, she would run along the quay, waving. 'Papa! Papa! A good catch today, *oui*?' And he would laugh and wave back, moor the boat and come ashore. He would sweep her up and hold her tight against the rough wool of his fisherman's jumper, which smelt of salt, of the wind and the sea.

'Hey!' She heard a shout. Her head swivelled.

'Is that you, eh? Is that really you? Sébastien's girl?'

Colette shielded her eyes. 'Henri!' She took a step towards the grizzled old fisherman, her father's long-time buddy. He had not gone out that night, the night her father died; he'd been coughing too badly and anyway he'd heard the forecast of the storm. She knew how guilty this had always made him feel, that his old friend had died alone at sea and that he had survived him.

'Come here.' He took her in his arms, a proper bear hug, and for the first time since she'd received Francine's letter, Colette felt her eyes fill.

He drew away, saw it and pulled her close again. '*Merde . . .* I knew that one day you would come home,' he muttered.

Colette nodded and swallowed hard, rubbed the tears from her eyes. 'I have to see Maman.'

'I heard about that.' He patted her shoulder. 'A bad business. Please give her my regards. And if there is anything . . .'

'*Merci*, Henri.'

'Anything at all.'

'Yes, I will tell you.'

'Well, then.' Finally, he moved away. 'I will let you go, little one.'

The endearment, her father's endearment, almost started her off again, but she managed to nod, give a little smile and a half-wave as she turned from him. '*Au revoir*, Henri.'

It was funny, she thought, her head had been so full of her mother, she had almost forgotten how it would be to see these old friends, these familiar places.

When she had left Belle-Île all those years ago she had only been looking forward; she had barely bothered to say goodbye. She had wanted to take the bus to Le Palais but her mother had insisted on driving her to the ferry. At the last minute, she had held Colette so tightly as if she couldn't bear to let her go. 'You are young,' she'd said. 'You think you can change the world, the past.'

Colette had pulled away and looked her in the eye. 'It is my future, Maman.'

'But you cannot.' Her mother continued as if she hadn't spoken. 'Trust me, you cannot.'

Trust her? In that moment, Colette had almost hated her. She was scared at the strength of the feeling. The past five years since her father's death had been the worst years of her life. Before that, she'd had him to run to if things got bad. After that . . . There was no one. So why bother to work at school? Why try to please anyone? Why not turn to boys like Mathieu with their warm hands and easy laughter? At least with a boy like Mathieu, Colette could feel. At least she would be noticed. At least she would be loved.

Her mother had pleaded and she had despaired. She had talked, she had disciplined, and finally she had washed her hands of her. 'Go your own way, Colette,' she had told her. 'Why not? You always do.'

And where do you go, Maman? she had wanted to ask

32

her. Where do you go when your eyes are far away? Who do you think of? Who do you love? Because it was not Colette's father – she had known that even before the row she overheard between them the night he died, even before she had lost him.

Colette bit her lip and walked on. Back then, she hadn't given a thought to how long she might be gone, when she might return – if ever.

Or why. She thought again of Francine's letter, still tucked in her bag.

'Why do you want to go alone?' Mark had asked her. And she could see the hurt in his eyes.

'Because of Maman.' So much between them was unresolved. Colette had been angry with her for such a long time. And those questions she needed answering wouldn't answer themselves. 'And because I don't know how long I might have to stay.'

Colette looked down at the small case she had brought, now trundling along the cobbles behind her. It wasn't only that. It was also because she couldn't go on letting Mark take over when things went wrong – this was her life, and she had to deal with it herself.

Mark had said that he understood. He said that if she didn't come back soon he would come and fetch her, and he'd laughed to show that he was joking. Colette had gone in to work that day and told them that she was really sorry but just as they were approaching the height of the holiday letting season she must leave to visit her sick mother in France, and no, she wasn't sure when she would be back.

Tracey had been sympathetic but brisk. 'We'll have to get a replacement, Colette. If you can't tell me how long you'll be gone for, then I can't guarantee your job will still be here when you get back. I'm sorry, but—'

'That's fine,' Colette said. She knew how things worked in the tourist industry. 'I understand.' So, she had lost her job – but what choice had she had?

Now that she was close enough, Colette looked up at the house of her childhood, unpainted since her departure, the dusky pink and lavender even more faded than before. Her mother *must* be sick – the red geraniums in the window boxes seemed tired and thirsty. Below, the flower shop was in shadow, looking sad and very obviously closed, a driftwood horse wound around with herbs, head down as if he might be grazing, standing outside. The horse hadn't been here before and Colette could guess where it had come from.

She walked up the hill, Rue Rampe des Glycines, towards her childhood home.

CHAPTER 5

Colette

'Maman.'

The front door was open so Colette had let herself in. She stood in the hall as if waiting in vain for the house to become home again. 'Maman,' she said again. The hallway was dim, the dark wood panelling dusty and unloved. She ran her fingers along it, smelt the scent of age, of damp, of something that was sharper and more medicinal. Where was she? Colette put a foot on the stairs, about to go up to her parents' old bedroom, when she heard a sound from the dining room. Of course. Her mother was sick, she wouldn't be upstairs. The door of the dining room was open. She heard the sound of movement, then a faint '*Bonjour?* Who is there? Francine?'

She hadn't told them she was coming; she could have tried ringing again but there had been no words she'd felt like speaking. The journey, the thinking, the memories – these had been strain enough. Colette pushed the door open wider.

Her mother was lying on what had been a spare sofa bed but she was an older, frailer image of the mother Colette had

35

carried in her mind since leaving. '*Bonjour, Maman.*' She took a step closer. She almost wished that Mark were here now, taking charge, that she was not alone. And yet . . . She took a breath and another step towards her.

There were lines where before there had been smooth skin, iron-grey-streaked hair where there had been only conker-brown. And her eyes . . . Her dark eyes seemed to have had the life washed out of them. Colette thought about what Anneliese had said about her leaving Sauzon a girl and coming back a woman. While Colette had been away, her mother had become an old lady. How could that have happened – without her even knowing?

'Colette?' Her mother was staring at her sightlessly, seeing but not seeing. 'Colette? *Comment . . .?*' She made as if to sit up.

'Francine wrote to me.' Her mother's pallor was white, almost ghostly. She was certainly very ill, as Francine had said. But worse, much worse than Colette had allowed herself to imagine.

'So, you came.' Francine had walked into the room behind her. She at any rate looked much the same as before – cold, upright and tight-lipped.

'Thank you for your letter,' Colette said stiffly. Francine was carrying a wicker basket. Colette saw fruit – grapes and bananas – and a thermos flask.

Francine shrugged and took her basket into the kitchen.

'Is it really you?' Her mother's voice was dry and brackish with pain and probably whatever medication she was on.

'*Oui, c'est moi.*' Colette moved closer still. She was near enough now to touch, to hold. She bent towards her. 'Why didn't you tell me, Maman?' She felt a surge of anger. Her mother had always been the woman of mystery, always holding something back – even if it was only a hug.

36

She flashed Colette a look that was very nearly a look from the past. 'I did not want to drag you back here,' she said, 'that is all.'

'But who is looking after you?' Colette's gaze turned to the pills and the glass of water by the bed. She would be anaemic, of course. Had they given her anything to help with that, anything to give her energy and strength?

'A nurse comes in every day,' her mother murmured now in this new voice of hers that Colette could hardly recognise. 'And Francine . . .'

'But shouldn't you be in hospital, Maman?' Colette realised that everything she was saying was emerging much harsher than she'd intended. 'To be looked after properly,' she said more softly. 'It's very good of Francine, but—'

'I hate hospitals.' Her mother's eyes, when she looked at her, seemed like a child's. 'Don't send me to hospital, please, *chérie*.'

'I won't.' Colette sat abruptly on the edge of the sofa bed. What would she do, then? Nurse her mother herself?

'They said I could die here.'

Colette put a hand to her mouth. 'But is there nothing they can do to help you?' she whispered. She couldn't bear it. How had this happened so quickly?

Her mother shook her head. 'It has all been done, *chérie*.'

Colette frowned. What had been done? Radiotherapy? Chemo? A bone-marrow transplant? But she realised she must ask Francine, get in touch with the hospital herself, to find out exactly what had gone on. It was not fair to expect her mother to tell her the details. She was too sick. She needed to be looked after.

'And the shop . . .' Her mother held out her hand. It was trembling. 'The flowers . . .'

Colette took her hand. Of course, she took her hand. Her mother's bones seemed so fragile, her skin so lifeless and dry, almost transparent. Always, the flower shop. As far back as Colette could remember, it had dominated their lives. 'Don't worry about that now,' she said.

But she saw that her mother was still fretting. 'Will you . . .? Will you help me, *chérie*? Will you see to things for me?' she asked. Her other hand was worrying at the edge of the sheet that covered her. Colette noticed the darkening bruise on the pale skin of her forearm.

'Things?' Colette glanced around the room at the heavy, dark furniture, so much a part of her childhood. The mahogany bookcase, the table now pushed up against the wall, wood panelling that seemed to keep everything in shadow. Just being in this room once again had dipped her back into the past almost as if she had never been away.

'Will you go into the shop? Will you see to the plants, check the orders . . .?' Her voice failed and turned into a deep and racking cough.

Colette waited for it to subside. She should have something to ease that cough. She should be putting something on that dry skin to give it moisture. And she had lost so much weight. Was she eating? Was it too late for eating? 'But Maman—'

'Please, Colette.' Her words came out in a rush now. 'You see you are the only one who can.'

The only one who can.

Her mother's eyes drooped. She was exhausted already, Colette could see. And now she was depending on her. It was an uncomfortable feeling. A switching of roles that she had not anticipated, which made things even more ambivalent than before.

Francine emerged from the kitchen. 'Time for a sleep, Thea,' she said. She nodded at Colette, gave a little jerk of her head.

'I'll go down to the shop.' Awkwardly, Colette patted her mother's hand. 'I'll see to things. Don't worry.'

A small smile drifted around her mother's lips. 'I knew that you would, *chérie*,' she said.

Colette took her case upstairs to her old childhood bedroom. Her emotions were so mixed, so churned; she felt sadness, horror, longing, but they had no order or priority, not yet. They were, she realised, as tangled as her feelings for Belle-Île itself. Even this room with the red-rose wallpaper and the dark shiny coverlet on the single bed took her back so sharply she had to hold on to the door jamb for a moment to find her balance. In the middle of the night sometimes, she had imagined coming back to Belle-Île. But she had never imagined it would be like this.

She drifted into her parents' old room. It was stale and musty; it no longer smelt of him, of course, and there was barely a trace of her mother's perfume. She trailed her fingers across the door of the walnut wardrobe. And had a flashback. It was almost twenty years ago and she was thirteen. She came in here looking for a scrap of comfort and had found her mother groping frantically through the clothes in the wardrobe.

'What are you doing?' Colette had stared at her in horror. He had been dead three days. He was her father, her darling.

'What does it look like?' Her mother's eyes were blank. Anger, Colette could have understood. She felt anger – towards the storm, towards the sea that had taken him. He was an experienced boatsman, had been a fisherman his entire life – even as a boy he'd gone out with his father most days. But when a storm hit Belle-Île-en-Mer there was no force stronger, or so

39

the islanders liked to say. He shouldn't have gone out in it. He knew it was coming. What had he been thinking?

Only Colette knew exactly what he'd been thinking of because she'd heard it all. 'Stop it, Maman. Stop it now!' She grabbed her mother's wrists, tried to pull her away.

'There's no point in keeping them.' Her mother eyed the pile of clothes already on the bed. 'He's gone.'

Yes, and you sent him there. She didn't say it, though; it had seemed too cruel.

That pile of clothes had looked so unutterably sad to Colette. This was her first loss and she knew instinctively that it was the greatest. The clothes were almost all that was left of him. His spare waxed jacket and waterproof trousers, his linen smocks and shirts in blue and grey, the smart suit he kept for weddings and funerals . . . And her mother was throwing them out. Throwing *him* out when he'd been dead for less than three days. Three days! Colette had slammed the door as she left their bedroom. What was wrong with her mother? Didn't she know how to feel?

Colette realised she was trembling now almost as much as she'd been trembling then. There had been so many other things – she'd lost track of the times her mother wasn't there for her, the times she seemed to push her away, the times her mother had failed to hold her. No wonder then that at thirteen she'd turned into what her mother called a wild child. No wonder, Francine had stood watching at the lace *rideaux* to see what she was getting up to, no wonder Colette had left Belle-Île.

But she was older now, she thought as she left her parents' bedroom. She had come back because her mother had leukaemia. She had come back to see her, of course, but that wasn't all. She had also come back to find out the truth.

40

CHAPTER 6

Étienne

It was the third day and Étienne thought he was getting somewhere.

The house details were being prepared by the *notaire*. Most
of the furniture had been sold and taken away. Étienne had a
large bag full of things to keep, including some photos, books
and one of his mother's embroidered cushions – a scene she'd
done depicting Morbihan Bay – and he was glad he'd brought
his car in the end, although being a two-seater there wasn't too
much extra space for baggage. Which was how Étienne liked
it. It might be lonely, but if you travelled light you'd never
let anyone down. Best of all, his mother's house was gradually
becoming free of clutter.

Free to breathe. Étienne put his hands on his hips and looked
around. Without the heavy old furniture, one could appreciate
the rich gleam of the wooden floors, which he'd polished on
his hands and knees yesterday. Therapy . . . The walls could do
with a lick of paint it was true, but if he did one room, he'd
have to do them all; one newly decorated would show up the

others, and he didn't have the time, not if he wanted to leave before the weekend.

He felt better too. Étienne's gaze strayed to the desk drawer. The desk was one of three items of furniture he'd kept – for now at least. A desk to work at and eat on while he was here, a chair to sit in, a bed to sleep on. Everything else had gone. He wondered what his mother would say if she could see the house now. Would she approve of its new minimalist style or would it shock her? Thing was, in this material world, everyone bought more and more layers to add to their life until in the end it was hard to see anything underneath.

In the drawer was the notebook he'd been writing in. He wrote every evening after he'd cleaned and decluttered. Pages of script that seemed to flow remarkably easily, about the boy he'd been, the family they were, the story of Belle-Île and what had happened here.

It wasn't what he should be writing, of course. Didier would have something to say about it. But it was cleansing. This was a new feeling and Étienne wasn't sure about it yet. Getting rid of the old. Was it possible? Probably not. But by the third day, being here didn't seem quite so hard. His morning questioning from Madame Riou at the boulangerie, his sedate walks along the harbour, his surveillance of the port and the ocean from the safe vantage point of his mother's house. These routines had slotted into his life.

Now, he sauntered out into the port where tourists queued for galettes and ice-creams and drank coffee or cider as they sat on the pink chairs at the pink tables at the harbour-front café watching the boats bobbing in the low water. He walked beyond the Hôtel du Phare and was just strolling back alongside the harbour wall towards the grey and pink café when he saw him. Another ghost. Only this time it was broad daylight. A child of maybe six or seven, brown-skinned with neat, narrow features and skinny legs dangling under his chair. The plate in front of him held a few crumby smears showing he had recently enjoyed a crêpe – possibly with blueberry jam and vanilla ice-cream.

Étienne stopped dead. He was weirdly conscious of the shallowness of his breath.

The child's mother looked up, instinctively sensing his presence, his stare. '*Monsieur?*' She half rose from her seat.

Étienne shook himself back to the present. '*Madame. Pardonnez-moi*. Please forgive me. It was just—' He stopped speaking. Because there he was – Denis, crossing the road to the café, a black leather bag slung over one shoulder. Older, of course, his brown face more weathered than before; lined, even, around the eyes and mouth. But indisputably it was Denis, as self-assured as he had always been.

'Denis?'

'*Putain!* What the—?' Denis stared at him, took a few seconds to adjust. 'Étienne Chevalier. God, man. Where the hell did you spring from?'

'Uh, well . . .' Étienne supposed that it was unsurprising. Denis's family had always come here every summer. Why wouldn't Denis continue that tradition when he had a family of his own? Even so, it had shocked him. 'I'm here to sell my mother's house,' he said quickly. 'She died, you see.'

'Oh, man, *je suis désolé.*' Denis clapped him on the back affectionately and this too brought back a sharp memory.

'You still come here for the holidays?' Étienne was still struggling with this concept, despite his own logic.

'Sure. Old habits, you know . . .' Denis hesitated and Étienne saw the flicker in his eyes. He knew what it meant, that flicker. 'But not every year,' he added. 'And not only in the summer.'

'Right.' They stood there looking at one another. Étienne wondered how he seemed to his old friend. Did he look successful? Damaged?

'So, this is my wife Adrienne.' Denis introduced the mother of his son. 'And you already saw Pascal.'

Étienne smiled. 'Pleased to meet you.' He took Adrienne's hand and they kissed politely on both cheeks. 'And yes, he's the image of you, Denis.'

'You think so?'

'Uh huh.' Étienne could see that his old friend was proud. And he was pleased for him, really pleased.

'And now?' Denis stood still but Étienne could sense a slight discomfort creeping in. 'You're a writer now, yes? I read your books sometimes.'

'Oh, really? Right. Well – that's great.' Étienne had never learnt how to have this kind of conversation. He didn't want to know what people thought of his books – he'd certainly never ask them. Enough, he thought, that they sold.

'What about you?' Something practical, Étienne guessed. Something sporty.

'Computers.' Denis grinned. Another stab of memory. 'IT technician.' He spread his hands. 'I fell into it.'

Étienne nodded. 'Sounds great.' Bullshit. And Denis knew that too.

'But would you not like to join us?' Adrienne was looking from one to the other of them, clearly surprised the invitation hadn't already been made. Étienne knew why.

'Ah, *merci, mais non*,' he said, before Denis could chip in. 'It is impossible. I have somewhere I have to be. Such a shame.'

44

He gestured vaguely towards the church and Place de L'Église. 'Business,' he added, for good measure. 'You know how it is.'

If he sat down, she would ask how they knew one another, she would ask about those summers. *And why did you not stay in touch*, she might say. *Why did you stop coming to the island for so many years?* Étienne could not deal with a conversation like that.

'Good to see you though.' Denis clapped his shoulder once again.

'And you.' Though Étienne wasn't as sure as he hoped he sounded. And this was why he'd never wanted to come back to Belle-Île. The ghosts were here. The ghosts would no doubt get him in the end.

The boy Pascal, clearly bored with his parents' dialogue with this stranger, had got up from his chair. Now, he began to cross the road to the harbour.

Denis was watching him. 'Don't go too far,' he called.

'Oh, Papa.'

Étienne caught Denis's eye. Another flicker. Another memory. Enough.

'*Au revoir* then.' He raised his hand in a wave. 'Enjoy the rest of your time here, won't you? *Bonnes vacances!*'

Étienne stomped back to the house, pulled the rogue exercise book from the desk drawer and stared out at the ocean. He picked up his pen.

CHAPTER 7

Colette

The shop had a dank feel to it when Colette pushed open the door. Stale water. Stale air. Rotting foliage. She left the door ajar and flung the windows open. Hands on hips, she surveyed the scene.

Everything was neat – of course, it would be. But everything was also untouched. Once-elegant crimson roses, blue and yellow-streaked irises and dark-centred sunflowers lay in the green buckets half dead and drooping. All of them should have been thrown out days if not weeks ago.

Colette's mother had always had her favourites; she used to have a regular order with her Dutch suppliers, depending on the season and availability, and Colette guessed that they were still delivering, and that someone – probably Francine – had stuck the blooms in a bucket of water and left them here to rot. Colette sighed. No wonder her mother was fretting. She would hate to see this neglect.

How long? Colette wondered. For how long had she kept to her bed? When was the last time her mother had been strong enough to even come in here? Colette found a bin bag under the sink and shoved the flowers in heads first, a few dank drips falling on to the tiled floor. She chucked the stagnant water down the sink, followed it with some disinfectant and set to, scrubbing out the buckets where old plant life still clung to the sides. There were few smells worse than foliage rotting in stale water.

Most of the potted plants had survived. She suspected that the Christmas cacti and other succulents had even enjoyed the neglect, and the slipper orchids with their delicate burgundy and white veiled flowers and mottled leaves were holding up well. Colette gave them all a good water and then found the secateurs and clipped back some of the brown edges and withered leaves, just as she used to when she was a girl. Her mother had taught her how to hold the cutters, how to prune, where to make the incisions to encourage new growth. For a moment she paused, remembering.

It had not been all bad. When she was young, Colette hadn't only been a daddy's girl. She had also loved to help in the flower shop whenever her mother would let her. She'd adored the heady scent of plants and flowers, loved to watch things grow. Her mother had taught her how to look after the cut flowers from the moment they were delivered, how to condition them by carefully removing the transit packaging, stripping and trimming the stems and giving them that vital long drink in a bucket of water. She had taught her how to inspect them, how to decide which ones must go into the cool room and which were ready for the shop or an arrangement. She had even taught her how to encourage a tightly closed lily bud to open, by placing it in a bright warm position, by spritzing it with water or even using a hair dryer on it. Colette

47

had listened to her mother talking to her flowers, watched her design and create her arrangements, witnessed the emotion when a daughter saw her mother's funeral flowers or a bride saw her bouquet for the first time. Colette understood the love.

By the till was a pile of delivery notes, orders and her mother's order book. Colette had always been able to decipher her writing, the round loopy scrawl. She set to, matching notes with entries and orders, making calls: *I am so sorry, my mother, that is we cannot fulfil your order at this time. My mother is ill. Yes. Thank you. I will.* She had been right about the supplier too – the orders had been scaled down considerably, but deliveries had not been cancelled. She picked up the phone.

'*Bonjour.*'

Colette looked up. Framed in the open doorway was a woman she recognised, though it had been a long time. '*Bonjour, Madame,*' she said, with a little nod.

'Oh, Élodie, please. You remember me, don't you?' Her voice was soft, almost musical.

The light shining behind Élodie through the doorway sent a shaft of brightness through the long fair hair which drifted down her back exactly as Colette remembered.

'Of course.' Colette was carefully polite. She didn't know her well, but she certainly knew of her. Élodie Blaise was older than her – in her mid-forties, Colette guessed – and she was an artist. Colette didn't think she'd had more than half a dozen brief conversations with Élodie, her entire life. Mostly, she'd just seen her striding out along the headland, her long hair flowing behind her; in earlier days with her older brother, in latter days walking alone. Élodie had lived with her mother Mathilde in the Old Lighthouse at the Pointe. Probably, she still did.

Colette's mother had lived there too, of course, when she first came here to the island as a young girl of eighteen to be the Blaise family's au pair. She had looked after Jacques and Élodie when they were young, been part of the family for some years. Which was why it had always seemed odd to Colette that her mother and Mathilde had never so much as acknowledged one another when they met in the street. She had asked her mother about it often enough in the past, but she would never tell her; it was another of her secrets. 'It is over, it is past, what has been done can't be undone,' was all she would say. What had she meant by that? Colette had absolutely no idea.

'How is your mother?' Élodie stepped inside the shop. She was small-boned and light as gossamer, Colette thought. An old-fashioned Faerie Queene in her floaty dress and espadrilles. She looked as if she belonged to a different era. And it wasn't just now that she was older – she always had.

'Not well, I'm afraid.' Colette picked up a cloth and began wiping the counter.

'So you came back.' Élodie was watching her curiously.

'So I came back.' Colette met her blue-eyed gaze.

'And you are looking after the flower shop for her.' Élodie made a graceful gesture with her arm which enveloped the shop, the untended plants, the flowerless buckets. 'How wonderful of you.'

Colette was embarrassed. 'Not really.' Not at all, actually. Not wonderful of her and not what she was doing. She was cancelling orders and closing the place down. After the death of her father, Colette had stopped helping in the shop. The scent of the flowers, her mother's abstracted expression when she tended them, only seemed to taunt her then.

'It will help her so much to know that you are here,' Élodie

49

continued as if she hadn't spoken. 'And she often speaks of spending time here in the shop with you when you were young. How much it meant to her. How she hoped you would take over the flowers one day.'

Colette stared at her. 'She does?'

'*Mais oui.*'

'You come to see her then?' Colette thought of Mathilde. She wouldn't like it that her daughter visited – unless they were friends again now.

'My mother is not my keeper.' Élodie smiled that sad, sweet smile of hers.

'And did you make the horse?' Colette liked him. He was graceful and yet his structure had been cleverly built up to make him muscular, strong; the driftwood gave him a texture and allowed the shoots and tendrils of the plants to wind around his body and long limbs.

Élodie nodded. 'Thea commissioned him a few years ago,' she said. 'I've made some little ones too for single herbs. She gave me the idea. They ought to be brought inside for the winter really' – she glanced out at the horse and Colette almost expected him to look up at her – 'in order to survive.'

So, she still worked at her studio creating her driftwood art. It suited her, she almost looked like an elegant piece of driftwood herself, floating around the place as she did. Colette smiled at the thought. 'He's lovely,' she said.

'Thank you.' Élodie made a move as if she would leave, but rather to Colette's surprise, instead, she took a step closer. She reached out, put a hand on Colette's arm, just for a moment. The touch was so light, Colette hardly felt it. 'You were lucky, you know,' she said softly.

'Lucky?' What did she mean?

Élodie wandered over towards the orchids Colette had watered. Again, she reached out and let the palm of her hand gently graze the flowers. That was the sculptor in her, Colette realised. She liked to touch things. 'I missed her so much when she left us,' Élodie said.

'My mother?'

'Oh, yes.' Élodie's eyed widened. 'I had a huge row with Mama about it.'

'Do you know why she left?' Colette tried to keep her voice casual. Maybe it wasn't such a secret in the Blaise household as it was in her own.

Élodie shrugged. 'Mama told her to.'

'Ah.' So she hadn't left of her own accord. Mathilde Blaise had told her to leave. What had her mother done to deserve that? Colette frowned. It must have been something bad. 'Didn't they get on?' she pressed. She wasn't even sure why it was so important to know. After all, as her mother had told her, the past couldn't be undone. But if it helped Colette understand her . . .

'Oh, yes,' Élodie said. 'They got on very well. Until—'

'Until?'

'Until the end.'

The end? The end of what – their relationship? Colette's mother's job, what? But Colette could see she'd get nothing further out of Élodie. She had that glazed look in her eyes again, as if she were keen to be somewhere else.

'May I go to see her now?' she asked.

'Yes, of course. She was sleeping when I came in here, but—'

'I shan't wake her.' Élodie drifted back to the doorway. 'But I will sit with her for a short while, if I may.' She turned. '*Merci beaucoup*, Colette.'

'*Au revoir*, Élodie.'

Colette continued to think about her strange visitor as she carried on organising things in the shop. It was the least she could do, she thought. It made her feel useful and it had given her an excuse to escape from her mother's bedside where she felt awkward, not knowing what to say, how to be. Élodie was right. It would make her feel better knowing that at least her shop was not in total disarray. Colette would have to sort things out with the supplier, though; it was ridiculous that flowers should continue to be delivered, as if her mother were still here, as if nothing had changed.

She phoned another customer, still thinking. Why had her mother stayed on the island after she left her job as an au pair anyway? It was the kind of job lots of girls must have done as a way of travelling, seeing the world – though in her mother's case she suspected it was more a question of getting away from Cornwall, from her parents, from a place that was stifling her. So perhaps that was why she hadn't gone back there. Even so . . .

'*Oui, Madame?*' The customer had answered. Colette ran through her explanatory spiel.

'Oh my goodness, no.' The woman sounded distraught. '*Merde*. I had no idea. I am coming over from the mainland. It is a special occasion.'

'Your aunt's eightieth birthday, yes.' Colette was patient – but people could be so selfish. 'We are sorry to let you down, to give you such short notice, but my mother—'

'Could you do it?' the woman asked. 'Please?'

'Oh no, I really don't think so . . .' Could she even remember how to put an arrangement together?

'I have no time to look elsewhere, you see. And it would

mean so much. You work at that lovely flower shop, don't you?'

'Not really. No, I don't. And I'm afraid I don't have the stock.' Despite this, Colette began to imagine what flowers she would use for the elderly woman's birthday bouquet: heady white jasmine growing in the hedges of their garden which stood for grace and elegance as far as she remembered, delicate scabious which always looked like a much-loved but elderly flower itself with its wrinkly lilac-coloured petals; some cosmos, feathery and delicate to symbolise tranquillity; and perhaps some old-fashioned scented stock – if she could get hold of it. 'Although—' Colette stopped short, not sure what had surprised her the most: her remembering the meanings of the flowers or her instinctive desire to take the order.

'*S'il vous plaît?*' The woman would not take no for an answer. 'Your mother was so helpful when I spoke to her several weeks ago. And it's not for a couple of days. I would be so grateful.'

'Very well.' Where had that come from? Colette wasn't sure. She only knew that she didn't want to let her mother's customers down. And she wanted to make the bouquet. 'It would have to be something simple and natural,' she said. For herself, she preferred flowers that way. For herself, she would not use Dutch suppliers at all; she would grow her own blooms on a flower farm with raised beds and a polytunnel and a special patch of worked ground . . . She shook this thought away. What was happening to her? It was as if the flower shop was casting some sort of spell.

'But that is her!' the woman exclaimed. 'My Aunt Marin – also my godmother, you know – is a simple and natural person. She is down to earth, not formal, you understand. And she loves the sea.'

She loves the sea . . . Everyone who came to Belle-Île loved the sea. It was there, all around. 'Excellent,' said Colette. 'Then it will be a pleasure for me to make her bouquet.'

She was thoughtful as she ended the call. Several weeks ago, then, her mother had been well enough to be working in the flower shop – at least part-time.

She slipped outside into the garden, a small square behind the house and shop. Here, her mother grew more herbs and some of her favourite flowers. Here, Colette was sure she could find more inspiration for Aunt Marin's bouquet. She felt a small jolt; a dart of adrenalin. It had been so long. These days the most she did was arrange flowers bought for her by Mark into a glass vase before putting them on the dining-room table. Mark . . . There was another jolt – this time of guilt.

In the sunniest corner of the garden next to the creamy viburnum were some pretty blue cornflowers and love-in-the-mist – which would be perfect with a sprig or two of lilac. If she could get hold of some in time, the scabious would bring in another more purply shade often seen in the ocean at this time of year, and the scented white jasmine would be like the crest of a wave. Colette could see the arrangement in her mind's eye. She would add blue stocks for colour and volume and a dark seaweed-green raffia to tie it all together.

It was all coming back to her. After-school afternoons working in the perfumed shop; sweeping the floor, cleaning the counters, trimming eucalyptus stems. 'There's a story behind every order,' her mother used to say, 'you just have to search for the emotion.' Colette knew that there were many times when her mother's flowers or her grasp of people and psychology had saved the day, that she had sometimes been a counsellor as much as a florist. Colette had even admired her for it – when she was not resenting those who took so much of her mother's time away.

Now, she was itching to get started. She looked back up at the house, at the window behind which her mother would be sleeping or perhaps still talking with Élodie. But it would have to wait until tomorrow. She looked over to the west, towards the cemetery. Tomorrow. She'd go to see her father tomorrow – she owed him that much at least.

CHAPTER 8

Élodie

Élodie was walking along the beach looking for driftwood. She did this most mornings. She never knew what she might find – but the best times were after a storm. She liked to watch them from the shelter of her small studio, which was close to the Old Lighthouse but entirely self-sufficient – she'd made sure of that. She would stand in front of the window before she went to bed, watching the night-time sea raging and rolling outside, the waves bucking and rearing; listen to the wind shrieking and the tide crashing on to the great granite rocks. And she would love it – both for the drama and for the haul she could expect on the beaches the following day.

The sea brought her gifts. Pieces of wood – all shapes and sizes that she could use and mould for her sculptures, her driftwood art; pieces of glass so old and pitted that she could only guess at their ancient history; shells that could be transformed, transfigured into jewellery, threaded on to leather thongs. It was a treasure hunt. And Élodie loved the sea for that.

She supposed that she had simply fallen into the work that

56

she did – and she knew that she was fortunate. When she was a girl, she and Jacques had spent hours beachcombing in the rocky coves, searching for special stones they could paint; shells and sea glass they could use to decorate some unsuspecting household item of their mother's – such as the edges of a mirror or a bedside lamp. They had made candle holders too and ashtrays, and their mother had never seemed to mind; the Old Lighthouse was still crammed with their early childish creations.

Even back then, they hadn't spent much time with other children from the island and their parents hadn't encouraged them to. Jacques and Élodie had been born here, but their parents had not and they were both considered outsiders – their father from Paris, their mother from just outside Rouen. Perhaps it was because their parents made no effort to integrate; behaved instead as if they might well be slightly superior to the Bellîlois, the people born on Belle-Île. And so Élodie and Jacques had felt like outsiders too. It was true that they were different from the other village children. They had made themselves insular, and the people in the villages seemed close and clannish to them. But Élodie and Jacques were never lonely. They had each other, so they could never be that.

Élodie bent to pick up a small piece of wood. It was rounded, which she liked; this showed it had spent a long time in the ocean, and it still had some red paint on one side. She ran a fingertip over it. Now, of course, her family were not outsiders – far from it. Now, it was Élodie and her mother who watched the visitors come and go. There was no sense of permanence; they each belonged to a new current of people who swept in with the sea and then out again, leaving the island behind them unchanged as ever. Although they sometimes bought her

57

artwork, these visitors meant little to her. Neither did Élodie have a lot to do with the people who lived around her – that hadn't changed. Did she need them? She spoke to her mother every day and for the rest, she had her work; this absorbed her. Sometimes, whole hours went by unnoticed. When she was lost in her art – that was when Élodie was happiest.

The wood had a good grain and an interesting knot too, adding to its character, and a curve at the top, so it might become a small part of an animal's head. She thought about it. It had the right kind of streamlined shape. A cheetah perhaps? She liked cheetahs because of how fast they could run – and it would certainly be a challenge to achieve that sense of movement in driftwood alone.

Over the years, she had moved on considerably from those first early ashtrays and mirrors. Now, her work varied in scale and could be anything from a miniature seahorse to a life-size stag, antlers and all – actually, antlers were one of the easiest things to accomplish from driftwood. Élodie smiled. She had learnt how to secure driftwood pieces to bases of marble or wood; how to fashion recycled copper into animal hooves, and how to make an armature – a steel frame – coated with fibreglass for a roughened surface on which to fit the wood, though for this she needed some help from Pierre who lived outside Le Palais and who would come over for a day or two when she took on the larger projects. But horses were her favourite – like the one outside Thea's flower shop, which had turned almost silvery in the coastal air.

Thea had been a big part of Élodie's childhood, this energetic Englishwoman from Cornwall, gluing their family together in that way she had. Élodie's father had always been difficult, though her mother Mathilde never used to be as fragile or needy as she seemed to be now. Their whole family was unstable. They teetered on the edge of something and Élodie wasn't sure quite what was below. Perhaps that was why her parents had employed Thea in the first place? Had they always needed someone to hold them together? Élodie could not remember a time when Thea had not been there.

The next piece of wood she found was smaller and had lodged itself between two rocks, half hidden by a thick ribbon of seaweed – it could be used as the limb of a small man, for there was a joint like a knee and the leg went off at an angle. She held it up, considering. A puppet man? The idea of making a complete puppet theatre had been running around in her mind for a while now; she could almost see the faces, the rectangular pieces of flat-grained wood with wedges for noses and round surprised eyes. Élodie put the driftwood in her bag.

In retrospect, Thea's departure hadn't come entirely out of the blue. Her mother hadn't been so nice to Thea for a while. They had been friends once, as she'd told Colette in the flower shop yesterday. But even as a little girl, Élodie had sensed their friendship disintegrating, even if she did not recognise that fact until much later. Her mother had become sharp and critical, she seemed to resent Thea's presence in the house. And yet Thea had come over from England to help her. ('Your mother cannot cope,' her father was fond of saying, though Élodie suspected it was he who made it difficult for her mother to cope.) And then Mathilde asked Thea to leave. But why?

Élodie stood up straighter to stretch her back, watched the tide rolling in, curling its pathway through the rocks of the cove, leaving its delicate foam trails to disintegrate into the air behind it. She loved these traces of the sea, the way it left its mark, just as Thea had left her mark on the family in the Old Lighthouse.

The first Élodie had known of her imminent departure was seeing Thea pack a suitcase, a set expression on her face as she placed items of clothing one by one – not folded as Mama would have done, but rolled.

'Where are you going?' Élodie had blurted. 'What are you doing?' Already, she liked to think that Thea somehow belonged to her. She was by nature a solitary child, preferring the company of her brother to any other, but she adored Thea. Élodie's mother was constantly asking her to do things, expecting her to be ready to go somewhere, to be on time for something she had already forgotten. Thea was not like this. Thea was easy-going; she always let her be.

'I am leaving, Élodie,' she said. She wouldn't look at her.

'But why?' Élodie stared at her. Thea was as much a part of their home as her mother or father – more than her father perhaps, for he was so often away, and often angry too. When he was around, their household changed, as if he had brought a tornado into the house with him. They were all aware of it. They stopped talking so much, laughing so freely. They slunk into the crevices of rooms and didn't risk sparking anything off. Élodie and Jacques would spend hours away from the house if they got the chance; often Thea went with them.

'I have to.'

'You cannot. *C'est impossible.*' Élodie had stood there, hands on hips, eyes blazing. 'Thea, you cannot!'

Thea had smiled then. She had bent down to Élodie's level and placed her hands gently on her shoulders, her head close to Élodie's. 'I have to, *chérie,*' she said. 'I don't want to. It's the last thing I want. But I have no choice.'

'Mama will not let you.' Élodie had been close to tears, she felt them welling inside, she didn't want to imagine how life would be in the Old Lighthouse without Thea.

'It is Mama who has told me to go,' Thea said.

Élodie had stared at her in disbelief. '*Non* . . .' She shook her head.

'I am sorry, my darling, but it's true.'

Élodie held her gaze for a few moments, registering what she was saying to her. Then she turned on her heel and stormed from the room. 'Mama!' she roared.

Mathilde was in the kitchen drinking coffee and reading the paper. She looked calm, but even then Élodie was not fooled. '*Oui, chérie?*'

'Why is Thea leaving?'

Her mother sighed and folded the paper. 'It is a grown-up matter,' she said.

'What grown-up matter?'

'Something that is too complicated for little girls to understand.' And that was all she would say.

Élodie cried and stamped her feet and even told her mother she hated her. Nothing made any difference. The only thing that pierced her mother's aura of calm was when she said: 'I will tell Papa. He will not allow Thea to leave.'

Her mother had glared at her then. 'You will not tell Papa, Élodie,' she said. 'And Thea must leave. There is nothing you – nor Papa – can do about it.'

And so, incredible as it seemed, Thea had left, though Élodie made her promise to stay close by. 'Don't leave the island,' she had begged. 'Don't go back to England – I will never see you again.'

Thea had looked as if she might cry. '*Ma petite* . . . I will miss you so much. But I don't know if I can . . .'

In the end though, Jacques too had pleaded with her and – much to their mother's undisguised irritation – Thea had stayed nearby in Sauzon. At first, they thought it was for a short while, at first Élodie was convinced that her mother would change her mind and Thea would return to the Old Lighthouse. But no. Thea opened a florist's shop with Lise from the village. She bought a second-hand motorbike to get around on and soon afterwards, she married Sébastien, a fisherman from Sauzon whose family had always lived on the island.

Life had gone on. Élodie saw her rarely; sometimes just a figure in the distance on the Pointe looking out towards the sea, towards her old home, sometimes on that motorbike wheeling around the country lanes. Later, as she grew up, Élodie saw her in Sauzon, sometimes they chatted. Thea had a daughter of her own by then, but she was always friendly and interested in Élodie's life – she seemed to hold no ill will for the way her mother had treated her.

Élodie had searched the rocks and beaches of several of their little coves – coves as good as private since you had to pass through the grounds of the Old Lighthouse to get to them. They could also be reached by sea but few bothered, even in the height of the tourist season; there were better beaches along the coast – if 'better' meant sand and fewer rocks under the surface when one swam. Élodie stood still for a moment and breathed in the fresh salt air; watched a cormorant drying himself on a flat slab of granite out to sea. She had collected a few driftwood pieces on the way and was especially pleased with some curly bits she needed for the wool of the sheep she was currently working on. She was lucky, she knew, to live here, to work here; fortunate that Belle-Île could be stormy, wild and unforgiving.

After Sébastien had died and Thea's daughter had left home, Thea and Élodie had taken to having coffee together from time to time. When they were chatting one day, Thea mentioned that she would love to see some of Élodie's work.

'Come to the studio,' Élodie urged. 'I'd really like you to.'

Thea smiled. 'That would be nice, but I'm not sure,' she said. 'Your mother . . .'

'Don't worry about her,' Élodie said. 'You know Mama. She might rage inwardly, but she'll keep out of the way.'

Thea had laughed. 'Well, maybe one day I will.'

And rather to Élodie's surprise she had come, one afternoon, looking rather hesitant, not on the motorbike, but picking her way carefully over the dunes and through the pink, purple and yellow succulents down the coastal path that led to the Old Lighthouse.

Élodie was delighted. She showed Thea some of her finished pieces – a small foal, a dragon, a complex spined fish. These were her current favourites but many more pieces were out there in galleries on the island, either sold or awaiting their new owner. Others she kept back, not quite satisfied with them, watching them almost warily as if they might tell her why. Sometimes they did – she would see what was missing or what had been overworked in the form and she could rectify it, but not always. Other times she remained frustrated with what was not quite right, what had not worked, and she would dismantle the piece with a sigh and use the wood for another purpose. It took time, but all her work took time. Time was what Élodie had most of, and work was what she most liked to do.

'Where do you find all the wood?' Thea's eyes were shining. She had always been so full of life; that was one of the reasons Élodie had missed her so.

'From the beach – mostly in winter. I dry it out first, store it in the barn and then, *voila*!' She laughed.

'It's amazing. The variety I mean – and what you make out of it.'

'I work with sea glass too.' She pointed to a lampshade. It had taken her a long time to find the right pieces, but when the light shone through, it had the pleasing effect of old stained glass.

Thea moved closer to examine it. 'How beautiful. I remember you and Jacques collecting sea glass from the beach when you were children.'

'*Mais oui*.' This saddened Élodie. Any mention of her brother could sadden her. They had been so close, they had done everything together once. But there came a time when she could not leave and he could not stay. And . . . She pushed away the thought of that. It was another thing she did not wish to remember.

'You must miss him,' Thea said softly. And she laid a hand on Élodie's arm.

'Yes, I do.' Life was solitary here on the island and normally that was how Élodie liked it. But yes, she missed him more than she could say.

'I would like to commission something,' Thea said. 'Something for the flower shop.'

'Oh.' Élodie was surprised. 'You really don't have to.'

'I know that.' Thea moved around the studio in between the driftwood animals, stroking a fishy spine here, a horse's mane there.

Élodie smiled. Thea seemed to have an understanding of the pieces, so perhaps she was not just being kind after all. She too was creative. Élodie had seen some of her flower arrangements, her baskets and bouquets. She had a delicate and artistic touch. 'What would you like?' she asked her.

'A horse,' Thea said with sudden decision. 'A horse with

panniers for plants and maybe some earth within his body for planting?' She nodded. 'I'll put him outside the shop.'

'Excellent.' Élodie very much liked the sound of this. And so, they discussed sizing and prices. Élodie quoted a price lower than usual because of what Thea had always meant to her and Thea pushed her up to 'what was fair'.

Élodie had worked on that commission for several weeks. She had to find the right image of a horse among the photographs of horses she had already taken, she had to work on a sketch and build up the plan. It always took time to select the right pieces; often, she had to go away, work on something else, come back to it with a fresh and objective eye. She started with some solid slabs for structure. The second layer of driftwood must go with the flow of the horse's muscles, provide that sense of contained movement, that sensation when one looked at the creature that it might almost gallop off into the sunset. This was fanciful of course, especially for a creature destined to hold flowers, but it was part of Élodie's process and so she stuck to it. For her, a horse symbolised energy and power; that was what she wanted to achieve. She needed to build him right, so that he had more hope of surviving the elements. But she would advise Thea that in the winter she should bring him inside.

When her work was completed, Élodie carried the driftwood horse to Sauzon, supporting his body on her lap, tied – and balanced precariously – to the handlebars; legs and hooves facing the oncoming traffic.

'I would have come to collect him,' Thea exclaimed, when she saw her wobbling along. But she laughed and gently touched his woody mane.

'No, no, I enjoyed the ride.' They had certainly attracted a few interested observers on the way. And as for Thea, Élodie could tell that she was delighted. The horse, which she had created with love, was going to a good home.

It was her mother who had told her that Colette was back.

'That's good,' Élodie had said. 'Will she stay this time, do you think?'

'I doubt it.' Her mother frowned. She was staring out to sea. The lichen on the granite shone like gold-dust.

'Thea needs her,' Élodie said. 'She is not at all well. So, whatever it is they have fallen out about, don't you think it is time to make up?' And for you too, Élodie was thinking. For you too.

'Have you seen Thea?' Mathilde's voice was sharp.

'Yes, I see her sometimes, you know that I do.' And you have to accept it, she thought. Élodie was an adult now; her mother could not dictate her life.

'And she is very ill?'

Élodie realised that her mother was trembling. She wasn't sure what this meant – just that everything concerning her relationship with Thea was packed with emotion. 'Yes, Mama,' she said gently. 'And you were friends once.'

'Yes,' she said. 'We were.'

Élodie let it pass. But now that Colette had returned to Belle-Île, she thought that other things too – good things perhaps – might also be possible. Élodie hoped that her mother would go and see Thea, that she could find it in her heart to forgive. She still did not know for certain why she had told Thea to leave, but by now she could hazard a guess. It was a matter best not mentioned, she decided, not now; probably not ever. But her mother needed to do something to put her life in order. And perhaps now, as then, it might be Thea who held the key.

CHAPTER 9

Colette

Colette walked up Rue du Port past Henri's house. The blue-painted, delicately wrought-iron front door was turning rusty in the salt air – just one example of what the tide, the rain, the salty breezes did to the houses, piers, jetties and cliffs . . . She paused to admire the lace curtains, at the windows of the low-roofed cottages featuring finely embroidered fishing boats and lighthouses. It was good to see that the island had preserved these elements of its culture and history. The sea was integral to Sauzon – the first fish canneries had been built here back in the mid-1800s, her father had been proud of this fact. *Her father* . . . Colette blinked back a tear. She was on her way to the cemetery to see him now.

She had dropped in at Francine's before she left the house. Yes, naturally, she would listen out, Francine said, her ironic smile telling Colette that she'd been watching and listening out for months while Colette wasn't even around. 'Sorry,' Colette said, 'of course you will, I know that.' Francine was good to help as much as she did. But Colette still found her as dour as she had in the old days.

The road soon took on a more countrified look: gardens with hollyhocks, plum and apple trees, ancient olives, a lonely pine stretching across the road. At the end she turned left, made her way under the cemetery's narrow arch through the green iron gate. *Every town that has a cemetery must also have a flower shop.* She remembered her mother's words once again.

The gravel walkways between the gravestones were deserted, the stone wall surrounding the cemetery adding to the air of isolation. The gravestones ranged from simple stone and white-painted concrete to polished granite and ornate marble; weeds sprouted around the graves, poking through gravel, searching for light. Colette knew exactly where he was. In the beginning, she had come here every day, gone home and said pointedly to her mother: 'I have visited my father's grave.'

Thea went too, of course; Colette saw her trudging with flowers up the hill, though she never spoke of it. Sometimes she even went there on that motorbike of hers – an old black and chrome Cimatti she'd had for years; Papa used to joke that he had more power in his little finger than that bike had in its engine. Her mother took no notice. She polished it till the headlights gleamed. 'That bike's served me well,' she'd say. 'It gets me away when I need to get away.' Colette's father hadn't seemed to mind, back then, that sometimes his wife needed to get away.

But Colette minded – she minded still. Did her mother feel guilty? She ought to. He would never have gone out fishing that stormy night if not for that row between them. Had her mother ever loved him? Or had it been a sense of duty that took her to his graveside – a desire to be seen to be doing the right thing?

68

Colette stopped short when she reached the grave. Her mother had chosen a polished grey granite, a simple cross. Colette had expected the granite to be bare, but there were fresh flowers, clearly only a few days old. She frowned.

Sébastien Lenoire. His name was inscribed on the tombstone; his lifespan. The words: *beloved husband of Thea and father of Colette. Lost at sea.*

They had found his body – it had washed up beyond the Pointe some days later. He had been laid out at home – cleaned up but still bloated, pale and so unlike the father she'd known and loved, that she could barely look at him. There had been a condolence book and people had come to write their thoughts and messages. It had been the worst time.

Colette laid her own flowers on the grave. She had brought sprigs of rosemary for remembrance, purple verbena and a pink and blue hydrangea from her mother's garden. '*Bonjour, Papa,*' she whispered. 'I'm sorry it's been so long. I think of you, though. All the time. You know that, don't you? I keep you in my heart.'

She knelt on the gravel beside his grave, bowed her head, whispered a prayer from her childhood, one she hadn't even known she remembered. The morning sun was warm and its brightness seemed to tinge the tombstones with gold. Colette closed her eyes. She hoped he was somewhere beautiful, some-where peaceful. And that he was happy there.

She remembered days she had gone out with him, in the small inky-blue and white fishing boat *L'Étoile.* His voice gruff: 'You can come if you are quiet, *ma petite.* But you mustn't scare the fish, remember that.' She had watched as he cast his net, waited with him for the haul. They had often stayed out until the sun was about to dip on the horizon, until the waters were calm and grey and they could row gently in. Only locals were aware that sailors must loosen their sails when entering Sauzon harbour; Colette knew that the wind coming from the cliffs could be strong and sudden enough to tip a sailboat right over.

Colette ran her hand gently across the polished stone – dusty from a few days without rain. She let the tears fall. By the time he died, she was older, she no longer went out in *L'Étoile*, though she still helped him with the gutting and filleting of the catch on the quayside. She'd never forgotten how to do it, either. Mark had marvelled at her fish-filleting and culinary skills the first time she'd invited him to dinner. 'Of course,' she had said. 'I'm a fisherman's daughter. A fisherman's daughter can never forget.' Sometimes she wished she could.

That night – the night of the storm – she had heard her parents arguing. It was unusual. And yet, had the atmosphere been strained between them of late? Colette was young, she had her own life now, maybe she had not noticed? Her father had his fishing, her mother the flower shop. It had always been that way. But when they were together they had seemed happy enough. She saw the way they looked at one another sometimes. She had always thought that was love.

Not that night, though. That night had been punctured with raised voices and silences. Colette had stepped out of her room to stand on the landing, to listen.

'What's this all about anyway?' her mother was saying. 'Why all the questions, Sébastien?'

A pause. 'Because, you see, Thea,' he said, 'I know the truth.'

'What truth? What are you talking about?' But Colette heard her mother's voice tremble. It made her listen even harder. She sounded scared. Why would she be scared?

70

'It's not a secret,' he said. 'Not any more. So why not come clean? Why not tell me everything?'

Colette waited. A secret? What sort of secret? And what did he mean by 'everything'?

'How?' Her mother's voice wasn't much more than a whisper. Colette had to strain to hear.

'Someone told me.' His voice changed. He sounded weary.

Another man? Was that it? Did her mother have a lover? Was that why she was always working late in the flower shop, why she went off for long walks by herself sometimes, why she went out riding her bike to 'get away', why she wore that air of perpetual mystery?

'Someone?' Her mother's voice was sharp. 'Who? There's only one person . . .'

'Never mind who. That's not important. What *is* important is that you have been lying to me, Thea, lying to me all this time.'

He sounded angry now too – and why wouldn't he be, if she had been lying to him, if there was another man? Colette felt her hands curl into fists. How could she do that to him?

'But—'

'Why, Thea?' His voice rang out and seemed to echo around the stairwell. Colette shrank back against the wall as if it might absorb her. 'Why did you do it? And why pretend – for so many years?'

So many years? Colette froze. She wasn't sure she wanted to hear any more. But she couldn't stop listening – not yet.

'Sébastien, listen to me . . .'

'Tell me the name of this man,' he demanded. 'This man who had you. This man who is—'

'What does it matter?' She was shouting now. 'What does

71

that matter, for God's sake?' Colette wasn't sure she had ever heard her mother shout like this before. She was crying too, her words indistinguishable.

There was a silence. Colette waited.

'Well, *chérie*,' her father said at last. 'You don't have to pretend any more. At least, you don't have to pretend with me.'

Colette heard footsteps, heard him lifting his fishing bag, heard him coming out of the kitchen and going to the front door. She peeked between the spindles of the staircase. His body was rigid, his face white and angry. *Papa*. But she didn't say it out loud.

'Don't go out tonight, Sébastien,' Thea called. She came after him, her face streaked with tears. 'They forecast a storm.'

He didn't even glance back.

'Don't go out . . .'

Papa.

He slammed the front door behind him.

Papa.

And Colette never saw him again.

Her knees were stiff and pockmarked from the gravel when Colette finally got to her feet. '*Au revoir, Papa*,' she whispered, and she straightened the flowers until they looked just right.

As she left the stone walls of the *cimetière* behind and stepped out on to Rue Amiral Willaumez, her mobile rang. She pulled the phone from her bag. Mark.

'Hello, darling.' His voice was bright. But Colette wasn't convinced.

'Hi Mark,' she said. She decided to go back a different way – it was a chance to take in the town, see for herself how much had changed.

'How are you? How's your mother?'

He was a kind man, Colette reminded herself, and he cared. She took a turn at Rue Roz er Mor. It was more or less untouched by development; a field of hay, another few scrappy plots of dry earth and wild grass scattered with fennel and cow parsley, leading to the narrow, steep *chemin* that led down to the Rue du Lieutenant Riou, the post office and the *mairie*. 'I'm fine. She's – oh' – she steeled herself – 'oh, Mark, she's very poorly. I'm not sure . . .' *How much longer she can go on*, she was thinking. But she didn't say it. She had spoken to the nurse who came in every day and she had done some research, desperately combing site after site in an effort to find out something more positive. She needed to speak to the doctor too, but she was very much afraid that it was just a question of time. She began to walk down the *chemin*, flanked by stone walls.

'That's awful, darling. I'm so sorry.' He sighed. 'I wish I'd come with you. I should have insisted. You shouldn't have to be dealing with this alone.'

'It's OK,' she said. She'd needed to.

'So – will you be staying? I mean—'

'For a while,' she cut in. There was no hope of explaining. Not to Mark, not to herself. There was so much she couldn't forgive her mother for. But she was still her mother. Colette emerged by the library, blinking as if she'd been in a tunnel. Perhaps it was a tunnel of her own making, she found herself thinking. And the church bell let out a dull clang, almost as if it were agreeing with her.

'I could still come over.' He sounded strong and firm.

'Maybe.' She could probably do with some of that strength. 'So . . .?'

'But not yet – she's very weak. I need to spend a bit of time with her first.' Which wasn't exactly it, but . . .

'Of course you do,' he soothed. 'But I want to support you through this, Colette. I want to help.'

'Thank you.' She made her way up Rue Saint-Nicolas towards the flower shop. She knew she was lucky to have him. But she also knew that he'd want to take over, do things his way. As she passed the rather grand villas in this road, she pictured Mark striding into her mother's sickroom, telling her what she should be drinking, eating, taking. And as for the flower shop – he'd think Colette completely crazy.

And I probably am, she thought. But – 'I'll let you know,' she said. 'I have to get back now. I'll call you soon.' And she breathed a sigh of relief as she replaced her phone in her bag.

She looked back in the direction she'd come, thought of the fresh flowers on her father's tombstone. Yes, he had been respected in the village, yes, he had lived here all his life. But he had no family left – only a wife who had betrayed him and who was now confined to her sickbed. Perhaps it didn't matter who it was. Perhaps she should just be grateful that someone cared. But Colette would very much like to know – who after all these years would still be laying flowers on her father's grave?

CHAPTER 10

Étienne

Today, Étienne was walking the other way – along the cliff path. Why not? Days were passing. There were other directions to take. It was just a walk, only a pathway.

He felt still fresh from the unexpected encounter with Denis, still smarting a little, aware that when he ventured out from his mother's pink house he was glancing from left to right, checking for the absence of that familiar face.

And now, walking the *sentier côtier* on this rather fine spring afternoon, the ghosts were still present, *naturellement*, pedalling on their bicycles along the thin strip of dry earth that made up the path. It was a test for them (wasn't everything?). Who could stay mounted the longest when the path began to climb? Who could go furthest without having to stop and get off? Who could build up the speed, the energy, the necessary momentum? They placed markers, but it was always Yann or Denis, the biggest and the oldest, who won – there was a lot of good-natured rivalry between those two. After that, they'd all have to push their bikes up the rest of the hill. No matter.

They were already looking forward to how it would be later – on the way down. Étienne could remember that sensation as if it were yesterday; how the wind stung his skin and tore through his hair, how they shrieked and whooped like wild things as their bicycles bumped at speed along the uneven and pitted path. And every so often, *mais oui*, one of them would go flying and pick himself up, dusty and grazed, before getting back on his bicycle again.

Étienne stopped. He wouldn't go any further. He had passed the little cove where they used to swim and had cut down to the lower walkway where they'd had to stamp their feet on the grass and the gorse to remind the fragile path that it really was one. He looked out to the ocean. It all seemed so peaceful. Just kilometre upon kilometre of barely ruffled sea sparkling in the gentle afternoon sun.

He sat down to survey the scene, automatically pulling his notebook and pen from the back pocket of his jeans. He'd been resentful, but now he was glad he'd come back to sort out his mother's house, though he hadn't expected to stay so long. It had given him more insight into the final years of her life, helped him to imagine her sitting in the window seat where there was the best light for her embroidery, heating up her coffee in the bad-tempered percolator, chatting to her friends in the boulangerie. Even so, although the cleaning, the sorting and the decluttering had been quick enough, the paperwork dragged on.

You are not the only client on our books was the subtext of Monsieur le Notaire's weary voice every time Étienne phoned his office. *There are still more papers to sign. And I must come to the house. We must make an appointment. You will be there for how long, did you say?*

Monsieur had come at last this morning. Étienne had been

76

expecting him to applaud his efforts at minimalism (*So —
what? Even now, a grown man, you need praise? You need approval?*
mocked that other voice of his again). But in fact, the *notaire*
had frowned.

'It is looking very spartan,' he had said, running a critical
fingertip along the top of the chair. It came away dusty.

Merde, thought Étienne. The one place he hadn't dusted,
the one place he'd missed. But he was damned if he'd apologise. Apologise for dust? That really would be the final insult.
'Spartan?' he echoed instead.

'Empty,' the *notaire* clarified, gesturing around the room as
if Étienne might not have noticed.

Étienne tried not to grind his teeth. 'I was under the impression that rooms appear larger when devoid of furniture,' he
said, not without a glitter of sarcasm.

Monsieur took a large white handkerchief from his pocket
and mopped his brow although it was neither hot nor airless in
the room and the window was open wide. 'Perhaps,' he said.
'But it can also help to make a place look lived in. Homely.
That too can be appealing, Monsieur Chevalier.'

Homely. How could he make the place look homely? Étienne cast his gaze around the room. Leave the stove greasy
from last night's supper? Crumbs from breakfast on the desk,
perhaps? A pair of dirty socks cast aside on the bed? Was that
homely?

'No matter.' The *notaire* sighed as he took his clipboard from
his black briefcase. He surveyed the form clipped to it. 'Will
you be staying to show people around?'

'Does that help make it more homely too?'

The *notaire* gave him a certain look over his reading glasses.
'Not necessarily, *non*.'

'Then, no.' Of course he wouldn't. Didn't he want to escape as soon as possible?

'Very well. As you wish.' Monsieur le Notaire put a tick – or maybe a cross – on the form. 'Sign here please.'

Étienne signed. And now – was he free to leave? Apparently, not yet. 'In one or two more days,' Monsieur le Notaire informed him. 'And then perhaps . . .'

Étienne thought of his notebook tucked away in the desk drawer and felt a strange shiver of relief. What was that all about? What was he even trying to achieve by writing it all down? Perhaps though, writing wasn't purely about achievement, he thought morosely. And he should know. He was supposed to be a writer.

He got up, dusted down his jeans and started making his way back along the path that was barely a path. Down below, the cove was gleaming and he was tempted. But no . . . He had to get back. There was still work to be done.

It was true that his mother had held a deep affection for Belle-Île, just as Madame Riou in the boulangerie kept telling him. Étienne supposed that his mother had always associated the island with the holidays – *les vacances* – much as she'd associated Locmariaquer, her home town, with work. And some might say there was no work harder than the oysters . . . Étienne understood because he'd seen how hard she worked, he'd seen what working in the oysters could do to people – women bent double with arthritic fingers and hands, rheumatism in their necks, weariness in their eyes. And of course, he too had been part of that blissful family summertime on Belle-Île.

But that wasn't the only reason Lucie Chevalier had wanted Étienne to come back here, surely? He drew closer to the cove where the water was a delicate pale green. Why had it been so important to her? He struck his way through the gorse and the bracken.

And then he got it. What an idiot he was sometimes. She'd wanted it because she knew it was important for him — not *to* him but *for* him; a subtle difference that Étienne appreciated. So. What had she wanted him to learn? What had she wanted him to discover?

There was a flash of movement in the cove below and he glanced down. It was a woman, a naked woman, her dark hair wet and curling around her narrow shoulders. He stared down at her — he couldn't help it — she seemed part elf, part mermaid. But in the next split second, she glanced up. He was too far away, but he instinctively guessed the horror that would be in her eyes. She'd thought it was safe. She knew the cove couldn't be seen clearly from the main cliff path. So, she knew the area, she must live here. He looked away almost immediately of course — he liked to think he was a gentleman if nothing else. But not before he saw her grab some flimsy item of clothing and hold it to her breast, as she headed into the lee of the cliffs and out of sight.

And even after everything: the loss of his mother, his soul-searching, that encounter with Denis, those ghosts and this place . . . Étienne had to smile.

Colette

Colette had forgotten how warm it could be here on the island in June. Long, sultry days, late dawns. Belle-Île was heated by the Gulf Stream, one of the reasons it had always been a popular holiday destination, she supposed. And now here she was, back where she had begun.

She'd slipped into a routine without really meaning to. Bringing her mother boiled water with lemon in the mornings, lingering long enough to open the blinds, plump up the pillows, sort out her mother's immediate needs. She'd breakfast then – on coffee and bread from the boulangerie. Then she'd go down into the flower shop. Flowers needed TLC on a daily basis – Colette remembered that much. They were hard to resist. And besides, it seemed to be what her mother wanted.

'Thank you, *chérie.*' She had grasped her daughter's hand surprisingly tightly when Colette told her about the customer and her Aunt Marin. 'Thank you so much, my dear.' And then: 'You know I will be feeling stronger soon, I am sure of it. If you could see to the shop for a short while every day. If you could water the plants and . . .' Burnt out by the energy she'd used, she sank back on to the pillows.

Colette hesitated. She hadn't come back here to run the flower shop. And yet . . . Hadn't she loved planning that arrangement for Madame Schneider's Aunt Marin? Hadn't she sniffed the fragrance of the jasmine and stocks and felt herself pulled once more into memories of her childhood world of flowers? It was all so confusing. But her mother wouldn't be getting any stronger. The opposite was true. Every day she was growing weaker.

'Very well, Maman,' she said. 'I will do that while I am here.' *But I will be leaving*, she ought to say. Belle-Île was no longer her home. But she didn't say it. For now, she was here. And besides, her mother had drifted off to sleep again.

Colette had been in touch with the doctor and talked to Francine about the original diagnosis.

'I saw she was looking tired.' Francine shrugged her thin shoulders. 'Losing weight too.'

Colette bit her lip. There were advantages to being the kind of neighbour who noticed things, she thought.

'She said she was fine. By the time I eventually persuaded her to go to the doctor, by the time she was diagnosed, by the time treatment was prescribed . . .' She sighed. 'Thea did not respond.' She said the words as if Colette's mother had had some choice in the matter and Colette gave her a sharp glance.

'Some of us think we do not have a lot to live for, you know?' Francine folded her arms as if this was explanation enough.

But Colette would not allow her old adversary to make her feel guilty. She had chosen to leave the island, but she'd had more than enough reason. 'She had her flowers.'

'Flowers – pff.' Francine gestured her contempt.

'Francine—'

'I know what you thought.' She hesitated. 'But you should give your mother a chance.'

'A chance?' Colette stared at her.

'A chance to explain. A chance to make amends.' Francine sighed. 'Things – they are not always exactly as they seem, you know, Colette.'

Colette frowned. 'What do you mean?'

But she shook her head, clearly thinking she'd said enough. 'Your mother was waiting for a bone marrow transplant when she was told that the leukaemia had relapsed and become incurable,' she said instead. 'The cancer was so aggressive, the doctor said she only had six months left to live.'

Six months . . . 'Which was when you wrote to me,' Colette said.

'Exactly.'

How had her mother felt when she heard that news? Had she wanted to fight it? Had she had the energy to fight it? Francine seemed to be suggesting that she hadn't had much to live for. And yet . . . Colette realised that she knew so little of her mother's life. There was the shop. But apart from that – what else did she have?

'I'll do what I can.' Not only in the flower shop, but to ease her mother's pain and discomfort.

'Good girl.' Unexpectedly, Francine put her bony hand on Colette's arm. 'I'll be here too,' she said. 'The nurse comes by every morning, and the morphine helps her pain, but don't worry, I cared for my Alain when he was sick. I know what to do.'

Colette nodded. 'Thank you.' She would never have dreamed she could be comforted by Francine, but she was.

Colette sat with her mother at various times during each day. But she never stayed too long. She didn't want to tire her, but more than that, she didn't know what to say to her. The past was still the past and despite what Francine had said, it wasn't so simply brushed away. Nevertheless, it no longer seemed possible for her to leave – at least not yet. Despite everything, Colette wanted her mother to know that she was there for her. This was not just about finding answers to her questions, not just about having the chance to say goodbye. But neither was it easy being here. And in the meantime – the flower shop let her breathe.

At 4 p.m. Colette slipped in to check on her mother. She was asleep again. Colette watched her for a moment, feeling an unfamiliar surge of tenderness, a gentle ache for what might have been. She could see the lines of pain etched around the creases of her eyes and mouth – new lines every day, it seemed – and a slackness to her jaw. Her eyelids trembled for a moment as if she might be dreaming. A nightmare perhaps? Colette moved closer. She could smell the lavender and thyme scent she had always preferred; but underneath it, the metallic smell of illness, of medication, of chemicals invading the body as surely as the leukaemia was.

Colette shivered. She plucked the bedclothes and pulled them gently over her mother's shoulders, hoping if she made her more comfortable then the dream might go away. She turned, left the room, closed the door as silently as she could.

Having let Francine know she was going out for a walk, Colette headed out past the Bureau du Port down to the harbour where crates of ropes, nets and oilskins perched on the uneven flags of the harbour wall. She breathed deeply, feeling a pang of guilt at her sudden sense of freedom. A few tourists were strolling on the promenade and outside the Hôtel du Phare people sat at tables enjoying their drinks and the views out to sea. Colette passed the fish stall on the corner, smelt the salty, gritty tang of the seafood combining with the sweeter smell of crêpes and galettes from the stall nearby. Being on the promontory, the Hôtel du Phare caught all the weather and was looking tired, she observed. But then again – weren't they all?

She headed up the path amongst tall hollyhocks gently waving in the breeze and the wild *fenouil* which often featured in local recipes. On the other side of the harbour mouth was the old boathouse, a few small tenders outside its olive-green doors. Sometimes, in the old days, children had got across there at low tide. Not that there was much to see – it was an isolated building and usually locked, but it had a certain atmospheric draw and still did. The boathouse was looking tired too, and the slipway that led down to the water was covered in thick seaweed and had fallen into disrepair.

Colette stayed on the *sentier côtier* which climbed steeply to give a stunning view of the pleasure craft carrying tourists into the sparkling harbour. Once, there had only been fishermen like her father. Even in her lifetime the village had changed dramatically. Pretty Sauzon, with its pastel-painted houses where men had fished and a canning industry had flourished, had sidestepped into a place of leisure and tourism. But not quite. Colette looked down. There were still working fish-ermen like Henri's son Pierre, there were those who lived here all year round, artists who had come – like Monet – to paint the landscape, and people who ran successful small businesses here, like her mother with her flower shop.

She picked up her pace. A small green lizard darted across the dry and dusty path in front of her and retreated to the crevice between two rocks. She reached the big hotel on the promontory. It hadn't changed too much. But for how long would there be a flower shop? Her mother was never going to run it again. Who would be interested in taking it over? Colette couldn't imagine. She had walked this path so many times before that her feet knew exactly where it was rocky, where it was sandy, which was the safest foothold. It was second nature, she supposed. It was home. This was the path that led to their nearest beach. Children often swam in the shallow glassy waters of the harbour, but the cove that could be reached via the steep steps from the grounds of this hotel was more private, more appealing.

But Colette couldn't stop now. She walked on, the *sentier côtier* still climbing, looking down on the open, shimmering sea; bright turquoise closer to the undercliff with the dark shadows of rocks beneath. The path clung to the cliff edge. There were yellow gorse and rocks under foot as it narrowed once more, giving out to pine and tamarisk bent from the wind, until the heathland of the Pointe du Cardinal opened out ahead. It was Cornish heath – no wonder her mother had felt so at home here. Colette picked her way over the parched clumps of grass and heather. As she reached the ragged edge, she looked down at the skinny inlet that snaked through the crevices of the cliff. It was even more scary than she remembered. There was a sheer drop and the black rocks beneath were treacherous.

She walked back through the pine forest where spiny needles lay thick on the pathway between the ribbed roots of the trees. Had she come back here simply because her mother needed her? Colette rubbed her hand across her eyes. Because she had wanted to find out the truth behind her mother's past actions?

Or were these simply excuses? Had she secretly been waiting for that call, those reasons to pack her bags and run back to the very island that had trapped her? Because despite that entrapment, despite her difficult relationship with the mother she had never been close to understanding, despite the fact that she had made a life for herself in Cornwall – with a job, a comfortable studio flat and a boyfriend . . . Mark. She stopped on that one. Mark. Despite all those things, she had to admit, there was a part of her that had ached to return.

Oh, for goodness' sake . . . Colette left the undulating path with its scent of fennel and sloes and cut through the bracken on the ghost of another path that was hardly there at all but nonetheless was one she still remembered. It led to a cove supposedly 'only accessible by boat'. In four minutes she was down. She kicked off her shoes. The water was shallow and palest green, the rocks shivering beneath the surface, matted with weed and barnacles. Seaweed lay in trails stranded over the beach and she could hear it cracking as it dried. The sand was gravelly between her toes as she walked down to the water's edge.

The wavelets curled over her feet, cool and refreshing, and Colette made a sudden decision. The bay was hidden from the main coastal path, half hidden from the lower one that only locals ever used, and anyway, there was no one around. She took a few steps back, pulled off her T-shirt and bra, stepped out of her denim skirt and ran into the waves, arms wide as if to embrace them. Although it had taken her father one stormy night, Colette had never stopped loving the sea.

The beach was deceptive. It was shallow at first and then a deep shelf could sweep you off your feet – literally. But Colette remembered. She swam a strong breaststroke between the rocks, then rolled on to her back, contemplated the distant waves, the horizon, the sky. This was a place she had often come to, sometimes with a friend, more often when she wanted to be alone. The beach itself was surrounded by an ancient marbled grey granite, succulents and other plants growing in its cracks and crevices, hanging over the walls and ledges. To the right of the bay, looking from the sea, was a narrow cave with a natural swimming pool that filled at high tide. She knew this part of the island so well; coming back here like this, it almost seemed that the paths were as close to her mind, to her heart, as the veins in her own body.

At last, feeling chilled, she let the tide take her in, wrapped her arms around her breasts and ran helter-skelter out of the water. No towel, of course. She'd never needed one when she was a girl. She'd just rub herself dry with her T-shirt and pull it on, run home and let the warm breeze do the job for her. It had been a while.

Colette heard a sound from the cliff top and looked up to see a man high above her stomping along the lower coastal path. Damn it. She'd assumed she was alone. And from the way he was stomping, this man looked angry.

She made a grab for her T-shirt, but he had seen her. He stopped dead in his tracks. Colette scuttled into the lee of a rock. It was ridiculous – who cared a jot about being seen topless these days? – but there was something about the way he stared at her . . . She shook the thought from her head. What did it matter? She rubbed herself dry and pulled on the T-shirt. It was revealing, but she'd jog back up the path. It would be fine. It had always been fine. Only, the man . . . She seemed to see again the way he stopped, the way he stared.

She pulled on her denim skirt. He was probably just a tourist who'd strayed off the main path. He'd be gone by now, no doubt heading for the bus stop already. Most people didn't stay long in Sauzon – unless they lived here. They came to the island on the ferry, saw the sights via the Belle-Île bus and returned on the ferry again a few days later. They were transitory. The people of Belle-Île – the real people, which for some reason she felt still included herself – barely noticed them. They hardly affected them or their lives at all.

He didn't live here, or she'd know. Chances were she'd never see him again. So she was safe – and next time she decided to go for a swim, she'd bring a costume and a towel.

CHAPTER 12

Mathilde

Madame Riou in the boulangerie had told Mathilde that Thea was ill even before her daughter Élodie had mentioned it. Madame Riou told her many things – that the woman in the pink house opposite had died, that her son had come back to sell the house, and did Mathilde know who he was? 'He was the one . . .' She prattled on. Mathilde usually ignored the gossip, but when it came to Thea, of course she could not. All these years and one would think she would have got used to it – Thea still living here on Belle-Île, Thea in her flower shop. But Mathilde had never dreamed she'd stay.

Thea had been the best friend Mathilde had ever had, which was funny, because Thea had come over here to Belle-Île, a young English girl of just eighteen, knowing nothing about children, or housework come to that, and Mathilde had not even wanted her at first. It had been Léo's idea. Most things in her life, she thought darkly, were Léo's idea.

Rather like Belle-Île itself. They had only been married a year, she was pregnant with Jacques and she'd been unwell – a bout of flu followed by bronchitis. 'Take her away from the dust and grime of Paris,' the doctor had told Léo. 'She needs fresh air. Pamper her a little. The baby will come soon enough and then she will be exhausted. Let us make sure the baby is healthy – and the mother too.'

'We will buy a holiday home,' Léo declared to Mathilde. 'Somewhere peaceful, somewhere to get away from the rush at weekends and in the summer. You can stay there as much as you want, my darling, and when you are there, I can visit as much as you want. Every weekend will be like a second honeymoon for us, *non*?'

It sounded an idyllic arrangement. Mathilde disliked the noise and bustle of the city, especially now that she was getting closer to her time. It was claustrophobic and in summertime it was sweaty and there were too many people crowding the streets. She felt limp, as if she could barely breathe. She had already given up her job, at Léo's insistence. 'You have me to look after you now,' he said. 'We don't need the money. You will have our child to care for too. There is plenty of time for you to go back to work later if you want to.'

Because of her illness, Mathilde was easily convinced. Léo was right. She still wasn't strong. She needed the space, the quiet.

'But where?' she asked.

Léo didn't want to spend much time outside France, he told her. France had everything: the best food, the most sweeping landscape, women among the most *chic* in the world . . . He looked down his long Roman nose at the Midi – the south of France was too busy and anyhow, had been spoilt by tourists. 'We will go and take a look at Brittany,' he decided.

Mathilde was happy to do what he wanted back then. She

had been besotted with Léo since the day they'd met at the party of a mutual friend. He was everything she'd ever yearned for – tall, elegantly dressed, good-looking with fine features that seemed to betray an aristocratic past; a gentleman who was intelligent, courteous and who clearly loved women. And he was successful too. He ran his own business, he had no baggage – he was not married and he had no children. In short, he was . . . '*Parfait*,' she murmured. Back then, Mathilde had believed in perfection; fantasised about finding a man like him. In retrospect, she supposed that Léo had filled the gap in her life; the gap left by her father, who had died of a stroke when Mathilde had just turned twenty-one. But she hadn't seen it like that at the time.

She had a little money – her mother had died long before her father and Mathilde had no memory of her, bar a sensation of warmth and the scent of freesias. She had been brought up by her father with the help of her grandparents and she didn't really miss her mother – how could you miss something you'd never had? Before she met Léo, Mathilde had a job as a personal assistant to a successful fashion editor, which had brought perks in the shape of a decent wardrobe of designer clothes which would otherwise have been beyond her reach. Léo, at any rate, had seemed impressed. He had gone out of his way to get her into his bed and into his life. They were married at the *mairie* less than six months after they met. Because when Léo wanted something, he generally got it – though Mathilde hadn't realised that at first.

They went over to Belle-Île for a few days to check it out. *La Bretagne* had attracted Léo because it was unspoilt and he liked to think he had a Celtic soul. Mathilde too was immediately drawn to the simple villages, the ancient forests, farmland and lush green meadows. The region seemed to be stuck in time. In the advanced stage of pregnancy that she was, this notion rather appealed to something romantic in her. But at the same time . . .

'Isn't it too far?' Mathilde remained uncertain. It had taken them six hours to get there in their *deux-chevaux* that day.

'Pff.' Léo dismissed her worries. 'That is nothing – if we can find the right place.'

There were houses in the villages for sale – but they all seemed so desolate. Neither of them were sure. In these small communities everybody knew everybody else, no one's business was private. Was that what they wanted?

But then on their last day on the island, they found an old lighthouse for sale and as soon as they saw it shimmering in the sea mist, Mathilde knew that it was the one. It had its own living accommodation – which could be easily extended – and there were rocky coves below that were more or less exclusive to the house sitting above them. It could only be reached by car along a dirt track from Sauzon or on foot via the coastal path and the dunes. It needed redecorating and possibly rewiring too. But it had windows all around which provided extensive sea and coastal views, the like of which she had never seen before – kilometres of sand, granite rock formations and the vast, lonely ocean.

'I love it,' she declared and clapped her hands.

Léo smiled indulgently. 'It's an unusual building and a wonderful location.' He frowned. 'But won't you feel too isolated, my sweet?'

'*Non. C'est parfait.*' Mathilde craved that isolation – at least in the beginning. In the beginning, Léo was there too. They spent hours wandering the beaches and the cliffs; he occupied himself with organising renovations to the Old Lighthouse – money no object – and she chose new blinds, rugs and wooden floors from catalogues. In the evenings they drove into Sauzon and ate seafood at the Hôtel du Phare, looking out on to the picturesque harbour. It was heavenly. Mathilde felt herself blossoming under the warmth of Léo's love and protection as the baby continued to grow inside her. And now she had a shelter too.

But of course, it couldn't last. Léo was a city man and he had business there, so he must return to Paris to work. They must be practical. They still had the house in the sixteenth arrondissement and Léo must be there during the week, at least. Mathilde understood – did she not? – that all this peace and solitude, this haven of tranquillity, must be paid for somehow? And Mathilde was able to smile as he left her, because she was the lucky one. She got to stay here on Belle-Île.

At first, Léo came back every weekend, smelling in some indefinable way of work and the city, and then when the baby was due he insisted on employing a woman from the village to come in every day, to do housework, cook meals and check that Mathilde was doing well. Like many of the older villagers she spoke a patois version of Breton and Mathilde could hardly understand her. She had a wrinkled and leathered brown face, her coarse dark hair was caught up in a tight bun, she wore a long black skirt and blouse and cast disapproving glances at Mathilde's brightly coloured sixties clothes. But she was a help and her presence seemed to reassure Léo at least.

'I would be here if I could,' he told her. 'And so you must promise – as soon as you have the first pains, telephone me and I will race like the wind to be by your side.'

When the contractions came, Mathilde asked the woman

to phone her husband, but he was not there, he was nowhere to be found. She gave birth, attended by the local midwife, accompanied by the village woman who gazed on with pitying eyes. And still Léo could not be contacted. Mathilde had never felt so alone.

It was a boy. Mathilde cradled this special boy, fed him, kissed the delicate fontanelle, promptly fell utterly in love with him. He was three days old when his father finally arrived from Paris, weary and contrite. Mathilde had already named their son Jacques, after her father, the father she had lost so young.

'My love, my love, *je suis désolé*,' cried Léo. 'How can you ever forgive me?' He talked of meetings, of being called away, of messages not being properly relayed. But the reality was that her husband had not been there when she needed him. He had left her here on this bleak and lonely island to fend for herself, and for the first time, Mathilde began to be afraid.

Jacques was such a pleasure though, such a wonderful distraction. It was so easy with him, to stay here in the Old Lighthouse, to allow Léo to spoil her and then let him return to the city for business, so that she could relax and be free to enjoy her new life with her new baby. And so it went on for the next year and a half. Léo came back at weekends – but not every weekend. Soon, once a fortnight was the norm, sometimes only one weekend in three. And Mathilde always understood.

But as time went on, she grew lonely. She went to Sauzon, looking out, she supposed, for other young mothers in a similar position. But the women in the village did not seem open to friendship and she felt like an outsider still. Jacques was adorable, but he was too young for conversation. She didn't get on with the woman they'd employed and in the end she told her to leave. Over the following months, Mathilde grew bored, dissatisfied and even mistrusting of her husband on the weekends when he said that he was too busy to come home.

And then she found that she was pregnant again. Jacques was two, running around everywhere, full of mischief and fun. She wanted to be glad about the baby. But how would she cope with two children to look after and Léo always away? Already, she was talking to herself, acting a little crazy sometimes. Should she go back to Paris with Léo? She didn't really want to; she had grown used to being here. It was a healthy lifestyle for Jacques, there was a satisfying if lazy rhythm to her days, and it was a refuge from the busy streets, the traffic, the people of the city. There had been unrest recently, not only in Paris; riots, demonstrations and strikes that threatened the entire French economy. She heard about it from Léo and on the news and realised how far away from it all she was here, how separate. But . . . Was that the answer? Because surely it wasn't right for a couple to spend so much time apart?

And that's when Léo decided. 'But, of course . . .' He snapped his fingers. 'We should have an au pair – that is the solution to our dilemma.' He looked thoughtful. 'An English girl – she can speak English to Jacques, it is never too early to learn.'

Mathilde wasn't sure. 'I can speak English to Jacques,' she said. Her father had ensured she had a good education, and Mathilde was thankful for that. But what of Jacques? Would the education he received here be sufficient for the son of a man of Léo's standing? They would have to see. For now, she wanted to stay on Belle-Île during her second pregnancy at least. But did she want to see Léo so infrequently? And did she want some English girl coming to ruin her peaceful existence with her son?

'Yes, yes, my love,' said Léo. 'I know that you can. But it will solve our problems, *non*? Everyone is doing it. She can live here with you and help you with the house, the children . . .' He beamed. 'And be your companion too.'

But you *are meant to be my companion* . . . Mathilde did not say this, though. Of course, her husband was far too busy and important to spend all his time with her. And did she want to move back to Paris, really, when she could be here on this blissful island on their own private beach, in the Old Light-house she loved? No, she did not.

They advertised in the English magazine *The Lady*. A few girls replied and Léo chose Thea. 'She is young,' he said. 'She sounds enthusiastic and she has learnt French at school.'

And so it was agreed, and Thea came to live with Mathilde and Jacques in the Old Lighthouse on Belle-Île.

Mathilde went to her dressing table, took the key from its hiding place under the bedside lamp and opened the top drawer. It had been a long time, so long that she had almost pretended this red leather journal wasn't even here. It was easy, she supposed, to brush these things under the carpet, to go on with life as if the past had never happened.

She had been tempted to read it so many times in the early days – of course she had, she was only human. But something had always stopped her. Perhaps it was guilt, or some vestige of self-respect that she clung to. Perhaps she was scared even to see the words, the truth that would no doubt be written there in black and white in Thea's unmistakable hand – reminding her of what had gone on that first year. It would be too painful – perhaps more than she could bear.

As time went by though, it had become easier to resist. The

diary was private. It would be wrong. Wrong too to destroy it, since it was not hers to destroy and more importantly because it encapsulated not only the bad things but also the core of a friendship that had been the happiest time of Mathilde's life. *Non.* Better simply to keep it safe. The diary was buried here in the drawer. The truth was buried too – it had had to be. But now . . .

She picked up Thea's diary, held it for a moment. It seemed incredible that it had been here for all this time and that no one knew this but Mathilde. It was her secret. Their secret.

In this diary, Thea must have spilled out all her secret hopes and dreams about her French adventure – and plenty more besides. It wasn't a conventional yearly diary – there was no date on the outside; it was just a thick notebook that she had often seen Thea writing in while she lived here.

From time to time, Mathilde had asked her what she was writing.

'How I feel about things,' she'd reply.

'And how you feel about people?' Mathilde had joked.

'That too.' Thea's dark eyes were dreamy. She often had that look about her, as if she were somewhere else. Mathilde never knew where, though. They'd shared confidences, but when she thought about it now, it was usually Mathilde sharing confidences and Thea listening in that easy way she had.

Mathilde had not taken the diary in order to read it. *Non.* Gently, she stroked her fingers over the red leather. She hadn't wanted to read it. She had only wanted to keep it safe.

But now Thea was ill and this had changed everything. Mathilde had carried so much bitterness in her heart for the girl who had come to Belle-Île, who had become her best friend. That bitterness had seemed indelible; there could be no way back. But was this true? Was it possible that things could be different? Should she go to her now – after all these years? Should she beg her forgiveness for what she had done, for Mathilde was certainly not blameless herself? Suddenly she needed to know how it was – from Thea's point of view. It became all-consuming, this need. Yes, this diary was private and perhaps what she was about to do was indeed wrong. But who would know? Who would care? There were things that Mathilde should have faced up to long ago. So, Mathilde would read it, and then she would know what to do.

Thea had come here at the end of the summer. Summer 1969. It all seemed a very long time ago.

CHAPTER 13

Thea: July 1969

I know it's weird to begin a diary in the middle of the year. But there was something special about today. So, I found this notebook and this is where it starts. I want to write it down, I s'pose. Everything.

Today began the same as every other Saturday morning in my life. I was cleaning the window display in the shop – not my favourite thing to do, but I'm lucky to have such a cushy Saturday morning job, I know that (and if I forget it, Mum keeps telling me) – and wondering whether or not to blow some of my wages in Kelly's Chippy opposite after work or maybe a Wagon Wheel from Adie's further up the street . . . when I spotted him. He was on the other side of the road striding down Fore Street towards the harbour. Really striding. Wow. I dunno. Just . . .

There was something about him. My mouth must have been hanging open like a fish and it's a good thing he didn't take a dekko across and see me standing there in the window of the newsagent's corner shop looking like a loon in my shapeless blue nylon overall, my hair tied back in a pony-tail and no lippie cos I was late for work and it would have to wait for tea break. Gawping . . .

But he was too wrapped up in looking at something else – and I soon saw why. He came to a stop by the chemist's. And there it was – parked by the kerb – all red, white and gleaming chrome. I craned round to get a better look. It was a classic. What a machine. Off the wall. Wow again. I was drooling . . .

I've got a bit of a thing about them – bikes. I reckon that's what I'm saving up for, my very own bike, that's why I don't spend all my cash on make-up and clothes or records, like some of the other girls I know. And I'm hoping that one day . . .

But how can I? How can I even dream about it? I may as well forget it. I'm never going to be zipping up and down Cornish lanes on warm summer evenings, wind in my hair and all that jazz, am I? No, because I've got Danny and Danny's saving up for a Ford Escort instead. It's much more practical than a bike, he says. Only, first, Danny's going to university to do a law degree (that'll be next September, the same time I go to teachers' training college if I do all right in my exams), then he'll work for a law firm to 'gain experience' (he actually says that), then he'll start up his own practice, then we'll get married (by then I'll have finished at college and be teaching) then we'll buy a house, then we'll have kids, then . . .

Aaaargghhh! Save me. It's so mapped out I can't even think about it. I want to just RUN.

It's not Danny's fault. Danny's lovely, he is. It's just that planning is his thing. Me? I don't know what mine is – not yet. I care about Danny. I used to think I loved him, but I don't know any more. Now, I catch myself looking at other blokes and I find myself wondering . . . I always wanted a boyfriend and Danny had so many ideas when we first got together, he made *me feel like a proper grown-up. But that was when I was fifteen and now it sounds pathetic. Now, I'm seventeen. I can't help it. Things look different now.*

Mum and Dad like Danny — that goes without saying. They would — they like his parents too. They're all in love with each other, as far as I can see. He's everything they want for me, their only child (unfortunately for me, at least if I had a sister or a brother we could share the pain). But what about me? What about if I don't want it any more? Could I break free? Would I dare to? This place is so dead it kills me sometimes.

Barb says I could break free, but it's easy for her to say — and it'd be easy for her to do. But she doesn't need to. Her dad's a scientist and although he's a bit weird (he sat us down in the garden of their cliff house up on Mount Pleasant the other day to tell us his latest theory about planetary influences on Earth and what effect this could have on our understanding of reincarnation) he lets her do stuff — like staying out really late and playing music really loud. He's all for experimentation (Barb says) and her mother's so easy-going she just shrugs and lets them all get on with it. Pretty good, huh? Barb has three brothers, so there's always plenty of other stuff happening. She also doesn't need to break free because she doesn't have a boyfriend and she doesn't have the most uptight and conventional parents in the world. She doesn't feel trapped — not like I do.

I've gone off on one of my tangents. I do feel trapped here in Porthleven and although I feel a bit scared about going to college, I'm excited too. I can't wait to get away, to be honest. There are folk living here who've never travelled further than Truro; some in Breageside who barely make it to the other side of the harbour. And I feel trapped in this house in Holman's Place. It's home, yeah. But it's also poky and dark with only a little patch of garden and it feels as if we live in the shadow of the chapel — literally, since the Methodist Church is right next to us.

But bikes are about freedom, aren't they? This one certainly is. It isn't from round here — he isn't from round here — I would have known if I'd ever set eyes on either of them before.

So there they both are — the bike and the biker — and there's me gawping, and something inside me does a double flip. I must have cleaned the same glass shelf at least five times. Thrilling things like this don't happen to me — not here in Porthleven. He has longish dirty-blond hair and he's wearing frayed blue jeans and a red T-shirt with some crazy black logo on the front. He's tall and he's skinny. Proper Mick Jagger skinny. He has a tatty fringed brown leather jacket slung over his shoulder. What can I tell you, diary? A treble flip wasn't out of the question, especially with the bike 'n' all. He's beautiful.

'Thea!' Marion called out to me from the shop. 'I need you to serve out here.'

'Coming, Marion,' I called. I didn't want another ticking off. Hastily, I shoved everything back on the shelf and edged out from behind the magazine racks to the counter. 'Sorry,' I told her. 'Those shelves were filthy.'

Marion raised a perfectly plucked eyebrow — no one can do this like Marion, I am in awe. It's partly cos she wears her hair — dyed Titian-red and a bit overpowering to be honest — piled up on her head in an ever so slightly tottering beehive. 'Really?' she drawled. She tapped a long, manicured red fingernail on the counter. 'Well, there's work to be done round here, young lady. No time for staring outside day-dreaming the hours away.' She looked over my shoulder, almost longingly, towards the window and the view we had of Fore Street. Frowned and tutted loudly. 'Riff-raff,' she pronounced. 'When did boys start looking so scruffy? I ask you.'

102

I looked out of the window and there he was – right outside the shop. He must've turned the bike around and now he was astride it and heading up the hill towards Torleven Road. He'd stopped for a moment to let a car coming out of Church Row go on in front of him and as he revved the engine, he turned his head, just for a second, and seemed to catch my eye. Wow again. It was a truly amazing moment. I grinned as he turned away and zoomed on up the road.

Marion made another cluck of disapproval, but that air of longing was still in her eyes. Scruffy? I dunno. He looked pretty amazing to me.

CHAPTER 14

Colette

Outside the flower shop the following day, Colette was pruning some of the sweet-scented herbs growing from the panniers of Élodie's driftwood horse, when she caught herself humming. She stopped abruptly. She had no reason to hum, no right to hum. She wasn't here to enjoy herself.

And yet. It was strangely therapeutic working in here for a few hours every day; she could almost forget her mother's illness, their estrangement, her life in England, and simply lose herself in the fragrances, textures and colours of the flowers she remembered so well. Colette patted the horse's textured mane. It might be made of driftwood but it seemed like a real creature Élodie had created here. And her mother had taken that creature and made it seem even more alive with the sage, marjoram and thyme growing in the panniers, and tiny erigeron daisies, campanula and ivy winding through the wood.

She had been thinking. Of course, the atmosphere between them was still strained . . . But her mother seemed a very different woman from the one Colette remembered, the one she had grown so angry with, who she had blamed for everything that seemed wrong with her life. Some things hadn't changed. That faraway look of hers was still there – but now it seemed as if she was looking forward instead of back. Colette shivered. She was softer, less defensive, more vulnerable. With good reason. And yet, still . . .

'Will you look after the shop for me?' her mother had asked again this morning. The morphine she was taking was slow-release and of course she slept a lot, but she still seemed brighter in the mornings.

'I'm doing that already, Maman, you know that.' She was keeping things ticking over, at least. Watering the plants, sweeping the floor, fielding orders and phone calls, taking in the deliveries. It had all come back to her. And her mother's records were as well-organised and easy to understand as they had always been.

Colette took away the glass on the bedside table and went into the kitchen to get some fresh water. The kitchen smelt stale, of day-old brioche and hot chocolate left to go cold. She decided to give it a good spring clean later – she shouldn't let Francine do everything. 'You should drink more fluids,' she said as she came back into the room. 'It hydrates the body. It clears out the system.'

Her mother gave what Colette assumed would be one of her famous shrugs, if she hadn't been lying down – which spoilt the effect somewhat.

'I meant – will you open the shop up again? Properly?' she persevered. Her brow was furrowed, though, with the effort of talking.

'Ssh,' Colette soothed. 'Why, Maman? What for? What

good will it do? When you're . . .' *Never going to be well enough to run it yourself.* But she couldn't say that.

'I hate the thought of it not being looked after,' her mother said. As if the flower shop were another child she had always loved more. 'I hate that people from the village can't just go in there, order arrangements and buy flowers as they always have. And . . .'

'And?'

Her mother held out a hand. She was having difficulty breathing; just speaking must have taken a lot out of her. 'Will you stay here a while, my dear?'

A while. Colette swallowed. How long was a while? She was spending a little longer with her every day. But for how long was she prepared to do it? What if six months became a year? What was she letting herself in for by deciding to stay with her till the end? What was she promising? She'd been here two weeks already. Mark wanted to come over, and she knew that he didn't understand her reluctance. But he'd be wanting to take her back to Cornwall with him. How could she tell him she was staying here for six months or more? How would he take it? Would he understand? That despite what had happened between them, despite the fact that she still hadn't got any answers, this time was precious. That it felt as though her mother was reaching out to her – which was something she had never done before.

'Yes,' she said. Because she couldn't let her die alone with only Francine for company. She couldn't leave her and apparently she couldn't leave the flower shop either. Not yet.

Her mother had been leaning forward and now she relaxed back against the pillows with a sigh. 'How long?' she whispered.

That could mean so many things. Colette reached out and stroked her hair gently from her face. 'I don't know,' she said. 'We'll see.'

'I'm not frightened of dying.' The pale eyelids flickered. 'But promise me . . .'

'Yes?'

'Keep the blinds open when you can, my darling.'

'Oh, Maman.' But how the sun must hurt her tired eyes.

'Let me see the sunlight. Let me have flowers.'

'Of course.' Colette bowed her head. 'I'll bring you some up.'

'Thank you, *chérie*.' She closed her eyes and Colette pulled the covers gently around her thin shoulders, quietly left the room. Some wild flowers, she decided. Some daisies and forget-me-nots. Maybe even some of that heady jasmine. And yes, she would stay a while. When she went back down to the shop, she turned the sign to '*Ouvert*'.

Later on, Colette took an order for a wedding bouquet. 'Something natural looking, *s'il vous plaît*,' the bride had said.

Something calming, thought Colette, for the bride seemed nervous. Lavender, perhaps. Its scent was soothing and it signified devotion and virtue, which had to be a good thing. She didn't ask why the bride required a last-minute wedding bouquet. She just set to designing a trailing, organic concoction with cornflowers as the centrepiece. The cornflower was so delicate; its fluttering blue petals seemed almost impossibly romantic. Colette decided to combine this and the lavender with a blue-green eucalyptus with leaves so thin they were almost ethereal, purple-blue thistle and white peonies, which symbolised a happy marriage.

When the relieved-looking bride had left, Colette ordered

107

these extra flowers from her mother's supplier – enough for the wedding bouquet and a few stems more. For . . . Well, she didn't know what for. At least not yet. The tunnel vision of the working florist, the mantra 'I will only buy what I need', was not working as efficiently as it might. But while she was here, she could still enjoy herself, surely? She could hum. She could imagine how she'd develop the shop if things were different and it were up to her . . . How she'd learn more about flower symbolism and natural healing, buy a field in which to grow more wild and meadow flowers. The earth of the island was high quality – swept by salt- and iodine-laden winds. She'd grow flowers, she'd plan designs and she'd create arrangements that reflected the seasons, the ebb and the flow of the tide here on Belle-Île.

Colette put the 'Closed' sign on the door and started packing up. But. She must remember that this was only temporary. She mustn't get carried away. She had no place here on the island, not any more. She didn't belong here and she wasn't going to let it trap her – not again. So she would do what she had to do – for the shop, for her mother, for her peace of mind. And then she'd return to England. That was home now. But in the meantime, the tranquillity she could find here . . . Well, it would give her a chance to unravel her feelings about her mother, about the island, about Mark.

The door rattled as someone – ignoring the Closed sign – opened it and strode in. Colette looked up in surprise. It was the man from the cliff path. She felt herself flush, though he wouldn't recognise her, she was sure, from that distance.

'Actually, I'm very sorry, but we're shut,' she said.

'So, it's you.' He made no move to leave the shop.

Ah.

He was staring at her. His eyes were very green and he seemed vaguely familiar. 'I hope you don't think I was spying on you?'

'Spying?' she responded weakly.

'Down on the beach yesterday.'

'Of course not.'

'And the door was open.'

Colette looked across. 'Was it?' She met his steady gaze. 'But the sign said "Closed".'

'Did it?' He frowned. 'Sorry, I didn't notice.'

They continued to stare at each other. What was it with him? He was quite tall and rather angular, not good-looking in any conventional sense. 'So what did you want?' she asked. It wasn't the politest of customer-speak, and her mother had taught her that she could think what she liked about customers as long as she also kept smiling, but he'd wrong-footed her. Colette rather suspected he made a habit of it. There was a wildness about him – in his hair which was dark blond and sticking up at all angles; in his clothes, a faded T-shirt, frayed jeans and well-worn leather sandals, and in his very green eyes.

'Want?' He seemed confused. Confused and perhaps even a little angry. His brows were drawn close. She looked at his mouth. He wasn't smiling.

'Flowers?'

'*Oui, naturellement*, flowers. What do you have?' He peered around the shop.

'Not a lot, I'm afraid.' She showed him the half-empty buckets. She was at least trying to resist buying more. 'Are you on holiday here?' she asked politely. She wanted to ask him what the flowers were for, but something was stopping her. She thought about suggesting some blooms from the garden but did she really want the intimacy of having him out there with her in that tiny space? Here in the shop she felt more in charge.

'Jesus, no,' he said.

Colette was taken aback by his tone. 'You don't live here?'

'No. No, I don't. This place . . .' But he didn't finish his sentence. And his expansive gesture took in the entire island rather than just Sauzon or the flower shop, Colette decided.

'You don't like it?'

'Like it . . .?' He tore his hand through his hair so that it was sticking up even more. 'God . . . It's not really a question of—' And then he seemed to recover his manners. 'Sorry, no offence.'

Colette shrugged what she knew to be her mother's shrug. 'None taken,' she said. 'I don't live here either.'

'You don't?' He was surprised. He looked around the shop again, looked at her.

She spread her hands. 'And I'm not on holiday either.'

'Clearly. So . . .?'

'It's my mother's shop,' she supplied for him. 'She's the florist – but she's rather ill. I'm looking after things for her.'

He nodded. 'I see. I'm sorry.'

'And the flowers?'

He gave a slight shrug. 'I don't care really. Something bright?'

Which wasn't the right attitude at all. Everyone should care about the flowers they bought. Colette tried not to look disapproving. He was the customer and the customer was supposed to be always right, only this one most definitely wasn't. Once again, she wanted to ask what – or who – the flowers were for, but once again she backed off. That was what her mother would have done, but for her that was all part of the service. She sensed that he'd find the question too personal, too intrusive.

110

He seemed like that type of man. The kind who wouldn't want to get close. Maybe the kind who didn't even like most people very much. Up on the cliff yesterday – as well as the anger, she reminded herself – he'd had a solitary look about him, a kind of sadness that seemed to cling to him. But what was he doing here on the island if he disliked it so much?

'Gerberas?' she suggested. 'I have a few of those.' She pointed to six orange and purple flowers, carefully wire-bound to preserve their height and dignity. He couldn't complain about them not being bright.

'*Parfait.*' He seemed relieved, pulled a battered wallet from the back pocket of his jeans.

'You want all six?' Supplies were truly dwindling. She'd have to bite the bullet, admit that she was really in business in earnest as her mother wanted her to be, and phone the supplier – fast.

'All six,' he said.

Lucky lady, thought Colette. Maybe. But she didn't say it. Too personal again. She wrapped the gerberas in brown paper, tied them with raffia and wished him good day. He was obviously a transitory visitor – he didn't even like the island – so she'd never see him again. And yet. And yet as she'd already thought, there was something familiar about his gait, the colour of those eyes. She searched her childhood memory. A summer visitor perhaps from the old days?

'*Merci,*' he said. 'And all the best.'

She gave him a questioning look.

'To your mother,' he said. 'I hope she gets better soon.' And he tucked the gerberas none too gently under his arm, poor things, and left the shop.

CHAPTER 15

Élodie

Today, Élodie was adding flesh in the form of driftwood to another animal sculpture. This one was a goat and had been on the go for a while like so many of her pieces, waiting for the right shapes of driftwood to come to hand. The curve of the horns was not easy, and the curious expression a challenge – that is, if one were even to attempt to capture it. The goat was bony and had a short stubby tail like a wire brush. She would get there – she hoped. She also hoped to distract herself from the letter in her pocket. Outside, the remnants of a sea mist still clung to the stratified layers of the granite rocks, still rested just above the ocean beyond. And from the other window she could see the outlines of the Old Lighthouse, grey and white, less solid than usual, almost blurring into the limpid sky.

The goat was dark brown with black markings indicated by deep indentations and knots in the wood and was reminiscent of the breeds that roamed the countryside around here. For Élodie, it particularly reminded her of a goat she and Jacques had seen on the beach one day, only a couple of weeks after Thea had left.

'Élodie, look!' Jacques had laughed that contagious laugh of his. There it was, munching on a sea cabbage, all alone, as if this rocky cove were its natural habitat.

At the sound of Jacques's voice, the goat had lifted its head from the sea cabbage and looked curiously around at the sea as if it too were rather surprised to be there.

'What a perfect tableau we make. A boy, a girl and a goat!' Élodie could hear the delight in her brother's voice. She smiled. She always wanted to please him. Didn't they all?

Jacques made friends with the goat, coaxing it to eat from his hand – he could always do that with animals; he had confidence, and a way of murmuring so softly that they knew he was a friend. He even insisted on taking the goat home with them, fixing some old fishing rope around its neck to use as a collar and lead and gently tugging it along. Surprisingly, the goat seemed willing to comply – perhaps it thought more food might be in the offing.

But their mother, still smarting from whatever had led to Thea's departure from their lives, only now discovering how important she had been (or so Élodie liked to think), had raised an objection.

'*Merde!* What in heaven's name . . . ?' she had begun, as she came out through the French windows at the back of the house to be confronted by the three of them.

'It is a goat, Maman,' Jacques had said.

'I can see that.' Their mother looked horrified. Élodie began to doubt the wisdom of bringing it here.

'I thought we could keep him,' Jacques said. His feet were planted solidly enough, but Élodie could see how hard he was finding it to stop the goat from dragging him off down the garden.

'*Non*, Jacques. Definitely not. We can't have it here. It will eat everything. *Tout!*'

And it was true that even as she spoke, the goat was straining at the leash, ears cocked, looking wistfully towards the delicious morsel that was their mother's climbing hydrangea.

'But he's brilliant,' Jacques said. Élodie recognised that sound in his voice – that stubborn petulance that meant he was determined to have his way. 'And he was on our beach. Look at that little tuft of brown between his horns. See the white shadows under his eyes? He's beautiful.'

The goat gazed back at Jacques as if it would like to return his adoration, but had more important things on its mind.

'It's a goat,' their mother said. 'A wild goat.' And the animal bleated loudly as if it had to agree.

Their mother shuddered.

'He can be our pet.' Jacques was undeterred. 'Me and Élodie can look after him. We can tether him to a post so he doesn't eat everything in the garden and—'

'We can't tether him,' Élodie had put in. She didn't usually disagree with her brother, but there was something in the goat's expression that told her she was right. 'We have to let him go. He needs to be free. That's what he's used to.'

'Exactly,' their mother had said. 'Listen to your sister, Jacques. She may be younger than you but she talks a lot more sense.'

This was unusual, because as they all knew, Jacques was their mother's favourite. And also, Élodie thought now with a touch of irony as she looked up to see the mist slowly lifting, the one to leave. She put her head to one side and surveyed her work so far. On a piece like this, she usually tied the wood in place first off and didn't screw it together until she was absolutely sure. Sometimes, on more delicate pieces, she didn't use screws at all, preferring the fragility of wire to hold things together. And sometimes she used glue – she had experimented for months before finally finding the right kind, invisible and strong. Experimentation – that was her watchword. Chaos might lead to creativity but experimentation led to discovery.

Jacques hadn't really minded about the goat. He released it and laughed as it bounded off. Jacques led a charmed life; there was something about him that made people want to please him. And there wasn't much he minded – apart from Papa, that was. He hated Papa for all sorts of reasons. With Papa, he could fly into a rage that scared even Élodie – almost. The problem being that Papa was the same. Jacques saw it as his mission in life to protect both his mother and his sister from Papa's anger. But it wasn't always possible.

In the days, months and years after Thea left, Élodie and Jacques were – rather like the goat – allowed to roam wherever they wished. Their mother couldn't seem to get a grip. They went to school – sometimes; other times they did not. Their mother was distracted, unwell, incapable – and without Thea at the helm, their family ship rocked precariously. Would they drown? Élodie suspected they might. Who could she cling to now that Thea was gone? Who would save her? Her mother had no solidity; she felt more like a feather in the wind being blown about all over. Small wonder, then, that Élodie and Jacques turned more and more to one another. Small wonder that they became inseparable.

Élodie eased a section of wood into place, but she was not careful enough, it wasn't the fit she'd envisaged. 'Damn you,' she said to no one in particular – maybe it was to Jacques or her father, or maybe even the unfortunate goat sculpture itself.

Time for a break. She was working on the sculpture but thinking of the past. She needed to let go. Usually, she could. But today . . . She fingered the letter in her pocket. Coffee, she decided.

She filled the percolator with water, added the filter and a generous spoonful of freshly ground coffee; screwed on the lid and put it on her little stove. She was self-sufficient here in her studio, with a bedroom, small bathroom en suite, tiny kitchen and adjoining workshop area. There was even a small barn which she'd had built with her early profits and in which she stored her wood and other materials for her work. This studio, reflecting her self-sufficiency, was not only so she could avoid her father, his temper and his infrequent visits to the Old Light-house, if she chose, but also so that she could be independent. She wanted to be her own person, to work irregular hours if she wanted to, not to be restricted by mealtimes or distracted by phone calls and chat. Élodie was close to her mother – but she still valued the space she could call her own.

She knew that she was lucky to have it. The little studio had always been here – originally it was some sort of summer house, built by a previous lighthouse keeper perhaps – but her parents had decided to renovate it in the early days, with a view to providing guest accommodation for visits from family or friends. *Family or friends* . . . In her childhood, Élodie could not recall any such visits; their little family had been isolated and seemed to prefer it that way. But when Élodie got older, when her artwork and the treasures she and Jacques collected from the beaches threatened to overflow from her bedroom, her parents had been more than happy to let her have the studio

116

to work in. Day by day, week by week, she had made it more hers. And when she finally moved in, no one had seemed in the least surprised.

The sun had dispersed the morning mist and so Élodie took her coffee outside to her little back terrace which faced the sea. The ocean was calm; she had to concentrate hard to hear the pulse of the tide, the sound that she sometimes felt was her heartbeat. At last, she took out Jacques's letter. She'd read it earlier, when it had first arrived, of course. It wasn't so unusual for him to write – maybe once every couple of months or so – but it was unusual for him to ask anything of her.

Come and visit, she read. *Come and see us here in Royan. I miss you. I need to talk to someone who understands. I'm at odds with myself, Élodie. And I really don't know why.*

What was wrong? Élodie's first instinct on reading the letter was to drop everything and go over there. She wanted to help her brother, wanted to sort things out for him. But it was complicated. There was her mother, her work . . . Was it right that he should click his fingers and they would run? The truth was that Élodie had not left the island for five years. She could – of course, she could, why not? – but she hadn't. And Jacques . . . There was his wife, whom Élodie had tried to like on the occasional visit they'd made to Belle-Île, when Jacques was sure his father wouldn't be around. But she had failed, because Karine was too bossy, too dominating. She seemed to control Jacques, and Élodie hated that because no one had ever controlled him before. Their father had tried – God knows – but Jacques had refused to let him, refused to comply. Karine didn't like her either, she could see. Élodie sensed that she disturbed her, that she disliked the closeness between herself and Jacques – or felt threatened by it perhaps?

Élodie paused in her reading and gazed out to sea. A breeze was building from the northwest; she could see the ruffles of white on the far crests. Later, at high tide, tempestuous waves would come crashing into the rocks and this would seem a different place. These moods of the sea, these turns of the tide, the inexorable ebb and flow . . . This was why Élodie loved it here.

She sighed. And then there were the children – her nephew Raphaël and niece Nicole. Élodie loved them – she would love anyone who was a part of Jacques, her beloved brother – though she barely knew them. She tried her best. She made sure she spent time with them whenever they visited. She showed the children the animals in her studio and had given each a small present – a miniature version of the animal of their choice, fashioned out of tiny pieces of driftwood from the beach. Nicole was a very compact and precise little girl, rather the image of her mother. Raphaël was so like Jacques; some of his expressions and gestures caught at Élodie's heart. She would like to see more of them. But. The 'but' seemed to fill the whole studio somehow. She didn't want to say no to Jacques, she had never wanted that, only . . . She grabbed some paper and a pen.

I can't come at the moment, she wrote. *There is too much work. And Maman* . . . She let this sentence drift. Jacques always knew what she was thinking; he could always fill in the spaces. He hadn't really forgiven their mother for the choice she had made; perhaps not Élodie either . . . *Can't you come here? You could all stay at the house when Papa is not around. Or* . . . Or he could come alone.

What's wrong? You know, Thea is very ill – Jacques would want to know this – *and her daughter Colette has come back here to Belle-Île*. It is possible then, you see, she wanted to tell him. Despite everything that has happened . . . it is possible to return whenever you wish.

CHAPTER 16

Colette

A few days later, Colette was tidying her mother's room, looking for a new box of tissues to put beside her bed. She'd have to run down to the grocery shop. And there were probably other things . . .

'In the top drawer, *chérie*.' Her mother gestured towards the mahogany chest in the corner. But it was a tired gesture, and for Colette it brought back a sharp contrasting memory of her mother's indefatigable energy. Her grandmother had said it too: 'Thea had so much life . . .' Sadness in her eyes.

An image came back to Colette – her mother on that old motorbike, the Cimatti, wind in her hair, whisking down the country lanes. Not any more. Now, she was fading, a little more each day. Now, it was an effort to sip water or to eat. Colette went to fetch the tissues. She didn't even know what had happened to that motorbike; she supposed her mother had sold it years ago. She took out the new box, spied a silk scarf she remembered from the old days and smoothed it with her fingertips. She could feel the tears welling inside. It was

119

red and blue and her mother used to wear it in a jaunty knot around her neck. Colette brought it closer, inhaled the scent of lavender and thyme, her mother's scent, still clinging to the delicate fabric.

And then she saw something else tucked towards the side of the drawer. She swallowed back the tears, drew a breath. It was her father's old wooden compass. 'What's this doing here, Maman?' Reverentially, she drew it out and held it up for her mother to see. The wood was stained and battered, the dark triangular markings faded. But it was just as she remembered it. She'd recognise it anywhere.

Her mother glanced across. Her eyes softened. 'Ah, yes. Bring it here, would you?'

'But . . .' Her mother had made no secret of the fact that she'd taken all his things – his clothes, his books and maps, his fishing gear – and given them to a charity shop in Le Palais. Colette had been furious, demanded to know exactly where they were, but she'd refused to tell her.

'And there's nothing left? Nothing?' she could remember raging at her. 'Nothing to remember him by?'

'There's nothing of him, Colette.' And her mother had turned her face away. 'There's nothing left of him.'

'You gave it all away,' Colette whispered now. 'Everything.' She didn't understand. She turned the compass around in her palm, felt its smooth grain, its reassuring weight.

'What does it do, Papa?' she had asked him when she was a little girl. She remembered the day so well. He had pulled one of her pigtails and bent down so that their faces were at the same level. 'It is a compass, *ma petite*,' he had said. 'Everyone needs a compass to show them the way.'

'Yes. And then I bought it back.' Her mother was waiting

for her to take it over to her, so Colette did. She placed it in her palm and sat down beside the bed.

'Just the compass?'

She stroked a finger over the beaten glass. 'A few bits and pieces.'

'But – why?' Colette stared at her. And how come she'd never known?

'I regretted giving it all away.' She was speaking with some difficulty. 'You were right. But you see, I was angry with him for leaving me.' Her voice grew softer still, so that Colette had to strain to hear the words. 'Oh, my dear, I regretted many things.'

Colette leaned closer. 'What things, Maman?' Was this her chance to find out more? But already she could see that her mother was tiring.

She took Colette's hand between her own. 'I didn't give you enough, *chérie*,' she said. 'I could have been a better mother.' For a moment, she seemed overcome.

'Enough?' Colette whispered the word.

'Enough time, enough thought, enough love . . .'

Colette patted her hand. 'Ssh now, Maman,' she soothed. Only, wasn't this what she wanted to hear? Wasn't this what she needed to understand?

'I put my trust in what couldn't hurt me. I let the past be more important than the present.' She took a shallow breath. 'I let my guilt come between us.'

'Guilt, Maman?'

'But never mind.' She shook her head. 'I never told you how precious you were, *chérie*. But you should know I always loved you.'

Colette nodded. 'I know that, Maman,' she whispered. Maybe she hadn't – but she knew it now.

'I'm glad.' And she smiled faintly.

Colette gently smoothed her mother's hair from her brow. She had some responsibility too. She had been a daddy's girl. She had loved them both, but it was always him she ran to. She had never stopped to think how her mother felt about it. So perhaps it was not only Colette who had been second best for her mother. Perhaps it was she, too, who had been second best for Colette.

But there was so much more that she didn't understand. Why did her mother feel guilty? Was it because of her lover – whoever he might be? Was it the row with Colette's father on the night he died? She stared at his battered wooden compass – he hadn't had that with him that night, for sure. What had happened in her mother's past that was so important and had affected all their futures so dramatically?

'Why didn't you leave Belle-Île, Maman?' She had been mulling this over ever since Élodie had come into the shop. Somehow, she felt that the answer might provide a clue. 'When you left the Blaise family and the Old Lighthouse? Why didn't you go home?'

Colette also owed it to her grandmother to ask this question. She was the one who had asked it first. 'That's what I can't understand,' she had said to Colette more than once, 'why your mother left that job and yet never came home.'

'I couldn't, *chérie*,' she whispered. 'I just couldn't.'

'Because you met Papa?' But Colette knew this wasn't the reason. Her parents had got together some time after her mother left her job as au pair. Hadn't Papa lost a piece of his heart when he first saw the young woman with the long curly brown hair climbing on to her motorcycle with a pannier full of flowers to deliver? Hadn't she first seen Colette's father from

122

the window of the flower shop, gutting and selling fish at his stall? Hadn't she gone down, bought some sea bass and talked to him – a little more each day? Until they were chatting regularly, meeting for a beer, until he was giving her sea bass or red mullet and she was cooking it for him? Until they went out together on her motorcycle on a trip to Donnant Beach? Until they fell in love? Wasn't that how the story went?

Her mother gave a little shake of her head, but seemed too tired to say more.

'Grandma always wondered why you didn't go home,' Colette murmured – so she too realised that she had been loved and missed.

'I know.' Her mother closed her eyes again. 'But Belle-Île had become my home, *chérie*,' she said. 'That's why. Everything I loved was here.'

'Yes, I see.' And perhaps her conventional grandmother, who had never really understood her daughter, had somehow understood that one thing. Home, she thought ruefully, was where the heart is.

Later, Colette went outside to look at the stars – they were so clear from here; there was less light pollution, she supposed. She stood on the pavement opposite the house. From here she could see down to the harbour and the hill and trees beyond; people still sat under the broad parasols outside the bar L'Abri-Côtier, and above this the little pink house with the mint-green shutters that faced the flower shop was closed up tight as a clamshell. It was low tide and some of the boats in the inner harbour looked stranded on the sand. Lights burned in most of the houses now, even the holiday homes were occupied; life went on behind the lace curtains. But from here she could also see how narrow these quayside houses really were; the backs of them only a few metres from their ornate, painted façades.

She thought about her mother and the flower shop and her father's compass, discovered in the drawer. She knew now that her mother had regrets, that she felt guilt, that something in her past had betrayed her trust. She also knew that her feelings for Colette's father were deeper than she had let herself imagine and that most importantly, her mother loved her – had always loved her. What other discoveries were here for her to make?

She pulled her mobile from her back pocket and called Mark. 'I'm staying here,' she told him after they'd said their hellos. 'I'm so sorry, but I have to.'

'How long?' That question again. His voice was tight with suppressed emotion. She didn't blame him for being annoyed. Mark just wanted her home.

'Until the end,' she whispered. In the darkness, she blinked back a tear.

'But that could be—' He stopped, seemed to realise what he was saying.

'Yes.' She had to be honest. 'It could be six months – or more.'

He sighed. 'But darling, I need to talk to you. Something's happened . . .' His voice trailed.

'What is it?' Colette wasn't sure she could cope with any more upset. She gripped her mobile more tightly.

He hesitated. 'I'd prefer to tell you in person.'

'Mark.' Colette closed her eyes. Even from here she could smell the herbs outside the flower shop, the fragrant white jasmine shrouding Francine's low wall next door. 'You know how much I want to see you. But it's complicated. I'm not sure that this is the—'

'Right time, I know. But you've been gone almost three weeks. You're my girlfriend. And I need to see you, Colette. I need to talk to you face to face.'

Colette looked towards the Hôtel du Phare. A man stood alone out on the quay, hands in pockets, gazing out towards the ocean. Three weeks – was it really that long? 'All right,' she said. 'Great.' After all, she'd dropped everything; dropped Mark and their life together and disappeared. How long was she expecting him to wait? How long was she prepared to put her life on hold? She watched the man walk out still further until he could walk no more.

'I'll come at the weekend.' Mark sounded happier now. 'I'll take a few days off – make a bit of a holiday of it.'

'Oh, Mark . . .' But she gave up. She turned back to the flower shop, to the house, to the tired geraniums in the window boxes and the faded lavender paintwork that she had always loved. 'I'll see you then,' she said.

CHAPTER 17

Thea

'Nice to see you with a smile on your face, hmm?'

Thea heard the words in a blur, through a doze, she guessed, because these days she seemed to doze so much of the time away. She supposed it was the morphine. The pain, the morphine, this damned sickness. But at least she was here, at home – not upstairs in her own bed, but not at any rate in hospital. Thea was grateful for that.

Francine was holding water to her lips.

'*Merci*, Francine.' Sometimes these days she felt like a child – vulnerable and dependent. But, *naturellement*, not with a child's energy. She caught Francine's eye and the look turned into a smile, into a cough, and Francine had to take the glass away before the water spilt.

She clicked her tongue in that way she had. 'So . . .?'

'It is good to see her,' Thea admitted. Her Colette back home. It was such an unexpected gift. 'Though you shouldn't have written to her.'

'Bah.' Francine swore softly under her breath. Once, Thea

had thought her neighbour a nuisance; an interfering woman who wanted to run the lives of others because she hadn't been able to run her own. Now, she knew better.

After Sébastien's death, Francine had tried to reach out to her; Thea supposed she felt sorry for her. But Thea hadn't wanted her help. She had been determined to maintain control – at all costs. And most of all, Colette would not suffer because of this, she vowed. But she'd been blind; ironically, she saw this now. Colette would suffer because she'd lost the father she'd adored. And loss always took its toll.

When Colette left the island, as month after month went by and her daughter did not return, Thea had crumbled. The flower shop helped a little – it always had. But if not for Francine . . . She doubted she could have carried on.

'You're a good woman, Francine,' she said.

'I just want to go to heaven.' Francine let out a short bark of laughter.

Thea smiled. 'And you will.'

'We'll see.' Francine straightened the bedcovers, disappeared into the kitchen to serve some nourishing stew that no doubt Thea would be unable to eat. Even the smell was turning her stomach. Only the scent of flowers seemed bearable now.

Francine had experienced more than her fair share of life's disappointments, Thea was to discover as she got to know her better, as she let her neighbour into her life. Since Mathilde, Thea had been wary of any female friendship that got too close, but Francine was a very different matter. Francine and her husband Alain had wanted nothing more than to have children of their own. Was this so much to ask? It seemed so. At any rate, it had proved impossible for them. Year after year, Francine did not conceive and eventually, when Alain suffered a stroke, she became his carer. Now, she was caring for Thea. A more nurturing woman Thea had yet to meet. If she did not go to heaven there was no justice, that was all Thea could say.

'You have talked with her?' Francine was standing in the kitchen doorway now, looking fierce.

'*Mais oui*, of course I have.' Thea closed her eyes so she didn't have to see her expression.

'*Eh bien*. What did you say?' She stepped closer to the bed.

Thea suppressed a sigh. 'I told her I had regrets.'

Francine let out a snort of derision. 'And that is all?'

'Francine . . .'

'Yes, I know, my dear.' She bent to stroke Thea's hair from her brow. It was comforting. Colette too had done that earlier and Thea had felt such a surge of love . . .

'I know you are tired,' Francine said. 'Don't worry.'

'I told her that I loved her too.' Colette had looked surprised – almost as if she hadn't known. It was hard for Thea to comprehend, but she could see now, looking back, what Colette might have thought: Maman always in the flower shop, Maman never having time for her. She wasn't to know that Thea had been afraid to love her, that she would far rather put her trust in a flower shop, that she was frightened to love a child she might lose. It was Sébastien who had wanted that child. Thea had done nothing to deserve her.

'But then Colette doesn't know the full story.' Francine spoke as though she had been following Thea's thoughts. Or perhaps Thea had been speaking aloud – who knew?

'No, she doesn't.' Thea opened her eyes and met Francine's candid gaze with a warning glance.

Francine raised her eyebrows in mock innocence. 'It is not my place to tell her.'

'No, it is not.' Thea made her voice as severe as she could under the circumstances. Francine had half-guessed the truth long ago. She had heard things and seen things. The rest, Thea had confided in a low moment when she had felt she couldn't go on, when quite simply she'd had to tell someone and Francine had been there.

'I realise it's not easy.' Francine's voice was softer now. 'But you know, as I do, my dear, that secrets can become toxic, dangerous even. You know that the truth is usually the best way to go, *n'est-ce pas?*'

She moved to leave her bedside, but Thea caught at her hand before she could escape. It was too easy for them all to escape from her sickroom, to melt away when Thea closed her eyes or was too tired to talk. And she was hardly in a position to stop them. On the other hand . . . And she smiled to herself. Being so ill, Thea could do and say as little as she chose as well. So, it was easy for her to escape too.

'It's just that I want to enjoy Colette for a while,' she whispered. She had learnt to live with her own sadness, but . . . 'I don't have long. I don't want anything to spoil this time with her.' Besides, this was not only about herself and Colette, it never had been. There were others to think of too.

Francine was looking at her with pity. 'Do you think I don't know that?' She sighed. 'I can imagine how you feel, *mais oui*, of course I can, my dear.'

'Just to know that she is nearby . . .' Tending the plants, pottering in her beloved flower shop as she once had with Thea when she was a girl. It was a wonderful thought, a much longed-for thought. It was more, so much more, than Thea deserved.

129

CHAPTER 18

Étienne

'*Bonjour! Ça va, monsieur?* Étienne?'

Étienne blinked and looked up, the sunlight reflected in the windowpane blinding him for a moment. The voice was familiar. He'd been lost in thought, but he realised that he was passing the boulangerie. *Merde* . . . he had forgotten to cross the street to avoid it. Madame Riou – who didn't miss a trick when she thought she could get a conversation out of it – was tipping an ovenload of freshly baked baguettes into a basket. She had her broad back to him, but apparently could see him anyway.

'*Très bien merci, Madame,*' he called back. '*Et vous?*' One had to be polite. One had to be sociable. This was a small village and his mother had lived here among these people.

'Come in, come in.' She turned to face him. Her cheeks were rosy from the heat of the oven. She had a friendly smile and probably meant well. She wasn't to know that Étienne was an avoider of conversations, of people. He wasn't exactly unsociable – or so he liked to think – he was simply selective, and he had found that a little went a long way.

But in this case, he felt he had no choice. 'I was just . . .' He gestured towards his mother's pink house. What? Going back there to tidy up – again?

Who would have thought there would be so many complications? Monsieur le Notaire had provided more forms and Étienne more signatures. Monsieur had been confident ('Yes, yes, it should sell, why not?') but also a little critical ('a rather odd house in its layout, you know, it certainly wouldn't suit everyone'). Monsieur had suggested that the place could look more homely and Étienne had bought flowers. Ah yes, flowers. He glanced back towards the flower shop.

'A bad business, yes, indeed.' Madame Riou beckoned Étienne further in and shut the door firmly behind him. 'A small pastry perhaps?' As if that might solve the world's woes. 'A *soupçon*? A taste?'

'Well . . .' They were delicious, as he already knew. He must look undernourished. Had he eaten lunch? He thought so. '*Pourquoi pas?* Why not indeed?' And reflected that he sounded rather like his father.

Madame bustled back behind the counter. Her crimson lipstick was slightly smudged and a tendril of black hair had escaped from her chignon. Her forehead glistened with sweat. Étienne guessed that she knew everything that happened in this village.

'A bad business?' he echoed. He leaned on the counter and, satisfied, Madame leaned too, towards him, dropping her voice to a confidential whisper.

'The mother – Thea Lenoire – she has leukaemia.'

'Oh, Madame, that is bad.' Étienne thought of the dark-eyed girl in the flower shop. No wonder she'd looked so sad. And yet although she'd said she didn't live here on the island, she had looked rather at home here, in the shop at least.

131

Madame nodded. 'Some might say it is a punishment. Not me,' she added quickly, and crossed herself for good measure.

Étienne frowned. 'A punishment for what, Madame?' Really, it was incredible that otherwise intelligent people still thought that way in this day and age.

'I couldn't say, I'm sure.' Though Madame's eyes gleamed as if she'd very much like to. 'Thea Lenoire is British, you know.'

Étienne's eyebrows rose. 'Hardly a reason to be punished,' he commented. Arguably.

Madame tittered. '*Non, non,* but *naturellement,* that is not what I meant at all.'

Then what did you mean? But Étienne didn't say this out loud. Actually, he realised, he did not want to indulge in tittle-tattle about Mademoiselle Flower Shop's mother, especially if the poor woman was so ill. As for her daughter . . . she seemed a lovely girl, an interesting girl. Following their two rather unlikely encounters, he had found himself looking out for her – by the harbour, in the shop, even on the cliff path. Why not? He was a writer but he was also a man. And he was very impressed by the gerberas – they'd given a whole new dimension to the phrase 'a splash of colour'.

He'd had no idea, when he first went into the flower shop . . . the last thing on his mind had been that girl skinny-dipping in the cove. Well, perhaps not the last thing, he amended, because he had given the image some thought, it was true. But his main concern at that moment had been the purchase of flowers – bright and welcoming to put smiles on the faces of all the potential viewers promised by Monsieur le Notaire.

Madame, however, was apparently not ready to stop talking. 'She came here years ago,' she said, 'when I was just a girl, you know.'

'Really?' Étienne tried to imagine this state of affairs and failed. He also tried to remember who had run the boulangerie in the old days – his old days, twenty years ago. Was it this Madame Riou? He rather thought it was. She obviously remembered him although he couldn't say the same about her. Boys of fourteen tended to have other more pressing concerns.

'She was not Thea Lenoire then, of course, not until she married Sébastien.' She gave a nod towards the harbour.

'Ah.' Étienne felt in his pocket for change.

'It is nothing.' Madame waved it away. 'She came here as an au pair,' she continued. '*Mais oui*. To the Blaise family in the Old Lighthouse. Mathilde and Léo Blaise.'

He hadn't heard of them, but Étienne's eyebrows rose another fraction at the way she spoke the name. Léo Blaise was clearly not on Madame's favourite-people list.

'Which is where you have it.' Sagely, she nodded.

'Indeed.' Étienne tried to sound as if he knew what she was talking about.

'Your mother was quite friendly with her, *bien sûr*,' Madame went on, hands on hips. She seemed to be expecting something from Étienne but he wasn't sure what.

'With Mathilde Blaise?'

'With Thea Lenoire.' She eyed him reproachfully for not keeping up. 'They were neighbours, as you know.'

'*Mais oui*. Of course.' It struck Étienne forcibly that here in Sauzon he was surrounded by his mother's friends, by the new life she had made for herself since his father died. Étienne knew very little of that life. He'd never asked about her friends, hardly admitted, even, that she had a new life. Which made him a selfish bastard, he supposed.

'She took it hard when her father died.' Madame passed him

the paper bag with his pastry inside. It felt like a transaction. But what exactly was he paying?

'*Merci*, Madame.' He glanced back towards the flower shop. 'Thea's daughter, do you mean?' It was a wild guess.

'Thea's daughter. And now she has returned, poor thing.'

Yes, she had returned.

'Thanks for the pastry,' Étienne made a mental note to give her extra money tomorrow when he came in for his croissant and baguette. There was probably no harm in her, but he didn't want to feel beholden. And in future, he'd keep his wits about him and make sure he crossed the road a bit sooner.

'It is nothing.' She shrugged and smiled. 'It is for your mother. And for you.' Her expression changed. 'You too have returned.'

'Yes.' Étienne thought of his notebook back at the house. He'd felt the compulsion to write this story longhand – as if his laptop were too far removed from real life. And it was flowing. So, some things at least were coming more easily. Not everything though. In reality, he couldn't quite get there. He kept trying, but could never make it all the way. A bit like women and relationships – the story of his life. He wasn't a commitment-phobe; he just didn't want to belong to any club that would have him as a member, as Groucho Marx had once famously declared. Not until he'd done something about sorting out his head, anyhow. And so.

'You too have not been back since—'

'I do not talk of that time any more.' In three strides, Étienne was out of there.

'Pardon, Monsieur, I meant no—'

He didn't want to hear what else Madame Riou might mean, might have to say. He'd been a fool to imagine that people

134

didn't remember, that the past had faded and that a man could start anew.

All he'd done since he got here was clear out his mother's house, walk and try not to think of the past. Why had his mother chosen to live here anyway? She'd always known his feelings about it. He could leave now, surely? He did not have to have this kind of conversation. He did not have to worry — Monsieur le Notaire would keep him informed.

And yet the past was here; it had seeped into every stone of the house, every pebble on the beach. It was in the sky, in the ocean and on that bloody cliff path. He wanted to get away from it and yet it seemed the past just wouldn't let him go.

CHAPTER 19

Colette

Colette stood by the smart white Vindilis ferry in the harbour at Le Palais waiting for Mark to disembark, trying to catch a glimpse of him among the sea of faces on deck.

She'd borrowed her mother's old Citroën, now parked up by the bus station. *As if I'll be needing it, chérie* . . . her mother had snorted with laughter in a brief burst of energy after the few spoonfuls of porridge Colette had managed to persuade her to eat this morning.

Colette was early and the boat was late, so before going to the harbour she'd wandered up the hill. She dipped into the Hôtel de Ville to check out the art exhibition there, then admired the pastel murals of Le Palais in days gone by at the old Rex cinema. She passed grand houses of coral, yellow and blue, with shabby shutters and wrought-iron balconies – the most impressive being Villa Henri (had an Henri ever resided there, she wondered?) – until she reached the town's original stone gateway, Porte Vauban. Behind the gateway was the *poterne du réduit*, a tunnel built in 1862 that led through the old ramparts.

And she thought she knew this place . . . Colette shook her head. There was so much history here on Belle-Île, so much more to discover. She knew certain facts, obviously, well known among the Bellîlois: that the ancestors of many of the townsfolk had come from Nova Scotia (not hers though, at least not on her mother's side), that pirates had once pillaged their churches and monasteries, that the Welsh had come to create the village of Bangor, that the island had been owned by the English for a couple of years in the eighteenth century. She knew that Belle-Île had always been home to farming and fishing, music and art – Monet, John Peter Russell the Australian impressionist painter and Matisse had been part of an artists' colony here. She knew that true Bellîlois like her father had their own dialect, traditions and identity. She remembered her father telling her that the island men had always wanted sons – for the work, for the sea – but that he was glad things had changed.

Colette smiled to herself. When she was young she'd barely appreciated all this, but now . . . She walked up to the top of the town-wall steps, overlooking the streets of Le Palais, the harbour, the open ocean beyond. Belle-Île-en-Mer – the beautiful isle by the sea, indeed. She had returned here with older eyes. Now she could truly see it.

The ferry-boat was coming in towards the harbour. It was time to get back to the bustling port, dominated by the high, sloping granite walls of the Fort. Time to meet Mark.

Down at the waterfront, she glanced up at the ferry, now docking. They needed to reconnect, she knew that, though she rather suspected that the disconnection was in her head, not Mark's. Because of everything that had happened, she told herself. Because of her mother. Because of coming back to this place.

People were streaming off the ferry now – young couples with neat suitcases, families with bags and rucksacks and buggies, elderly people holding on to the hand-rail, children impatient to get to the—

'Colette! Darling!' And then he was there, in front of her, tall and reassuring. 'My God, it feels like so long since I've seen you.'

Colette felt herself begin to relax. It would be all right, she thought.

Mark wrapped his arms around her and gave her a long kiss, oblivious to their surroundings, to the other people disembarking around them, to the officials directing the cars down the ramp . . .

Colette disentangled herself, laughing. She looked up, spotted the man from the cliff, the man who had come into the flower shop and bought all her gerberas. He had a black weekend bag slung over one shoulder. He was waiting to get on the ferry, to leave the island. And he was looking straight at her. Again.

She gave a mental shrug. What did it matter? Sometimes life was like that; the same people turned up in different and unexpected places. There had been something appealing about him, she had to admit, despite that rather tortured look in his green eyes. But he was leaving. He was a stranger. He didn't like the island, he'd as good as said so, and he was, as she'd first suspected, just a visitor, no more.

She turned to the more solid reality of the man by her side. 'It's good to see you, Mark.' She tucked her arm in his. 'Come on. I'll show you the sights of Le Palais another day – we should get back to Maman.'

His face clouded. 'We can have lunch first though, can't we? In one of these appetising little cafés?'

Colette followed his gaze. The original promenade villas and hotels were still stately if a little faded, and under their green and blue wooden shutters stood little crêperies, bars, boutiques and cafés. The waterfront of Le Palais did look appealing, and Mark had had a long journey. She smiled. 'Of course. That would be lovely.'

Perhaps just for a moment, she could sit outside a café in Le Palais and pretend that all was well with her world. Most girls would be glad to have their boyfriend to themselves for a couple of hours before heading home. Her mother could wait for the lunchtime soup that Colette must persuade her to eat, to keep up what little strength she seemed to have left. Her mother could wait to be introduced to Mark – Colette had kept her waiting long enough already. Be like most girls, Colette, she told herself crossly. Be glad.

CHAPTER 20

Colette

They soon found a restaurant with a view of the busy harbour and a menu Mark approved of. It was the kind of place that would be the first choice of many tourists on their first visit to the island, Colette thought. Smart waiters, red umbrellas, a menu with photographs of the food (as if it had to be seen to be believed), plenty of tables crammed on to the wide terrace and an uninterrupted view of the bay.

'So, what's happened?' Colette asked him as they tucked into the *fricassée de coquillages* Mark had ordered. The thyme balanced the lemon and the wine in the light creamy sauce and the seafood was fresh and delicious. 'What did you want to talk about face to face?' She gave him a little nudge with her knee to show that she was teasing.

'Ah.' He paused – as if for dramatic effect. 'I've got the chance of a new position.' Mark looked so proud. He smoothed back his neat dark hair and beamed.

'Wow.' Colette squeezed his hand. 'In the estate agency?' He was already the manager. She speared a clam and savoured the sweet taste of the sea. She was probably biased but shellfish seemed to taste so much better here on the island.

'In a different branch.' Mark straightened the collar of his stripy T-shirt which didn't need straightening — it already looked perfect enough.

He looked so like a British tourist abroad, she found herself thinking. Colette smiled and took a sip of her small glass of dry white wine. She didn't mind, though. Mark always dressed smartly and he'd tried his best with the tailored charcoal-grey shorts and even a straw hat which he'd now placed on the seat beside him. But he looked not quite right for the island — as if he was trying too hard. The image of the man in the flower shop popped unbidden into her mind — lazy and lounging, his T-shirt faded and yet somehow looking just the thing. But he didn't belong here either, she reminded herself. And he'd already left. She dipped a prawn in the sauce still on her plate.

'A bigger branch do you mean? Truro?' She supposed that would mean a longer commute. But Mark wouldn't object to that. He'd enjoy being in charge of more people — and he'd be good at it too.

'Truro?' Mark let out a bark of laughter. 'You're joking.' He picked up the last mussel and prised the half-open shell further apart.

'Where then?'

He didn't answer at first. 'Coffee, darling?' he asked instead. He leaned back in his chair. He seemed in his element, taking charge.

'Mm, please.' Colette pushed her plate away and let her gaze drift for a moment to the bay. The ferry had departed now of course, but there was a yacht swooping through the mouth of the harbour and another pleasure boat chugging in behind it. 'So if it's not Truro . . .?'

Mark caught the attention of a young waitress and ordered their coffee. He smiled at Colette – a triumphant smile, she thought – and reached for her hand.

She waited. Let him have his moment. He deserved it.

'Think more the big city,' he said.

Colette frowned. 'Plymouth?'

'No, Colette.' He shook his head at her and gave her hand an indulgent pat. 'That just shows how parochial you are.'

'Parochial?' The sun was in her eyes and Colette thought that she might be getting a headache.

'Look at you.' He leaned closer and scrutinised her. She fidgeted in her seat. 'A stylish Frenchwoman . . .'

'Half-French,' she reminded him.

'But born in France,' he went on. 'You're a woman who deserves to be spoilt, my darling. You should be living such a different life, enjoying the variety, the culture that a big city offers.'

Colette blinked at him. She didn't remotely recognise the woman he was describing. 'So, where's the job, Mark?' And did she want a different life? Once again, her gaze drifted out to the blue ocean. The UK seemed so far away already, another world.

'London.' He squeezed her hand enthusiastically. 'London, Colette, the only place where property business is big business; the only place – apart from New York anyway – where you can get anything you want at any time of day because the city never sleeps.'

She might be parochial, Colette thought, but at least she didn't talk in clichés. She suppressed a brush of irritation. She was tired. She was worried about her mother. She wanted to make things better between them. She didn't want her to die . . . 'London,' she echoed. 'Whereabouts in London?'

'North London,' he said. 'Enfield, to be exact.'

Enfield . . . It meant absolutely nothing to Colette. Even their conversation seemed surreal, as if Mark was talking about one thing and she was hearing another.

'What do you think of that then?' He was beaming like a small boy. 'That's news, don't you reckon? That's news that needs to be said face to face.'

Colette didn't know what to think, what to say. 'Mark, that's . . . that's great. I mean I didn't even know you'd applied for a transfer. I didn't even know you wanted to move – to London.' Or to anywhere, she thought. He certainly hadn't discussed it with her.

'London? Who could say no?' He laughed and Colette smiled back at him. 'It's a hell of a lot more responsibility, darling. And a sizeable pay increase obviously.'

'Obviously.' Considering how expensive it was to live there.

'And it only just came up.' But he looked away towards the boats in the harbour as he said this and Colette wasn't sure whether to believe him. More likely he'd applied for it ages ago and decided only to tell her if he got it. She couldn't blame him for that, though – every man had his pride.

She nodded. Thanked the waitress who appeared with the coffee. 'London,' she said. 'Wow.' Again. It was so far away. He wouldn't be commuting from Cornwall, not to London.

A woman scurried along the waterfront carrying a basket full of colourful fruit and vegetables. Colette watched her. She was a local, not a tourist, it was easy to tell from the way she was dressed, the confident way she moved. Belle-Île had been a haven for tourists for many years, evident from the grand hotels

143

in Le Palais, the tall villas, the black and white and sepia photographs one could see in bars and cafés of past days not much less busy than these . . . but there was still an undercurrent of the old life here, the life that Colette remembered. There were still fishermen like her father, flower-sellers like her mother; there was still a colourful market in Le Palais selling fresh fish and seafood, vegetables grown in the local fields and glasshouses; *charcuterie*, *fromagerie*, shoes made by island cobblers. There was music here – and there always would be. And there were still the original bars with a fug of cigarette smoke hanging over the rough wooden counters and stone flags. At the windows of the houses, with their ancient leaning walls, hung delicate lace curtains featuring horses, galleons – all manner of embroidery. Belle-Île still had those traces of reality, of history, and Colette loved it for that.

She'd been to London, of course, not long after she first arrived in the UK; she'd seen some of the sights – Madame Tussaud's and the Natural History Museum – witnessed the changing of the guard at Buckingham Palace, wandered around a few galleries. More recently she'd gone with Mark; they'd ridden on the London Eye and visited the David Bowie exhibition at the V&A (her mother would have loved that too – Colette remembered her playing the *Ziggy Stardust* album when she was a young girl). But Colette had been relieved to get back to the quiet of Cornwall, to be honest; to the slower pace of life. Mark was right. She might be half-French but she was as parochial as they came and she rather liked it that way.

'Perhaps it's because I grew up on a small island,' she said to him now, 'that I'm such a small-town girl.' She gave a little laugh to show she hadn't taken offence.

'Don't be silly, darling, you're not a small-town girl.'

How was he so sure? She'd always known that Mark wanted a chic French girlfriend – he'd said as much. And she knew that he liked to look after her – to pamper her, even. But did he want the real her? Colette wasn't convinced. Did he even know the real her?

She watched as Mark looked around him and tried to see it through his eyes. From the waterfront promenade, various streets led up the hill towards the remains of the old fortifications where she had walked earlier. There were many interesting shops and galleries to be found on the way; tempting patisseries, chic boutiques and interior decor shops, boulangeries with the original black and gold signage – none of which Mark had yet seen. At the moment there was a fascinating exterior exhibition of the photographs of Pierre Jamet, taken between 1930 and 1960, which was slightly before Colette's mother's time but certainly during her father's. The pictures were all in black and white: children playing in the sand and doing gymnastics on the beach, families running into the sea, women in forties and fifties dresses reading magazines and kissing their husbands goodbye at the waterfront ferry. *En vacance* in Belle-Île-en-Mer, thought Colette. The island had always had so much to offer.

'It's really small, isn't it?' Mark was shaking his head. 'My God, I looked the place up after you left and I couldn't believe it.'

'Couldn't believe what?' And this coming from a Cornishman? Colette kept her tone mild but her internal hackles were raised. Interesting. It seemed that she could say she couldn't wait to leave Belle-Île, she could feel trapped here, she could stay away for years. But let an outsider criticise the place and she was as defensive as if it were a member of her own family. And perhaps it was, in a way.

'There's really nothing here.' Mark's expansive gesture

145

embraced the entire island, not only the bit of Le Palais that he had already seen.

'Oh, I don't know,' she demurred. 'You might find more here than you think.' Secluded coves to swim in, sandy beaches shelving into turquoise sea, coastal paths and rural hideaways, quaint villages of stone houses and ancient churches, light-houses and galleries of arts and crafts. Markets, restaurants, boutiques and bars.

'If you didn't want to come and live in London, I wouldn't take the job,' Mark told her.

Colette glanced across at him. Did he mean that?

'My life's with you,' he said.

Oh, Mark . . .

'So, what would you do instead?' she asked him after they left the café and were walking beside the harbour towards the little black bridge.

'I'd stay with you in Cornwall,' he said.

'You'd be happy to do that?' She was touched.

'I'd be perfectly content.'

Which wasn't quite the same thing. Two different scenarios drifted through Colette's head. One featured her and Mark in London, living in a tiny flat because that would be all they could afford. Traffic noise would send them to sleep at night and traffic noise would wake them in the morning. They would have access to all the films and shows they could possibly want to see; they could eat anything they wanted to eat any time. They could go to exhibitions and concerts and live gigs in Hyde Park. They would be part of the buzz that was London. They would be together – but what would she *do* there? Scenario two featured them in Cornwall. But they would only be there because Colette had said no to Mark's job, to the promotion he was so excited about. How could she possibly do that? They would be together – but how long would it be before he hated her?

They climbed the stone steps up to the car park by the old Citadelle. 'I had no idea you wanted to leave Cornwall,' she said again. 'I mean, you were born there, I always assumed you wanted to stay there.' This was the most surprising part – that she simply hadn't had a clue.

'Exactly,' he said. 'I was born there – and now it's time to get out, just like you did.'

'Well, yes, but . . .' She had got out, true enough, but there had been all sorts of other reasons.

They reached her mother's car. He glanced at it. 'You're driving this thing?' He laughed.

'It's my mother's.' Colette unlocked the Citroën. 'I had no idea you wanted to move to London.' And yet it made sense. Mark was an ambitious man. Now she came to think of it, Colette was surprised he hadn't left before.

He leaned over the top of the car towards her. 'It'll be exciting, Colette,' he said. 'Just imagine.'

Colette tried. 'Let me think about it.' She opened the door and slid into the driver's seat. 'And then we can talk about it some more.'

'OK.' He unfolded his body into the seat beside her and glanced around the car's interior.

It was full of the detritus of her mother's existence – terracotta pots stacked in the back, a trail of soil across the passenger-seat footwell, an unopened bag of compost and some old newspapers. 'Sorry about the mess,' she said.

He leaned over and kissed her. 'I don't mind a bit,' he said. 'I'm just glad to see you.'

147

'Me too.' And she was. But it was more complicated than that. It had been more complicated even before she heard Mark's news. Colette felt as if she were being thrown around on some fairground ride. She'd lost her sense of direction entirely. She no longer knew which way was up. And she hadn't even told Mark that she was working in the flower shop . . .

CHAPTER 21

Élodie

Élodie walked down to Sauzon to post her letter to Jacques.
It was a pleasant June day and she sensed the summer shift in
the air, in the breeze as it blew her hair from her face, as she
walked the path she knew so well into the village. She and
Jacques were so close that even after all these years and such
a long separation, she imagined she could still feel his moods.

And today reminded her of another day many years ago,
only months before Jacques left the island, when Élodie was
fourteen, Jacques seventeen, when they had been walking along
the coastal path – not into Sauzon, but back from Donnant
Beach. It was another of those June days that seemed to go on
for ever, days when Élodie had almost thought that anything
was possible as she and Jacques walked barefoot across the sand,
swam in the pretty bay, gasping at the chill that remained in
the water although it was already summer.

It had been a sunny day on the beach, but heavy too, the very
air making their feet lag as they walked back along the path.
Gradually, the sky grew darker and their feet felt still more

leaden. Élodie began to wish they had not walked so far, but it was always too easy. They started fast as though they both wanted to get as much distance between them and the Old Lighthouse as they could, then they would talk and dawdle, walk and wander on some more, and suddenly they would be still on the coastal path but many kilometres away.

Although the sky had turned from mid-blue to a dark bluey-grey, the first drops of rain took them by surprise as they splattered on to their arms, their legs, their faces.

'*Merde.*' Jacques grabbed her hand. 'Let's make for the forest.' The pines were only fifty metres away. Heads down, they ran.

Lightning streaked across the stormy sky, a growl of thunder seemed to reverberate through Élodie's body. 'Isn't it dangerous?' she gasped. 'The trees? The lightning?' Under her feet, the pine needles were already sodden and her hair was damp and sticking to her face and scalp.

'*Merde*,' said Jacques again. 'But we'll get soaked.' He looked around, blinking through the rain; pulled her further into the wood. 'Hey, what's that?'

Élodie looked. It was a bivouac, a kind of rough shelter built from branches and twigs, even fir cones. 'Who . . .?'

'Let's go and see.' Jacques led the way, crashing over to it. 'Hey! *Bonjour!* Is anybody there?' He laughed, and in the electric eye of the storm his laughter sounded wild, almost mad.

Another fork of lightning lit the sky and immediately the thunder grumbled back at it. The storm was on them.

'Come.' Jacques bent, then crawled into the bivouac through the wet leafy opening, still pulling Élodie behind him.

She felt something damp – a fern perhaps – brush her face, wetness on her hair, and then she was in. Safe and sheltered, they drew breath, laughed, looked around them.

There was nothing in the bivouac, just some old matting. Élodie couldn't help wondering who had built it, who had used it and what had happened to them. But Jacques sat down on the matting, exhaled loudly, opened his arms and drew her down next to him. Élodie relaxed against the body she knew so well, her head on his chest, snuggled in close. They were quiet. She could feel his breathing, hear his heart beating, while outside the rain lashed down and the storm ranted and raged all around them.

Jacques stroked her hair, gently smoothed and untangled the rain-matted tendrils with his fingers. 'I love you, Élodie,' he said.

'I love you too, Jacques.' She sighed, comfortable and replete, although they'd exhausted their supplies and eaten nothing but a few squares of chocolate and an apple each for hours.

He bent his head. 'And I want you to understand that when I leave—'

'*Comment?*' She pulled away from him. What was he saying?

'That I am not leaving because of you.'

'Leaving?' she echoed. It was impossible to contemplate. 'Leaving Belle-Île, do you mean?'

'Yes,' he said, 'and you must leave too. I will help you, of course – when the time comes.'

Élodie didn't know what to say. She knew him so well, and yet she had not thought . . . She searched his face. He looked different. It was Jacques's face, his velvet-brown eyes, but those eyes were glazed with an emotion she'd never seen there before. It was, she realised, a kind of nervous anticipation.

'But what about Mama?' And her voice sounded cold to her own ears. Because if Jacques was leaving, then who would look after their mother?

Jacques turned away – but not before Élodie saw the flicker of resentment. 'Maman makes her own choices,' he said.

Élodie understood what he was referring to. She'd heard that conversation between the two of them only the other day: 'Don't you ever get fed up with the way he treats you? Won't you ever tell him to go?' Jacques had said to her.

'He's my husband, Jacques,' their mother had replied.

'And I'm your son.'

Élodie had watched from the doorway, knowing that this was a special private moment between her mother and her brother but unable to peel herself away from the scene. She watched their mother reach for Jacques, she saw her hold him close and she witnessed her trying not to weep. Élodie was young but she knew how difficult this decision must be for her, she knew how much her mother loved them both.

'I cannot stand it, Maman.' Jacques was still speaking, the anger clenching every word. 'I cannot stand *him*.'

'Hush, Jacques.' She stroked his dark hair as if he were still her young child. Jacques even looked like their father – he had the same handsome darkness about him, the same fine features and sudden, charming smile.

'It will be him or me, Maman. You know that, don't you? Sooner or later. Him or me.' He drew away from her then. He stood straight and tall. *I am a man. I will help you if you let me.*

'Jacques . . .'

'You must decide.'

And she had; in her own way, she had.

Already, Élodie had reached the postbox. She hesitated for a moment, the letter in her hand.

In the end, though, Jacques hadn't made the decision to leave Belle-Île at all – it had been made for him. And under those circumstances, Élodie wasn't sure he would agree that it was always possible to return.

CHAPTER 22

Colette

'It's not that I think you're crazy,' Mark said, 'opening up your mother's flower shop, making up orders and arrangements for all the old customers, letting her think that you're looking after the place, that nothing has changed . . .'

Though he obviously did. 'I *am* looking after the place,' Colette protested.

'Yes, of course you are, and I understand why.' He looked ahead of them, out into the distance, down the street of neat candy-coloured houses with their white shutters and dark-grey slate roofs. 'But things *have* changed, Colette, that's the point.'

'I know.' But there was such a thing as damage limitation.

They were walking around Locmaria and had just left the church. It was the simplicity of the building that always touched her – the pale blue of the ceiling against the white stone arches, the vibrant clarity of the stained-glass windows, the dome outside and the figure of Christ, white and vulnerable on the Cross. Colette wasn't sure exactly what she believed – but she believed in something.

She had explained to Mark why she was looking after the shop (*I feel I have to – it upsets her so*) on the way back to Sauzon after that first lunch in Le Palais three days ago. And Mark had seemed to accept it. Colette guessed that he wanted to see for himself how things were, before he suggested any changes – she knew he wouldn't be able to help himself. He had plenty of things to think about too: a prospective promotion, a move to London, a girlfriend who had promised to stay on the island of Belle-Île in southern Brittany – at least for the foreseeable future.

Colette's bedroom was so small that Mark had suggested they sleep in her parents' old bedroom instead. 'I can't,' she told him at first. It felt weird, wrong even.

Mark had laughed – 'You're being ridiculous, darling' – and she supposed he was right. It was just a bed, just a room. And so, she'd agreed – but she still hoped her mother hadn't realised.

In the mornings, when she was attending to her mother's needs and looking after the shop, Mark strolled around the harbour, bought himself an English newspaper and a coffee and chatted to people – not to locals, but to tourists visiting Sauzon. He would return to the house for a late lunch, and in the afternoons Colette did as she'd promised – she showed him some of the sights of Belle-Île, while Francine took care of her mother. Mark had appeared interested in the villages, the grand lighthouse, the rocks at Port Coton and the church at Locmaria – all the places Colette cared about, wound up with her memories of her childhood and her father as they were – but she wasn't totally convinced. Even so, she was glad that he was here, on her territory; it gave her at least the illusion of having more control.

'I simply can't see the point of pretending,' Mark continued as they walked down the hill to Port Maria. 'Obviously, the flower shop will have to go. Isn't it more sensible to start sorting things out now, rather than later?'

'More sensible perhaps.' Colette looked around her. This was one of her favourite places on the island. Like the village itself, the bay was quiet, simple and peaceful, being protected by the granite cliffs around it. The waves lapped gently into the cove over the small rocks and the seaweed. The sea was pure green and translucent; the sand, golden-brown. 'But I'm doing it for her, I told you.'

'Is your mother ever going to be well enough to run the shop again?'

'No, but—'

'So, are you going to run it? After she dies?'

Colette flinched.

'Obviously not.' He answered for her. 'So, you'll have to put it up for sale, won't you? I know you don't want to hear this, darling, I know you don't even want to think it, but it's the obvious thing to do. That's all I'm saying. What's the point in putting off the inevitable?'

Colette felt bombarded. 'There is a point,' she said. There was still her mother. Mark was acting as if she didn't exist. She bent to take off her sandals, she liked to walk the sand barefoot, feel the damp grains squeeze between her toes. 'It would break her heart.'

'Like she broke yours?' he countered.

Colette had no answer to that. 'I don't want to argue,' she said. Though right now she was losing patience and that too seemed inevitable. This was exactly why she'd resisted Mark's offer of coming over here. It wasn't his business and yet here he was taking over, being sensible and practical and not allowing his thoughts to be clouded by emotions. But emotions mattered. Her mother mattered too. 'Let's sit down for a while.' She pointed to the rocks by the far cliff path. From there you could sit and look out to sea.

Mark made a bit of a meal of climbing up the path – one would never guess that he was a Cornish lad, though he'd always been a bit of a townie too – and they flopped on to the rocks. 'I don't want to argue either, darling,' he soothed. 'I'm here to support you, you know that.'

'And I'm grateful.' Though at the moment she didn't feel it. When she was still reeling from the death of her grandparents, she had been so appreciative of Mark's support, for the help and security he seemed to provide, even for his advice and guidance at times. But now . . . Colette glanced up at the house that stood at the back of the bay, perched a little way up the grassy cliff looking out to sea. As far as she knew, it had always been there, ravaged by weather, but still peaceful somehow. She liked the narrow oblong windows on its first floor, the off-white walls and elegant grey arched shutters. It was a lovely house and a perfect setting – but no one ever seemed to be living there. Now, she was trying not to feel annoyed with him. This was her mother and she was dying. Didn't Colette know the best way to handle things? Hadn't she grown up here? Didn't she know – more than anyone – how important the shop was to her mother? It felt as though Mark was simply charging roughshod over all the things that meant so much to her.

'You're too much of a softie, darling,' Mark said. 'I'm trying to protect you from yourself.'

But wasn't that all she had – herself? Colette watched a white gull crest the waves. She wanted to pick her way through the rocks to the sea; to paddle, to wash away what Mark was saying. The sun was shimmering on the water further out, but the shoreline was in the shadow of the high granite cliff, the undergrowth, the bracken.

'Anyway, you can only sell the place if she actually owns it,' Mark said. Clearly, he had no intention of letting the subject drop.

Colette sighed. 'What do you mean?'

'Well, does she own the shop or does she rent it?'

'I'm sure she owns it.' Though Colette realised that she had no idea. So, in a way, Mark was right. She was letting emotions cloud her judgement, she was being hopelessly impractical. She straightened. Even so . . . There were two small fishing boats high up on the beach; one red, one indigo and white, next to what was left of the old jetty. The blue and white boat made her think of her father. Had he bought Colette's mother the flower shop? She didn't think so. She knew her father's family home – the place where he'd grown up and lived until he married Colette's mother and moved into the pink and lavender building over the shop. It was an unassuming enough cottage set back from Sauzon harbour that had been in his family for generations.

Colette had visited once when her grandfather was still alive – had seen for herself the spare flint walls, the ancient black iron cooking pot positioned on a rack over the embers in the stone fireplace under smoke-blackened beams. In the front parlour were two pictures. One was a photographic portrait of her grandmother wearing a traditional *coiffe Bretonne* – a delicate lacy headdress – a serene expression in her handsome dark eyes. The other was a black and white picture of the big old sardine nets being pulled up on the quay; her grandfather told her proudly that he had been there when the picture had been taken, on the edge of that scene with the other fishermen in their rough baggy trousers and shirts and flat Breton caps. It must have been a very different life back then. Her father had insisted an inside lavatory be installed and the original dirt floor had been flagged many years before, but other than that the cottage remained unchanged.

Colette frowned. Her mother couldn't have had money of her own when she came to Belle-Île; she was too young. So, did she own the flower shop or were there mountains of debt? 'I'll find out for certain,' she told Mark.

'You'd better.' Mark shook his head in apparent despair. 'Because if she rents it, then there might be bills to pay, rent due, insurance that needs sorting out – who knows?'

'Mmm.' He had a point.

'At the very least, you should be looking after her affairs, Colette.'

'She's not dead yet.' She tried not to snap. He was only thinking of her best interests, only trying to help.

'But she's not capable of looking after things herself,' he pointed out – perfectly reasonably, she had to admit.

'I suppose not.' Colette let her gaze drift out to the sea. She'd like to send this conversation out on the waves, never hear it or take part in it again.

'And then there's the house.'

'The house?' She wasn't sure she could take much more of this, not now.

'Oh, Colette, darling, honestly. You don't seem to have a clue.' He put his arm around her and patted her shoulder. 'I think it's about time you found out a lot more about your mother's life and finances – don't you?'

Colette wished he would stop doing that too. She tensed. What was wrong with her? This wasn't how she'd envisaged their day out. She wanted to spend time with Mark and she had missed him — but she also wanted to get back to her mother's bedside. Everything that Mark said was true. But that didn't mean Colette had to see it the same way as he did. She and her mother had been estranged for so long and Colette had still not completely forgiven her, although she was trying to understand. But despite everything, she was her mother and she had loved Colette. They might not have very much time. And Colette was determined that during these last weeks and months she would do all she could to make her final days as pain-free as possible.

He could say what he liked, but she wasn't the same person she had been when she first met Mark. Time had passed; she was older — perhaps stronger too. And now, as far as her mother was concerned, there was only her, just as Francine had said. And so Colette would do things her way.

CHAPTER 23

Thea: July 1969

Tonight was a dead loss. Danny and me — we had different agendas from the start. He wanted to spend some time together — go for a walk, have a coffee then watch TV round at his place. I don't know, it didn't sound that thrilling, I suppose. I wanted more. We could have bought some cider and drunk it up at Loe Bar. We could have gone back to his place, stayed in his room, listened to some music . . .

OK, I wanted sex. No, not even that. We haven't managed sex yet, although not for want of trying. It's been a mixture of us being scared his parents are about to walk in (we've only tried when they're safely out of the way), Danny not wanting to hurt me (which is sweet, but if it hurts first time like everyone says, then I'll just have to put up with it), and the fact that both of us are virgins and don't really know what to do. We've got carried away quite a few times since we first got together, but we've never gone all *the way. It's like it's just too far for us.*

But I didn't even want sex. Not tonight, not especially. What did I want then? Sometimes I'm not really sure. I feel angry and

160

I don't know what with, I feel sad and there's no reason. I feel frustrated and I'm not sure why. OK, so tonight . . . I wanted to feel wanted, really wanted. I wanted . . . Oh, I dunno.

It's painful to want so much.

Anyway, it didn't happen. Nothing happened. I went round to his place. His parents are better off than mine and they live in one of those Victorian piles on Bay View Terrace overlooking the sea. Shabby but grand. It's a million times better than this place to be honest, but Danny's parents inherited some family money, which was why they could afford it; it's not like they're stuck up or rich or anything.

We kissed. It was nice. Danny had put some smoochy Marvin Gaye on the record player – I prefer Bob Dylan and the Rolling Stones, but I don't mind a bit of Motown – and we were busy getting in the mood. His hand was snaking under my T-shirt, so I decided to go for it. I started to unzip his jeans, and he pulled away like a frightened rabbit.

'What?' I sighed.

'Just . . .'

'What?'

'Not here.'

I sat back. We'd both been breathing heavily but now he'd completely broken the mood. 'Where then?'

He shrugged.

'Why not here?' We could hardly go to a hotel room. We were in his bedroom – his territory, his own private space. His parents had gone out to The Ship for a drink. It couldn't be more perfect. Where else was there?

'I dunno.' He scrambled off the bed. 'It feels wrong.'

'Wrong?' I echoed. You don't expect that. Your mother might say it – but not your boyfriend.

161

'And anyway,' he added, gathering ammunition. 'I haven't got anything.'

I narrowed my eyes at him. What boyfriend hasn't 'got anything' when his girlfriend's coming round for the evening and his parents are out? I'll have to go on the pill. Everyone's doing it. Why not me? If I do go to see Dr Reeves about it, he won't even be allowed to tell my parents, or so Barb says; it would be confidential.

The answer is that Danny doesn't really want me to go on the pill. 'It seems a bit well, cheap,' was what he said when I suggested it. Which is exactly what Mum would say.

I spent a while pondering on why my boyfriend keeps sounding like Mum these days. I didn't come to any conclusions. But if there is a generation gap, then it strikes me that Danny and my mum are both on the same side of the chasm.

'We could just mess around?' I said. 'We could . . .'

But he wasn't looking at me now. He was looking out over his parents' neat back garden where the grass is shorn within a quarter of an inch of its life and where weeds don't dare make an appearance. 'Perhaps we should wait,' he said.

But how long for . . .? I ground my teeth. Barb says it's bound to be a confidence problem. She says if I'm patient, then it'll happen. Just when you're least expecting it, she says. But I can't help wondering if there's something wrong with us. We've both got the right equipment but no clue how to use it. What we need is an instruction booklet, but all Mum's ever given me is a little white leaflet about periods. Barb's been more forthcoming – she's slept with two of her boyfriends already – but even with Barb I don't want to seem too naive. It's pathetic really.

'Why do we have to wait?'

He shrugged again. 'I love you, Thea,' he said. 'But I respect you too.'

162

Right at that moment I didn't give a toss about respect. I got to my feet and adjusted my clothes so that I looked half-decent. I pulled on my purple skinny-rib cardigan. Then I made for the door. I walked out of that house and along the terrace path, which was dark and deserted.

Oh, he came after me – Danny will always do that. He caught me up halfway down the narrow pavement. I ranted and raged a bit about how he didn't fancy me and he stroked my hair and told me that he did, that it was as much as he could do to hold back, that it will be different when we're both eighteen (how, exactly? Will someone wave a magic wand?) and even more different when we get engaged, that he doesn't want to be one of those blokes who take advantage of his girl, that he loves me and values me and respects the wishes of my parents and . . . I know. I know all that. But I still can't help wishing he'd rip my clothes off and pounce.

'Anyway,' I told him, 'I want to go home.' And I wouldn't let him walk me, either.

I turned up Fore Street by the chemist and headed for our house. There were a couple of lads hanging around outside Wimbleton's Butchers. I've seen them before – they're a year older than me and live on the other side of town. 'All alone, love?' one of them called out to me and they both laughed as if he'd said something hilarious.

'Best way to be,' I snapped back at him.

'Ooh, touchy.' They laughed again.

I tossed my head and turned into Holman's Place. Sometimes I believe it 'n' all.

Mum and Dad were still up watching TV when I got home. Some comedy, the volume up far too loud. No one's deaf – my theory is they're afraid of the silences.

'Hello, love. How's Danny? Did you have a nice time?'

'All right, thanks.'

163

They always say the same thing. I always say the same thing back. Either we're all stuck in one hell of a rut or we are actually The Most Boring Family on Earth. At least we're all safe though, eh?

Next weekend I'm going to the Hall disco with Barb (Danny can do what he likes). It's always the same old crowd but at least it's something. And tonight I know who I'm gonna be dreaming about. Biker guy. I may never see him again, but one thing's for sure — I'm not gonna give up looking.

Cos it's not a rut. It's a bubble. A big, glossy, soapy bubble. And there's two things I want to do. Prick the bubble so it bursts. Then see what's outside. There's a mad, bad, exciting world out there, I know it. And I want to see exactly what it is that I'm missing.

CHAPTER 24

Mathilde

Thea had wanted to get out there and see exactly what she was missing . . .

Mathilde put the diary to one side and let out a small sigh. And that was how these things started.

She remembered when Thea had first arrived at the Old Lighthouse. She'd had no idea of Thea's story then, of what had led her to answer their advertisement in *The Lady*. Léo had gone to pick her up in the car, brought her over on the ferry.

'*Bonjour*, I am Mathilde.' She had held out her hand and given Thea a swift but close scrutiny. She liked to think of herself as intuitive; she would know, she'd told Léo, as soon as she met her.

'*Bonjour*, Madame.' The girl was younger than she'd expected, smaller too. And there was a brightness and an energy about her – especially when she reached out her arms to Jacques and started playing and swinging him around as if she'd known him for ever. Mathilde liked that. But there was a sadness in her too, a shadow around her eyes that alerted Mathilde. What was her story? Had something happened at home? Had she already, at such a young age, been disappointed in love?

She wondered what Léo and Thea had talked about on the way over. Had conversation flowed between them? Or had he focused on the road and then read a newspaper on the ferry while Thea stared out to sea, wondering what she was letting herself in for? What had he told Thea about Mathilde? Had he said she was needy, unstable even – or would he let Thea find that out for herself? Had he been attracted to her? Mathilde felt her knuckles clench. Or did he see her as a gauche, naive English girl to whom he must be pleasant and caring, rather like a surrogate father?

'Thank you for giving me this chance,' Thea had said, shaking Mathilde's hand rather energetically. 'You won't regret it. I promise you won't regret it.'

Mathilde hoped not.

'Shall we have some coffee?' Behind Thea's back, Léo rolled his eyes at Mathilde. She guessed that this was what he'd had to listen to all the way here.

'Yes, of course,' she said. 'But let me show Thea to her room and then I have to put Jacques down for his nap.'

When she came back downstairs, Léo had lit a cigarette and was smoking it by the French doors. He looked restless. As if he couldn't wait to be gone, Mathilde thought.

'So, will she do?' Léo asked her. 'Are you happy?'

'I think so.' Mathilde switched on the coffee machine.

'Because I only want to make you happy – you know that, don't you?' He came up behind her and put his arms around her waist.

'That's nice,' said Mathilde.

He burrowed his face into her neck. 'Mathilde,' he said.

166

'You'll stay tonight?' Mathilde turned around and held him, almost cradled in her arms. Did she sound desperate? she wondered. Somewhere inside her, she almost felt that she was losing him.

'*Oui*,' he said, 'but I'll leave in the morning.'

'And when will you be back?' She couldn't help herself; she felt incomplete when he was gone.

'I don't know. *Je ne sais pas*.' She could hear the irritability in his voice. 'I'll phone you. I'll let you know.'

Mathilde looked up to see Thea standing in the doorway. How much had she heard? How much had she understood? 'Is everything all right?' Mathilde asked her in English and in her breeziest voice.

'Oh, yes,' Thea said. 'Thank you. It's lovely. *Merci beaucoup*.' She smiled shyly. 'Everything is absolutely fine.'

Thea: July 1969

I heard them gossiping up Fore Street today, outside Adie's and Gladys's. It's usually the same women and the same time of day. The gossip shops they call them. They're both grocers and Adie's has been there donkeys' years, so Marion says. It's weird to have two grocers existing side by side selling exactly the same stuff, and what's even weirder is that according to Marion it's a religious divide. Methodists on one side, C of E on the other. I told Mum about it and she muttered something about being glad we're not a church-going family − though if we were, we'd be close enough to pop next door whenever we wanted. We might not be church-going, but our family − my parents, that is − are about as conventional as they come.

Normally I take no notice of the gossips. But they were talking about change, that's the thing, and I couldn't help but stop and listen. Seems it's in the air. Adie's and Gladys's shops are being taken over and made into a launderette and no one can quite believe it. I can see the use for a launderette, me, but to some people it's the beginning of the end. Change – that's how it gets folk. To some it's a good thing; others are scared half out of their wits.

Change is exciting. Perhaps that's what I need. And I can't help it. I think of Danny . . .

So, me and Barb got ready for the dance at her place – no one around then to tell us our skirts are too short or we're wearing too much make-up. 'This is 1969, Mum, for heaven's sake' . . . doesn't go down too well in our house. Mum'll be stuck in the 1940s till the day she dies, I reckon. Joan Prewett from down the road got herself pregnant last year and Mum suggested her mother might die from the shame of it. That's how liberated my parents are.

Barb's dad gave us a lift up to the Public Hall. 'Have fun, girls,' he said with a slight frown of disinterest, as if he might be going home to write an academic paper about molecular changes due to photosynthesis or something.

We paid our money, pushed open the double swing doors and we were in. Music pulsated around the room. Creedence Clearwater Revival's 'Proud Mary'. The DJ was up on the stage at the other end of the hall surrounded by equipment, the big stage curtains were draped back. A few people were dancing already on the wooden floor, the disco lights spinning around the hall streaking pathways all over them.

'A bit different from the jumble sale,' I whispered to Barb and we both bent double in a fit of the giggles. The Public Hall's a bit of a joke to us but we appreciate it nonetheless, it being a gift to our town from a local landowner and the only place in Porthleven where anything remotely interesting ever happens. It was even used for boxing matches back in the forties, Barb's dad told us, and during the war GIs gave a party there for the youngsters of the village. Nowadays it's used for all sorts: horticultural shows, film shows, amateur theatre . . . And dances like this one.

We got shot of our summer coats, checked our make-up in the Ladies' and then we were on the dance floor, no hanging about. Steppenwolf's 'Born To Be Wild' came on and I gave a whoop. Barb grinned. It sums up so much for me, that song; it's like it's telling me to wake up. Change, you know? And here we were – off and running . . .

Two hours later we were still dancing, though we'd stopped for a few soft drinks and no doubt we were starting to glow under the disco lights. Everyone was. I've never seen so much activity in the Hall. Barb's mascara had left dark smudges under her eyes, her fair hair was damp and there was a glistening of sweat on her forehead. But who cared? We were having a great time.

There were boys there as well as girls of course – we knew most of them. Porthleven's not a big place in that way. But a lot of the boys were just hanging round the sidelines, too self-conscious to get on the floor, talking to their mates and pretending to look cool. Danny wouldn't have come even if we hadn't had that barney the other night – he isn't into dancing at all. But the girls – they were loving it.

I swung my head down so that my hair blinded me then tossed it back and blinked. I stopped dancing right in the middle of Tommy Roe's 'Dizzy'. Oh, my God.

'What?' Barb grabbed my arm, shouted above the din. 'What, Thea?'

*I tried to keep moving, tried to pretend. But . . . 'It's him,'
I hissed into her ear.*

'Him?' Barb swung round.

*'Don't look.' But it was too late. He'd seen me and he'd seen
Barb and now he lifted his hand in a casual wave as if . . . as
if . . .*

As if we knew each other. I smiled and raised my hand too.

*Barb's eyes were huge when she looked back at me. 'Biker
guy?' she mouthed.*

*I gave a little shrug of affirmation, tried to look indifferent.
Who was I fooling? No one probably.*

*The music slowed as if the DJ up on the stage knew far more
than we did and I glanced at my watch. It was getting late. Slow-
dance time. Elvis's voice started crooning like melted chocolate.
And there he was. Biker guy. Walking towards me.*

*'Dance?' He was giving me that look again. Close up it was
even more powerful than last time. I couldn't believe he remembered me. Couldn't believe he was here – asking me to dance.*

*I nodded. Speaking was out of the question. I stepped into
his loose-limbed embrace. I could hardly breathe. I was shaking.
I must be shaking. Not only were we dancing, we were slow
dancing. Elvis was giving it some and here I was in biker guy's
arms.*

*I couldn't see Barb. I couldn't see anyone – I was too close to
him and he was too tall. He pulled me in a bit closer still and I
rested my head against his shoulder. It felt as if it belonged there.
It was like a dream. It couldn't be real. But it was. He smelt of
leather – or his jacket did – and cigarettes. And oil too or petrol,
or something that made me think of his motorbike.*

*'You here on your own?' he murmured. He sounded Cornish.
So where did he come from?*

170

'Yeah.' I didn't count Barb. When you're with a girlfriend you have an unspoken agreement, should a fella appear. I wouldn't leave her in the lurch – but for now she didn't exist for me. I was all taken up and loving every second.

'I'm Jez.'

Jez. What a great name. Jez. It really suited him. It seemed to hum in my head along with the music. Jezzzz.

'You?'

'Thea,' I whispered.

'Right.'

'Where have you . . .?' Come from, I was going to say, because it felt as if he'd appeared in the hall by magic. But then I realised how stupid it sounded. 'Where have you left your bike?' I said instead. Which also sounded a bit feeble, but what the hell, I'd been taken by surprise, I was unprepared.

He chuckled into my hair. 'You like the bike, huh?'

I felt goose bumps on the back of my neck. 'I like the bike,' I confirmed. Did he even know who I was, where he knew me from, that I was the girl in the blue nylon overall from the corner shop?

'It's outside.' He jerked his head. 'Wanna see?'

Was he joking? 'Yeah. I could do with some air.' Mum says she's been having hot flushes for fifteen years and for the first time I could understand the feeling.

We exchanged a look. Sometimes you just know, don't you? And as the music died, we walked right out of the double doors side by side as if it was the most natural thing in the world to do, leaving Barb standing there open-mouthed and staring. I winked at her as I walked past, hoped she'd get it.

'There you are.' He nodded towards the bike which was in a dark corner by Wellington Terrace. I went up to it. Reached out a hand towards the chrome, still gleaming in the darkness.

'You can touch it,' he said. I looked across at him. He was smiling as if he was used to this reaction.

'Where d'you live?' I asked him.

'Helston.'

'Right.' That explains why I've never seen him before. But I would have thought there were more exciting things to do in Helston than go to the small-town Porthleven dance. So . . .? I ran my hand along the black leather seat, slightly damp to the touch. Rested the other hand on the handlebar. Oh my. There was such a sense of unleashed power about this machine. It scared and yet captivated me at the same time.

'Wanna go for a spin?' He sounded casual. Clearly, he had no idea that I wanted that more than anything in the world at this precise moment.

I shrugged. 'OK.' As if it hardly mattered one way or the other. 'I'll have to get my coat.' Yes, and square it with Barb.

'I'll wait here.' But I could tell from the restless way he shoved his hands in his pockets and rocked back on his heels – he wouldn't be waiting very long.

I tried not to run back inside. Barb was standing by the swing doors as if unsure what to do next. Another slow song was playing but people were beginning to disperse and drift away.

'What's going on, Thea?' Barb hissed. 'What are you doing?'

'Looking at his bike.' I grabbed her arm and pulled her towards the cloakroom. 'He's taking me for a ride.'

'I bet he is.'

'Very funny.' I wondered if she was jealous.

She put her hands on her hips. She can look very fierce sometimes, can Barb. 'What about Danny?' she asked.

'Danny isn't here,' I said, somewhat unnecessarily. 'And it's just a ride on a bike . . .'

She gave me her 'Who are you kidding?' look. And she was right. Who was I kidding? Of course, it wasn't just a ride on a bike. Who could tell what else it might turn out to be?

'Tell your dad I've made my own way home,' I pleaded. He wouldn't think anything of it — I only live a few minutes' walk away after all.

'All right,' she said.

I was already practically out of the door.

'But Thea . . .'

'Yes?'

She touched my arm. 'Be careful. You don't know him from Adam, remember.'

I nodded. 'I will.' Although in a way I do know him, in a way I've known him all my life — as if somehow he's already a part of me.

I slipped back through the double doors and out of the hall. He was still waiting there in the dark, smoking a cigarette. The tip of it burned like a beacon. When he saw me he grinned, dropped it on the ground and stamped it out with the back of his heel. 'All set?' he asked.

I took a deep breath and mustered a smile. 'All set.'

He jumped on to the bike and beckoned to me to do the same. I put my hand on his shoulder and swung my leg over.

He started the engine. I felt it racing through my body — the rush, the warmth, the thrill. I've never felt anything like that before.

'Hold on tight,' he yelled.

And I did.

And she did. Mathilde shut the diary quickly, as if she could pretend to herself that she had not been reading it. It was wrong – but now that she had started, how could she help it? For years she had shut Thea away in a part of her mind and heart that she never opened, not any more. But now she needed to know what had happened back then. She was determined to face up to it. This diary was a window on to the past; an insight. How else could she discover what she needed to know?

And Thea – how was Thea doing now? Mathilde suppressed the guilt and considered this instead. Should she go and see her? Should she return her journal now, after all these years? She smoothed her fingertips over the old and battered leather. Perhaps she should.

But . . . Mathilde looked out of the window towards the isolated cliff top, the rocky cove below; the silver-grey of the morning sky, the sandy path that led towards the shifting dunes. And she wondered what else had happened that night . . .

It's a dream, a night dream. That's how I felt as I held on to him, as the wind tore my hair from my scalp, as we swept down the road, as we swished past houses, gardens, parked cars, the occasional night-time wanderer – setting the tarmac on fire. The bike, his bike, us on the bike, breaking the night-time silence; slicing into it, filling it, overpowering it. Taking over the night. And I was part of it. Me. I thought of Mum and Dad at home in bed. Not knowing. Hearing the bike, maybe. Sighing. Rolling over. Going back to sleep. Not having a bloody clue. And I laughed.

I held on tight, I clenched my knees, I leaned when he leaned into the bend. It felt as if we were stuck to the road, moulded, streamlined. It was chilly, I was sure, but I couldn't feel it; I was immune, invincible. I burrowed my face into the battered leather of his jacket. Leather and engine oil. It smelt sweet and delicious. Like heaven – just like heaven.

I closed my eyes. Felt the freedom. It was there to touch, to know, to find. I can't explain that. But it was there, with him, on his bike. And it was something I've never known with Danny.

Danny. But I couldn't think about him now. This was bigger, this was better. And it wasn't a dream.

He stopped the bike by the beach. What now? But we stayed on the bike, watching the moon spotlight the water. We didn't say a word. But I felt it — I felt it more than I can say.

Afterwards, he took me back home; slower now, me yelling directions. I stopped him on the corner, jumped off the bike. I felt mad and dizzy. I hated that it was the end of the evening, the end of this adventure. Surely it couldn't go on?

'So,' he said, 'fancy a day out tomorrow?'

I couldn't breathe, let alone speak. He wants to see me again. It isn't the end after all. I thought of Danny. How could I? An evening spin on the bike is one thing, but . . .

'Or are you busy?' His cool blue eyes raked over me. He was everything I wanted. How can I go back to Danny after this?

'No, I'm not busy,' I managed to say.

He grinned. It was heart-melting. 'Great.' He beckoned me closer, cupped a hand around my head and pulled me closer still. 'Great,' he said again. And then he kissed me.

And then he kissed her. Mathilde's gaze drifted once again towards the window, towards the ocean. 'Oh, Thea,' she whispered.

She had thought at first that Thea would come storming back to the Old Lighthouse when she discovered her journal was missing, that she would demand Mathilde return it immediately. *It's my personal property*, she would say. *You have no right . . .*

175

Which was true enough. But if Thea had done that, Mathilde would have denied all knowledge back then. This journal was her insurance. More crucially, it was evidence. Evidence of what had gone on. That was why she had taken it that day.

What she should have done, was burn it. She should have built a huge bonfire in the garden, thrown on Thea's journal and watched that evidence create beautiful flames. *Something beautiful out of something so terrible*. That would have been some compensation, perhaps.

But she could never bring herself to do it; to destroy Thea's past, Thea's memories, like that, despite everything. The journal was not, she reminded herself, hers to burn. Nor hers to read.

Nevertheless, she opened it once again, flipped through the pages, taking care not to get too ahead of herself, not yet. She needed to read it, she needed to get to the part . . . But it was hard. Thea's words reminded Mathilde of her voice and of what Mathilde had lost. Her son Jacques, who might have been lost many years before, if not for Thea. Thea's friendship, the bond between two women that had been so special, so precious. How had it all gone so wrong? And Léo – still here, but so often at a distance, still ruling their lives.

Yet again she asked herself – should she go and visit Thea, before it was too late? Élodie would be pleased. Élodie had never understood why Thea had left their family in the first place. But how could Mathilde ever explain to her? It was so long ago. But how could she forgive Thea? And how could she forgive herself?

CHAPTER 25

Colette

A few days after Mark had left, a man came into the flower shop.

'*Bonjour, Mademoiselle.*' He greeted her with an outstretched hand. 'Philippe Lemaire at your service.'

'Monsieur Lemaire?' Colette paused in the act of cutting the stems of the lisianthus, neatly, at an angle of forty-five degrees, exactly as her mother had once shown her. She didn't know the name, didn't recognise the man. He was smartly dressed, in his early forties, rather smooth, with flicked-back dark hair, brown eyes and a rather mean-looking mouth. He didn't seem like a tourist, nor did he seem like a customer. 'How can I help you?'

'This place.' He gestured around the shop. 'I like it.'

'That's nice.' Colette raised an eyebrow. He was very sure of himself too.

'Forgive me.' He smiled, but Colette didn't smile back – not yet. She was getting a bad feeling about this visit already. What did he want from her? – she had a feeling there was something. 'I came here to take a look around the village for a few days.'

177

'Oh?'

'I live on the mainland at present.' He regarded her thoughtfully. 'But I am looking to move to Belle-Île.'

'That's nice,' Colette said again, politely. Though what this had to do with her she couldn't begin to guess.

'To Sauzon perhaps.' He continued to stare. Colette shifted position. She felt more than a little uncomfortable.

'I see.' She was beginning to.

'The fact is . . .' He went to the door and stared out over the harbour. 'This place has a great view *n'est-ce pas*?'

Colette acknowledged this with a nod.

He turned. 'I'm aiming to buy a music bar, you see.'

'A music bar,' she echoed. 'I'm not sure that we have one here.' There were bars of course. Quiet bars which served great food and sometimes had live music too. Bands played on the waterfront at festival time and of course there was the famous opera in August in Le Palais. But . . .

'Precisely.' He rubbed his hands together. '*Mais oui*. Which is why we are thinking of opening one.'

'Ah.' Colette immediately envisioned the worst kind of music bar ever. The kind where tinny music played all night long and people got increasingly drunk and increasingly loud. The kind of place that would shatter the peace of quiet little Sauzon.

'This would be the perfect venue.' He spun around. '*Parfait*. Space for an outside terrace with a view of the harbour. Plenty of room inside too. Accommodation available for the manager on site—'

'Hang on a minute.' Colette held up her hand. 'This place is not for sale.' She refused to think about what Mark had said – at least for now. As she'd decided, she was doing things her way.

He looked crestfallen. Then he recovered and wagged a finger. 'But a little bird told me . . .'

Colette stood up straighter. 'The bird was wrong,' she said. Her mother would have a fit. 'This is a flower shop not a music bar and anyway, as I told you, it's not for sale.' At least not yet, she added silently to herself.

'Hmm.' Again, he regarded her closely. 'You own the shop, Mademoiselle?'

'*Non*. It is my mother's.' At least as far as she knew . . .

'Then . . .'

'We're not interested.'

He took a step forward. 'But perhaps in the future . . .?' He let the words hang, reached into his pocket and withdrew a business card. He held it out to Colette.

She ignored it and strode over to open the door. Bloody cheek. And who was that little bird? That was the trouble with villages like this one – everyone knew everyone else's business and people talked. She thought of Madame Riou in the boulangerie. She certainly talked.

Philippe Lemaire shrugged and put the card on the counter. 'If you change your mind,' he said. 'Sometimes it is not so easy to sell business premises. Sometimes one must accept that situations change, that things must move on. We should all try to live in the present moment, *n'est-ce pas*, Mademoiselle?'

'Thank you, Monsieur Lemaire. Good day to you.' Colette didn't look at him as he walked past her. She wouldn't tell her mother, she decided. Why worry her even more over something she could have no control over? But Colette realised that this was her responsibility. And sooner or later she'd have to face up to it. Mark was right. She should be looking after her mother's affairs. She still hesitated to interfere, but she had a duty to be practical and Lemaire's visit had unsettled her enough to push her into action.

'You must tell me, Maman, if there are things I should be taking care of,' she said to her after lunch.

'What sort of things, *chérie*?' She shifted uncomfortably in the bed and Colette saw her wince.

'Financial things. Maintenance things.' She thought of Mark. 'Practical things like bills or rent that need to be paid. I'm sorry, Maman, but—'

'Thank you, my dear.' Her mother looked at her for a long moment. 'The ledger is in the desk drawer,' she said. 'Perhaps you can take a look for me and make sure that everything is up to date.'

'Of course.'

'But there is no rent to pay. The house is mine. The shop is mine. You have no need to worry, *chérie*.'

'I see.' Colette considered this. She felt bad for even mentioning it. But how on earth had her mother managed to buy the place? Had Colette's grandparents helped out? She doubted they could have afforded it – and they'd never said. Was there some mysterious benefactor? She would look in the ledger, she decided; it might help her find out.

CHAPTER 26

Élodie

Élodie had seen her father arrive without prior warning at the Old Lighthouse, which was annoying as she had intended to go and talk to her mother about Jacques. She'd had another letter from him this morning and there had been more developments. He was talking about giving up his job, even leaving Karine. Élodie might not like Jacques's wife very much but this was serious. What about the children? She was worried. Jacques was clearly under a lot of strain and he could be unpredictable.

But she couldn't talk to her mother about him when her father was around. He always maintained that Jacques could come back any time – and Élodie knew that her mother often sent sad letters to her son telling him this: *Papa has forgiven you. Please come back to see us more often. Please can we be a family again?* Élodie could well imagine. And she could also imagine Jacques's reaction . . .

She paced from room to room, unable to focus on her work, not even soothed by the sight of the ocean. She picked up the photograph of her brother she kept on the small cabinet by

181

her bed. She had taken it herself, captured him in a carefree moment on the beach when he'd picked up a crab from one of the rockpools and held it aloft, laughing. The wind was in his dark hair, the sun lighting up his smile. It was one of Élodie's most precious possessions. She ran her fingertip over his face in the photo, his dear face, and put it carefully back on the cabinet.

But those carefree moments couldn't last. How was it possible in a family like theirs?

That afternoon in the bivouac had shown her that tensions would mount, that something had to give. Jacques had already decided to leave – it was just a question of when. Élodie dreaded it for herself and for her mother. She wasn't sure which of them would miss him the most. She worried that it might push her mother completely over the edge.

She glanced out of the window at her father's car, which looked ridiculously out of place parked on the dirt track outside the Old Lighthouse. And then it had happened – that awful afternoon. Their father was here for the weekend, and from inside the house Élodie heard the tell-tale signs of him beginning to lose his temper. She recognised the situation immediately though she didn't know how it had started. Perhaps he had drunk more wine with lunch than usual, perhaps their mother had asked him to come to Belle-Île more often. It hardly mattered why it had begun.

'Nag, nag, nag,' she heard her father say. 'Don't you know how lucky you are to have all this? Not to be bothered with having to work for a living? *Tu me gonfles*, Mathilde – you're really pissing me off.'

Élodie slipped outside. 'Let's go down to the beach,' she said to Jacques, who was in the garden reading. She hoped he hadn't heard what was brewing inside.

But he had. He shook his head. He got to his feet. He walked into the house.

'Why are you such a bastard, Papa?' Élodie heard him say. '*T'es un salaud!*'

'You stay out of this.'

'I will not.'

'*J'en ai plus rien à foutre.* I don't give a flying f—'

'Shut the—'

Seconds later, Élodie heard a crash and ran into the kitchen to see her father on the floor. It was obvious what had happened. 'Jacques!'

Her brother looked unrepentant. His fists were clenched. Mathilde was helping Léo to his feet.

'Get out,' her father snarled at Jacques. '*Dégage!* Now!'

Jacques waited. Élodie waited too. She knew he was expecting their mother to defend his actions, to speak out for him, to tell her husband that he was the one who should leave, even. But she said nothing.

And it was just like it had been with Thea. Élodie watched another person she loved pack their bags. She watched another person she loved leave her. And there was nothing she could do.

CHAPTER 27

Colette

It was now two weeks since Mark's visit and Colette had checked her mother's ledger and gone through all the out-standing post and emails. Everything seemed to be in order, all payments up to date. There was no clue, however, as to where the money to buy the shop might have come from. This made Colette think of Philippe Lemaire. His visit continued to bother her, and then yesterday she had received a letter in the post from him, making a firm offer for both the house and the shop.

Colette could barely believe the presumption of the man. But it was a reasonable offer, which made it even worse. She hadn't told either Mark or her mother about it yet. Her mother might suggest they accept – to make things easier for Colette – but she knew how much this would pain her. And Mark would definitely urge her to accept – though for very different reasons. Heigh-ho.

A few days ago, her mother had asked if she would read to her. The expression on her pale face was wistful.

'Of course I will.' Colette was glad to. It seemed to soothe her and it was something Colette could do to distract them both from other things that remained unasked, unsaid.

She had chosen D. H. Lawrence – *Sons and Lovers*, the English version. Colette enjoyed the hypnotic rhythm of the words; Lawrence's prose was like poetry and seemed to slip off the tongue.

Colette had not experienced the pleasure of reading aloud to an infant, not yet. But she remembered her mother reading to her when she was a child, in English and in French: fairy stories, tales of knights and dragons from Brittany; tall tales like *The Tiger who Came to Tea*. She had loved being read to. And she loved that she could now give some of that pleasure back. Whatever had happened, whatever her mother had done and whatever mysteries lay in the past, Colette was here. She wanted to ease her pain.

'It sounds like such a perfect day.' She sighed as Colette finished the chapter. 'Spent in the sun with the one you love.'

'Or the one you are longing to love,' said Colette, thinking of Paul and Clara in *Sons and Lovers*. When it came to love, longing and landscape, Lawrence was the best.

'Yes, that too.'

Colette smiled. 'What would your perfect day be, Maman?'

'*Le jour parfait* . . .' Her mother's milky-brown eyes seemed to glaze over with a memory. And then she came back to the room. 'I have a picture,' she whispered.

'A picture?' Colette looked around. There weren't many prints or photos. There was one taken at her parents' wedding, her mother's nut-brown hair long and loose, threaded with flowers (always flowers, thought Colette) and curled around her shoulders, her dress a froth of cream silk and lace. Colette's father looked less confident in his slightly ill-fitting grey suit. Nevertheless, they made a lovely couple. There was a photo of the three of them too – Colette just a babe-in-arms with her proud parents; a school photo of her in uniform; one of her father standing beside his boat *L'Étoile*. And that was about it.

'In the shop,' her mother said. 'In the bottom drawer of the desk.'

Her voice seemed to hold such a note of urgency that Colette ran down to fetch it. She was curious too. Would the photograph hold clues to any of her mother's old secrets? Who would be in the photograph? *What* would be in it? She pulled open the drawer and found it almost immediately, face down in a brass frame. A boy – a confident-looking boy with dirty-blond hair stared unsmiling back at the camera. He was good-looking, though – Colette could see the attraction. And he looked vaguely familiar. Was this her mother's first love perhaps? And the place. That was even more of a surprise.

'This was taken at Loe Bar,' she said, when she returned upstairs. Colette had walked there many times. Mark's house was on the Loe Bar Road; they had often taken a stroll along the coastal path and around Penrose Woods. It was a glorious beauty spot. But what had it been like in her mother's day? Much the same, from what she could tell from the photo.

'Yes.' Her mother was looking at the photo with some longing.

Colette placed it gently in her hands. Later, she'd stand it on the chest of drawers, she decided. Her mother should be able to see it, if it was that important to her. 'So who's the boy?'

Her smile was wan and misty. 'His name was Jez,' she said. She traced a fingertip over the image.

186

'Was he special?' Colette smiled. He looked as though he was.

'Yes, he was special.' She paused. 'He was the kind of boy who changed things.'

'Things?' Colette wanted to ask exactly what had happened at Loe Bar and why it had been such a perfect day. But her mother's face told her that it was a private memory. She put the photo in its frame down on the coverlet, pushed it further away. It was another secret, Colette realised. Otherwise why would the photo be tucked out of sight in the desk drawer in the flower shop? After all, it had been a long time since her father had died, a long time since her mother had been with anyone who would have minded.

'And how is Porthleven these days?' she asked Colette softly.

'Probably a lot busier. But it has something – doesn't it? Something unique?'

Her mother let out a tired and throaty chuckle. 'You know, I couldn't wait to get away from the place,' she said. 'And then once I'd gone, I missed it like hell.'

'But you never went back.' Colette perched on the edge of the bed. She was feeling more comfortable with her mother these days, easier. Even so, she recognised the wariness as it returned to her mother's eyes.

'After a while, you begin to develop ties to a new place,' she said. 'The landscape starts meaning something to you.'

Colette nodded. It had been like that for her in Cornwall.

'You start to make friends.'

'Like Mathilde?'

Her mother sighed. 'Yes, like Mathilde – in the beginning.'

Their conversations were full of empty spaces, Colette thought. Empty spaces that only her mother could fill. 'And

187

you never wanted to go back to Cornwall – even for a visit?'
she persevered. This was what surprised Colette the most. Her
grandparents had said they never fell out with their daughter
– not really. One minute, she had a long-standing boyfriend
who was nice and steady. (Colette guessed that Jez was not
that boy; he looked neither nice nor steady, especially not
steady). They said Thea had intended to go to teacher training
college. But she never did. She just upped and left one day and
that was that. They waited and waited for their daughter to
get whatever it was out of her system. When they realised she
wasn't coming back, they went to see her in Belle-Île, though
Colette had got the impression her mother never made them
feel particularly welcome. But . . .

'I never made things right with my parents,' she told Colette
now. 'Not really.'

'But when you heard they were ill . . .' Colette remembered
how angry she had been that her mother hadn't come over to
see them, hadn't even attended their funerals. It was hard to
understand.

'So was I,' she whispered.

Colette stared at her. Of course. Francine had mentioned
a relapse. Her mother had been ill for much longer than she
knew.

She bowed her head. 'Too ill to travel, the doctor said. I
wanted to be there, but—' She didn't need to say more. She
shifted uncomfortably in the bed and Colette adjusted her pillows for her. She could see how exhausted she was from this
long conversation. She shouldn't have tired her so.

'Will you do me a favour, my darling?'

'Yes, Maman, what is it?'

'Will you go to your father's grave?'

Colette blinked at her. She hadn't been expecting that.

'Every week I have taken him fresh flowers,' she said. 'First me and then Francine when I asked her to.'

'Every week?' Colette thought of the flowers she'd seen on his tombstone. They were from her mother? She hadn't even considered that.

She shrugged her thin shoulders. 'What other use is a flower shop?' she whispered.

Colette took her hand. 'Of course, I will do that, Maman,' she said. 'And now you must rest.'

'*Merci, chérie.*'

Colette watched as her mother's eyelids began to droop once again. 'You loved Papa, didn't you, Maman?' she murmured. It came to her – a truth she had allowed herself to forget.

'Yes, my darling, I did.' Her hand went limp in Colette's. 'He might not have believed it in the end. But I loved him more than I can say.'

CHAPTER 28

Thea: July 1969

It was a perfect day.

In the morning, Mum was asking lots of questions like 'Where might you be going, young lady?' and 'Danny knows where you're off to, does he?'

'If he comes round,' I told her — and he probably would — 'give him this, will you?' I handed her the note. I wrote it all down last night.

It doesn't matter what's going to happen with Jez — though something already has. I've woken up. There was my life, neatly mapped out, everyone knowing who I am, what I'm doing next. But not me. I don't know who I am and I don't want to know what I'm doing next.

And there was last night and Jez. Suddenly I feel I've got the chance of being someone different, of having some other life instead of the perfectly pre-planned safe one — if I want it. And I do. I want to grab it. I want to be that different person. Who knows? The chance might not come again.

'What's this then?' Mum eyed the yellow envelope suspiciously.

'It's sealed,' I told her.

She bristled at that. 'It's your business, Thea,' she told me, 'not mine. But I hope you're not doing something stupid, my girl.'

Not stupid, I thought. But crazy. Wonderfully, amazingly, spontaneously crazy. I feel bad towards Danny. I do. I don't want to hurt him. I have to push away the thought of his soft brown hair, the caramel and chocolate colour of his eyes. But he doesn't want me, not really. Not this me. I've changed, and I've got to be the person I want to be. I have to do this.

Jez brought cheese and pickle sandwiches – a bit squashed but wrapped in foil so that was all right – and some lemonade in a bottle; his mum made it, he said. It might not sound much, but we were hungry. We'd ridden to Penzance and back, snaking through the narrow Cornish lanes, me hanging on to his waist and loving every second of it. Every day could be like this, Thea. Every day.

By unspoken agreement, we didn't hang around in Penzance; we came back to Porthleven – almost as if we were daring someone to see us, to question what we were doing. Did I worry about being spotted on the back of Jez's bike by Danny? No. I almost wanted to be.

We rode past the cottages on Loe Bar Road to where the landscape alters. There's a green hill and stone walls threaded with thrift and daisies; Tye Rock stands proud on the cliff beyond the tamarisk trees. The sea, I realised as I looked down, was the exact same shade of blue as the sky. We stopped in the car park leading to Loe Bar and made our way up the steep coastal path and then down towards the water. Jez carried the picnic bag slung over his shoulder. We were laughing: high on the ride, the speed and the wind in our faces. I'd never felt so alive. As we got closer to the sea, the grass became greener and springier under foot, the path edged with white cow parsley and purple thrift.

We ate the picnic sitting on the beach at Loe Bar, watching the water. It was peaceful and the food tasted better than anything I've ever tasted before. Loe Pool is Cornwall's largest freshwater lake. It's quite a place. I've hardly ever gone there with Danny, but Mum and Dad took me there quite often when I was young. Me and Jez . . . well, that was something else. We talked about stuff – really talked. I told him about teacher training college and The Plan (not mentioning Danny of course). Somehow – I don't know how – I managed to put Danny to one side for today, as if he belongs to a separate world. And perhaps he does; he belongs to the world I'm determined to leave behind. It still rankles – what he said about waiting. I don't want to be respected. I don't care about that. I want to be loved.

'That's nice,' Jez said. But his expression said something else. That's boring? *Maybe, maybe not. Maybe that was just in my head.*

When I asked him about his plans, he said he didn't have any.

'What, none at all?' I tried to imagine this. 'That sounds good,' I said – 'cause it did. It sounded like freedom to me.

He shrugged. 'I'll see what happens.'

Well – yeah. But you could make things happen too. 'Will you go away – from Helston, I mean?' He told me he was a motor mechanic, still learning the ropes. But I don't see him here in Cornwall. I see him somewhere else – America, maybe, like Easy Rider, out along the highway. Would I be riding pillion? I don't know.

''Spect so,' he said. 'I wouldn't want to live in this dump for ever.'

I looked around us as we sat on the pebbles of the Bar. The afternoon sun was spooling over Loe Pool, illuminating it into translucence. And on the other side of the Bar the ocean seemed

192

to stretch into eternity. I know what he meant. This isn't the liveliest place – nowhere in Cornwall is the liveliest place – and it drives me mad too at times. But it is beautiful. Nowhere else has beaches like Cornwall's, desolate moorland, rocky cliffs and coves. It really isn't a dump. And I think he knows that too.

We stayed down at Loe Bar all afternoon, talking. I've never talked so much to a boy before. Danny and me . . . well, we've known each other for ever. It's different with Jez. Jez is new, he fascinates me. I watched the way his shoulders moved under the black T-shirt he wore and I wanted to run my finger along the bone that jutted from his neck to his shoulder. It makes me shudder inside now, just thinking about it. I looked at the shape of his jaw, the way his mouth moved as he spoke, as he smiled, as he laughed. I watched him brush back his raggedy fair hair – it's long, he could almost tie it back if he wanted. And I watched his eyes. They're cool blue, the colour of Loe Pool in the winter. They told me nothing and everything all at the same time. But at least I could see that he wanted me.

I was thinking that I should get back, that Mum would be starting to worry, when Jez suggested a walk up the hill to Penrose Woods. He said it casually. 'If you like,' he added, as if it meant little to him either way. But I wasn't fooled. There was a wired energy about him that was sexy and electric. I could almost taste it.

I felt a surge of excitement. 'Sure.' I tried to sound equally cool. But I didn't want to go home – not yet. I didn't want the afternoon to end. When I went home I'd have to face them – Mum, Dad, maybe Danny too. The longer I put that off, the better.

He bent towards me. 'There's too many people around here,' he whispered into my hair and I shivered. So, if I'm honest, I knew what was coming and I went with him anyway. It wasn't a trap. No way. My eyes were wide open. I couldn't wait.

We walked up the hill hand in hand and nipped through the gate into the wood. He took another pathway and pulled me with him, laughing softly in that way he has. 'Here,' he said, and we sat down on a grassy mound in the middle of the trees. We were alone.

We lay back and looked up at the sky through the criss-cross branches of a thin-needled pine that had been bent and almost flattened by decades of strong coastal winds. The green bank blanketed with pine needles felt soft beneath me. I felt that if I closed my eyes I might float away.

He leaned on one elbow and gazed down at me. 'You look like Guinevere,' he said. He spread out my hair on the grass around me. 'With that curly hair and those big seductive eyes of yours.'

Big seductive eyes? But I let this pass. 'Tell me about Guinevere,' I murmured. Because this was a magical place. I wouldn't have been surprised to see elves or goblins peering from the under-growth, fairies dancing on the grass by a clear-leaved beech tree. It was romantic too; the trees formed a canopy above us, the lake was still visible behind. When Jez stopped talking, all I could hear was the rustle of the wind in the trees and the distant throaty murmur of the sea.

'She was beautiful too,' he said. And he told me the story of Guinevere's love for Arthur and Lancelot and how she craved adventure and romance with Lancelot but still loved Arthur beneath it all. As he was talking, I watched his mouth; saw how full his bottom lip was compared with his top lip, noticed the slightly crooked eye tooth. The story of Guinevere reminded me a bit of me, Jez and Danny, even though Danny's hardly kingly by any stretch of the imagination and from the way Jez was kissing my neck, he's very far from being a respectful knight looking for his lady's favour. His fingers moved deftly under my top, stroking

194

my stomach in ever-widening circles that were making me glad I was lying down on the forest bed.

'How did she choose between them?' I wanted to prolong the conversation – the other stuff was lovely, but the way I was feeling was scaring me a bit. Not because of Danny, but just the intensity of it. I've never felt true intensity with Danny, I realise; we've never let it go that far, or maybe we don't have it in us anyway. But it is in me. I know that now. This is who I am. This girl who wants this boy.

I've already chosen. I thought of the note I'd written to Danny. I'm sorry, but I want something different. I'm not sure what, not yet, but it's not us. *Has he read it? Has he gone out looking for me? Was he about to appear here in the woods in our secluded little glade? Did he know – somehow – about Jez?*

Jez's kisses grew deeper. There was a wildness in the air, a heat in my body, a sense of abandon. Should I stop him? Now – before we went too far? Danny's sad brown eyes swam into my view. What had he said? I don't want to. I haven't got anything . . . *For heaven's sake. We're seventeen years old. Not fourteen and certainly not seventy.* But. *But you want this, something whispered inside me, you want this, Thea. You want him and everything he stands for.*

We were both breathing hard and fast. The scent of him – Brut and engine oil – seemed to mingle with the flavours of the wind and the sea. It was intoxicating. I looked into his face and I saw my desire reflected in his cool water-blue eyes. There was a moment – a yes or no moment, a free choice. I let out a breath. I knew that moment could change everything. My plans, my life, even my future for the years to come.

195

Mathilde looked out into the distance. Thea had never told her about that day, although she had confided snippets about the boy, about Jez.

For a couple of weeks, Jez was everything. It was a mad time — too mad for me even to write about it. I saw him every day. Mum and Dad knew. Mum tried to talk to me. 'What do you think you're doing, Thea?' she asked me. I didn't answer her. But I knew what I was doing all right. I was living. And loving every second of it.

Danny came round. He'd read my note and he was confused and hurt. 'What about our life together, Thea?' he asked me. 'What about our plans?'

I felt bad, course I did, I'm not made of stone. But he was at a distance from me now. Everything was at a distance, unfocused and blurred. My parents, Danny, all those plans of ours. The only thing I could focus on was Jez. We've had times when we went for a drink or a walk or a ride. Other times when we've made love, fast and furious — always outside, because we had nowhere to go. We didn't go back to Penrose Woods, though. Usually we rode out to some deserted place — and no, I never asked myself how he knew of these deserted places — or if we were short of time we sneaked out to the Wrestling Fields beyond Barb's house. That made us laugh. We did a different sort of wrestling, and I was loving every second of it. How he made me feel. Alive.

But then I got to wondering — what next? We got on well, it was a buzz riding on the back of his bike and we were having sex whenever we could. But we'd somehow stopped talking about anything important. There's more to life than motorbikes and sex. What was the purpose of it all? Where were we going? And what the hell was I going to do about college? It was the end of July and college in September was looming ever closer.

I talked to Jez about it one day. 'Do you think you and me will stay together?' I asked him.

He laughed. 'We are together.'

'Yeah, but . . .' I wasn't sure how to say this – it sounded a bit desperate. 'How long for?'

I love you, Thea. *That's what I wanted him to say.* You're the best thing that's ever happened to me. Of course, I want to stay with you. You're everything to me. *He might even ask me not to go away to college like I'd planned – and what would I say if he did?*

But he didn't say any of those things.

'What about when I go away in September?' I asked him.

He shrugged. 'What about it?'

'Well . . .' I dunno. He didn't even seem to care about me going away.

He said: 'Why worry about the future? We're here now, aren't we? Having fun?'

And that's when I realised. Those things I wanted him to say were things that Danny would have said. And that's what I'd turned my back on, so I only had myself to blame.

The following day Jez didn't turn up on his bike after work like he always did. Nor the day after. His parents didn't have a phone so I had to wait till the weekend to go over to Helston and see him. I expected him to be ill – why else wouldn't he have come? – but there he was in his parents' garage fiddling with that damned bike.

'Jez?' It was my turn to be confused.

'Oh, hi, Thea.' He grinned, and I felt my legs do that weird melty thing. But he didn't come and grab me or kiss me or apologise for not coming over.

197

'I just wondered where you were.' It was pathetic, but I couldn't think what else to say.

He frowned and looked past me. 'I thought we should cool it for a while,' he said. 'You're a great girl, but . . .'

'But?' I thought of that perfect day out on Loe Bar. But . . .?

'But I'm not looking for anything serious,' he said. 'I thought you felt the same.'

I do! I wanted to shriek. I do feel the same.

'But I love you, Jez,' was what I actually said. Total humiliation — here I come.

He laughed weakly. 'Well, that's er nice, but, like I said, I'm not after love.' He looked a bit embarrassed and he still wouldn't meet my eye. Clearly, he wanted me out of there.

'What are you after then, Jez?' I asked. At least I didn't throw myself down on the floor of the garage and beg him to take me back.

'Just a laugh,' he said. He grabbed an oily rag from the bench and rubbed his hands with it. 'A good time, a lark, a bit of fun. You know.'

'Right.' Freedom, I thought. And wasn't that what I'd wanted too? I felt a stab of regret — about Danny. Right now, what wouldn't I give for his warm smile, the sound of his gentle voice talking about our plans. I turned round.

'See you then, Thea,' he called.

I swallowed. 'See you, Jez,' I managed to say. I'd lost everything.

And then I was at the bus stop, waiting to go back home. As I stood there I thought about things a lot. I've had it with Cornwall. My first taste of freedom hadn't worked out but I certainly wasn't going to crawl back to Danny with my tail between my legs. I wanted to go to bed and cry over Jez for days, but I wasn't going to be that person either. No. I would do something different *and exciting. Something independent. I'd show them the sort of person I could be.*

In Porthleven I bought a copy of The Lady. *I knew that it featured advertisements for au pairs and nannies. A girl could go and stay with another family and learn a bit about another country, another culture, even get pocket money or a small wage while she was there. It sounded perfect.*

I circled an ad from a family in France – not too near and not too far. I was good at French at school and there was only one child – a young son. I went down to the phone box and put through a call to the number listed. The man who answered sounded nice and kind, and better still, he spoke half-decent English too. He wanted someone rather quickly, he said. His wife was lovely but she needed someone to be around. They lived in southern Brittany, on an island called Belle-Île by the sea. 'It will be home from home for you,' he said in his rich, deep voice. I gave him my details and told him I'd take the job. I couldn't believe it. But I'd done it. I might be heartbroken but I'd done it. I was out of here.

Mathilde felt slightly guilty reading about Thea's heartbreak, although it was so long ago. She had no right, she reminded herself, to be reading Thea's diary at all. She should take it back to her – right now. And she would. She really would. But this was helping her to understand. This story fitted the jigsaw of Thea's life; everything now made sense. There were a few more pieces. But it was getting clearer. Thea was that girl, and Mathilde could see why she had run away.

CHAPTER 29

Élodie

Élodie decided to go next door anyway. She should say hello to her father, and maybe he'd be occupied on his computer as he so often was and she could take her mother aside, tell her about Jacques.

She slipped out of the studio and wandered across to the Old Lighthouse. The sun was trying to come out from behind the clouds and a lone gull shrieked as it flew the thermals high above. Élodie breathed in the fresh salty air and headed to the back of the house. Unfortunately, it was her father who was sitting by the French doors, speaking softly into the phone. Instinctively, she took a step back.

'Call a plumber, *chérie*,' he was saying. Élodie paused. She knew that voice – it was his caressing voice. She'd heard him use it before – usually when he was talking to one of his women. 'I am not there to take care of it. You know I would if I could.' There was a pause. '*Oui, oui*, but I have to. It is business, you know that.' Another pause. '*Moi aussi*. Me too.' His voice grew softer still. 'Until then, *chérie*. I will be back very soon.'

Élodie rolled her eyes and shook her head in silent despair. *Merde*. So it was still going on, even now he was in his seventies, for God's sake. She clenched her hands into fists and turned the other way, staring out towards the cliffs and the sea. Her mother must know about his affairs. All these years. How did she stand it? By putting her head in the sand? By pretending it wasn't happening?

'Yes, yes, of course I do. You know I do.' Her father's voice was a mere whisper now. And what about the woman in Paris? Did she know about his wife, his children? Did she know that he still slept with Mathilde when he was here? Did she know about Belle-Île-en-Mer?

'But of course, yes. *Au revoir*, my petal, my sweet.'

Élodie cringed.

As he ended the call, he started whistling. To Élodie it felt like the final insult.

She stepped towards the house and into view. Her father jumped guiltily when he saw her but recovered smoothly. 'Élodie. Dearest. How lovely.'

'Do you live with her?' she asked him. 'In Paris?'

'What can you mean?' Her father frowned and then rearranged his features. 'Ah, but we are honoured . . .' He smiled.

Like a wolf, she thought.

'. . . by a visit from the charming and talented artist next door. Who happens also to be my daughter. *Bonjour*, my darling.'

'*Bonjour*, Papa.' Élodie accepted his kiss on both cheeks. 'How long are you staying?'

He spread his hands. 'A week maybe. Less? More? We shall see, hmm?'

He certainly didn't like to be pinned down. 'Doesn't

she mind?' she asked him. She stepped closer to the open doorway.

'She?'

'The woman on the phone. Your mistress, or whoever she is.' Élodie didn't bother to keep her voice down, though her father was waving his hands around to get her to hush.

Instead, he pulled her none too gently away from the doorway. 'You should come back with me to Paris, Élodie,' he said. 'You have grown up far too sheltered here on this little island.'

'You think so?'

'Yes, I do.' He cocked his head to one side and scrutinised her. 'You talk like a peasant girl.' He clicked his tongue. 'And look at you. What on earth are you wearing?'

He was so good at changing the subject. Élodie looked down at the navy linen shift she often wore for work. 'Perhaps I like being a peasant girl. An island girl.'

'Of course, there are no decent shops in this outback,' he said. 'I will give you some money.' He reached for his wallet in the back pocket of his grey chinos.

He was still a debonair-looking man, she thought. There was a dark shadow of stubble around his jaw, and his grey hair was well cut and made him look more distinguished somehow. He had kept in good shape too, and of course he had the money to dress well. But he didn't stop to consider that it was he who had brought them here to the beautiful island he now called an outback – and in a way, he who kept them here too.

'You must go to the mainland – to Nantes, if you won't come to Paris. It's hardly the same, but . . . And buy yourself something decent to wear.' He extracted three hundred-euro notes and held them out to her.

Élodie knew his game. She walked past him and into the kitchen and he followed her. He put the money down on the kitchen table, added another hundred for good measure.

Élodie raised an eyebrow. 'Where is Mama?'

'Resting.' He took her arm. 'Now, see here, Élodie—'

She glanced pointedly down at the hand holding her. She knew what he was thinking. '*Are* you living with her, Papa?' She looked into the familiar brown eyes – so like Jacques's eyes. They did look alike, yes, and they were both volatile too. But there were also many differences between them. And yet . . . She frowned. She knew nothing of her brother's personal affairs these days. Was he faithful to Karine? She had no idea. Once, Élodie had known everything about him, once she had idolised him. But now . . . She couldn't help but feel resentful. He was the golden boy, always the favourite. And yet he had escaped all this. He had succeeded in slipping away.

'*Non.*' He sighed. '*Tu me fatigues*, Élodie. You're beginning to annoy me. And keep your voice down, will you?'

Again she looked down, and he finally let go of her arm.

'But still she has to call you when she needs a plumber?'

'Don't lecture me.' He wagged a finger. 'You're my daughter. You don't have the right to question how I live my life. No one does.' She could see that he was keeping his temper with some difficulty. It didn't take much; she, Jacques and their mother all knew that to their cost.

'No, Papa, of course not, Papa.' She kept her voice soft. She didn't have to push him any more.

'Nor dictate to me . . .'

Élodie shrugged. 'I wouldn't dream of it.' But she had lost her respect for him a long time ago. And because of their father,

203

Jacques had left long before he'd planned to, hardly ever came here to visit in case he should run in to him.

'And if you tell your mother—'

'Tell me what?' Élodie's mother stood in the doorway. She glanced suspiciously from one to the other of them.

'Papa was on the phone,' Élodie said sweetly.

Her mother's eyes narrowed. She looked from one to the other. 'Not to her? Léo? Didn't you tell me it was over between you?'

So, she had known. They had talked about it, argued about it. And yet still her mother believed that something would change. When exactly? When he was eighty years old and ill and needed a wife to take care of him perhaps?

Mathilde stood, hands on hips, her blue eyes both angry and sad. But Élodie could see she was tired of it, weary of these conversations.

'Yes, I did. And it was true.' Her father glared at her. '*Merde* . . . Élodie overheard a conversation and misunderstood. That is all. Right, Élodie?'

Élodie glanced at the money on the table. She saw that her mother had seen it too. 'I don't understand why you even bother to carry on coming over here, Papa,' she said. 'Why don't you just stay in Paris? Someone over there obviously needs you far more than we do.'

'Why you—' He took a step towards her.

Élodie stood her ground. Jacques had always stuck up for her before but there was no one to help her now. She had no doubt pushed it too far, but . . . 'And perhaps you should both admit that your marriage is a sham,' she went on. 'You go from her to *ma mère* and then back to her again. What is the point? Why do you need two of them?'

Her parents were both staring at her in amazement but suddenly she realised that she couldn't stop, she had to go on. Perhaps she had simply held it in for too long. 'You give them both only a part of you and expect that to be enough. But why should it be enough? And why should you betray them both like this? It isn't fair.'

Her father recovered first. 'Why, you little bitch!' He was on her in seconds, his hands on her shoulders, shaking her. '*Tais-toi*, Élodie, be quiet!' Élodie felt her teeth rattle.

'Get off her, Léo!' Her mother's voice rang out as strong and true as Élodie had ever heard it. 'I said, get off her!'

'Mathilde . . .' He let go of Élodie and turned to his wife.

'*Ta gueule!* Shut up!' She held up a hand. 'It's true. Élodie is right. You are a complete bastard. Our marriage is a sham and I am a fool to put up with it.'

He took a step towards her. Élodie held her breath, but once again his mood had changed. 'But it is not true, Mathilde,' he said. 'You know that I adore you. I have always adored you.' His tone was injured now.

'*Non.*' Mathilde stood straighter, taller. Élodie was proud of her in that moment. It took great strength to say no to Léo . . .

'*Non?*' He barely seemed to understand the word. '*Mais—*'

'What you have always done, my dear,' she said, 'is continue to be unfaithful to me. Women in Paris. Women in the village. Even Thea.' Her voice broke. She glanced quickly at Élodie and then away. 'Even Thea, who was my friend,' she said quietly.

'Thea?' He gaped at her. 'The au pair? What are you talking about? That is nonsense. I never had sex with Thea.'

Mathilde tossed her head. Clearly, she didn't believe him. 'Our marriage is a sham,' she repeated. 'Élodie is right. It's time we both admitted it and brought it to a close.'

205

Élodie held her breath. But her father's face crumpled. 'You don't mean that?' He was pleading with her mother now, his eyes looked afraid. He went to her, took her face in his hands in that way he had. 'Mathilde . . .'

'Oh, but I do mean it, Léo.' She pushed him away, went to Élodie and took her in her arms. 'Are you all right, *chérie*? *Ça va?*'

'*Oui, Maman.*' Élodie smelt her perfume – that scent of citrussy musk that her mother always wore. She squeezed her tight to reassure her, to say: *I am here.*

'Élodie is right,' her mother said for a third time. And Élodie was reminded again of that time with Jacques and the goat. 'It is time for you to leave, Léo.'

Élodie's father glared at them both, turned on his heel and stormed from the room.

And still her mother held her close. 'At last,' she whispered. It seemed to Élodie that she was speaking not only to her, but also to herself. 'It is over.'

CHAPTER 30

Thea

Thea closed her eyes for a moment. How wonderfully restful it had been to listen to Colette reading Lawrence. Thea had loved his books as a girl. She'd relished every hungry moment as Paul obsessed over Clara, and as for Mellors in *Lady Chatterley's Lover* . . . She chuckled. That had pretty much been Thea's sex education back in the day. She'd borrowed the book from a girl in her class whose mother was a lot more liberal than most and the copy had been passed around from girl to girl, getting more battered and dog-eared on each journey.

She opened her eyes and stared out at the afternoon sky. Colette had left the shutters half-open so that a shaft of sunlight fell across the bed, but not on Thea's face, not in her eyes. That was thoughtful. Thea felt the familiar guilt curdle in her belly. Not just guilt about not being a better mother to Colette, but also guilt about not being a better daughter. She listened hard to the outside noises: to the voices drifting in from the street outside, the slam of a car door, an engine being started up. She kept trying, but she couldn't quite hear the sea.

Thea had not been there for her mother, any more than she had been there for Colette. She hadn't made soup, rubbed cream into her dry hands, brushed her hair, or opened the curtains to let the sunlight in. Nor had she brought her flowers. They'd had each other, her mum and dad; this had been one excuse. And there had been too many reasons for Thea not to leave Belle-Île. First there was the Blaise family, then the flower shop. Then there was Sébastien – finding Sébastien in the midst of all that heartache had been such a joy. And then there was Colette.

But she should have gone back to visit. Once again, Thea closed her tired eyes. Why hadn't she? Had she been so scared of them finding out the truth? Scared to leave her new-found happiness and precious little family even for a week to see her parents and go back to Porthleven?

Naturally this had caused a few rows, naturally her parents had not understood. And this had made Thea more stubborn. 'You can come here,' she'd told them. 'But I can't leave the shop.'

And so they'd come over, stiff and unhappy, twice, maybe three times, for visits that they probably all found excruciating. 'What is it with your family?' Sébastien had asked her. 'You act like strangers.' And he was right. So, what had gone wrong for theirs? Why couldn't they reach out to each other? Thea simply did not know. Perhaps there were just too many things that she couldn't see from her mother's point of view and too many things that her mother couldn't see from Thea's.

Thea opened her eyes again to look over at the chest where Colette had propped the photo. Jez had been her first love, she supposed, if first love meant spending every minute of every day dreaming about how someone made you feel. She didn't know him, though, and Jez patently had no idea what was

208

going through Thea's head. He was her first love, but more than that, he'd been her escape route, the trigger that took her life in another direction. Jez had enabled her to break off with Danny, and when he dumped her so unceremoniously . . . he'd unwittingly enabled her to leave Porthleven too.

From here, she could hardly make out his features, that blond hair, those cool blue eyes that had inspired such passion. Jez – so obviously the opposite of Danny, so attractive because of it. She'd been so sure that he was exciting, that he represented the freedom she was craving. But Jez hadn't been exciting, not really. He was just a boy. He'd simply been there at the right moment, walked with the right kind of swagger. He'd liked motorbikes and so did she. Which was why, when she started doing flower deliveries on Belle-Île, when she needed transport, her trusty Cimatti had given her that elusive taste of freedom all over again.

Jez had only wanted a bit of fun – fun as in uncomplicated sex, that was. There was nothing wrong with that – hadn't Thea wanted much the same thing? But like most girls, she'd also craved some emotion – something to hang on to, to reassure her after everything she'd given up for him. Not for him though, she reminded herself. For her.

As for the rest . . . she supposed she'd projected it all on to the unsuspecting Jez. It must have terrified him, a boy who didn't even make plans for tomorrow, when she'd started with the awkward questions. Thea smiled now at the memory. He must have been so freaked out when Thea asked him about his plans for the future – however distant that might be – when he'd finally twigged that she wanted more. Where was he now, Jez? Was he still a garage mechanic or did he have his own place? Did he have a wife? Kids?

Here, her thoughts faltered.

Colette had assumed she'd kept the photo because Jez was her first love, and in a way he was. But it was more than that, and less. That day at Loe Bar had been just as she'd told Colette – a perfect day. Perhaps the last perfect day.

Once again, Thea closed her eyes. She could smell the jasmine Colette had put in a vase on the windowsill, honeyed enough to cast a welcome sensory veil over the room. Francine thought that she should tell Colette the truth, that she should let them all get on with the inevitable repercussions while Thea slipped from the world. But was that fair? It would be disruptive certainly. It was also a bit of a cop-out. Would they even believe her? She thought of Mathilde and that promise they'd made. How ironic it would be if Colette and the others put it all down to the ramblings of a sick woman . . .

Sleep was close now. It used to be slow in coming, or she'd go straight off and then wake at four in the morning, alert and yet exhausted, thoughts and memories racing around her mind as if it were a dog-track. Despite the distance between them she thought more often of her parents as she grew older. As she'd told Colette, she would have gone back there at the end, but she simply didn't have the strength.

'I'm so sorry, Mum,' she'd told her when she phoned – only days before her mother's death, as it turned out. She was sorry for so many things – for leaving, for letting them down, for not being the daughter they wanted and most of all for not coming home.

'You never have to say sorry to me, Thea,' she'd replied. 'I'm your mother.'

But she was wrong. Thea did have to say it. And perhaps Francine was right – perhaps there were other people to whom she should be saying it too.

CHAPTER 31

Colette

Down in the flower shop, Colette decided to go through the drawers of the desk, in case there was anything else hidden here that she should know about. She'd already found the ledger and now the photograph. What other secrets might it hold?

Sure enough, in the middle drawer she came upon a book that she remembered. *Flowers and Healing*. She stared at the vivid orange marigolds on the cover, opened the first pages, knowing already what she would see. *For Colette*, she read, the words written in her mother's loopy handwriting, *who loves flowers as I do*.

She stared at the words. Yes, she did love flowers, but somehow, she had almost forgotten that fact, almost forgotten this book that her mother had bought her all those years ago. Slowly, she turned the pages. She had been thirteen, it was just months before her father's death. After that . . . She had turned away from her mother and turned away from flowers too. She had forgotten about the book and yet, just as she had kept her father's compass, Thea had kept this book. Had she thought that one day Colette would return?

211

Yes, of course, she had been interested in flowers. But not in exactly the same way as her mother was. Colette had envisaged something quite different – a flower farm, perhaps. Not just flowers that could be used for sending messages, or flowers brought in from Holland, but flowers grown locally and organically, whose natural healing properties could be used to help people in a different way.

She continued to turn the pages, reading snippets. She recalled some of it. That anise could be used to combat stress, about the calming qualities of bergamot tea. Calendula was an antiseptic, cauliflower could build up one's immune system. Once upon a time, these recipes were well known and well used; not written down in a book but as knowledge passed from grandmother to mother to daughter. People didn't nip down to the chemist so much as go to their own back garden. Remedies were natural and prepared with love and care. She paused. There were recipes in this book for poultices, massage oils, creams and lotions; for infusions, for honey and tea. The book was so full of possibilities. Why, she could even use it to help her mother. It was one way, at least.

Later, Colette walked down to the harbour and sat for a moment next to the lighthouse watching the boats. It was late afternoon and the yellow light was slanting over the sea from beyond the hill behind her to the west. This was the perfect place to catch the last of the day's sunshine; part of the little town was in shade already, but visitors would be sipping cocktails on the sunny terrace of the Hôtel du Phare for a few hours yet. The cooking smells were making her hungry – she could smell fish and garlic and the caramelised sweetness of crêpes and galettes from across the quay. A yacht was approaching the harbour entrance and she saw the harbour master zigzag

212

across on his red inflatable to welcome them and direct them to a mooring. He stood up in his RIB, displaying an impressive sense of balance and steering ability. Colette smiled. Things were well organised these days in Sauzon.

She thought of her mother's's perfect day at Loe Bar with the boy in her photograph. If it had been so perfect – why did she ever leave Cornwall at all? What had happened to that boy, to Jez? Did he still live in Porthleven now that he was a man? It was a strange thought – that Colette might even have come across him there and never known. She thought of Mark. He remained very much on her mind; not least because he called her every day. Colette knew that he was waiting – for her to say she'd made a decision, for her to say she was coming home. He was convinced she'd tire of the island, that all the things that had pushed her away from Belle-Île first time around would come back and haunt her; push her away again. But they hadn't. She no longer felt trapped in the way she had before. It was different now.

'You should do what you want to do,' she had told him before he left on the ferry to Quiberon. 'Go where you want to go.'

'But what about you?' he'd asked her.

'I'm here,' she'd said. 'And so at the moment I can't make any promises.' She guessed it wouldn't be long before he would have to make his decision. She didn't know what it would be though – he hadn't given her any clue. Instead, they'd chatted about safer things – a documentary he'd seen on TV, friends back in Porthleven, the weather. Nothing, Colette thought now, that mattered.

She heard a sound coming from beyond her field of vision, and she half-turned. The mint-green shutters of the house behind her were being flung open and a man appeared at the window. Colette couldn't help staring at him. He was very

213

familiar. It was the man from the coastal path who had come into the shop and bought all her gerberas. How odd, she thought. He was gazing out to sea. He looked distracted. He seemed troubled. Why was he back here again? And so soon?

She was about to look away when he glanced down and saw her. He seemed surprised to see her too. He nodded and disappeared from the window.

A few minutes later, he was standing by her side, hands in his pockets, still looking out to sea. It was a calm evening and the breeze had dropped. The boats moored in the harbour were still and Colette was conscious of a sense of waiting in the air.

'The flower lady,' he said.

She smiled. 'The gerbera man.'

'I was wondering,' he said.

'Yes?'

'Could I trouble you for some more?'

'Gerberas?'

He shrugged. 'Flowers,' he said.

'Now?' He seemed to keep his own hours and clearly expected her to open up whenever it suited him.

'If it's not too much trouble.' He smiled.

It was a nice smile. She got to her feet.

In the shop, Colette showed him the stock.

'More flowers than before,' he commented. He was wearing jeans and a T-shirt, different but similar to the one before. She noticed again the green of his eyes, the way they crinkled at the corners. This time he wasn't frowning. And it suited him.

'A few more, yes,' she admitted, half feeling as if this was something she should be ashamed of.

'Not closing things down after all, then?' He rocked back on his heels, still observing her.

214

'Not yet,' she said. For a moment she wondered if he was the 'little bird' who had spoken to Philippe Lemaire. But, no. She didn't believe that he was. For one thing, he hardly knew the place and he wasn't even here most of the time. For another . . . She didn't think he was the gossiping type.

'And your husband?'

'Pardon me?' She paused in the act of rearranging the irises in the bucket.

'Boyfriend?'

'What about him?' Colette remembered that this man had witnessed their kiss of reunion when Mark had first arrived. It seemed such a long time ago now. Since then, Mark had told her about his promotion and she had promised to stay on the island to care for her mother. Since then . . . She straightened, hands on hips.

'He's gone home again, *oui*?'

'*Oui*.' Though what business it was of his . . . She turned again, held up some snapdragons. 'These are very bright. I seem to remember that's what you like.'

'Sorry.' He held up a hand, tore it through the sticky-up hair. 'I'm being too inquisitive. I apologise.'

Colette shook her head. 'It's fine. He was only here for a few days. And I'm going to be around a lot longer than that.' She laughed, but it sounded hollow to her own ears.

'You don't want to be?' Yet again, he was pushing to know more. Colette felt it in him. He wasn't being inquisitive exactly; he just seemed curious about what made people tick. And she rather liked that.

'I feel I have to be,' she said. 'As to what I want . . .' She hesitated.

'Yes?' He really seemed to want to know.

'I have no idea what that is.' She laughed again – and this time it sounded real.

He laughed too. 'I know the feeling,' he said. And suddenly they stopped laughing. In a way, they were both outsiders. It was strange, but something seemed to pass between them, as if they had discovered a shared bond.

'*Et les fleurs?*' Colette filled the awkward silence. She was still holding the snapdragons.

'They tell you to make it homely,' he said. 'Isn't that what they say?'

'They?'

'Estate agents.' He rolled his eyes.

For a moment, Colette was confused. How on earth did he know about Mark's job? Then she realised. 'You're trying to sell the house?'

'*Mais oui.*' He took the snapdragon from her, sniffed it, held it aloft. '*Eh bien. D'accord.* I think that this will do it.'

He seemed to have a higher opinion of the power of flowers than most. 'Six?' asked Colette.

'Six.'

She hesitated.

'What is it?' He frowned.

'Oh, it's just that odd numbers look better – in a vase, I mean. Perhaps your wife or your girlfriend could . . .'

He glared at her. 'I will do it myself. Seven then.'

'Or five?' she ventured.

'All right, five.' He got out his wallet. Like him, it was scuffed around the edges. 'Though I must say your sales technique is unusual.'

'Is it your house?' she asked. It didn't seem to fit. Clearly, he didn't live here. 'A holiday home?'

He shook his head. 'It is my mother's house.' And something in his face seemed to close up.

'Ah.' And he resented having to come over here, having to take the responsibility for the sale, was that it?

'She died.' His mouth tightened.

'Oh. I'm so sorry.'

He shrugged, but she wasn't convinced by the casual gesture. 'So now I have to sell the house.'

She wrapped the snapdragons in brown paper. 'I see.' So that was the only reason he was here on the island – to sell a house that he had inherited from his mother. She could see why he was angry too, and why he was sad.

'Don't bother with that.' He pointed to the raffia. 'I'm only going to be ripping it off in five minutes.'

Colette regarded him curiously. 'But if your mother lived here – why do you dislike the island so much?' she asked. 'What has it done to you?'

He eyed her darkly. 'We spent every summer here when I was a kid,' he said. As if that were an answer.

'Yes?' She realised that this was where she remembered him from. Not that she'd had a lot to do with the holiday gang as they called them and anyway, he was a few years older than her. But she remembered him nonetheless. He had been tall and gangly and had sticky-up hair even then.

'And that,' he said, 'was enough.'

'You didn't enjoy your holidays here?' Colette was surprised at that. She considered the island an idyllic place to spend a few weeks in the summer – and it was perfect for children too. Endless warmth and perfect days on the beach – what could be nicer? She wanted to find out a bit more about him. He interested her. That sadness in him could

217

simply be because of his mother's death, she supposed. But she suspected it ran deeper still. What had happened to this man? Where did he live? What did he do? And why did he draw into himself so quickly if he thought someone was getting too close?

'Did *you* like living here?' He had virtually turned the question around.

Colette considered. 'I was happy growing up,' she said. 'But after my father died . . .'

'*Mes condoléances*.' Now it was his turn to sympathise with her loss.

'It was years ago,' she said. 'I was only thirteen. But after he died, things got much worse. I didn't get along that well with my mother—'

'Your mother who owns the shop?'

'Exactly.' She had no idea why she was telling him all this.

'And I felt trapped. I left when I was eighteen. And I never came back.'

'Until now,' he said softly.

'Until now.'

He gave her the money for the flowers and Colette busied herself at the till, handed him his change.

'So, where is home for you now?' he asked.

'Porthleven in Cornwall, England.' Though even as she answered the question, Colette wondered whether it really was. What held you to a place? What made it home? 'And you?'

'Oh, I haven't travelled so far.' His gaze shifted past her towards the harbour and the ocean. 'I live in the Gulf of Morbihan, over on the mainland, in Locmariaquer.'

'I know it. It's a lovely town.'

'Yes, it is. A land of mists, myths and megaliths.' He laughed and Colette wondered why. Perhaps he too was a bit lost when it came to the question of home.

'So why are you back here again so soon?' she asked.

'There is a prospective buyer. There are things to sort out, to discuss.' He pocketed the change and picked up the flowers.

'Good luck then,' she said. 'I hope the sale goes through.'

He nodded. '*Merci*,' he said. 'It has been nice . . .' His voice trailed. 'Sauzon is a small town, *n'est-ce pas*?'

'Yes.' She smiled. Very small, Mark would say. Far too small for him.

'*Eh bien*, then I think I will be seeing you again.'

CHAPTER 32

Mathilde

At first, Mathilde could hardly believe that Léo had gone. He had left that same afternoon – tight-lipped and silent, not even deigning to throw her a final look of reproach as he walked out of the door and to his car. And yet, in reality, he had left a long time ago and so really, nothing had changed. But Élodie had been proud of her – she'd told her so – and told her too that she should be proud of herself. Mathilde was glad that she had found the courage. All those years . . . All those affairs; those seemingly small slights and cruelties. They had melded into one. One thing that had made her what she was. Diminished her, made her less of a woman, less of a life force. And certainly not proud of herself: that was something she could never be. And she couldn't blame Léo for that.

There was another day she wasn't proud of, and it was the day that had altered the relationship between herself and her new au pair, the English girl who seemed so young, so raw. Mathilde hardly knew what to do with her. Would she ever fit in? She almost couldn't imagine it.

On that particular day, Thea had been with them less than a month. The two young women were polite with one another – but not friendly, not warm. Mathilde wanted Thea to know that she was not part of the family, not really, and that she was there on sufferance – only of value as long as she kept herself useful. How cruel she had been, she realised now. It didn't cross her mind to wonder how Thea was feeling – all alone in a strange country and isolated from her family, her friends, everything she knew. At that time, Mathilde was concerned only with herself, with Léo and with her son. That took all her energy.

'I shall take a picnic down to the beach for lunch,' Mathilde had told Thea. 'I will take Jacques with me. He can play down there and then come back for his nap later.'

'Are you sure, Madame?' Thea had seemed doubtful. 'I can watch him here. Or I could come down to the beach with you?'

'There are chores to do, I'm afraid, Thea.' Mathilde knew her voice was crisp. But really, did the girl think they were paying her to have picnics on the beach? And Mathilde could look after her own son, for heaven's sake. She'd been doing it since he was born. Thea was here to do the housework, and to be here to help where needed when the new baby came.

'Of course.' Thea bent her head. 'That's fine. What do you want me to do?'

Mathilde wondered when the girl would start thinking for herself. She hated giving orders. 'Clean up the kitchen first, I suppose. And then prepare the vegetables for dinner perhaps.' She softened. 'When you've done that, you can come down to join us.'

'OK, will do.' The girl had begun with a smattering of French words and phrases which she threw into conversations with a childish enthusiasm. But already, she seemed to be gaining confidence and would now speak to Mathilde in stilted sentences, until Mathilde took pity on her and switched to speaking English. To Jacques, Mathilde had requested that Thea speak English as well as French; this was part of the reason she was here, so that Mathilde's son, who might be held back by his schooling here in certain ways, might benefit from a bilingual experience.

Thea was cheerful enough and unfazed by anything she was asked to do – as if she quite relished the distraction from her thoughts. Once again, Mathilde found herself wondering – why exactly had she come here?

Down on the beach, Mathilde settled herself by some rocks so that she could sit up and watch Jacques as he played in the rockpools. This was the best beach to come to with him. Some of the coves were too rocky, too dangerous, with jagged granite that could pose a risk if Jacques were to clamber over it – and he was already an adventurous child. This bay, in contrast, had a substantial patch of pale-brown sand, with trails of shells and weed where the tide had come in and deposited them. There were a few little pools for him to explore with his fishing net and a narrow opening between high granite rocks which she and Léo had often swum through and out to sea.

Mathilde seemed to lose her breath and her composure for a moment. They hadn't done that for a long time. Now, of course, Léo was here less often and there was always Jacques to think about, to care for. Perhaps, though, now that Thea was here too, Mathilde and Léo could do more things together once again, rediscover some of their old closeness . . . This thought was a pleasing one. Mathilde laid the picnic out on a white tablecloth she had brought down for the purpose. There was a baguette, Brie and tomatoes, some orange squash and two tiny *tartes Tatin* from the patisserie in Sauzon.

'Jacques!' she called. He was so happy playing on the beach; she loved to watch him toddling around on his fat little legs, his dark curls dancing in the breeze. 'Come and eat.'

They ate in companionable silence; Mathilde watching the waves, Jacques throwing bits of crust and cheese for the sea-birds. And when lunch was finished, he went back to his rockpool and Mathilde sat back against the rock, watching him contentedly. There were succulents growing from the crevices in the granite and this made the rock surprising comfortable, especially with the cushion she had brought for her head. She thought of Léo. Would he come next weekend? She'd only seen him once since Thea had arrived. She would have to show him how good things could be between them now that Thea was here to help care for their son. She didn't want the arrival of the au pair to make him feel even less indispensable and free to stay in the city at weekends if he so chose. On the contrary – they were a family but they could also be as free as a childless couple if they so chose.

On the other hand . . . Mathilde returned to the subject that was so often on her mind. Should she return to the city after the baby was born? Because maybe they could have an au pair there too – why not? Mathilde laid her hands on her belly as she watched Jacques play, shrieking with delight when he spotted a scuttling crab or a tiny shrimp. She wasn't sure, but she thought she should probably do something new. Going back to Paris would be one solution. But could she do it – after this? She let her thoughts drift. She would so much like the baby to be a girl. She knew that Léo wanted a girl – and

223

perhaps a girl would have the power to keep him here with them rather more frequently . . .

A sudden shout disturbed her and she sat bolt upright, not sure for a moment where she was. The beach. *Mon dieu, oh mon dieu!* The panic hit the pit of her stomach. *Jacques* . . . She leapt to her feet, her eyes scanning the sand, the rocks, the water. And then she realised. Then she saw. Thea was in the sea thrashing about. Even as Mathilde watched, even as she gasped, Thea had swept Jacques up in her arms and was striding back through the waves towards the shore.

'Jacques!' Mathilde ran down to the water's edge and made a grab for her son.

But Thea was stronger. 'Let me.' She put him gently down on the beach, her hand supporting his head; she bent forward so that her ear was next to his mouth.

That moment seemed so long. His skin looked so cold, almost blue. Mathilde crouched next to her son. 'Jacques, Jacques.' She put all her desperation, all her anguish, into these words. She took his hand and massaged it between her own.

'He's breathing.' Thea turned him on his side, firmly patted his back.

He was breathing. Thank God he was breathing. He came to and spluttered, opened his eyes. He looked so frightened. Mathilde held him to her and now Thea sat back on her heels and let her have him. He started bawling; hiccupping and crying, his face turning a blotchy red. He was alive. He was fine. Mathilde and Thea exchanged a look of delight and relief, a very special look.

They took him back to the house, Mathilde carrying him awkwardly in her arms. She could not bear to let him go. She sat with him then on the sofa, Jacques snuggled under a blanket, Mathilde gently stroking his curls and crooning softly. 'My boy, my boy.'

It was Thea who cleared up and brought the remains of the picnic back up to the Old Lighthouse, putting the food away in the fridge, throwing away the rubbish, folding up the dainty white tablecloth.

Later, when Jacques was sleeping, Mathilde went to find her. She took her hands and held them tight. 'You saved his life, Thea,' she said. 'I cannot thank you enough.'

'I'm just glad I was in time.'

Not a word of reproach, and God knows, Mathilde deserved it. 'I fell asleep,' she whispered.

'I know, Madame.'

'Mathilde, please.'

'Mathilde.' The name was clearly awkward on Thea's tongue.

'I have been taking something – a tablet to help me sleep,' Mathilde confessed. She sighed. There had been so many bad nights. But how could she have fallen asleep when she was supposed to be watching her child?

'Have you tried a herbal remedy?' Thea's eyes were kind. 'In your condition, it might be better for you anyway.'

Mathilde nodded. 'I think you are right.'

'I can make some tea,' Thea said. 'My grandmother used to swear by it. It's only a herbal brew – but it might relax you.'

'*Merci.*' Mathilde was humbled. She hadn't been kind to this girl. She had not welcomed her into the family, she had given little thought for how homesick she might be feeling. She had thought only of herself. And yet Thea had turned out to be her guardian angel. Her precious boy's guardian angel. 'I am not fit to be a mother,' she muttered. 'I don't deserve Jacques. I don't deserve this baby either.' She shuddered. 'If

225

Léo knew about this, I think that he might kill me.' Which sounded melodramatic . . . But she knew her husband, and she sensed the violence in him. She knew how much he wanted this new baby too.

Thea's eyes widened. 'I'm sure he would not,' she said staunchly. 'But he will never know. Your secret is safe with me.'

Your secret is safe with me . . . Mathilde felt a tear creep down her cheek. How close she had been to losing her son. 'If not for you . . .'

'But you know, that is why I'm here.' Thea seemed to grow bolder. She reached out and put a hand on Mathilde's arm. 'Please don't be upset. You do deserve to be a mother – you really do.' Her voice broke. 'You are an excellent mother to your boy.'

Mathilde wanted to believe her, but she could not. She looked away, out of the window towards the cruel sea that had almost taken him.

'It was just one moment,' Thea said. 'One small mistake. You were so tired. Everyone makes mistakes. That's what makes us human.'

'Thank you.' Mathilde took Thea's hands in hers. How had this young girl become so wise?

'Don't feel guilty. Don't feel bad. Please.'

Mathilde swallowed back her tears. 'You are a lovely girl, Thea,' she said. And she embraced her. 'I am so glad that you are here.'

Now, Mathilde imagined Élodie's voice. *And how did you repay her, Mama? How did you thank that guardian angel for saving your son? You sent her away, that's how. You deprived her of everything she loved, everything she held dear.*

226

Mathilde turned the pages of Thea's diary. It was true. And she needed to ask Thea's forgiveness for that before it was too late. Had Thea betrayed her? Had she seduced Léo behind her back? Planned to take her place? To live in the Old Lighthouse with Léo and the children? She had always been so sure . . . She had seen it with her own eyes, had she not? Heard it with her own ears. And yet Léo had denied it. But what did that signify? Very little. Did Léo not deny everything?

But before that, there had been a better time, a happier time for both her and Thea. A time when they had helped one another and supported one another. A time when they had laughed together and looked after the children together and . . . They had been the best of friends. As for the rest — surely the guilt was not hers alone?

CHAPTER 33

Colette

After her morning in the flower shop, Colette made a late lunch for them both, then washed up the dirty dishes in the small kitchen. There had been a delivery early on, so she'd spent most of the morning sorting, conditioning and inspecting – in between answering the phone and taking two new orders. One was from a friend of Henri's who wanted to say sorry to his wife – her mother would probably have asked what for and then chosen the flowers accordingly, but Colette contented herself with suggesting white roses; simple, pure, sincere. The other order was for funeral flowers, which she tried not to feel depressed about as she gently suggested a flower basket that could later be taken to the hospital or a local care home, if the relatives would like. How long, though, before she would be preparing funeral flowers for her own mother? The thought had made her shudder.

Yesterday evening she had made up some massage cream with fresh lavender flowers and almond oil, using the recipe from her *Flowers and Healing* book. She'd taken it into her mother's room first thing this morning, gently massaged her arms and hands – which seemed so skeletal and frail, it was heartbreaking. She had said very little, but Colette knew she would have enjoyed the softness and the fragrance, and she was glad. The sense of touch too – such an important sense that was often so lacking in life today, especially for people like her mother with no partner to give her that kind of intimacy, warmth and consolation. Colette had made her some milk-thistle tea too; she'd read that these plants could help repair damaged cells and reduce toxins and they were growing wild on the island this summer – there were even some in her mother's garden, which fortunately hadn't been weeded for quite a while. It wasn't much, she knew, after all these years, but it was something.

'You should get out for some fresh air.' Francine had come into the kitchen. 'Thea's fallen asleep, but I'll watch her.'

'Thank you.' Colette touched her sleeve. There was no trace of the bitterness she remembered in her old neighbour. Perhaps she had always felt protective towards Colette's mother. Perhaps she had been trying to mend the relationship between mother and daughter, not prise them apart as Colette had always assumed.

She left the house and set off past the Hôtel du Phare, heading for the coastal path and the cliff. She heard the wet rustle of water slapping on the hulls of the boats as they shifted closer to each other and then apart. Colette took a deep breath. It was a warm afternoon, the mellow sunshine highlighting the grass and trees, the breeze gently ruffling the ocean. Her mother had loved days like these – as if the afternoon light gave her licence to dream. And her father . . . Well, the sea was in his blood; had been in his family's blood for generations. Any day that was a good day for fishing was the right kind of day for him.

Colette's footsteps stamped a pattern in the dry earth. She glanced down at the walkway below, at the water bubbling over the rocks. In the distance she could see the passenger ferry going over to the mainland. She thought about her parents' relationship – the love she had taken for granted as a child and how her impressions had changed after her father's death. She remembered her mother's face, taut and unfeeling. But had it been unfeeling? Now, she wondered – had she simply been trying to hold back her emotions? Trying to stay strong for her daughter, for her own sanity even?

Yesterday, Colette had again visited the cemetery to lay more flowers on her father's grave. Afterwards, she had gone to the Church of Saint-Nicolas; she hadn't been brought up a believer – her father had attended church as a matter of duty, but her mother had never bothered and Colette had taken her lead. Despite this, its white walls, wooden pews and polished stone floor and arches had soothed her. Its simplicity and purity were representative of the island somehow. As she left the church, descending the granite steps, she noticed the tiny stars of coloured confetti on the ground. There had been a wedding – even someone she knew perhaps. She'd had a coffee and a pancake in the groovy pink and grey crêperie round the corner before going back to the house, back to the flower shop. She'd been wrong, she thought. Belle-Île was hanging on by its fingertips. But change was in the air.

Now, she came to the fork in the path surrounded by bracken and buddleia where one could take the steps down to the beach or continue towards Le Cardinal. She went on. There were two access points to this little cove surrounded by tamarisk trees and it was a beach she knew well. But for today . . . She shielded her eyes from the sun. She needed to walk out some of her frustration. And she needed to think. The truth was that her mother had truly loved her father – Colette knew that now. Her mother had returned to Le Palais, had bought back his precious compass; she had continued for years to lay flowers on his grave. These actions didn't sound like those of a woman having an affair. And yet . . .

The familiar path opened out in front of her. Colette had hoped that getting up high like this would allow her to find a different perspective, to see more clearly. But her mind was still chaotic with questions, her thoughts still tangled. Did she miss Porthleven? Did she miss Mark? What did Belle-Île mean to her? And was it part of her future or merely a slice of her past, a slice which she was unable to let go of?

As she rounded the headland, she saw a getting-to-be-rather-familiar figure sitting on the grass-tufted rocks and staring out to sea. His long legs were stretched out awkwardly in front of him, his arms straight, palms digging into the ground. Colette hesitated. She felt uncomfortable. Would he think she'd fol-lowed him here? That was ridiculous, but nevertheless, she decided to walk on by. He seemed even more caught up in his own thoughts than she was. He looked as if he wanted to be alone. She walked on, head down, hands swinging at her sides.

'Hey, Mademoiselle Flower Shop!' His voice carried.

She stopped walking and turned around. 'Hey.'

'Are you avoiding me?' He cocked his head to one side as if curious, but not in the least offended. He jumped to his feet and took a few steps towards her.

'Non.' Colette stayed where she was. 'But you looked as if you wanted to be alone.'

231

He shook his head. Blown by the wind, his hair was as usual sticking up at all angles, and kept there by his restless fingers tearing through it, no doubt. 'I already have more solitude than I know what to do with,' he said gloomily.

'How come?' She walked back towards him. He was wearing the same faded jeans, with another different T-shirt. This one proclaimed that the revolution was only a T-shirt away. She raised an eyebrow.

'I work on my own,' he said. 'From home.'

'What do you do?'

'Shall we sit down for a minute?' He indicated the spot where he'd been sitting. 'If I was wearing a jacket I'd lay it down on the grass for you.'

'Very gallant.' She smiled. 'But there's no need. I come equipped.' And she untied her hoodie from her waist and sat on that. She hugged her knees close to her.

'Very organised,' he shot back, dropping into his former position. 'As you can see, I travel . . .'

'Light?' Though she noticed the notebook sticking out of his jeans pocket. It was spiral-bound and crumpled.

He nodded. 'I'm a writer,' he said. 'Ghastly thrillers, for my sins.'

Colette had never met a writer before but it made immediate sense. She could almost see him pounding away at a keyboard, tearing his hands through his hair as he dreamed up his next plot. 'Ghastly thrillers set on Belle-Île?' It wasn't really that kind of place. She could imagine it more as a setting for a romance. She looked across towards the sea shimmering softly in the light breeze against its backdrop of blue-grey sky. 'Isn't it all a bit too peaceful?'

'Probably.' He followed the direction of her gaze. 'But you know what they say.'

She gave him a quizzical look.

'Still waters run deep.'

Hmm. 'And even peaceful places have their secrets.' She thought of Loe Bar and the photograph she'd found in her mother's desk drawer. A perfect day at Loe Bar. What had made the day so perfect for her mother – the place or the boy? It had to be the boy. And yet she had left him, hadn't she, to come to Belle-Île, looking for a new job, a new life?

'They also have their tragedies.'

Colette glanced at him. His expression had altered; he looked so sad again. His mood seemed to change faster than the tide, the wind. 'Tragedies?' she asked. Grist for the mill, she would have thought, for a writer.

He met her scrutiny head on. 'Secrets?' he enquired.

'Touché!' She laughed. 'Actually, it's my mother who keeps all the secrets.' She had no idea how to go about unlocking them from the depths of her mother's heart, and she wasn't even sure she had the right.

'Such as?' He leaned back, still watching her, seeming interested in what she had to say.

So she told him – hoping he wouldn't put it into one of his books. She told him about her parents, about her childhood, even about the row she'd overheard before her father's death that night at sea. She told him how her mother had behaved afterwards and finally she told him what she'd discovered since she'd been back here. It spilled out from her, all these things she had never told a soul. She had no idea why. Perhaps it was the setting – the sea and the late afternoon honey-coloured sun and the lightest of breezes on her face and brushing softly through her hair. Or perhaps it was the man – some quality as a listener which he seemed to possess.

'And now you're thinking, was I wrong about her all those years ago?' he said.

'I suppose so, yes.'

'And you haven't asked her?'

'*Non.*' She didn't want to press her, to tire her, to upset her. And it all seemed too much. Colette lay back on the grass. It was so lovely in this spot, she could feel the sun warm on her skin. It was easy to forget the problems, her mother's illness, that offer from Lemaire, and Mark, still in Porthleven, but no doubt anxiously waiting for her return. She missed him – of course she did – but right at this minute she didn't seem to have the head space to think too much about what was happening in their relationship, where it was going.

'But you know that you should ask her these questions,' he said, 'while you still can.'

His voice was so soft. She opened her eyes to look at him. He was very perceptive.

'I had difficulties too,' he said. 'In my childhood. While I was growing up.'

'What happened?' She wanted him to confide in her, she realised, as she had confided in him.

But he shook his head. Did that mean that nothing had happened or that he wasn't willing to talk about it? He plucked a long piece of grass and began to chew it thoughtfully. Colette watched his eyes cloud over with the memory.

'And what was the tragedy?' she asked him. It was a strong, emotive word – not one to be used lightly.

He looked away. 'Tragedies happen everywhere, *n'est-ce pas?*'

he said. 'And people love to read about them, do they not? Death, disaster, murder. You name it.'

So, were they talking about his writing or about real life? Colette propped herself up on her elbows. 'Can't you write something else?' she asked. She didn't know anything about these things, but she imagined that writers could choose their subjects and their themes.

He gave her a sharp look. 'It's not so easy,' he said. 'One has a contract, you know. And readers with certain expectations.'

'Mm.' That made sense. 'Maybe you could write under a pseudonym?' she suggested. 'Become someone different for a while.'

He laughed. 'If only it were that simple.'

'But you'd like to?' she pressed. She felt as if she were getting somewhere.

'I'd like to write a real story,' he said. 'Something that means something. A story that's written from the heart.'

From the heart . . . 'A true story?' she whispered.

But she felt him clam up again at this. Colette knew that she was getting some glimpses of the real man. He would let someone get so close. And then . . .

He seemed to shake the memory away.

And then back off, she thought.

'Shall we walk some more?' he asked. 'What do you think? Do you have the time? Is there somewhere you have to be?'

'Not really.' Her mother would be sleeping, Francine was looking in on her and Colette didn't want to end this encounter – not yet. It was still light, still warm. The sea below them was like silk unfurling until it moved gently in to the rocks to break and fizz. And there was more, she felt, to be said.

'*Eh bien.*' They got to their feet and walked further along

235

the stony, undulating path lined with blackberry bushes and yellow gorse. Perhaps she had opened up to him too much. But now the serious mood between them had passed. Now, they walked on along the path, talked about the flower shop, about his mother's house and the prospective buyers who didn't seem to be able to make up their minds whether they wanted the place or not.

'And in the meantime,' she teased him, 'you have to keep coming back.'

'Yes.' And he gave her a different look this time. 'We have both done that, I think – returned to the island almost against our will.'

'Yes, we have.' They had both had difficult childhoods – apparently – and perhaps they both had ghosts to lay. 'But now that I'm here . . .' She hesitated. Could she really say it out loud? Would that make it more real?

'*Oui?*'

'. . . I'm happy to be staying around for longer.' She looked about her, at the boats moored at the inlet far below them at Bordery Beach, on the silvered shingle. The world hadn't broken into pieces. Everything was as it was before. And yet . . .

'Belle-Île is a lovely place,' he conceded. But he was eyeing her curiously. Did he – like Mark – consider it not much more than a pretty backwater; great for a few days but hardly likely to fulfil one's needs for any longer than that?

'Yes. But it's not just that.' They lingered on the crest of the hill and Colette knew they should turn back. It was getting late, she must see to her mother; it wasn't fair on Francine to leave her for too long. 'Better head for home,' she murmured, and they both turned around. Ahead of them – a few kilometres away by now – lay Sauzon and its scenic harbour; the duties and memories it held.

'What is it then?' he asked.

She wondered how to explain. It was about times she remembered with her father – and her mother too. It was about this coastline and the tiny beaches she kept glimpsing below, lapped by turquoise water and shadowy rocks, and even this cliff they were walking along. It was something about the wild winter winds and the size of the island itself – the containment of it, she thought. 'I suppose it's home,' she said.

He was frowning, looking down at the ground, his arms loose at his sides, his stride lengthening so that she had to practically run to keep up with him as the path wound through the thick expanse of bracken which led into the pine forest. 'People leave home,' he growled. She had apparently hit a raw nerve. She thought of Mark and London. He had said much the same thing. But one thing she knew – she didn't belong in a city.

'Yes, and people come back.'

He stopped suddenly. 'Will you? Come back for good, I mean?'

Did he think she would be utterly mad to contemplate such a thing? And although he had said that he disliked Belle-Île, that he wanted to sell his mother's house and be shot of the place, Colette wondered for the first time if this was true, if there was perhaps another side to the story that he hadn't told her – yet.

'*Je ne sais pas*,' she said. She felt a stab of betrayal towards Mark. Did he know how ambivalent she felt about this place? 'Will you?'

He swore softly. '*Merde*. I couldn't, even if I wanted to,' he said.

And although she waited for him to go on, she knew that

237

he'd said all he was going to say for now. That was how he was – exceedingly adept at prising information out of other people and exceedingly good at keeping his personal affairs to himself. She wondered if this was a writer thing.

By the time they finally got back to Sauzon harbour they were laughing at his impression of the potential buyer of his mother's house. '*It's small, but perfectly formed.* Ma would have loved that.'

'But would she have wanted to sell her house to him?' Colette asked. She didn't remember his mother very well; apparently she had only come to live here permanently while Colette was away. *Holiday people.* They'd never taken too much notice of them. And yet here was this man buying flowers from her shop and somehow becoming someone who she wanted to spend time with. He was rather a tortured soul and she had no idea what kind of secret sadness he was hiding, but all the same, she sensed a kindred spirit, someone who might understand her.

'*Non.*' And suddenly he was serious again. 'She would have wanted me to come back here to the island – to visit, perhaps even to live here in the little house by the harbour she loved.'

'Why would she want that for you?' It had only been a holiday home at first and as a family they had never lived here permanently. It might mean a lot to her, but if his mother had only moved here after his father had died . . . Colette sensed that his answer might give her more of a clue about this man and his past.

'Because she knew that you can't move forward until you have faced up to the shadows.' For a moment he was still, looking out to sea as if those very shadows were still there, lurking behind the crests of the waves. And then he turned back to her and the moment passed. Not the shadows, though; they were still there, and not only because evening was now drawing in.

'Listen to us,' he said.

'Yes.' Just listen . . .

'It's crazy, you know.'

'Yes, I know.' Colette glanced across at him. She had been thinking much the same thing. A stranger who had simply come into the flower shop, a man who was clearing out his mother's house in order to sell it, as she might have to do one day not so very far in the future. A man who didn't even live here on the island . . .

'These conversations.' He didn't need to say more. Personal conversations, deep conversations; even – in her case – intimate and confiding conversations. He was intuitive; he was making her recognise some home truths about what she was really doing here. They were walking towards the quay now. The path was dropping steeply to the harbour below.

'And yet I don't even know your name,' she finished for him.

'Exactly.' His eyes had been troubled, restless, but now she could see that spark of humour in them too. They were a shade of green that looked like the water in one of the bays. She felt a sudden flush of shyness.

'Étienne,' he said. 'Étienne Chevalier.'

'Nice to meet you, Étienne.' She smiled. That surname was familiar too – like him. She wondered if her mother might remember.

'I'm—'

'Colette!' The voice came from in front of them. They hadn't noticed him standing there at the end of the path, waiting.

'Mark,' she said. 'What on earth are you doing here?'

CHAPTER 34

Colette

Mark's second visit to Belle-Île had not gone well so far.
He had been tight-lipped ever since he'd discovered Colette
and Étienne walking together on the cliff path and he'd been
unwilling to even discuss it.

She had introduced the two men. Étienne had extended
a hand and murmured, 'Pleased to meet you,' though she
imagined she heard the irony in his tone and she didn't dare
meet his eye. Mark had squared up to him as if they were about
to do eight rounds, barely managed a handshake and a gruff
'Hello'. Honestly. Men.

'What on earth are you doing here?' she asked again as she
let Mark and herself into the house. 'Why didn't you tell me
you were coming?'

'Warn you I was coming, you mean,' he said.

'Oh, Mark.' It didn't take a genius to know what he was
referring to. 'He's just a . . .' What? Friend? 'A man who
came into the flower shop,' she said lamely. Which sounded
ridiculous.

Mark didn't deign to reply. But he gave her a look that said he didn't believe a word.

'What's happened?' she asked him after she had checked on her mother. She wouldn't be able to read to her – not tonight – but she didn't seem to mind. She was tired, she said, she'd watch the television for a while, she would be fine – though Colette knew from experience that she'd be too weak to do that too when it came to it. 'And do you think you could manage some supper later?' Colette asked her. She had planned a simple vegetable stew with cauliflower and carrots but now that Mark had arrived, perhaps she'd do that for her mother and give Mark her version of Boeuf Bourgignon – always her father's favourite meal. 'Maybe a little,' her mother said, 'if it's not too much trouble.' And she had smiled that new smile of hers, which was so much more serene.

They were in the kitchen now, Colette cooking the supper, Mark sitting at the table looking morose and drinking wine. 'I don't understand.' She wanted to fill the awkward silence. 'It's lovely to see you, Mark. But why the big mystery?' She felt wrong-footed, as if he'd been trying to catch her out somehow. Or was that her guilty conscience?

'I had this feeling that you were slipping away from me.' He eyed her searchingly.

'That's not true.' And yet . . . With every day that she was spending here, Colette was aware that a change was taking place. It was almost as if she was finding her feet.

He shrugged. 'And I wanted to surprise you.'

'You certainly succeeded in doing that.' Colette tried a laugh, but it didn't sound convincing. She finished chopping the beef and tossed it in the seasoned flour. She wanted to go and put a reassuring arm around him, but realised her hands were too floury, so she rinsed them under the hot tap instead.

'I imagined you'd be here at the house,' he said pointedly. He took a large gulp of wine from his glass. 'Playing nurse.'

She bridled at that, changed her mind about putting her arms around him. 'Most of the time, I am,' she said softly. He was hurt, that was all. She wasn't playing, though. Her mother was dying. That was hardly a game. It was just that sometimes she needed to take some time out away from the house, and Francine seemed to sense that, seemed to want to share the burden. Colette needed to see the ocean and the sky; she needed to regain her sense of perspective. Mark should be sensitive enough to realise that. She shouldn't have to spell it out for him.

'I can't help feeling that I'm losing you.' Mark poured more wine. He looked so forlorn that despite her misgivings, her heart went out to him. It must have been horrid to turn up here, not to be able to find her, and then to see her walking with Étienne on the cliff like that.

'You're not losing me.' But Colette could see why he'd felt the need to come back here. Poor Mark. She wasn't being fair to him. Did staying on this island until her mother passed away mean that they had to break up? She wasn't sure. She thought about it every day – what she was doing here, how she was putting her life on hold. But lately she'd also started thinking – maybe this *was* her life? She was finding that she enjoyed the French way of doing things. She was enjoying speaking the language of her girlhood again; she was feeling that she belonged. And if so – what did that say about her relationship with Mark? About Cornwall, which was supposed to be her home? About the love she and Mark were supposed to share?

'Are you sure?'

'I'm sure.' If she said it decisively enough, it would be true. Colette dried her hands on a towel, came up to where he was sitting and dropped a light kiss on his head. 'You know why I'm here.' And as Étienne had said – a strong love survives a separation. One only had to look back at history to see that.

She opened her mouth to say this, but thought better of it. It probably wasn't a great idea to bring Étienne into this conversation. Instead, she retreated to the stove, heated the oil in the pan and tossed in the beef to brown.

'Has anything happened?' Mark asked her. 'Is everything with your mother still the same?'

'More or less. She's not getting any better, if that's what you mean.' Colette had noticed that Mark hadn't gone in to say hello. She wanted to remind him – *my mother matters. She's still alive and she matters.* But she knew he hadn't meant to be rude; he was just distracted.

'And has anyone shown any interest in the place?' He looked around the kitchen.

Colette frowned. Once an estate agent, always an estate agent apparently. 'Why would they?'

'Oh, I don't know.'

Colette thought about Philippe Lemaire. He and Mark would definitely be on the same page. She opened her mouth to tell him about the man's visit, about his offer for the flower shop and the house. But once again, she changed her mind. She knew what Mark's reaction would be. He would say she couldn't turn down an offer like that – under the circumstances it would be pure madness. And she would say . . . What would she say? So, she wouldn't tell him. There was no reason why

243

he should run into Philippe Lemaire or that little bird who had told Lemaire that the flower shop might be for sale.

Mark picked up his glass and slugged back more wine. 'It certainly looks like you're busy making friends.'

'Hardly.' The beef was sizzling. Colette removed it with a slotted spoon and rapidly deglazed the pan with a splash of red wine. The aroma of beef clouded the air.

'Oh, c'mon, Colette.' His tone was injured now. 'What's going on? Have you known him long?'

Colette really didn't want to be having this conversation. 'Nothing's going on. I hardly know him at all. I've only spoken to him a couple of times.' She tipped the contents of the pan on top of the beef in the casserole and turned her attention to the peeled shallots. A toss of hot oil and they would be nicely caramelised.

'But clearly he isn't just some bloke who came into your mother's shop.' Mark took another large gulp of the wine. He'd knocked back half a bottle already and she had the feeling there was a lot more to come. 'Obviously, he means more to you than that.'

'Not really.' Colette was glad she had her back to him. Once again, she deglazed the pan. 'He lost his mother recently. We got talking. You know how it is.'

'I can guess,' he growled.

'Oh, Mark.' Colette added the rest of the cooking liquid and the bouquet garni. This was a rich stew and would take a while to slowly simmer.

'I'm not stupid.' Mark rocked back on his chair. 'I could see you responding to him.'

Responding. Now, that was a loaded word. Had she responded to Étienne Chevalier? Colette stopped in her tracks.

There was a certain bond between them, yes, there was a lot they shared, as she'd already realised. She was curious to know more about him too, but . . . wouldn't she feel the same way about any mystery?

Of course she would. Mark was being ridiculous. And jealous. Colette slammed the lid on the casserole and opened the oven door to put it inside. The heat hit her in a rush to the head. 'We've got some things in common,' she said, in what she hoped was a placatory tone, 'that's all.' And a connection? She thought of that moment when Étienne had done his daft impression of the man buying his mother's house. It had made her laugh and there had been a moment . . . But Mark hadn't been there and that was all it was – one moment of connection.

'What things?' he asked.

'Oh, you know . . .' She found she really didn't want to talk about it. And she didn't relish being cross-examined either. 'Our mothers, this island . . .' Her voice trailed.

'He must be more than a customer in the shop, if you went off walking with him,' he went on. 'I came to the house, I called your mobile. Even Francine had no idea where you were.'

Colette snapped. 'I didn't "go off walking with him",' she said. 'And I didn't take my mobile with me. I left it here – at home.'

'At home?' He raised an eyebrow.

'Figure of speech.'

'Isn't that a bit irresponsible of you, Colette? What if your mother needed you? What if Francine was trying to get in touch with you? How would she know you'd gone out walking with some bloke—?'

'I didn't.' Colette ground her teeth. 'I bumped into him while

245

I was out on the cliff.' There was a big difference. She didn't like the way Mark was referring to Étienne as 'some bloke'. 'And sometimes I just need to get away.' She realised that she was gripping the edge of the counter and that her knuckles were white.

'Whatever,' he muttered.

Colette sighed. Why was she even bothering to try to explain? Why was she even cooking for him, come to that? What she'd really like to do now was forget the Boeuf Bourgignon, forget Mark and her mother and take an evening stroll alone along the harbourside, watch the street lights reflected in the smooth water, hear the sounds of other people's lives and know that she was here, taking a peaceful moment for herself.

'You see, Colette . . .'

She dragged her attention back to him. She should be more sympathetic. She knew it was difficult for him with her not being around, but—

'. . . I did come here for a reason.'

'Oh?' She set the timer. 'Something to do with the job offer?' She had thought as much. Mark was the kind of person who had to spill things out and if there was big news he had to spill it out in person.

'No.' Mark got to his feet and pulled her away from the kitchen counter. 'Come and sit down. I'm sorry I got so uptight. Have some wine.' He handed her the glass.

'OK.' She sat. 'I do understand – and I'm sorry too.' She took a sip of the wine and put her glass back down on the table. In a minute, she'd go in to check on her mother, see if she was ready to try and eat something.

'Thing is, Colette, I've missed you so much since you went away.' He took her hands.

'I know. I'm sorry.' Colette looked down at their hands

interlocking. 'I've missed you too. You know that.' And she had. She'd missed the familiarity of him, the safety, the knowledge that whatever else happened, Mark would be around for her; that he'd take her out for a drink or dinner, make her feel appreciated, even adored; that he'd make her feel better, try and solve her problems. Life was so much easier with Mark just around the corner, that was for certain.

'I'm glad,' he said. 'I wasn't sure.'

Colette felt a stab of guilt. Because some days, she too wasn't sure. 'There's a lot on my mind,' she reminded him. 'Which is why I probably haven't been as . . .' What? Attentive? Caring? '. . . communicative, as I should have been,' she said.

'I get that, of course I do. And I want to help you.' Mark was gripping her hands really quite hard. She sneaked another look at the level in the bottle of red on the table – three-quarters empty now. She extracted a hand and grabbed her glass. She had some catching up to do. 'Thanks.' She took a sip. 'But like I told you before, things are pretty much the same. Maman is—'

'Colette.' He cut her off. 'This is about us.'

She stared at him. 'Us?'

He let go of her other hand and fumbled in his pocket, extracted a small black box.

Oh, my God. Oh no, she thought. Please don't let this be what . . .

'Colette, darling.' He opened the box. A diamond solitaire glittered up at her. She blinked back at it. *Oh, Mark.*

'Will you marry me?'

'God, Mark.' She couldn't take her eyes away from the mesmerising diamond.

'What?' He smiled.

'Well. This is such a shock.'

He eyed her quizzically. 'Really? But you know how I feel about you.'

'Mm.' Still she eyed the diamond in the black box. Unlike her, it looked very sure of itself. It was very confident, the setting very ornate. Very Mark, she found herself thinking.

'And I've just been telling you how much I miss you.'

'Mm. But we . . .' – she chose her words carefully – '. . . haven't been together for very long.'

'We've been together long enough for me to know what I want.'

He sounded so confident, so sure. Colette envied him that. 'But we haven't even lived together.' In this day and age shouldn't they at least try each other out as living partners, before they contemplated such a commitment? This whole thing seemed so sudden.

'Only because I haven't been able to persuade you to.' He pushed the box closer towards her. 'I'm hoping that this will.'

'Oh, Mark, it's beautiful, but—'

'Don't you want to marry me?' He leaned closer. She smelt his aftershave, an oaky fragrance; nice, but slightly at odds with the meaty and herby scents in the kitchen. 'Don't you love me, Colette?'

She felt herself being pushed into an uncomfortable corner. It was a feeling she'd had before with Mark; when Mark made decisions and expected her to comply, when he organised her life and expected her to sit back and be grateful. It was all very lovely, but . . .

'Is this about the job?' she asked him.

He frowned. 'What do you mean? How can it be about the job? It's a proposal of marriage, Colette. I want to marry you and for us to be together.'

'But does this mean you've accepted it? The new position?' She had that feeling – that this might be Mark's way of bringing her back to him, of ensuring that she too moved to London. She hoped she was wrong.

'No, that is . . .' He barely hesitated. 'It's because of how much I love you, how much I miss you. I told you.'

She saw it again – that faint flicker of annoyance. 'But you have said yes to London?' She looked down at the ring and back up at him. 'Mark?'

'Yes, yes I have.' He bowed his head. 'But if you really don't want to go, I stand by what I said. I'll back down, I'll say I had second thoughts.'

I don't want to live in London. But Colette didn't say it. She remained silent and in that split second, he took the ring from the box and placed it firmly on the third finger of her left hand. It fitted perfectly. It would.

Colette stared at it. 'Mark, I don't know,' she began. How could she even begin to explain her reservations? That she wasn't sure she loved him enough? That she didn't want to move to London and yet neither did she want to stand in the way of his ambitions? That she hadn't imagined that this was how a proposal of marriage would feel?

'Why don't you know?'

'It's not you,' she said quickly. How could she put it so that he wasn't hurt? 'It's just that I'm not sure I'm ready for marriage. And the timing . . .' The ring was hard and sparkling and didn't feel quite right. She twisted it uncertainly. Maybe it was just her and all the emotions churned up by coming back to Belle-Île to look after her mother. Maybe it was the fact that her mother was dying. Maybe she was being a fool. Marriage to Mark might after all provide answers to everything.

'I understand, my darling.' And again, Mark was holding her hand. The ring cut into her finger. 'And I'll give you as long as you need – because I want you to be as sure as I am.'

'Really?' Colette gave the ring a little tug as if she might take it off again. After all, if she was still thinking about it . . .

He put his hand on hers to stop her. 'But will you wear the ring – while you're thinking about it, I mean? It looks so beautiful on you. I knew it would. Will you wear it for me?'

He wanted to lay claim to her, she thought. But he looked so eager and so loving – how could she refuse such a simple request? It seemed too cruel. Colette struggled for the right words. 'I'm flattered,' she said at last. Which weren't at all the right words. But she was so tired, so unsure. How had it come to this? 'And—'

'I want to be with you,' Mark cut in. He'd always been better at words than she was. 'I want to look after you.'

'I know. Thank you.' She really should be grateful. What had she ever done to deserve a man like Mark anyway?

'So, will you wear it – for me?'

She hesitated. 'I'll wear the ring, Mark,' she said, 'but I really do need more time.'

'You have it.' A smile spread across his handsome features. 'You have it, my darling. And in the meantime, let's celebrate.'

'Celebrate?' she echoed weakly. With her mother in the next room sick and dying?

'In our own quiet way,' he added quickly. 'Just you and I together here on your little island before I have to get back to Cornwall.'

My little island, she thought.

Mark patted her hand. 'We can have such a wonderful life together, you'll see. And it's going to start right now.'

CHAPTER 35

Étienne

His mobile rang and Étienne put down his pen and reached for it absently, his mind still half on the page in front of him. He shouldn't still be doing this, it was all wrong, but at the same time it felt right, and that was the problem. Bloody hell.

'Didier,' he said. Didier Lamar was his agent and also a friend. This was a good thing in many ways, but not all. The bad part of it was that Didier knew him rather too well. There was no escape with Didier.

'How's it going? Am I interrupting anything?' Didier's tone was hopeful rather than apologetic. 'Are you right in the middle of . . .' – he let his voice trail – '. . . anything?' Such as the new novel, he meant.

'I've started it.'

'Because . . .'

'I know.' Étienne was aware that he had a deadline. He was also aware that signing a contract to do two books this year could have been a mistake. He had agreed to his publisher's suggestion for several reasons. He thought it would be a good

251

distraction from things he didn't want to dwell on, and no one could get things done as efficiently as a busy person; everyone knew that. There wasn't a great deal of research needed for the sort of books he wrote (fact: he didn't like it, but it was true). He could write very quickly once he had the plot nailed and once he got properly in the zone. He also knew very well that keeping a high profile was usually a good thing – his readers wouldn't forget who the hell he was. Then again all the good could come to nothing if he wrote a dud. A writer was only as good as his last book. What was possibly even worse was writing nothing at all.

'When you say "started it" . . .?' Didier pressed. Again, he left the sentence hanging.

'I've done the first chapter.' Étienne stared moodily out of the window towards the busy little patch of promenade below. This wasn't entirely a lie. He had created a new Word document and typed 'Chapter 1' at the top of it. He had made some notes about what he might put in this first chapter; he also had a rough though incomplete outline of the entire plot in his head. Yes, in his head. He didn't like to write it down. Not even on Post-Its. Once he wrote it down it began to feel too set in stone; he might find it too hard to deviate, to allow himself to go off on a creative tangent, to let the characters do their own wandering over and beyond the page . . . All that stuff. If it was merely in his head, on the other hand, he had both the premise and the flexibility. Writers, he reminded himself, were paranoid and sensitive creatures.

He craned his neck to get a better view of the harbour. The fishermen had returned with their catches and there was a not unpleasant odour of fresh fish, ripe and salty, lacing the air.

'That's great.' Didier paused. 'Do you want to whizz it over? I could take a look and check it out for page turnability.'

Page turnability. One of Didier's favourite phrases; one of Étienne's least favourite phrases. Yes, obviously Étienne knew it was important that readers should want to keep turning the pages – especially in his genre – and it was rather integral to the whole reading experience. But what about lingerability?

He rolled this word around in his head, rocked his chair back and surveyed the sky. It was very clear, very blue. He thought of his conversation on the cliff with Mademoiselle Flower Shop – or Colette, as she was apparently called. What about writing something thought-provoking that actually affected your readers in some way? A good way? Something that made them write emails to you saying things like *This really reminded me of when I was going through a similar experience . . .* or even *You helped me so much at a difficult time in my life, thank you.* Something from the heart, he'd told her.

Étienne rocked the chair back to floor level again and shook his head in despair. What a tosser he was, really. He was lucky enough to be published, for his books to be wanted, for readers to give them their time. Why be arrogant enough to think he could write something life-changing? Who did he think he was – Jean Paul Sartre?

'Maybe later,' he told Didier. Which would tell Didier that either (a) he hadn't written a word or that (b) he thought it was crap. Let's face it – if he had any faith in it whatsoever he would want the gratification of instant approval from Didier, as he always did.

'Right,' said Didier.

Étienne noticed that the windows of the flower shop had been flung open. She was in there then. Did that mean her boyfriend had left for England again, or maybe that he was in the flower shop too, or perhaps he'd walked down to the harbour for an English newspaper? How would he fit into the picture if she decided to stay here on the island?

He craned once again but he couldn't see the guy's tall figure. Only the blue water of the outer harbour, the boats, the endless ocean beyond. Étienne hadn't liked him – the boyfriend. He was uptight and possessive, that much was obvious. It was in his eyes: *she's mine*. And yet Colette hadn't struck him as the type who could belong to anyone. She should be a free spirit. He thought of the sadness in her face when she'd told him about her mother. He'd been moved by that; had wanted to tell her something in return. But it wasn't so easy, was it, to share confidences? He looked down at the pages in front of him. Easier, though, to write it down, it seemed. At least when he was here in situ.

'I've got to sort out my mother's house first,' he told Didier. Though it was sorted, really. This new buyer wanted to buy it, the seller wanted to sell. Étienne just had to accept the offer – or not. 'Then I'll get down to things properly. On my honour.'

'*Eh bien, mon ami.*' Étienne could almost hear his shrug. Clearly, he didn't have a high opinion of Étienne's honour. And he had little idea of how right he was. 'You're on the island then?'

'Yes.' He was a good friend, but Didier knew nothing about Belle-Île and Étienne's history there. No one did. Definitely not easy.

'For how long?'

He found himself thinking of Colette's dark eyes. Of how she had looked that first afternoon down in the cove when he'd accidentally caught her skinny-dipping. He chuckled to himself. 'Not sure,' he said.

'And are you writing while you're there?' Didier was trying to sound strict now, he could tell.

'Yeah, I am.' And that at least wasn't a lie. In fact it was surprisingly easy to write here – especially with the sea view and all. The trouble was that it was a different sort of writing.

On this visit, just like the last, Étienne had scribbled and scribbled – longhand, from the heart – until the early hours. It left him exhausted – mentally and emotionally drained. After that first time, he'd put the pages away in the top drawer of the desk in his mother's house and he'd gone back to his real life back home in Locmariaquer, which was in some weird way also his fantasy life, the life he lived most of the time. He'd tried to start the new novel, he'd walked and he'd thought and he'd got almost nowhere. The characters were in place but they were dead as dust. The plot had a narrative arc but it didn't sing to him.

This time when he'd come over . . . He'd opened the desk drawer and gone back to his other writing, his secret writing, greedily, like an addict. Every day he wrote another few thousand words. And so it had gone on. The past would not loosen its grip.

'That's great,' said Didier.

Étienne thought guiltily of his deadline, fast approaching. 'But it is going slowly,' he warned. Best be prepared.

'I gathered.' There was a pause. 'In fact, I was thinking of coming to Locmariaquer to see you.'

Only I'm not there. It was home and he should get back there. That, after all, was where he worked, where he did what he did for a living, laptop and all. But . . .

'Will you be around next week?'

'Er . . .'

'We could have a beer, have a chat about the book, talk things through . . .'

Étienne knew he must agree. He had a deadline and he had to find a way to reach it. But he was also on a treadmill and he kept getting the urge to jump off. Although if he jumped, what then? 'I'll call you,' he said.

'But—'

Étienne saw Colette coming out of the flower shop alone. There was something determined in the way she was walking. He liked the way her hair swung around her shoulders, the way she always paused when she came out of the house or shop as if she needed a minute to properly take in her surroundings. He liked the fact that she was a girl who thought about things; he liked that a lot. 'Very soon,' he said. '*À bientôt.*' He ended the call.

And opened the window wider. 'Hey!' He called out. '*Bonjour*, Colette.'

She jumped and looked around. 'Oh, hi.' She seemed to flush as she looked up at him. 'Étienne,' she said. She wasn't far away. Close enough for a conversation, close enough for him to see the lighter brown highlights in her hair. She was wearing a denim skirt and a blue flowery top. She looked a bit like a summer's day, he thought. And very inviting.

'It is a beautiful afternoon.' His gesture embraced the sky and the ocean. He felt suddenly cheerful. Here they were, on the ground and sort of on the balcony, like Romeo and Juliet (only the other way about) and the sun was shining, beckoning him outside. Forget work – surely life was for living? 'Are you going for a walk?' He wondered if he should invite himself along. It would be good to talk some more, only . . . 'Sorry about the other day. Is your boyfriend still here?' He was

256

talking more than he usually did and she seemed confused by this. Only, he didn't want her to simply walk away.

'Yes, I am,' she said. 'And no, he's not, he left last night.' She glanced nervously from left to right as if she expected him to suddenly leap out from behind the harbour wall. Étienne couldn't blame her – the guy did seem fond of surprises.

He nodded. So far so good. Not that he had any intentions towards her – with his record in the relationships department, she was far too nice for him. And clearly, she was taken. But he liked her, he liked her a lot. And he found that he wanted to spend some more time with her. He had a few questions he'd like to ask her. Like, was she beginning to find some sense of peace here on the island? He hoped so. And, was she glad that she'd come back here? He thought that maybe she was. She certainly seemed to be getting into that flower shop business of her mother's. So, she wasn't an outsider – not like he was. And yet . . . 'Shall I . . .' – he pointed to where she was standing – 'come down?'

'Oh.' She still seemed a little flustered. 'I'm just off to see someone actually.'

'Ah, right.'

She lifted her hand to shield her eyes from the sun and something sparkled. Étienne frowned. She wasn't very far away and he could see clearly now. Wasn't that the third finger of her left hand? *Really?* After what she'd told him on the cliff, he found that very hard to believe.

'But there's no need to apologise,' she said. 'Mark was fine. In fact . . .' Her voice trailed.

Étienne waggled his finger at her. 'Are congratulations in order then?' He kept his voice light but in fact he was disappointed. Not for his own sake – but because quite obviously the guy was an arrogant tosser.

'Um.' She looked down at the ring as if she was surprised to see it there. 'Not really,' she said. 'Well . . . I suppose.'

Étienne laughed. But suddenly he didn't want to know any more. 'I might be gone before you come back,' he said.

'Oh.' She took a few steps closer. 'You've sorted everything out then?'

Not really, he thought. But it was a decent price. He didn't like the man who was buying it, but since when was that a reason for not selling? He pushed his mother's voice away from his mind, her worried hazel eyes, her frown. 'I think so,' he said.

'So quickly?' She seemed surprised, and maybe – he liked to think – disappointed. Perhaps for her, he was a diversion. Perhaps she treated men the way he'd always treated women. That would be a turnaround.

'Why not?' He shrugged. What was there to hang around for, after all? The past couldn't have him. It could stay locked up exactly where it was. What had happened in the past was unforgivable. It would always be unforgivable – nothing would change that. He had a book to write – and it wasn't this book. There was absolutely no reason for him to stay.

'Right then.' She continued to gaze up at him. 'I hope it all goes well for you, Étienne.'

'And for you, Colette.' Étienne raised his hand in a gesture of farewell. 'And for you.'

CHAPTER 36

Élodie

Élodie saw a figure approaching along the winding coastal path lined with succulents, and stared at it fiercely until – rather to her surprise – it turned into the person of Colette. She smiled. Not many people came this far; it remained an isolated spot and Colette's advance reminded her vividly of that one time Thea had visited her studio, when she'd commissioned the horse with the panniers for her flower shop. Colette was a lot younger than her mother had been then of course, but she cut a similar figure in her blue skirt and patterned top, her dark-brown curls blown back by the sea breeze, slim arms swinging loosely at her sides.

Was she coming to the studio? She must be. Where else could she be going? Only to the Old Lighthouse, and under the circumstances she'd hardly be going there. Thea had been reluctant to come to this northerly end of the island in case she bumped into Élodie's mother, and Élodie had thought she understood. But now she wasn't so sure. What had really happened between Thea and her mother and how was her father involved?

259

Élodie had been quite young when she'd first worked out for herself the manner in which her father operated, his apparent inability to remain faithful to his wife. It hadn't been hard to put two and two together and make a guess at the reason for Thea's dismissal. It was a classic. Her father had come on to the au pair and the au pair had been unable or unwilling to say no. It didn't sound like Thea, but Élodie assumed her mother must have virtually caught them in the act for her to be so sure, and she had to admit that if this was the case, then she didn't blame her for telling Thea to leave. Thea understood Élodie and Jacques. She played the best games and wielded the best sticking plaster. But she had betrayed Mathilde and betrayed their friendship.

But had she? Élodie's father had sounded very sure when he'd denied it the other day. So. Perhaps *something* had happened – but something that wasn't quite so simple.

Élodie dusted off her hands – she had been doing some sanding – and left the studio, heading out on to the coastal path to greet her visitor. She had so few and she preferred it that way. Why encourage them? She had no need of people coming to look at her work. Sometimes she took pieces to markets to sell. More often she offered her work to art and craft shops in the villages who in turn sold it to tourists and took commission. It was a good system and left Élodie free to focus on collecting her materials and on her work. However, she found she was rather glad to see this visitor. 'Hi there,' she called.

Colette raised her hand to wave. She was a nice young woman; Élodie had always liked her, always assumed this was because she was part of Thea. Élodie had allowed much of the closeness between herself and Thea to dissipate when she'd worked out the reasons behind her dismissal. But their closeness had never gone entirely – how could it? Thea was a huge part of her childhood – and these days she made it her business to go and see her, to maintain the friendship that her mother still refused to acknowledge. Thea was very ill. Élodie wished that Mathilde could soften towards her now. Perhaps one day . . . She hoped that her mother wouldn't leave it until it was too late. But in the meantime, Élodie thought, perhaps she was acting as the bridge between these two women who had once been so close.

Thea . . . Was it bad news? Was that why Colette had come? Her heart seemed to stall. 'Were you coming to see me, Colette?' Her words were lost in the wind. She walked more quickly to meet her, raised her voice. 'Is everything all right? Your mother . . .?'

'*Bonjour*, Élodie, oh, yes, *merci*, she is much the same.' Colette reached Élodie's side, stuck her hands in her pockets and smiled a little uncertainly. 'A bit weaker perhaps, that is all.'

Élodie was rather surprised by her own sudden burst of affection for the girl. She took her by the shoulders and kissed her lightly on both cheeks. Colette seemed a bit surprised too from the look in her eyes, though she submitted to the embrace with good grace. Of course, she had been living in England for years and no doubt they were less demonstrative over there. But her smile was warmer now.

'How lovely to see you,' Élodie said. 'Would you like to take a look around the studio? Could I get you some coffee?' *Don't gush, Élodie*. Perhaps, yes, she should get out more.

'*Mais oui, merci*, that would be very nice.' Colette began to follow her towards the studio. She paused and looked out to sea. 'It's so beautiful here,' she said, almost wistfully. 'So peaceful.'

Élodie paused too, tried to see the view – her view – through someone else's eyes. The flat-topped rock surrounding them was carpeted with succulents like *griffe de sorcière* and *cinéraire maritime*, plants and grasses at their brightest at this point in early summer, the entire cliff covered in blooms of fluorescent orange, pink and purple. In the autumn the flowers would have faded, the foliage would turn to a dull amber; in the winter the undergrowth would die down to a brackish brown and in the spring it would be green and silver with the dazzling yellows of mimosa, broom and gorse beginning to flower once more. The rocky bays and narrow inlets were surrounded with longer grasses and tamarisk trees and the landscape of the dunes metamorphosed into jagged granite at the Pointe. Beyond the bays and the Pointe, the ocean slowly rolled; slumbering or crashing, rushing or creeping, depending on the moon and its mood.

'It is beautiful, yes,' Élodie said. 'And certainly never boring. Naturally, I am used to it. But I hope I never stop loving it just the same.'

'The view from my mother's shop is glorious too,' Colette went on. 'But this is so much wilder. To work with this land-scape right there in front of you . . .' – she turned to Élodie, eyes shining – 'must be so inspiring.'

Élodie felt humbled. And yet so often she took it for granted. 'Yes,' she said, 'it is.' Though she was taken aback by the passion in Colette's voice. She glanced at her again. She seemed different somehow. 'Are you all right?' She hesitated. 'Is everything OK?' After all, they were not exactly friends. How deeply could she delve into the girl's state of mind?

'I'm fine.' Colette reached up to brush the hair from her face that had been stuck there by the wind, and Élodie noticed the ring on her finger. You couldn't not notice it really – a large solitaire.

Colette saw her looking. 'Mark came over from Cornwall,' she said in explanation. 'My boyfriend, that is.' She looked down at the ring – a strange look, almost as if she were blaming it for something.

'And you got engaged?' Élodie had never met Mark, but in her opinion Colette didn't look like a young woman madly in love. In fact, she looked a bit lost.

'Not exactly.' Colette put her hands in her pockets once more as if to hide the ring from sight. 'I promised him I'd wear it while I was thinking it over – his proposal, I mean.'

That was rather odd. Élodie raised an eyebrow. 'And have you?'

'I've thought of nothing else.'

Élodie nodded. Not that she remotely understood. Belle-Île was a small place and Élodie was a solitary person. She had wondered sometimes if perhaps she simply didn't have it in her to feel that way, wondered if all her emotions were wrapped up in her family – in Jacques and in her mother – and in her art. But that was enough for now. If Colette wanted to confide in her, she would. She was here, that was nice enough in its own right. 'Come in,' she said, leading the way to the studio. 'This is it.'

'Where it all happens,' Colette said and followed her inside.

'Where it all happens indeed.'

She made coffee while Colette looked around the studio, exclaiming over this sculpture or that piece of decorative art. Élodie noted that her taste, too, was rather similar to her mother's. However, she seemed most taken with a driftwood heron which had taken an age for Élodie to complete, mainly because of the interleaving of the wafer-thin shapes that were the feathers. The eye was a leaf-shaped knot in the wood; the bill tapered to a smooth, pale point. It was finished, but she hadn't yet delivered it to the gallery she'd promised to take it to.

'You're very talented,' Colette said. She bent down, looked into the heron's face.

Élodie laughed. 'And you're very kind.' She put the tray on a small table outside the studio and they sat down on the wicker chairs. So why had she come? Élodie waited. She knew it wouldn't merely be a social call.

Colette fiddled with her teaspoon. 'I came to see you because someone was in the flower shop this morning asking about your work,' she said at last.

'Oh?' Élodie took a sip of her coffee. It was black and very strong – just as she liked it, a hot-wire to the brain.

'He had seen the horse.'

'Ah, yes, *le cheval aux fleurs*.' Élodie put down her cup and passed Colette the milk. 'And what did he want, this man?' She tried not to sound weary. She was pleased with compliments – though not flattered. And she welcomed commissions, of course. She had to live. But she'd prefer to work on a piece because it drew her, rather than because there was pressure to complete.

'He wanted to know your name.' Colette looked across at her. 'I told him. I hope that's all right?'

'Of course.' Élodie laughed again. 'It's not a secret. And it's carved on the mane.'

'The mane?'

'Of the horse. Maybe he wants a horse for himself, is that it?'

'I don't think so.' Colette added milk to her coffee and stirred it.

'What then?' Élodie was only mildly curious. She was fortunate enough to sell almost everything she could make. Many tourists came to Belle-Île and many of them had money and wanted to take home a souvenir of the island. Élodie worked slowly, but she didn't need to earn much in order to live. She was far from desperate for more clients. She was lucky – she realised that; at least, in some ways.

'His name was Armand Dubois.' Colette tucked her hair behind one ear. One of Thea's gestures, thought Élodie. They were so alike. And what a pity it was she'd stayed away from her mother and the island so long.

'Nice name.' She considered. 'I don't think I know him though.' She frowned. 'Is he a tourist? Does he live here on Belle-Île?'

'He lives on the mainland,' Colette said. 'He owns a gallery. He asked me to give you his card.' She unzipped the purse she wore slung over one shoulder and extracted a blue and green business card. '*Voilà.*'

'A gallery?' Élodie took the card. Modus. It was in Auray. She'd never heard of the gallery, but then she wouldn't have. She went over to the mainland so rarely and she'd never been ambitious enough to approach any galleries there direct.

She let out a small sigh and allowed her gaze to drift towards the ocean. It was sleek and silky today, almost unruffled by wind, which was rare in itself. There were times, yes. But this was the life she had chosen for herself soon after Jacques had left. He needed to leave – she could understand that – after what had happened between him and their father, and so she must stay. She was only sixteen. And besides, someone had to stay with their mother, someone had to keep an eye on her. It had hurt – to keep refusing to join him in those early days; to read his letters so full of his plans and his new, interesting life, to witness how easily he seemed to have left them all behind. It had even hurt when he finally told her that he had met someone, that he was to be married. Not because she would deny him such happiness, but because that's when Élodie knew that she'd lost him for good.

'I thought I should come over straight away and tell you,' Colette went on, breaking into her thoughts. 'Maman said she didn't have your number and anyway . . .' – her voice trailed – 'it could be very exciting, couldn't it? It could lead to something?'

'Mm, thanks.' Élodie put her head to one side. 'Yes, I suppose it could.' It was a nice business card: contemporary and bright. But . . .

Colette leaned forward. 'He was very nice. And he loved the horse, Élodie.'

'Good, good.' Absently, she tucked the card under a book on the table.

'You will call him?'

Élodie regarded her thoughtfully. She really seemed to care. 'Probably,' she conceded. Or maybe not. She would see.

Colette sat back in her chair and picked up her coffee cup. She was drinking it faster now, as though she might soon be gone.

'You know, my parents have finally split up,' Élodie said conversationally. She wasn't sure why she wanted to tell her this. Perhaps she simply wanted to talk about it? She'd already written to Jacques to tell him. *You can come over here now, to visit*, she'd written; *he's not around, he's gone, our mother has finally done it*. Mathilde had found the strength from somewhere – who knew where? And she didn't seem to regret her decision

– although she was acting a little strangely. Yesterday she had come over to the studio, hung around watching Élodie work until at last she had downed tools and asked her mother what was up.

'Nothing,' she had insisted.

'You're not lonely, Mama?' Though why should she be? – being apart from her husband was hardly a new experience for her.

'No. It's just . . .' And she had shot Élodie a look of entreaty.

'What, Mama?'

'I was only thinking . . .'

'What is it? What were you thinking?' Élodie was trying to be patient. She wanted to get on with her work but it seemed that her mother had something she wanted to say to her.

'Oh, nothing, *chérie*. I'd better get back to the house. There are things I need to do.'

Élodie had watched her disappear from sight, not as upright these days as she had once been, her fair hair now silvery. She still had a certain elegance though, the charm of the older woman once beautiful, and she was still slim and dressed well. Whatever it was, she'd do it in her own time, Élodie thought. She would be fine.

'Oh, dear, I'm so sorry,' Colette said at her news. She sounded very concerned.

'I'm not. It was long overdue.'

They both laughed.

'Their marriage – it wasn't good?'

Élodie sensed her treading carefully. 'It wasn't good for Mama,' she said.

'And you didn't get on with your father?'

Élodie sipped the last dregs of her coffee. It was cold now

267

but she never minded that. 'He has always been a serial wom-aniser,' she said. 'And he can be violent too.'

Colette let out a small gasp. 'Oh.'

'My mother has had much to endure her entire married life,' Élodie went on. 'As for whether I got on with him . . . Let's say I tolerated him. Let's say I work and live in this studio so that I'm near Mama but so that I always have a bolt-hole – in case I need to get away from him.'

'Goodness.' Colette's mouth was open now and her eyes wide.

'It is nothing new.' Élodie shrugged. She could see Colette struggling to get a hold on it all. It was a lot of emotive infor-mation and her mind must have gone into overdrive. Perhaps Élodie shouldn't have said quite so much. She wondered if this was how it was with people. You remained solitary for days and months. You weren't sociable, you didn't share. And then someone came along – someone unexpected like Colette who was part stranger and part familiar – and it all spilled out. Everything. You lost all your inhibitions and told that almost-stranger the story of your life.

'Did my mother . . .?' Colette began. 'I mean, do you think she was one of the women?'

Oh, dear. Élodie hadn't thought far enough ahead. She didn't want Colette to think badly of Thea all over again. 'I shouldn't think so,' she said breezily. 'I think the women were all in Paris and kept well away from *ma mère*.' She pulled a face.

'But . . .' Colette seemed troubled. 'I always knew there was someone.'

'Someone?'

'I heard my parents arguing the night my father died.' Colette bowed her head. 'It was obvious that my mother was having an affair and that my father had just found out about it.'

268

'I see.' That must have been a hard argument to witness.

'And yet my mother loved him.' Her eyes were confused. 'Do you think it was your father she was seeing?' she asked Élodie. 'Papa said that the thing – my mother's secret, that is – had been going on for years.'

'Oh, you poor girl.' Élodie was beginning to understand why Colette might have left Belle-Île in the first place.

'It happens.' Colette attempted a shrug but Élodie could see how affected she was, even now.

'But maybe it didn't happen with my father,' Élodie said gently.

'Why should you think that?'

'Because . . .' And Élodie repeated to Colette what her father had said that afternoon. 'He completely denied it,' she said. 'And really, at that point he had no reason to lie.'

'Do you believe him?' Colette looked sceptical.

Élodie considered. 'I think I do, yes.'

'So why did your mother accuse him of it then – she must have had grounds for suspicion?'

'*Je ne sais pas.*'

'And why do they still not speak to one another even now – my mother and yours?'

'I don't know that either, *chérie*.' Élodie put her coffee cup down on the table. Her mother had wanted to tell her something though, hadn't she? And perhaps this concerned whatever it was that had driven her and Thea apart. 'But if you like – I can ask her.'

CHAPTER 37

Colette

Colette was in the shop changing the water in the flower-buckets when a woman came in to order a christening bouquet. She lived in Bangor, she said, and hadn't been to Sauzon for a while, but now her grandson was to be christened and so she had come for some special flowers.

'I wonder if I could speak to Thea about it?' she asked. 'Is she around?'

Oh, dear. 'I'm sorry to have to tell you that my mother is not at all well.' Colette was still not used to saying this. She saw the woman's expression change. 'Were you friends?' she asked cautiously. 'I'm afraid I've been away for a long time and . . .' Her voice trailed. And I no longer know who my mother's friends are, she thought.

'Not friends, exactly, no,' the woman told her. 'But I am very sorry to hear this news.' She eyed Colette with curiosity. 'She never mentioned a daughter.'

'No.' Why would she? Colette had never come back here. She couldn't blame her mother for letting her go. She had

270

insisted on being released if not forgotten. *But she loved me.* She had told Colette this, and Colette believed her. Perhaps she had always known but never acknowledged it.

'The christening is for my son's child,' the woman went on conversationally. 'As for my daughter – she has been away travelling. She has met a man and fallen in love, you know how it is.'

'*Mais oui.*' Colette thought of Mark. Did she know how it was? Did she really? She had taken the ring from her finger because she didn't want to damage it while she was working. And she had done this with a small but unmistakable sigh of relief.

'He's Dutch – my daughter's boyfriend, I mean. He has a degree in horticulture.'

'Really?' Colette was dealing with horticulturalists in Holland – that was where her mother got most of her flowers. They always had lovely fresh blooms in stock and of course people wanted certain varieties in their arrangements. But . . . She looked around rather wistfully. It was very different from her vision of a garden of flowers – meadow flowers, healing flowers. Maybe if she had such flowers, she could make lotions and potions too – not only for healing but for cosmetics made the old-fashioned and natural way. Maybe she could make jams and biscuits, sell massage oil and wild bouquets. She could have artists coming in to paint still-lifes of her flowers; she could sell those too. If she were going to run a flower shop – which of course she wasn't, why would she? – that was what it would be. An alternative flower shop.

She shook herself back to the conversation, for the customer was still talking about her daughter and the horticulturalist boyfriend. 'That's very interesting,' she said. Though actually,

271

she wanted the woman to give her the order and leave her in the shop to get on, for there was plenty to do and Colette was at odds with herself today, not really in the mood for chat.

What would her mother think of her ideas for an alternative flower shop? Colette sighed. She had to accept that her mother would soon be leaving this life and she must be wondering what would happen to her precious shop once she'd gone. Colette worried about it too. That offer from Lemaire, that threat of the shop becoming some kind of music bar, was never far from her mind.

'I do hope your mother feels better soon,' the woman said. She seemed nice, she seemed concerned.

'My mother is dying,' Colette told her starkly. Why pretend? At least then the woman would know why Colette was not in the mood for talking to strangers.

'Oh, my dear. I'm so sorry to hear that.' The woman took a notepad out of her bag and wrote a number down, ripped the page out and gave it to Colette. 'This is me,' she said. 'If I can be of any help at any time, please do not hesitate . . .'

'*Merci beaucoup*.' Colette took the paper. Her eyes filled and she could barely read the words the woman had written. *Béatrice Charron*, followed by a phone number. 'You're very kind.'

'And I would still like the christening flowers – if you can do them, if it is not too distressing for you, my dear.'

'*Mais oui*, I can do them.' Colette tucked the piece of paper into the pocket of her jeans. She needed to keep working, keep doing. 'I'll take down some details.'

After the woman had left the shop, Colette made some orders, did a couple of pencil sketches for the christening bouquet, and began to tidy up. But as she swept the floor and watered the pot plants, she felt herself welling up and pretty soon she was weeping uncontrollably. She shoved the 'Closed' sign on the door. What was the matter with her? What had started her off? She blew her nose loudly on a green paper towel from the roll she used for mopping up.

Her mobile rang and she answered it quickly, before she could change her mind. It was Mark and she'd already ignored his last two calls. She didn't feel ready to speak to him. She didn't have an answer and she knew that was what he wanted.

'Hello,' she sniffed.

'Colette?' He was all concern. 'What is it? Has something happened? Is it . . .' – he paused – '. . . your mother?'

Yes, it was her mother. She was growing so weak, and it hurt Colette to watch. But it wasn't just that. Why not tell him? Colette needed to offload and he was practically her fiancé. She looked mournfully at the diamond ring sparkling on the counter next to the sink. It almost seemed to be mocking her. Nevertheless, she went over and pulled it back on to the third finger of her left hand as if Mark might be able to spot from Porthleven that she wasn't wearing it. 'It's everything,' she said. 'The house, the shop, Maman . . .'

'What's happened, sweetheart? Do you want to come back to Cornwall – is that it?' He sounded hopeful.

'How can I?'

'And what about the shop?'

'Someone came in.' Colette told him about Philippe Lemaire and his interest in the property.

'Oh, Colette darling.' Mark sighed. 'It's not so awful. These things happen. People hear that places may soon be up for sale. Everyone knows your mother is ill. You can't blame people for trying.'

'I suppose.' Though she did. Lemaire's approach had been tactless and insensitive, to say the least.

'And you know, it wouldn't be the end of the world to get something sorted out.'

Colette gripped her mobile more tightly. Her boyfriend, the estate agent. Her fiancé, the estate agent. Mark clearly wasn't concerned and he had a point – she knew she must keep things in perspective. But he had no idea how much her mother would care.

'But then it wouldn't be a flower shop.' Couldn't he see? After all her mother's hard work.

'Things change, Colette.' His voice was clear and firm. 'And why shouldn't they? After all, there are nightclubs in every town in the world practically, and—'

'Nightclubs?' Colette shuddered. 'He said a music bar.'

'Music bars then.' Mark's voice softened. 'It's an option, isn't it, darling? Don't you think it's a good thing? To have options? After all, it could save you a lot of time and energy after, well, after . . .'

'Yes.' It had been pointless trying to tell Mark how she felt. He would support her, yes. He would have sympathy, yes. He would even look after her – and Colette relished this; she had never really felt looked after since her father had died. But he was never going to understand.

CHAPTER 38

Colette

Later, in the house, she made some wild garlic and cauliflower soup for her mother and told her about the customer.

'I remember Béatrice Charron,' she said. She took a small sip of the soup but Colette knew this was more for her, Colette's, benefit than because she wanted it.

She smiled. 'Maman, you remember everyone. I don't know how you do it.'

Her mother smiled weakly back at her. 'I always hoped you would take over the flower shop, *chérie*,' she said.

Did she think . . .? 'But Maman . . .' *I haven't*, she wanted to say. She really hadn't. She hadn't decided anything, and besides, there was Mark's proposal to consider now. Even so . . .

Her vision of a garden of flowers was only that, she reminded herself – a vision. She didn't run a flower shop and she didn't live on this island, or even in France. The flower shop had always been her mother's dream, not hers.

'You were always such a dreamy child,' she said, and Colette could hear the soft note of affection in her voice. 'What are you thinking about now, my dear?'

Colette blinked at her. It was the first time she could remember her asking this question. And surely her mother had been the dreamy one? Then she caught the smile in her faded brown eyes and went over to the bed to take the tray. 'Have you finished, Maman?' she asked.

Her mother nodded. '*Merci, chérie.*' She leaned back on her pillow as if just those few sips had exhausted her.

Colette sat down and took her hand. 'Flowers,' she confessed. 'I was thinking about flowers, Maman.'

Thea seemed satisfied at this. She closed her eyes.

'But that doesn't mean . . .' Colette hesitated.

'I know,' she whispered. And she squeezed her hand to show her that she didn't need to say more.

But something was prodding at Colette like an itch that wouldn't go away. She knew she shouldn't scratch it, but . . . 'She didn't even know you had a daughter,' she said. 'This Madame Charron from Bangor.'

Her mother gripped her hand a little harder. 'Colette, my darling,' she murmured.

Colette was surprised at her strength. 'I do get it,' she said. 'I don't blame you for not talking about me. Why should you? It's not as if I was ever around.'

'Sometimes, it hurt too much to talk about you,' her mother murmured. Her eyes were still half closed, as if remembering, and her breath seemed to catch in her throat. 'Sometimes, I didn't want that pain.'

'Oh, Maman.' Colette buried her head in the bedcovers, felt her mother's hand lightly smoothing her hair just as she had when Colette was a young girl. She *had* blamed her, though.

276

She had blamed her for not loving her father enough, for not loving her, Colette, enough, for loving her flower shop more. For not saying the right things and not doing the right things. Colette had never realised how much her mother was struggling. And now that she was making so many new discoveries, she was wondering how much of what she had believed for so many years was true.

She heard her mother take another shallow breath. 'I had my regrets, yes. I've told you that.'

'Yes, Maman.'

'I put my trust in what couldn't hurt me or leave me.' Each word seemed to emerge with some difficulty now.

'Oh, Maman.'

'I even let your father have all your love.'

Colette bent her head.

'But I always knew that I had a daughter.' Her mother's voice broke as she spoke the words. 'I always knew. And I always believed in you, *chérie*.'

I always believed in you . . . Colette inhaled her mother's perfume mingling with the lavender-and-almond massage oil, laced as always with the medical smell that seemed to fill the sickroom no matter how wide she opened the windows or how often she brought fresh flowers to put on the windowsill.

Colette hadn't believed in her mother, though. Her heart had belonged to her father, and when he was gone . . . She hadn't given her a chance, she realised. She had believed in neither her grief nor her love. She had rejected her and everything she stood for – the shop, the island, her own home. Perhaps there had been someone else for her mother – very likely, Colette would never know, unless Élodie found out the truth. But it

277

wasn't for Colette to judge her parents or her parents' marriage. It was time to forgive, way past time to forgive.

'And perhaps that is what matters the most, hm?' It was just a whisper. She seemed exhausted now as though the last strength had been sapped from her.

'Yes, Maman. That's what matters the most.'

They sat together in silence for twenty minutes or so, hands clasped, her mother drifting in and out of the sleep that Colette hoped was some release, at least. She hoped that Thea knew how precious this time was for her. She had come over to Belle-Île to help, to be there for her last days, out of a sense of duty to start with, not love. But now . . . This time had turned out to be a gift for Colette – a chance to make things better.

'Tell me what you've been doing.' Her mother was awake again. 'I like to hear your voice, my darling.'

'I went up to the Pointe yesterday afternoon,' she told her. 'To Élodie's studio. Someone came into the shop asking about her.'

'Oh?' She shifted her weight, clearly in pain, and Colette adjusted the pillows to try and make her more comfortable, felt the angular jut of her frailty under her cotton nightie.

'He said he owned a gallery. He liked the horse.' Colette smiled as she remembered Élodie's reaction. It wasn't exactly what one might expect from an artist hearing that her work had been admired by someone who could potentially help further her career. As for Armand Dubois – Colette had liked him, and he'd seemed sincere. She'd gone to see Élodie because she'd thought it might be important, but also because she'd wanted to get away for a while. Élodie was a strange one, but Colette felt drawn to her. And who else could she talk to? Before Mark's proposal she could have talked to Étienne. But not now. She'd sensed his surprise, his disappointment even. She was almost glad that he'd left the island once again. She didn't want him to witness her confusion, the sense of emotional desolation she seemed to be going through right now.

'That's good.' Her mother nodded and licked her dry lips. Colette held the water glass for her. The nurse had suggested a straw and her mother seemed to find this a little easier to manage. 'She should spread her wings.'

Colette thought about what Élodie had said yesterday afternoon. 'Maybe she stays on the island to be with her mother.' She hesitated to bring up the subject of Mathilde. Mathilde – who might well be the key to some of her mother's secrets.

'Perhaps.' She was giving nothing away. 'But she could still go over to the mainland from time to time, don't you think?' Her milky-brown eyes were focused on Colette as if she was finding it hard to concentrate, or as if she was wondering where this conversation might lead. She frowned with the effort it must be taking. 'And how did you get on – you and Élodie?'

'We got on well.' Colette liked her. She was enigmatic and appealing. Colette rather hoped that they might become friends. *Come again*, Élodie had said to her. *And I will tell you what I can find out from Maman.* Her blue eyes had shone as if she was enjoying this new camaraderie, this shared mystery.

'I'm so pleased about that.' Her mother relaxed against the pillows once more. 'She is lonely, of course. Ever since Jacques left the island.' She sighed. 'They were so close, those two.'

As if an invisible thread tied them together, Colette remembered thinking, as if an invisible wall shielded them both from the world. She supposed that as their au pair, Thea would have grown to love them both. Jacques had clearly found a new life for himself away from Belle-Île. But why had Élodie not found someone to love?

279

'She was telling me that her parents have split up,' she said.

'Ah.' She didn't seem surprised. 'Poor Mathilde,' she murmured. 'She always knew that he would leave someday.' There was no hint that this news might unlock any of her secret memories.

'Maman – do you think that you and she . . .?' Colette let her voice trail. *Could ever be reconciled*, she was going to say.

Her mother held her gaze for several seconds before she looked away towards the window. 'It's probably too late,' she murmured.

'But what happened between you?' Colette took another risk. Her mother was having a good day; she seemed strong enough to talk about this. And Colette so wanted to find out the truth. Étienne had talked about the shadows of the past, and he was right. They were far-reaching and they could prevent a person from moving on. *Ask her while you still can*, he had said. 'Was it him? Was it Léo?'

Her mother shook her head but didn't quite look her in the eye. Her fingers began picking at the quilt. 'I will always be deeply ashamed,' she said. 'I will never forgive myself for what I have done.'

'But, Maman, what have you done?'

'I can't . . .' Her voice trailed into nothing. She looked listless, frightened. She shot Colette a look of silent appeal.

'Whatever it is,' Colette said quickly, 'it is past, and you mustn't worry about it.'

When her mother looked at her again her eyes were less scared but her voice sounded like a child's. 'Mathilde and I,' she began, 'both have good reason to be ashamed.'

'Ssh now.' Colette stroked her grey-streaked hair, wispy and fine as a newborn's. She didn't want to talk about it if it was going to have this effect on her. She was ill. It wasn't fair.

'I wrote it down,' her mother whispered, 'but now it is lost.'

'Did you keep a diary?' Colette was intrigued. What wouldn't she give for a sight of that diary. She'd find out all the answers then.

But her mother was distracted. She took Colette's hand and turned it around. 'A ring, *chérie*?' she breathed.

Colette looked down at the ring, shining, bright as a star. She'd put it on again when she'd finished in the shop, felt compelled to. But now . . . She'd take it off again, she decided. She was getting a bit tired of trying to explain. 'Mark gave it to me,' she said. 'But . . .' She pulled it from her finger. It resisted at first but she tugged more fiercely and when it came over the knuckle it left an angry red mark behind. She rubbed at it with her forefinger and placed the ring on her mother's bedside table. 'I don't know what to say to him, Maman,' she said.

'Do you love him?' She whispered the words.

'I don't know.'

Her mother seemed to be searching her face. But it was clearly taking some effort; Colette could see that she was tiring again now. 'You'll find your pathway, Colette,' she said at last. 'Most people do in the end.' She gave her hand a final pat and rested back against the pillows, eyes already beginning to close.

In seconds, she had drifted off into a deeper sleep and Colette moved over to the window that looked out over Sauzon's harbour. She glanced down at the small square by the lighthouse where Henri the old fisherman stood talking to Claude Macon, one of his cronies from the old days. She looked back down the road towards the crêperie run by Anneliese then across at the mint-green shutters of Étienne's mother's house – now firmly closed to show that there was no one at home. As she'd always told herself, Étienne Chevalier was a transitory visitor. He was always going to leave the island.

What *was* her pathway? Colette looked down at her finger, the knuckle still sore from Mark's ring. Did she have any idea? Was that why she had first gone to Cornwall, spent time with the grandparents she hardly knew, travelled around, found it hard to settle? Was that why she had come back here? Because she was lost? Because she was still looking for that pathway? She was half-English and half-French. So, where did she belong? She thought of her father's old wooden compass. *Everyone needs a compass to show them the way.*

Colette turned sharply from the window. She pulled down the blinds. The sun was suddenly too bright, the harbour almost too pretty. And why did she feel so much like crying again? These conversations with her mother were so intense at times; these gatherings of memories so important, now that there was so little time left. But . . . She slipped out of the house and knocked on Francine's door.

'*Oui?*' Francine had opened the door almost before she knocked. Nothing new there then. No doubt she was keeping watch, as usual, through the *rideaux*. But now, Colette no longer minded.

'Francine – could you hold the fort here if I go away for a few days?' From Quiberon she could take the train to Rennes and then get a flight to Exeter – that might be the quickest way. Mark would meet her there or she could take the train to Penzance. Anyway, she'd make a few calls and she'd work out the best route.

'Will you come back?' Francine was watching her closely.

'I will, I promise. It's only a few days.'

'Of course, it is no problem at all. I wish . . .' But Francine did not say what she wished.

'*Merci.*' Colette nodded. 'There are some things I have to do, you see.' She had left all her stuff in the studio and her car outside – it had been quicker to get a flight to France and that was all she'd been thinking at the time. Now . . . 'There's something I have to put right.' And since she'd made the decision, Colette felt lighter somehow, as if a burden had been lifted. 'Then I'll come back to stay – until she doesn't need me any more. You can trust me on that.'

'That's good.' Francine seemed satisfied.

'And the flower shop?' It was a lot to ask, she knew. 'Can you manage that too – just an hour or two a day perhaps?'

Francine clicked her tongue in that way she had. '*Bien sûr,* I'll do it for your mother,' she said. 'But you know I cannot look after it the way that you do.'

'*Merci.*' Colette reached across and gave her a kiss on the cheek, then another on the other cheek.

Francine stared at her in surprise. 'When are you leaving?'

'Soon,' said Colette. 'Maybe tomorrow morning. I'll tell my mother. I'll let you know, shall I?'

Francine smiled. Colette had the feeling that she'd hardly seen her smile before. 'Good luck,' she said.

'Thank you, Francine.' It might be only the first step of Colette's new pathway – but it was a beginning, at least.

CHAPTER 39

Mathilde

Once again, Mathilde suppressed the pang of guilt as she flipped through the pages of Thea's diary. It seemed incredible now that she had kept this journal hidden and unread for so long. And yet it had unleashed so many emotions — sometimes dangerous to show — and she had sensed that this would be the case. She couldn't deny that it was painful reliving those times, discovering Thea's feelings about her life, their friendship, and this was what Mathilde had dreaded. But there was also joy in the remembering, and it was this that she hung on to.

She was reading about Thea's arrival at the Old Lighthouse, her immediate connection with Jacques, her reservations about Mathilde herself. *But I like her*, she read. *I thought at first that she has an easy life, but she doesn't. Léo's a tricky one.*

Mathilde tensed. Here we go, she thought. This was one of the things she had to know.

He tried to come on to me almost as soon as I arrived, followed me into my bedroom, this wolfish grin on his face. 'You're a very pretty girl,' he said. 'Très jolie.'

I'm not sure how to handle him, to be honest. He's tall and handsome with dark, wavy hair, aquiline nose, sensual lips . . . but I'm still heartbroken over Jez and it's hardly appropriate. In fact, it's embarrassing. He's my employer and he's married, to Mathilde — poor woman. 'Such a pity,' I told him sweetly. 'But surely, much too close to home.'

For a moment, I thought I'd blown it — after all, no man likes rejection, and especially a man with an ego like Léo's — but I could see my words had struck a chord. And he wouldn't want to look for another au pair, not so quickly.

'Hmm,' he said. 'Eh bien. We'll have to see if we can find a way round that, don't you think?'

I threw him a look — regretful but firm — and crossed my fingers behind my back. What have I done? What have I walked into? Only time will tell.

Mathilde shook her head. *That unfeeling bastard . . .* Why hadn't Thea told her? Not immediately perhaps, but as they became friends? Although, would she have believed her back then? Mightn't she have told Thea to pack her bags even earlier? It was a sensitive subject. Later, of course, she had her suspicions. Why, she'd even suspected that Élodie . . . Mathilde sighed. The truth was that she would always have believed her adulterous husband rather than an English girl who had just moved into her house. The truth was, that she had never wanted to face the truth. Until now.

Mathilde knew exactly where she was when she first found out the truth about Léo.

She was six months pregnant, Thea had been with her for two months, though in recent weeks she had not seemed quite herself – as if something was bothering her perhaps. Mathilde hoped she was not thinking about leaving them and returning to the UK, she wasn't quite sure how she would manage without her. Their closeness had developed since the near-drowning incident, which Mathilde could not think of without feeling the same panic in her belly as she had felt back then. Now, the two of them often spent evenings together after Jacques had gone to bed, chatting and sharing stories of their past. Thea didn't say exactly why she had left Cornwall, but she had confided that there had been a boy, and Mathilde had been able to fill in the gaps. 'We have found each other at the right time,' she told her.

On this particular day, Mathilde was standing in her bedroom – their bedroom, but that was becoming rather a joke; Léo, she had come to realise, did not find a pregnant wife as alluring as a svelte one. She was looking out to sea, towards the beach where Thea was rock-hopping with little Jacques. *Take care!* she wanted to shout. But she did not need to. Thea was so good with him. She was holding his hand and if her boy should slip, Thea had him; she would take his weight and help him find his balance once again. The older he grew, the more time Jacques wanted to spend by the ocean. He would sift sand in a sieve purloined from the kitchen, hunt for crabs and shrimps with his little net, paddle contentedly in the shallows for hours, happy just to be by the water. His bad experience in the ocean that time had altered nothing – thank the lord.

The phone rang and Mathilde moved lazily to answer it on the bedroom extension. It had been like this with Jacques too, this slowness of movement, this sense of well-being that came in the sixth month once the baby was well established in the womb.

'*Bonjour, Madame.*' It was a woman's voice. 'I trust that you are well?'

Mathilde frowned. 'Very well, thank you. And to whom am I speaking *s'il vous plaît*?'

'You do not know me,' the woman replied. There was a bitterness in her voice and Mathilde automatically put a hand on her belly as if to protect her baby from it. 'But I know you.'

'Is that so?' Mathilde kept her voice calm. She considered putting the phone down but decided against it for now. She would see what this woman wanted first.

'Because I know your husband Léo,' the woman went on conversationally. 'In fact, I know him rather well.'

Mathilde did not like the insinuation. 'Who is this?' she snapped. Her hand tightened on the receiver. 'And what are you implying?'

'Very convenient for him to keep you far away,' the woman said. Her voice was like silk. 'It made things so easy for us. But he doesn't want me now. After two years, would you believe?'

Two years? Mathilde found herself unable to speak. But neither could she put down the phone. It seemed she must hear more.

'It is a long time, *n'est-ce pas*? A long time after which to simply click one's fingers and discard a lover, *non*?'

'What is your name?' Mathilde managed to ask, though her stomach was churning and there was a pain in her head, in her eyes.

'Renée Poulin,' the woman said. 'I am not married so you may as well know.'

And that was not all she wanted her to know, thought

Mathilde. 'You want to hurt him,' she said. 'As he has hurt you.'

There was a click and Mathilde realised that she had ended the call. *Two years?* She sank on to the bed. Her husband had kept a mistress for two years – almost the entire time she had lived on Belle-Île. Was that why he had moved her here?

She drank some brandy that night, even before Jacques had gone to bed.

'Are you all right, Mathilde?' Thea asked her. 'Has something happened?'

Yes, something had happened. Her world had fallen apart.

Mathilde had to tell someone. 'I found something out today,' she said. And she told Thea about the phone call.

She drank more brandy that evening and she cried – a lot. She ranted and she railed and she became self-pitying. 'Look at me,' she said. 'Why would he want me when the women in Paris are so elegant, so chic . . .'

Thea tried to comfort her but what could she say? Léo had betrayed her in the worst possible way – she could not deny it. Mathilde knew that many men took mistresses but she had always thought that Léo was different, that he was above such things and that the love they shared was special. And to take a mistress for two years, while Mathilde was carrying his two children in her belly . . .

It was past midnight when she phoned Léo.

'Who,' she demanded in a somewhat slurred voice, 'is Renée Poulin?'

'*Comment?*'

'Don't lie to me, Léo,' she cried. 'Not any more.'

'Have you been drinking, Mathilde?' Léo's voice was dangerously low. 'Have you risked the health of our unborn child?'

No apologies, no admission of guilt. What could she say? She accused him and he admitted nothing. And he was angry – with Mathilde.

He came over, though, the very next day, pushing past Thea, taking Mathilde in his arms, talking to her, reassuring her, holding her.

'I know Renée Poulin, sure,' he said. 'But she is a crazy woman. I turned down her advances and now she's consumed with bitterness, damn her.' He was so angry, so righteous. 'I will never forgive her for upsetting you so.' He held her close and he made love to her that night so tenderly.

'I am sorry, Léo,' Mathilde said. 'But I miss you. And you know, you are here so little . . .' Her voice failed at the expression in his dark eyes, his anger.

'Just remember, Mathilde,' Léo told her. 'Everything I do is for us, for you, for our family. It is all I care about. Everything I do.'

When he left, he told her that she must take more care of herself and of their unborn child. 'Promise me, Mathilde.' He put his hands on her throat and very gently, he squeezed.

Mathilde gasped for breath. 'Léo . . .'

'Promise me.' There seemed to be no love in his expression now.

'I promise,' she whispered.

'Because I could never forgive you,' he said perfectly calmly, 'if your actions led to the loss of our baby.'

Mathilde felt a slow shudder run through her body. She was left in no doubt of the threat. She told herself that she believed him about the woman Renée Poulin. She told herself this because she was his wife and she was pregnant with their child and because she was frightened and wanted to believe him. Otherwise . . .

She had made a great many mistakes, Mathilde knew that now. Léo had changed her life in countless ways. He had brought her love, passion and her family whom she adored. But she had been weak and that had been the biggest mistake of all. Because that mistake had led to so many more.

CHAPTER 40

Colette

Louise had insisted on picking her up from Exeter airport and was there to meet her when she arrived. She had tried to call Mark but couldn't get an answer; hopefully he'd ring her back so that she could at least tell him she'd be there in Cornwall late this afternoon. By necessity, it would be a flying visit. Last night, looking down into the still blue waters of Sauzon harbour, watching the boats come in, the harbour master in his red inflatable, swerving his practised pathway around them . . . she had felt herself not really there on the island, but in some sort of limbo. Perhaps it was in her head. But there were things she had to do, and she needed to come back here to Porthleven to do them.

'We're sorry to lose you, of course,' Louise told her as they reached the outskirts of the town. 'It's been lovely having you in the house.'

'And lovely to be there, Louise, you've been great.' Colette stared out of the window, taking in the familiar landscape as they drove down Methleigh Bottoms (nowhere had names like

Cornwall, she thought ruefully) with the green stretch of Gala Park to their left.

'But we understand that you can't keep the studio on indefinitely.' She turned to Colette briefly before refocusing on the road ahead. 'Would it help if we let you keep it on at half price for a few months?'

'Oh, Louise, thank you.' Colette gave her a warm smile. In truth, paying rent for the studio while she wasn't working had used up most of her savings in the past weeks. 'It's so kind of you both.' And especially good of Louise to come and pick her up from the airport. It was a two-hour drive – she was an absolute star. Colette realised that she would miss her – in the years that she'd lived in Porthleven, Louise had become a friend almost without Colette realising it. 'But it's not just about the money.'

Louise nodded. 'And Mark's going ahead to London, you say?'

'Yes.' They turned left along the road by the harbour. There was Koto Kai's where they'd had their last dinner together before she left Porthleven, the glass studio and the letting office where Colette had worked until recently. Funny, she thought, but it seemed so long ago. 'It's a big step up the ladder,' she said. 'He deserves it.'

'Oh, yes, I'm sure he does.'

But Colette caught Louise's curious glance and she knew what she was thinking: how would Colette settle in London? Wouldn't she find it too different from the small-town atmosphere of Porthleven, the wild Cornish landscape, the proximity of the ocean in all its moods and colours?

They drove down Harbour Road and up Salt Cellar Hill, took a sharp right on to Peverell Terrace. It wouldn't be so easy to say goodbye, she knew that. This place had, after all, been home for a long time.

In the studio, Colette didn't hang around. Fortunately, the rooms were rented furnished; the only piece she owned was her grandmother's old rocking chair. She wanted to keep that – it could go in the car, she decided. There was plenty of other stuff too – it was amazing how much one could accumulate in two years. She began to go through it, trying to be as ruthless as possible. Soon, there was a sizeable rubbish pile (Adam had said he would help her get it to the tip), a charity shop pile and a 'to keep' pile. She would take two suitcases and the rocking chair back to Belle-Île, she decided; no more.

Mark called when she was right in the middle of it. 'Are you OK, darling?' he asked. 'Sorry it took me so long to get back to you. It's been really hectic . . .'

'I'm here,' she said.

'Here?'

'In Porthleven.' Colette stretched and looked out of the window. It was late – dusk was already drawing in over the harbour, and she should eat something soon. Her stomach was empty and she felt light-headed; she'd skipped lunch, she realised.

'In Porthleven?' he repeated as if he couldn't believe it. He wasn't in London already, was he? Surely, he would have said? Colette hoped she hadn't left it too long.

'Yes,' she said.

But: 'Oh my God, you're joking. How . . .? When . . .? Where are you? At your place?'

Colette had to laugh. 'I tried to let you know. I decided on the spur of the moment really.' Though it hadn't been a whim, not at all.

293

'But that's wonderful.'

'It'll be a really short visit.' Colette felt bad when she heard the enthusiasm in his voice. She hadn't been fair to Mark. She had upped and left with barely a day's notice and she had failed him when he'd told her about his new job, his great opportunity. She had been unable to tell him how long she'd be gone and she'd even failed to answer his marriage proposal. All this indecision . . . It wasn't like her, she usually knew what she wanted; she'd certainly known when she left Belle-Île at the age of eighteen. She'd known how she felt about the island and she'd known how she felt about her mother too. But now . . . It seemed that all her preconceptions were crumbling in front of her eyes. And she had to take action. 'Yes, I'm here at the studio,' she said. 'Can you come round?'

'Try and stop me,' he said.

Adam let Mark into the house and he ran up the steps to the studio. Colette met him at the door.

'Colette, darling!' He held out his arms and she walked into his embrace without hesitation. He was different here, she realised. On his own turf, his confidence didn't seem misplaced. He knew exactly who he was and where he was going.

She slipped out of his arms before he could kiss her. He took her hand. Frowned. 'Where's the ring?' he asked.

'Here.' She moved into the studio, retrieved it from a black velvet pouch that had once housed a favourite pair of earrings. She held it out to him.

He stared at the ring, at her. 'What . . .?' Then he looked behind her into the studio. 'You're clearing out your things.'

'It's pointless paying for a room when I'm not here,' she said.

'But where are you taking it all?' He looked hopeful. 'You could leave it at mine.'

This was even harder than she'd expected. 'I've decided to leave Cornwall, Mark,' she said. 'At least for now.' It hadn't been an easy decision, but at least she'd made it. She loved Porthleven, she had made friends here, she liked living in her studio facing the sea. Her mother had been born here and her grandparents had lived here most of their lives. But it wasn't the place Colette wanted to call home.

'So . . .?' He was frowning. 'Does this mean you'll be coming to London with me?' He looked at the ring she was still holding. 'Is it too small? Is that it?'

Colette shook her head. 'It fits perfectly, Mark,' she said. 'And I'm so sorry.'

She saw him struggling with this. Wanted to reach out to him, even to take the words back – but she couldn't. In some ways, she and Mark were on the same wavelength, but in other ways they were very different – too different to make a life together.

'You're turning me down? You're saying no?'

'I have to. I'm sorry.' She should have done it straight away, she knew that; she should never have given him hope. But should you marry someone because they're familiar, because they're safe, because you feel beholden? There were other reasons. But however long she looked at those reasons, they weren't enough.

'You don't want me?' It was the first time she had seen him look broken and it made her feel worse than ever. Why did she do this? Why did she hurt people? She'd hurt her mother too and hopefully it wasn't too late to try and rectify that. But what had Mark done – except look after her and support her and ask her to be his wife?

'I do love you,' she said. 'But not in the right way.'

'Then you don't,' he said mournfully.

Perhaps. 'I don't want to marry you,' she said. 'I'm sorry. I'm not ready to marry anyone. Perhaps I never will be ready to marry anyone.' She tried a bright laugh as if that might make it better, but she just sounded slightly hysterical. 'And I don't want to move to London. It's not me.'

'Then I won't go.' Mark slammed his palm down on the chest of drawers.

Colette flinched. This was what she'd been afraid of; this was the reason she knew she had to make the decision now. 'You have to go,' she said. 'It won't make any difference. I told you, I'm leaving Cornwall.'

His eyes narrowed. 'Where are you going? Back to your godforsaken little island?'

She stiffened. He was hurt, that was all. 'For now, yes,' she said. She would take her car with her this time – there would be nothing of her left in Cornwall. 'I'll look after Maman and the flower shop until . . . until the end. And then . . .' *Yes, Colette, what then?* 'And then I'll decide,' she said staunchly. 'Where I want to be. What comes next.'

'You're a fool,' Mark snapped. 'You've had an offer for the place, haven't you? You should take it. You're lucky that Lemaire chap came along. You might even do well out of it.'

'Please take the ring, Mark.' This was always going to be the hardest part. But she'd had to do it in person. No way was she going to refuse Mark in a text or a phone call; he deserved better than that. And the last thing she wanted was for him to come haring over to Belle-Île again to try and make her change her mind. This had to be done here and now.

He snatched it from her palm and shoved it in his pocket. 'Most girls would jump at the chance,' he growled.

Colette knew he felt bitter. But: 'Please don't.'

'I'm offering you a hell of a lot here, you know, Colette.'

'I know you are.' And perhaps she was a fool to turn it down. But she wanted him to leave now, leave her to get on with clearing out her life.

'I'm a bloody idiot,' he said. 'For ever thinking that you and I—'

'You're not.' She caught at his arm. 'We had a good time, Mark,' she said. 'We were happy.'

He shook his head, looked down at her hand until she let him go. 'I was a stopgap for you, that's all. You wanted someone to care for you when you were grieving for your grandparents and I was what you needed – then.'

Colette said nothing. It hadn't been exactly like that, had it?

'You never even wanted to move in with me . . .'

'I wasn't ready to.' Lovers didn't have to live together. They didn't have to stay together for ever. Sometimes they simply went their own ways.

'It seems you're never ready, Colette,' he muttered. A thought seemed to occur to him and his eyes narrowed. 'Is this about that bloke I caught you with?'

'Mark!' Colette flushed.

'So it is.' He looked triumphant now.

'No, of course it's not. I told you.' Colette could stamp her foot in frustration. But in a way he was right. It wasn't about Étienne exactly . . . But in truth, she had responded to him. She had felt – something, however insubstantial, however fleeting. And that wasn't right. How could it be? If she was in love with Mark she wouldn't even look at another man.

297

'I should have seen what you were. But I'm grateful to you for making your mind up – at last. Fact is, I'll be better off without you, Colette.' And with that, he stormed down the stairs and left the house, slamming the door behind him.

Yes, you probably will . . . Colette sighed. And she'd hoped they could still be friends.

'Are you all right, Colette?' It was Louise, calling up the stairs.

'Fine.' She sat down on the bed and let the tears fall. Why did endings always have to be so sad? She had hated doing it. And in a way Mark was right – she had led him on, she had needed him, she probably should have finished the relationship months ago. And she should never have worn his ring. But there was a time when it had seemed right, when she had hoped that he was the one. She wasn't sure when things had changed, when she had realised that perhaps Mark didn't want the real her, that she felt trapped, that she wanted more . . . Going to Belle-Île had clarified their relationship for Colette. Mark hadn't belonged there and he hadn't understood. She hadn't missed him nearly enough . . . And now, despite the tears, Colette felt a burden lifted. *First steps* . . .

CHAPTER 41

Élodie

Jacques was due to arrive this afternoon and Élodie could not settle to the driftwood puppets she was making. She'd found some small pieces with flaking paint in red and blue and was pleased with the effect. This was a new idea, a new way to get movement into her work. And she'd felt the need to move to a smaller scale, to get away from her animals for a bit. It was frivolous perhaps – this piece was more toy than decorative art – but it was different, and she knew it was important for her work to keep evolving.

Jacques. How long since he had been here? Two years? Three? It was a combination, she suspected, of him not wanting to bump into his father, and his wife Karine being unwilling to make the trip. But now . . . It was the first time since his marriage that he would be coming here alone and it was this that had unsettled Élodie. She had discussed it with her mother. *Has something happened? What could it be?* They didn't even know how long he would be staying – he hadn't said, perhaps because he didn't know. *Eh bien*, Élodie told herself, as she carefully worked with her chisel to mould the contours of the wood, *we shall find out very soon.*

An hour later, she heard the car bumping along the track and ran outside, eager for her first sight of him. The car drew closer – going much too fast, he'd probably get a puncture on that stony surface, and that was Jacques all over: a risk taker, a devil-may-care. Élodie smiled and waved. She could see him in the driver's seat now, he waved back and she ran towards him, propelled by some force she had no hope of understanding.

He braked, flung open the car door, jumped out and caught her in his arms. 'Élodie.' He buried his face for a moment in her hair.

She stroked his dark head – his hair was longer than before, curling around the collar of the pale-green cotton shirt he wore – inhaled the scent of him which had hardly changed, though it was masked by a new citrussy aftershave. 'Jacques,' she whispered.

He laughed and lifted his head to look at her.

She held his face and laughed back. The same Jacques – velvet-brown eyes, tanned face, easy smile. A few more lines perhaps . . . She traced them with her fingertip. And there was a certain unkempt look about him – the dark shadow of stubble around his jaw rather suited him. 'It's good to see you.' An understatement if ever there was one.

'And you, *ma soeur*. You are beautiful as ever.' For a moment, he was serious, his eyes grave. And then the moment passed and he grabbed her hand. 'Come. Get in the car. Let's go see Maman.'

Élodie ran around to the passenger seat, feeling light as air. How she had missed him – the look of him, his voice, the touch of his hand. Her childhood companion, her dearest brother.

300

'So, I want all the news.' He sneaked a sidelong look at her. 'How is she?'

'Mama? Oh, pretty well, I think.' There had certainly been a sense of peace since their father had left – in the Old Lighthouse and in Élodie's studio too. Her mother went about her business as always, but she seemed more thoughtful, as if she were coming to terms with her new life – but still reflecting on the old.

'She's not sad then, to see him go?' Jacques frowned and Élodie knew exactly what he was thinking – if their mother wasn't sad to see their father go, then why hadn't she told him to leave years before?

Élodie placed a hand over his on the steering wheel. 'It took a long time for her to find the courage, Jacques,' she told him. 'She's been dominated by him for so long. You know how it is.'

'How it *was*,' he said.

'Yes, "was".' And yet still Jacques was like a child, she thought. He still minded that their mother hadn't chosen him rather than their father when Jacques had made her choose. He'd probably never truly forgive her for that. 'It's complicated, *n'est-ce pas*?' she said. 'Marriage.'

He gave her another long look. 'Later,' he said. 'First, let's see Maman.'

They drove up to the house and Élodie wondered how he saw it, this place of his childhood. No longer a lighthouse and yet not just a house . . . White and grey with a tall tower, a weathervane and a pale-red dome that betrayed its history. Forever isolated, always serene – even in the storms that hit their part of the coastline. Around it, the wind could shriek and the sea could smash into the rocks. But the Old Lighthouse had weathered every storm. It had stayed solid and invincible.

301

They got out of the car and Élodie ran her fingers over the white stone wall. It was warm to the touch.

Inside, Jacques happily submitted to his mother's hugs and kisses and allowed himself to be spoiled by them both. Mathilde had prepared a massive late lunch of salad, meats and cheeses with bread and pickles and they ate this together with a bottle of fruity red Bergerac, chatting of this and that – but not about why he was here or what might happen next. They talked about the children too and Jacques showed them recent pictures on his phone of both Nicole and Raphaël. 'They are growing so fast,' Mathilde said wistfully. 'I wish . . .'

'Soon, Maman, I will bring them to see you soon.'

'And how is Karine?' their mother asked.

Jacques drummed his fingers on the wooden table. 'We have decided to separate,' he said.

'Oh, my love.' Mathilde reached for his hand. 'I am so sorry. What happened between you?'

Jacques glanced across the table at Élodie. She sat very still and watched him. 'Karine and I were never love's young dream.' He broke off a piece of crusty white bread and chewed it thoughtfully. 'We were attracted to each other in the beginning, of course, but we married on a whim.'

'On a whim?' Mathilde stared at him in surprise. 'But why?'

'Why do people get married who really shouldn't be together at all?' he shot back at his mother. 'It happens, *non*?'

'Yes, of course.' Mathilde seemed flustered. 'But I thought you loved her. I thought you were happy.'

'Happiness, *merde*!' Jacques pushed back his chair. 'What is it, really? What do you think, Maman?'

Élodie frowned. She hoped he had not come back to continue haranguing their mother. She understood how much strength it had required for her to break the grip of their father's domination. What more did Jacques want from her now?

'I married Karine because I was unhappy,' Jacques said. 'And because I thought she could make me happy – there's a difference.'

Mathilde nodded. 'I see.' But her eyes were sad.

Élodie said nothing. But she reached out a hand and placed it over her mother's. And received a grateful smile in return.

'It's ironic really.' Jacques laughed but there was no humour in it. 'I hated my father because he was such a dictator, and then I married someone who turned out to be a female version.'

'You also had two children,' Élodie reminded him. Although she adored her brother, in her opinion Jacques had always found it a little too easy to shrug off his responsibilities.

'*Oui, les enfants!*' Mathilde gasped. 'What about the children, Jacques?'

He shrugged, but Élodie was not fooled. She knew Jacques and, responsible or not, she knew how much he loved his children. 'Karine will have custody, *naturellement*,' he said. 'I can see them every other weekend.'

'Is it enough?' Élodie asked.

He met her steady gaze. 'It has to be enough,' he said.

'And what about your job?' Mathilde asked. 'Is that still going well?'

'Maman, it never went well.' Jacques picked up the bottle of wine and refilled his glass. 'I am an accountant because I am good at figures – no more, no less.'

'You've left the company?' Élodie guessed. She could see it in his face – a sort of desperation.

'I'll find another job.'

'But, *les enfants* . . .'

Jacques pushed his chair further back from the table. 'I cannot help that, Maman,' he snapped. 'Don't you hear what I'm saying? I've left my job and Karine has the house. For now, I have nothing. Nothing.' Once again, he put the glass to his lips.

Élodie shot her mother a warning look. It was perhaps odd, but because her father had been so volatile, she and her mother had almost let themselves forget that Jacques had inherited so much of that volatility. He was not so arrogant and he was certainly not violent, but there were strong similarities; he was his father's son. They would find out more, of course, when Jacques was good and ready, but for now, they should change the subject.

'I wrote and told you that Thea is very ill,' Élodie said.

'You did.' Jacques's expression grew grave. 'How is she?'

'Not so good.' Élodie glanced at her mother. There was no obvious reaction but Mathilde was like that – most of her emotions were kept under the surface, it was the way she maintained control. Élodie turned back to her brother. 'Would you like to go and see her this afternoon? We don't really know . . .' *How long she has left*, she was going to say. But she found herself unable to voice it quite so starkly.

'Sure.' Jacques's face brightened, though his eyes remained sad. 'Poor Thea. Will she remember me, do you think?'

'Of course she will.' Élodie smiled. How could anyone forget Jacques?

'She saved your life once,' said Mathilde, quite out of the blue.

They stared at her.

'What do you mean, Maman?' Jacques leaned forward across the table.

Mathilde's face took on a faraway look. 'You and I were

304

on the beach, Jacques. I was pregnant . . .' She smiled sadly at Élodie. 'And then, Jacques, you went into the water.'

'Always the adventurer,' Élodie teased.

'I fell asleep, my darling.' There were tears in Mathilde's eyes now as she gazed at him. 'I had been sleeping badly, I'd taken something, the sun was so hot. But there's no excuse, none at all, it was unforgivable.' Her words came out in a rush. 'Thea came down from the house and saw you. She waded in, pulled you out of the sea and managed to get the water out of your lungs by slapping your back.' Mathilde paused for breath. Her hands were shaking. 'She saved your life, Jacques.'

'Wow.' Élodie was impressed. 'Good for Thea.' She hadn't heard this story before. And it made it even more surprising that her mother would continue to hold a grudge against her. Thea had saved Jacques's life and Thea had most probably not slept with Mathilde's husband. So, what in God's name did Mathilde have against Thea? Why did she hate her so?

'Absolutely.' Jacques lifted his glass in a toast. 'Even more reason to go and see her then, eh, Élodie?'

'I never wanted you to know.' Their mother still seemed upset. She was wringing her hands. 'I felt so bad about it. Can you ever forgive me, Jacques?'

'Of course I can, Ma.' He winked. 'I already have. Perhaps I should blame Élodie instead for keeping you awake at night.'

'Élodie?' Their mother seemed confused. And then her brow cleared. 'Ah, yes, I see.'

Élodie reached out to squeeze her mother's arm. She had noticed, lately, that Mathilde's thoughts were muddled sometimes. 'It's all past now, Mama,' she said. 'Don't worry.'

'So, shall we go and see her together, Élodie?' Jacques got to his feet and pushed back his chair. 'Just like the old days, eh?'

'Why not?' But there was a glitter to his eyes that worried Élodie. Jacques wasn't well, she was sure of it. He had told her that he was at odds with himself. But he had also said that he needed to talk to someone who understood. She was that person and always had been.

'Will you come, Maman?' Jacques extended a hand to their mother.

'Not today.' She said this a little too quickly. She got to her feet and began clearing the table. 'But you two go – yes, why not? And please . . .'

'Yes, Maman?' Élodie paused. This was progress – of sorts.

'Send Thea my regards.'

They decided to walk to Sauzon. 'Just like the old days,' Jacques said again. But Élodie knew that nothing was like the old days; that might be what Jacques wanted to think, but it was an illusion. She glanced back at the Old Lighthouse on the Pointe. It was lit up by the afternoon sun, stark against the vivid blue of the sky.

'You never liked Karine, did you?' Jacques asked her as they walked along the sparse grass of the coastal path.

'What makes you think that?'

'I knew and she sensed it.'

'We're very different.' Élodie had tried. She had made an effort with Jacques's wife, but found no warmth, nothing she could relate to. She gazed out towards the ocean, watched a fishing boat negotiate its delicate way around a rocky outcrop and out to sea.

'And she was jealous, of course.'

'Jealous? Of our closeness, do you mean?'

'*Mais oui*,' he said smoothly. 'But what was it you didn't like about her, Élodie?'

Élodie began to feel slightly uncomfortable. She had never been uncomfortable with Jacques and yet it had been a long time. She wasn't used to these kinds of conversation. She was used to walking this path alone, used to watching the cormorants dive into the waves, the swallows returning in spring. She was used to just thinking. 'I suppose I worried that she was controlling you,' she said at last.

He let out a short laugh. 'Oh, she tried.'

'Though of course there is always one person in every relationship who is the stronger,' Élodie went on. 'And one person who is more accommodating. Not everyone likes confrontation. Nor is everyone good at compromise.'

She had expected Jacques to laugh and tease her as he certainly would have done once upon a time, but he turned on her almost with a snarl. 'And what makes you such an expert, little sister?' he asked. 'How many men have you had relationships with?'

'Not many,' she admitted. A few disastrous dates and a couple of short relationships that had turned out to be only friendships. When she was younger, she had made some effort. Lately, not so much. With every man she met there was always something missing. 'But you know, I like to think that I am an observer of human nature.' She looked down at the ground.

He took her arm. 'Yes, you are. Sorry, my dear. You are very wise, I know that.'

Élodie smiled as she half-turned towards him. 'And you know, there aren't many eligible men around here.'

Behind them, the Old Lighthouse was now small in the distance. She thought she could see her mother standing outside, but was that even possible from here? The path hugged the coastline; way below lay one of the rocky bays carved from granite which she and Jacques had explored many times. She could see the deep chasms in the rocks, the sea fizzing and foaming through every crack. There was no one else around, the path was deserted. Like the old days indeed. Élodie took his arm and they continued walking, more slowly now. They took the fork of the path that led them gradually away from the coast towards stubbled yellow fields with bales of hay and the first smattering of houses visible in the distance.

'You could go further afield.' He glanced across at her. 'You could go over to the mainland.'

'Like you did?' He thought life was so simple: do what you want to do. But there was her mother to think of. And besides, her work was here, her studio, the landscape she loved.

'Not necessarily to live.' He paused and they both stopped to look around them, at a field of golden barley swaying in the breeze, at the rolling sea now in the distance, the endless sky. 'You could visit the mainland more often. You can meet people when you visit places.' He nudged her to show that although he was teasing, he knew and understood her solitary nature. 'You could take your work to other galleries, other places on the mainland.'

'I could.' Élodie thought of the business card Colette had given her. What was his name, that man? He had loved the driftwood horse, Colette had said. She had tucked the card away somewhere. But . . .

'You should, Élodie.' Jacques sounded very sure. 'It's not good to hide yourself away like this. Not all the time.'

'Perhaps I will.' She picked up pace as they reached the out-skirts of Sauzon. She might surprise him, surprise herself too.

CHAPTER 42

Étienne

This morning, Étienne had written a whole chapter – just under two thousand words – of his new thriller. He'd printed it out and read it back to himself. Then pressed Delete on his keyboard and torn up the pages. He decided to go for a walk instead, along the path by the mudflats that wound along to the Neptune Hotel and on past the oyster beds. He needed to do something.

He shut the front door of the cottage, thinking as he always did that it was in the perfect location – even if not perfect for writing, right now . . . And that he loved it. It was a two-bedroomed fisherman's cottage built in 1821 and it faced the sea, the large expanse of sand and mud, with boats moored in the harbour beyond. In the garden in front of the cottage, lavender, fuchsia and oleander grew alongside a walnut tree, and there was a small stone outhouse draped with lichen and moss which had once been used for washing and gutting fish. He knew this because it had been his grandparents' cottage, on his father's side, and it was Étienne's inheritance when they died. The place was special.

His grandfather had worked the oysters as had his father – in the old days all producers came to the trade that way, though it was a desperate living – but *Grand-père* had fished too in the barren summer months, and Étienne's grandmother had planted up the garden so that the scents of the flowers mingled with the sharp whiff of the sand, the ripeness of the fish and shellfish, all combining in the salty air.

The trouble was, Étienne thought, as he swung out of the gate and along the path, his total inability to focus on this book. Usually, he didn't have to try. Once he started, it was simply there; it became part of his consciousness, as real as his other reality, a place he went off to for a few hours every day, momentarily dazzled and confused when he came back from that world in order to get on with the rest of his life.

He passed the Neptune Hotel, which was a bit run down but had an old-fashioned café where he went to sit sometimes for a change of scenery, with low beams, stone walls and a great view of the sea. *Behind the Night*, he had called the book, which had seemed an evocative, even enigmatic, title to begin with and now sounded ridiculous. Night was night; there was nothing behind it, not really, only things that happened in it – usually bad things, if he had anything to do with it.

Étienne was now walking along the sea wall where stone steps led down to the beach. Although it was by the sea and close to the island, being in the Gulf of Morbihan, this landscape was very different from Belle-Île. This was very much a working beach. The water lapped gently enough across the sand and low rocks. There was a rectangular sea pool with bigger stones around the edge where the water was still as a millpond – a *bassin* for the oysters – and small wooden boats dragged ashore to sit in the mud amongst the trails of green and brown seaweed until the next fishing trip. There was all the paraphernalia for shellfish farming – always had been. Clams, whelks, mussels – their shells littered everywhere. And the oysters. Always the oysters.

As far as the thriller went, Étienne had done everything right. He had thought about his plot last night directly before going to sleep – this was a technique he'd used over the years that brought several consequences. One, it was a quiet time, a still time and so – if he was lucky – random thoughts could pop into his head and help him with a plot hiccup. Two, it planted his story in his mind so that it could (ideally) germinate during the sleeping hours, the idea being that in the morning the premise would be fully formed or a plot problem smoothed away, allowing him to write fluently for a few precious hours the following day. Three, it sent him off to sleep. And Étienne valued his sleep.

Beyond the working boats – fishing craft and flat-bottomed barges used for the shellfish – Étienne could see yachts and pleasure boats way out in the Gulf. He paused to take in the scene. A series of knobbly peninsulas reaching into the ocean like twisted fingers, the Gulf of Morbihan offered little coves, bays and muddy estuaries in which the cherished oysters could thrive.

For his father, being 'in the oysters' meant permanently watching the weather – hours the old man would spend staring out to sea worrying about the predators that might finish off his precious catch. Starfish were the worst, he'd told Étienne. 'They can't finish an oyster off quickly, see. They hug and they hug – exhausting it in a long and futile fight.' Étienne shivered. His father's story made him think about quarrelling lovers destined to die like Romeo and Juliet, Tristan and Isolde.

This morning, he had also made notes in his exercise book – how he saw the chapter developing, what his protagonist (Troy – perhaps that name was a mistake, perhaps the character was impossible to take seriously?) was thinking and feeling, how the story would progress.

Étienne made himself a pot of strong coffee, switched on his laptop and . . . found himself thinking about that other damned story, the one he went back to every time he returned to Belle-Île. Undeterred, he swept it from his mind and wrote the opening chapter of *Behind the Night* – determinedly, for almost two hours. But when he read it back . . . It wasn't going in the right direction, it lacked tightness, it wasn't even bloody interesting. So he tore it up.

He grinned at the little seabirds running along the shoreline amongst the rocks. There was something so comical about the way they hurried to escape the approaching tide just in time. A pine tree in a garden hung over the low path that was also a wall, and he ducked. He had to get that other story out of his head, that was the thing – and there was only one way he knew of. It was lurking like some prehistoric creature, lumbering after him whenever he so much as closed his eyes. There was no doubt in his mind. *Merde*. He had to finish the bloody thing.

He'd left it there, in his mother's house, in the desk drawer, thinking that this would stop him dwelling on it, and more crucially, writing more of it, of course. Étienne noticed the swallows diving. The gulls too. They were after the leftovers from the oyster shells, crab shells, tiny shellfish too small to be of interest to any other being. If he didn't have the manuscript, how could he write it, how could it affect his life? (Hah!)

Though of course this nameless story belonged to Belle-Île, not Locmariaquer; he wasn't sure he would ever be writing

312

any of it here. He hadn't been able to chuck it, though, like all the stuff he'd cleared out of his mother's place – a collection hoarded over the years, everything from lace antimacassars to ceramic vases, to a driftwood shark which he'd decided to keep after all and had hung over the doorway as a sort of ironic welcome to visitors. It had made him laugh, anyway. Yes. Étienne would have to rescue his manuscript before the sale went through, but that was weeks, maybe even months, away.

He passed the oyster shack, the fishponds of Locmariaquer, and smiled, thinking of his father. Having given his own life to the oysters, it had been hard for him to understand that his son might want something different. 'What you want is neither here nor there,' he had said. But things were different now – and fortunately for Étienne, he had rather more say in his destiny than his father would have liked.

The path was now at one with the beach. Back on the mudflats, a few people passed by with their knives and baskets as Étienne supposed they had always done – ankle-deep in the muddy sand, looking for wild mussels, clams, crayfish from the tidal ponds. In the distance a motorboat sped through the water puncturing the smooth mirrored sea.

Étienne continued through to the yard of the sailing club, and on to where the path became softer and earthier, lined with long grass, approaching a tall row of pines. He climbed up the steps to the viewpoint area where an orange buoy signalled the entrance to the Gulf and the sea surged back and forth, draining and filling according to the tide. A small statue of a woman and child looked out to sea, waiting for their man to return. Same old story, he thought. He leaned on the wooden rail. Sometimes this view was hazy, sometimes clear. From here to the southwest he could make out the blurred outline that was Belle-Île. At any rate, there was a pleasing sense of openness here. Étienne looked towards the arc of the beach in the distance, where holiday pursuits replaced oysters and children built castles in the sand.

A girl was walking across the shore towards him and he thought about Colette. It struck him that he'd been spending a bit too long thinking about her. What was going on? Why should he give a moment's thought to a free-spirited girl running a flower shop on a godforsaken island, who was about to be married to some arrogant English bastard? He had to laugh at himself. It was crazy, but he kept thinking of her sad dark eyes and that contrary spring to her step. She was just an island girl with a way of reaching out to him, but he'd missed a chance with her — a chance of telling her what had really happened that summer on Belle-Île, of explaining why it haunted him still. He didn't even want a girlfriend, though. And he certainly didn't want one who was engaged to someone else. But there was something about her. She was present, he thought. Every time he had ever seen her, ever talked to her, she was fully there in that moment. And that, somehow, had imprinted her on his mind.

His mobile rang and Étienne pulled it out of his jeans pocket. He reluctantly decided to take the call. It was Monsieur Morel, the buyer of his mother's house. He should go through the *notaire* of course, but he had a habit of cutting out the 'man in the middle' as he liked to put it. Étienne would put it another way: the man was a control freak. But since he had little time for Monsieur le Notaire himself, he didn't object. '*Oui?*'

He listened while Morel launched into his monologue, thought for a moment of the impression of the man he'd done for Colette up on the cliff path in Sauzon. She'd really laughed, her eyes had lit up, and he'd thought — couldn't help thinking

314

– wouldn't it be great to do that more often, make someone laugh like that? Dumb, eh?

Étienne suddenly realised what Morel was saying. He'd had a survey done – '. . . but of course, *naturellement*, with an old property one has to make all the checks, *n'est-ce pas*?' – and there were problems with damp.

'Everywhere on Belle-Île has problems with damp,' Étienne pointed out. He continued along the beach where the dunes started to rise and the landscape changed once again. And this was one of the beauties of Locmariaquer. There was a sense of space here too, of timelessness. It was in the desolate landscape – the stone, the slate, the dunes, the *menhirs*. This morning he had woken to the usual sea mist, so delicate, as if clinging to the coastline by gossamer threads. The light – as it gradually filtered through – was green and silver and he'd wished he could paint it, not just write about it.

'You think so?'

'It's the nature of Belle-Île,' he told Morel. It was the way the seas pounded into the harbour only metres away from the house, the spray and the rain lashing into the walls and against the windows and shutters. The manner in which the wind howled and blew its salty, whistling pathway into every tiny crevice and crack. All that was during the winter, of course. In the summer, thankfully, it was very different.

'Even so,' said Monsieur Morel, 'the problems, they have to be fixed. Air bricks, a new damp course . . . And then there is the roof.'

'The roof?' The sea was very calm and the sun was glinting on its glassy surface. Étienne noticed that there were people swimming. Perhaps he too should take a dip? He was tempted. But no – he should be at home writing, after all.

'*Mais oui*. You must have noticed some slates have blown off. These need to be replaced, at the very least. My surveyor thinks a new roof will be in order within two years.'

Étienne was already bored with this conversation. A writer should be free to follow the tracks of his imagination. Instead, he must worry about slates and roof and damp. No wonder he could not get on, hey? 'So, what are you saying, Monsieur?'

'I am suggesting that we adjust the price of the property in order to take these new findings into account,' he said.

'Hardly new findings,' Étienne tore his fingers through his hair and stared moodily towards the trees on the far promontory of Pointe de Kerpenhir. 'The place was for sale as seen. I never pretended it was perfect.'

'Perhaps,' said Monsieur Morel. 'But even so . . .'

'What price are you suggesting?' Sometimes Étienne just felt like giving the damned house away. But then he would recall his mother's face – her joy when after years of slaving away in the oyster trade, her husband was made foreman and earned more money and they were able – with the help of the sale of her mother's house inherited after her death – to buy a small holiday home on Belle-Île, her dream. His mother had given up working in the oyster trade then – his father had persuaded her. 'I will not see you crippled by it,' he had said to her, and Étienne was glad. It had been a hard trade, a punishing trade. The hands of the oyster-workers were raw, swollen and chilblained, cut and deformed by constant salt water and handling rough shells.

Monsieur Morel named a figure substantially lower than the figure previously agreed.

'*Bordel de merde!*' Étienne swore. Yes, he wanted to get rid. *Sorry, Maman*. But that was taking the piss. 'Forget it,' he told

Morel. He glanced back at the broad arc of the beach and began to make his way up to the top of the dunes.

'*Comment?*' Morel was clearly taken aback. 'You are telling me that now you do not want to sell?' He sounded outraged, as if it were Étienne who had created this problem and decided to back out of the arrangement.

'At that price, *non*,' Étienne said staunchly. The sun was ahead of him now and he pulled his shades out of his pocket. He'd put the place up for sale again. Where was the problem? He'd go back over there. After all, he had left a part of himself in the drawer of the desk. And he had to pick it up sometime. He had to finish it sometime, he reminded himself, trying not to wince at the thought. So that he could move on.

'Then perhaps we should discuss the matter further,' said Morel. 'Surely we can come to a compromise . . .'

Now that I have called your bluff . . . All of a sudden, Étienne almost hated this man. That house had been his mother's dream and he didn't want Morel to have it. He wasn't right for the place. He was too petty, too mean-spirited. He simply couldn't imagine Monsieur Morel flinging open the shutters and greeting the harbour, the morning, the pretty girl in the flower shop . . .

Étienne would have liked to show her this beach, the high grassy dunes so different from the rocky outcrops on the island. He would have liked to maybe eat some oysters with her, experience that fresh, briny taste with someone he sensed would appreciate it. This thought surprised him. Bloody fool.

'I do not think so, *non*,' he said. And he continued along to the spot where the road ended, where the standing stones continued to stand as timeless as the Gulf itself, the oysters, the ocean.

'*Eh bien*,' said Monsieur Morel, for the first time sounding rather unsure of himself. 'This is most irregular. I will of course contact the *notaire*, but—'

'Do as you like. The deal's off.' Étienne ended the call.

He felt a rush of adrenalin, a surge of excitement. He'd go back to the island – right away. OK, he was behaving like a jack-in-the-box, but his mother was right. 'It happened, Étienne,' she had said. 'Worse things happen, you know.'

And yes, he knew about all that too. He had grown up with Breton stories, tales of hardship and heartache, and he had borne witness to how difficult it could be to make a living. But Locmariaquer was a charmed location in so many ways, lying on the placid Gulf of Morbihan as it did, and increasing experimentation and mechanisation had changed the oyster business considerably. His father would look at the way things were now, mind, and most likely he would turn in his grave.

'Yes, Maman,' he whispered. 'Hard things happen.'

'And now you must get over it.' She had said that too. Perhaps that was why she had always kept the place, always tried to get him over to the island, to face up to those shadows. That was more or less what he'd told Colette, more or less what he believed. But that didn't mean it was possible.

Étienne reached the dolmen. The prehistoric burial chamber had ancient inscriptions and a flat roof consisting of a huge slab of granite. He sat down on the ledge at the entrance and put through a call to Didier. 'I need an extension,' he said, once they'd exchanged the usual pleasantries.

'It's not going well?'

'There's something I need to write first,' he said. He might as well admit it. 'I need to get it off my chest.'

'A different genre?' Étienne could almost hear Didier's frown.

'Something personal,' he said.

'Autobiography?'

'Not in a commercial sense,' Étienne clarified before Didier's money-making brain could go into overdrive.

'I don't know,' Didier said. 'I'll speak to them. I'll do my best. But it's an indulgence—'

'It's not an indulgence,' Étienne cut in, 'it's something I have to do, *mon ami*.' Otherwise I might never write another bloody book, he thought. He ran his palm along the smooth grey stone of the dolmen. Who had built this? How had the stones been transported and erected? What had this place been like in those ancient days? How could anyone really know? All the time his mother was alive and Étienne stayed in Locmariaquer he could almost ignore the past; at least he could put it to one side. But as soon as he went over there himself, as soon as he walked those cliffs and found himself near that place . . . It had returned to him even more powerfully than ever before. The writing he had begun there told him that much, if nothing else.

'*D'accord*.' Didier could obviously tell how important this was. 'Get on with it then, Étienne. Soonest, eh?'

'Soonest.' He'd go back to Belle-Île and he'd face up to the shadows. His mother's house not selling was a sign. Meeting Colette was another. Because, yes, what had happened was and always would be unforgivable. But until he faced up to the past and the fact that he had done it . . . He had the feeling that he wouldn't be going anywhere.

CHAPTER 43

Colette

Colette parked the car outside the house and went straight inside. Her mother was awake, and she could hear Francine moving around in the little kitchen at the back.

'Hello, Maman.' It might be her imagination but she sensed her mother had grown even more frail in these past few days while she'd been away.

'Colette.' She brightened, lifted her head a little from the pillow and smiled a tired smile. 'It is so good to see you, *chérie*.'

'And you, Maman.' And she realised that it was true.

Francine came to stand in the doorway, drying her hands on her wrap-around apron. 'There you go, Thea,' she said briskly. 'I told you she'd be back soon.'

But Colette saw a crease of concern on Francine's face. '*Bonjour*, Francine,' she said. 'How has she been?'

Francine nodded. 'Pop by later,' she said. 'I'll fill you in.' She untied her apron strings. 'But for now, I'll give you two a bit of time alone.'

'*Merci*.' Colette noticed that her mother's lips were cracked and dry and the soreness in her mouth and throat was preventing her from talking very much, so she consulted her book of flower remedies that she was now keeping handy in the kitchen and got busy – making some mint tea and a mouthwash.

She held the straw to her mother's lips as she sipped.

'I saw Élodie,' she whispered when Colette had taken the cup away. 'I saw Jacques and Élodie.'

'That's nice.' Colette sat by the bed holding her mother's hand. She smoothed her wispy hair from her brow. Her forehead felt damp to the touch. Colette was glad that Élodie had come over. And Jacques Blaise was visiting too. It was good of them both.

Her mother's eyes had grown misty. 'Now that his father has gone . . .' Her voice drifted.

Colette mentally finished the sentence for her. Now that his father had gone, Jacques might be free to return. He had nothing against his mother or sister. Quite the contrary. According to Élodie, it was Léo he'd fallen out with, Léo who had kept him away. 'What about his wife and family?' she asked. Not to mention his job.

But all she got in reply was one of her mother's shrugs – so weak and insubstantial that it was hardly there, but Colette recognised it just the same.

When Colette left her to sleep and went to speak with Francine, her fears were confirmed. 'Something has changed,' Francine said. 'Her breathing, it is slower, more difficult for her. It won't be long now, my dear.'

Colette reached out, held the other woman in an awkward embrace. Francine was a good neighbour, had been a fine friend to her mother. Without her . . .

321

'She will soon be released.' Francine nodded as she drew away.

'Yes.' Because this was how she was determined to think of it too. She hated to think of her mother in pain. When she was ready to go, Colette hoped that her mother could just slip away peacefully one night, and that she, Colette, would be able to be glad for her.

While her mother was sleeping, Colette went to get her things from the car. She pulled the biggest suitcase from the boot with some difficulty. It was heavy. She lugged it from the pavement to the front door and went back for the second. Then the rocking chair. It wasn't big – her grandmother had been a dressmaker and it had been her sewing chair – but it had a small drawer under the seat and was awkward.

'Can I help you with that?'

She peered through the rocking chair runners. It was Étienne, grinning widely – presumably at her predicament – and already gently pulling the chair from her grasp. '*Merci*.'

He left it with the cases by the front door and returned to the other side of the car. They eyed each other warily over the top of it. 'Moving in more permanently, are you?' He raised an eyebrow.

'No choice,' she told him, not quite truthfully. 'I had to move out of my studio flat in Cornwall.' And it was rather sad – that this chair was about all she had to show for it. Porthleven had been good to her. She had enjoyed living there and relished the sense of family roots she had found in the small town. But she had also known that it was time to leave. Now that her grandparents were gone and she'd broken up with Mark there wasn't enough left to keep her there.

She realised that Étienne was still looking curious. No doubt he was wondering why she hadn't simply left her things with Mark in England. She decided not to elaborate. 'What are you doing back here anyway?'

He shrugged. 'The sale of the house fell through.' He looked beyond her to the mint-green shutters of his mother's house. She turned. The shutters were open. In the window was a desk covered with papers. It looked as if someone had left the room very suddenly. It also looked as if that someone was very occupied.

'Wrong person?' They exchanged a smile. Colette thought of what he'd told her on the cliff top – about his mother, who definitely wouldn't have approved of the fastidious Monsieur Morel.

'Wrong person.' He came round to her side of the car, stood very close. Colette was taken aback. She hadn't thought for a second that he would be here in Sauzon – again – and yet there was also an inevitability about it, as if perhaps their paths had been destined to cross. Rubbish, she told herself firmly. Absolute rubbish. He was still just a visitor, still trying to sell his mother's house so that he could be free of the place. And as far as Étienne was aware, she was engaged to another man. She steadied her breathing. But despite all this . . .

Étienne took her left hand and examined it. His touch was warm. 'No ring,' he said.

'No ring,' she confirmed.

Once again, he raised an eyebrow. 'Wrong person?'

She had to laugh. 'Wrong person.' Touché. So now they had another thing in common.

'So, shall I help you get this lot into the house?' He gestured at the cases and rocking chair still parked by the faded lilac front door.

'Please.' She realised that he was still holding her hand and she looked down at their two hands. His skin was a different shade of light brown to her own, more olive, more French, whereas Colette had her mother's colouring – dark brown hair and eyes but lighter skin. His hands were rougher than she would have expected for a writer, his fingers long, his nails square cut. He was dressed as usual in jeans, and a faded blue T-shirt with buttons at the collar, undone. He looked very at home here all of a sudden, Colette found herself thinking.

He let go of her hand but didn't move away. 'I wondered where you were. When did you get back?'

'This morning.' She'd arrived quite late in Roscoff last night, driven south and stayed overnight in Lorient before catching the early ferry from Quiberon.

'And how is your mother?' He seemed concerned.

'Very weak, I'm afraid.'

'I am sorry.' Étienne bent his head.

'Thank you.' Colette opened the front door and they started taking everything through.

'And has she told you any more of those secrets of hers?' Étienne murmured, when they were outside again.

'Not really.' Colette shook her head. Though there had been that mention of a diary. Had she really lost it? Or might it be here somewhere among her other belongings? Colette wouldn't hold out any hope. She picked up the last bag. 'And she seems to have so many.'

Étienne followed with the rocking chair. He glanced back and seemed to look beyond her, towards the sea perhaps. 'Secrets and tragedies,' he said softly. 'We all have them, *n'est-ce pas*?'

Colette remembered their previous conversation up on the

cliff. She had confided in him and yet he had closed up to her – just like one of his books. There was a dreaminess to him that reminded her of her mother. She did not want, she told herself firmly, any more secrets.

'And this?' He gestured towards the rocking chair still sitting at the bottom of the stairs. 'What shall we do with this?'

'I'm not sure.' Colette ran her fingers lightly over the oak patina. 'I'll move it when I decide. Thanks, Étienne.' She accompanied him to the door.

'Perhaps later . . .' he began.

'Later?'

'I have been thinking.' He frowned.

'Yes?'

He seemed to come to a decision. 'When you've settled in and done whatever else you have to do for your mother . . .' He held her gaze. As always, she was struck by the green clarity of his eyes – '. . . we could go for an afternoon stroll perhaps?' He paused. 'Is there someone who could sit with her?'

'Well, yes, but . . .' Colette hesitated. Francine wouldn't mind. And besides, Thea was sleeping so much of the time now. 'I've only just got back, so—' She caught the look on his face. 'Is it important?'

His mouth tightened. 'There is something I would like to say, something I would like to show you.'

Francine materialised from next door, nodding to Étienne as she did so. 'Monsieur.'

'Madame.' He shot her that smile of his.

'You look as though you could do with a bit of fresh air and exercise.' Francine addressed Colette. 'Travelling is tiring, *n'est-ce pas*? But we are sitting down the entire time, so we wonder how this can be.'

Colette blinked at her.

'Indeed,' said Étienne.

'Go for a walk, Colette.' Francine was almost shooing her away now. 'You will be back soon enough.'

'OK.' Colette wondered if she was venturing into dangerous territory. She straightened her back. She was intrigued. She was keen to see what he wanted to show her, hear what he wanted to say. But from now on, she would be in control, she decided. She would only go where she wanted to go. Nowhere else. Not any more.

CHAPTER 44

Colette

'So how did he take it?' Étienne asked her as they climbed the *sentier côtier*. Colette had no idea where they were going, but there was something; a glimmer of understanding dawning in her mind.

'Mark? Not well.' She glanced across at him. He had a sweater slung over his shoulders though it was still very warm. It was hard to believe that it was still only mid-July, that she had been on the island for only six weeks in total. And yet she remembered those summers on Belle-Île that had seemed to go on for ever. It would be another six weeks at least before the weather would close in and Belle-Île would become an entirely different place. And what of herself? Would she still be here?

She looked down. The sea was dark teal and shining, lit up by the yellow late afternoon sun. She knew this change would come; hadn't she seen it throughout her years growing up here? But sometimes there was little warning; the breeze would shift direction and the winds and rains of autumn would be upon them. But not yet, she reminded herself, not yet. Right now, she did not want that ever to happen.

'*Je suis désolé*. I'm so sorry to hear that.'

She glanced suspiciously across at him. He didn't look sorry in the least. 'It was my fault,' she said.

'How so?' He frowned.

'I should never have let him think I might say yes.' And that was the history of her relationship with Mark, thought Colette. They had often wanted to do different things and yet she had not spoken out enough, she'd been too weak, too compliant, she'd allowed herself to be railroaded too often. Until it came to the question of returning to Belle-Île to be with her mother. Mark had many good qualities – he was loving and he'd been supportive. But he didn't want her to be herself – she realised that now. He needed someone who would want to move to London, who would fully appreciate him and the importance of his career. And it had taken what had happened with her mother to make her see how wrong they really were for each other.

Étienne put a hand on her arm and Colette realised how fast she'd been walking, her feet keeping pace with the thoughts shooting through her brain. She slowed, glanced across at him ruefully. 'Sorry.'

'But at least you told him in person.' Étienne took his hand away and they continued walking at a slower pace. 'That was brave.'

It hadn't felt brave.

They'd reached the pine trees and she wondered again exactly where they were heading. Into the woods perhaps? She shivered, but he stayed on the coastal path. Still, Colette was glad she'd done it. She didn't even feel bad about losing

Mark. She felt stronger, freer. She had no idea what was ahead, but that was a good feeling too.

He smiled.

'What?'

'That swing in your step,' he said.

Colette smiled back at him. 'And why did you come back, Étienne?' she asked him. 'Not just to put more flowers in the house to make it look homely for prospective purchasers, surely?' The tease was a gentle one. He was unpredictable but she was confident he could take it.

'I needed to come back because of unfinished business,' he said. 'A bit like you perhaps.'

So many parallels, she thought. It was almost uncanny. 'Because you haven't finished writing that story?' He hadn't told her that he was writing it exactly – but she'd seen the evidence on the other side of the shutters. And she remembered what he had said before. *A real story, something that's written from the heart*. Was that what this was all about?

'That's part of it, yes.' He paused, glanced out towards the ocean. They had left Sauzon behind; they were walking alongside the turquoise coves with the jagged rocks, heading towards Pointe du Cardinal. 'That's what I wanted to explain to you. The story I seem to need to write is about what happened here on Belle-Île. I guess I have to be here to write it.'

Colette waited, but he didn't elaborate.

'When we get there.' He pointed ahead. To wherever 'there' might be . . .

'How long will you stay for this time?' she asked him. She watched a butterfly with brown speckled wings flit past.

'As long as it takes.'

As long as it takes to do what? she wondered. To write? To

come to terms with whatever he had to come to terms with? She had no idea and he clearly wasn't ready to tell her yet. She sneaked a look at him. 'And what about your thriller?' she asked. 'How's that going?' Could writers write two stories at the same time? It must be hard. She imagined it was a bit like being two different people.

'It's not.'

Ah. They couldn't then.

'What about you, Colette?' Étienne stopped walking as the path opened out into the Pointe. He turned to her once more. 'How long will you stay?' He made it seem like a loaded question.

'At least until my mother dies.' It was the first time she had spoken these words out loud. 'After that – I don't know.' They exchanged a look. So, he was staying until he wrote out his story and she was staying until her mother died. *For as long as it takes* . . . What a pair they were. And in the meantime? She hoped they could be friends. Colette liked his company, she knew that much. And she also knew there could be more between them. She was aware of it, like an undercurrent or the subtext of one of his stories, running just below the surface. But that would be in another place, another lifetime. The last thing she intended to do was launch herself into another relationship straight after breaking up with Mark. With her mother and the flower shop she already had too much on her mind. And for that, she needed to focus – and to be alone.

'So, here we are.' He looked around.

'Pointe du Cardinal,' she whispered.

There was a wild look in his eyes now and it was Colette's turn to put a hand on his arm. 'What is it, Étienne?' She kept her voice gentle. But it was all coming back to her, the tragedy

330

he had spoken of on the cliff when they were here before, the amount of time he spent up here on this coastal path as if daring himself to go further.

'Down here.' He began to scramble along the ghost of a narrow grassy path over the rocks and moorland. 'Come.' He held out his hand and she took it, followed him down the slope towards the edge of the cliff. And the memory of what had happened that summer came back to her as if it were yesterday. It had shocked them all to the core. The whole island had reverberated from it.

'Étienne . . .'

'I will tell you.' He took a deep breath. 'I will show you.' And he led her further down the rocky path, until they stood close, so close to the ravine.

CHAPTER 45

Mathilde

During the last few days, Mathilde had enjoyed having Jacques in the house. He saw to things that had been neglected, even before Léo had left. He chopped logs and kindling so that she would have a decent supply during the winter ahead, he fixed a picture back on the wall in her bedroom and put a new shelf up in the kitchen. Mathilde felt energised by his presence. She dusted and vacuumed the place, washed cushion covers and throws as if it were spring, put them on the line to dry and watched the squares of burnt orange, red and midnight blue billowing in the sea breeze. Now that Léo was gone, she found herself thinking, she could redecorate and bring a few more colours into the house to replace the white walls he'd always preferred. She clung to that thought – it was a cheering one.

After Jacques and Élodie had left to visit Thea the afternoon he'd arrived on the island, Mathilde had walked out of the house and watched them until they were out of sight. She went round to the back of the Old Lighthouse; stood in her usual place, her thinking place, the spot that meant so much to her, looking down at the cove where she had almost lost her son that day. If not for Thea . . . It was calm, the sea illuminated by millions of pinpricks of light, all moving, all shifting as the tide rolled in, as the waves splashed and curled around the rocks, creeping into the crevices, effervescent on the sand. The sky was clear, a dark, pure blue; she could hear the occasional seabird scooting and crying – otherwise there was simply the usual solitude that she had become so accustomed to. Solitude, but not always peace of mind.

Mathilde did not object to them seeing Thea. She had minded Élodie's visits there at first. She had been fearful, jealous even. But how could she mind now? Thea was dying, and besides, none of it had been her fault; she had given in to Mathilde's idea because she thought it was for the best, because she had nowhere else to turn. She had trusted Mathilde. Mathilde sighed and turned away. And this was how she had repaid her.

Sooner or later, she must address the situation. These things could not be put off for ever. Élodie had said that Thea was weaker. 'She won't be long for this world, Maman.' And although there was no word of reproach from her, Mathilde knew what Élodie was thinking. *If you are going to see her, if you are going to talk to her, you must do it now.*

Mathilde could not bring herself to read the next section of Thea's diary. She was not quite ready to remember. She felt the usual stab of guilt at reading any of it – after all, this diary was Thea's personal property, her own private account of what had gone on . . . But Mathilde had to know, she had to face it. So, she turned the pages until she came to the bit where Thea left the Old Lighthouse, the final part. Had Thea continued to write a diary after this one? Mathilde had never considered

333

that. But she thought not. The secret was Mathilde's to reveal. It would take strength – and she would have to consult with Thea of course – but she knew that she must do it. It had stayed hidden for long enough. Everybody deserved the truth.

Mathilde guessed what would be written in this part of the diary. She recalled only too well her own possessiveness, the way Léo bullied her – the children too, especially Jacques – and how she had been unable to control her jealousy. It had been a bad time. Mathilde had felt that Thea had betrayed her. She'd felt that Thea was trying to take what was hers – Léo, the children, her life here on Belle-Île. And so she had told her to leave. She had stolen this diary – it could tell too many stories of what had really gone on here that spring of 1970 – and she had destroyed the precious friendship between herself and Thea.

But perhaps, thought Mathilde, it wasn't too late to make it right.

Thea: March 1976

I was in the kitchen making coffee for me and Mathilde – this is unusual; these days she doesn't seem to want me to do anything for her at all – when Élodie ran in. Mathilde was sitting at the table but she ran past her to where I was standing at the stove. 'Look at my picture,' she crowed. 'Thea, look at my picture.'

I glanced at it, my attention half on the percolator. 'It's lovely, darling.' Usually, I'm around when she does this sort of thing, then I can get her to show Mathilde straight off. God knows, I don't want the situation between us to get even worse. Though the truth is, I don't know what to do. I'm at my wits' end. She's consumed with jealousy. It's driving me crazy. Why did I do it? Why? It was such a terrible, stupid mistake. I've never regretted anything in my life so much . . .

Mathilde stopped abruptly when she read these words. She had never known that Thea regretted it quite so much . . .

'It's us,' Élodie said. 'It's me, you and Jacques. And Mummy.'

I looked more closely then. The figure of Mathilde was standing a little way away from the other three. The figure seemed lonely, isolated, apart. It was unintentional on Élodie's part – but sometimes a child can see things without realising their significance. I knew in that second that Mathilde mustn't see her drawing.

'Hey, Élodie, why don't you show Maman that jigsaw we finished,' I said, clutching at straws, admittedly. 'Then I'll bring Maman's coffee into the sitting room, and we can—'

'Show me the picture, Élodie.' Mathilde can always read me like a book.

I sighed.

Élodie ran over to show her. Mathilde's face . . . It went pale and her mouth pinched up in that way it does and she grabbed Élodie with a desperation that always frightens her and makes her wriggle – which only makes it worse.

And then Léo walked in.

'How are my girls?' he bellowed. Élodie escaped from Mathilde's clutches and ran to him. He lifted her up high and swung her around until she screamed with delight. Mathilde winced.

Léo put her down. 'And you, my petal?' He squeezed Mathilde's thin shoulders while I surreptitiously grabbed Élodie's picture and hid it behind the kettle. After all, he didn't feature in it at all so I didn't want to take any chances. Élodie adores Léo (which makes me a bit sad, I have to say) but she's slightly scared of him too and I know that's only going to get worse. That's another thing that haunts me. Jacques already stands up to him – that could be his downfall – but Léo never has as much time for his son. It's always girls for him.

Élodie ran off to fetch his slippers. Mathilde said: 'Coffee, Léo, darling?' and gave me one of her looks.

I made the coffee and then made my escape.

I'm writing this later. It's after midnight and everyone's in bed. Just now, he came into my bedroom. I was only half asleep; like Mathilde, I don't sleep so well these days. I know we can't go on like this, but . . .

I sat up and stared at him. He was wearing that belted black velour dressing-gown of his and his feet were bare. 'What's wrong?' I switched on the bedside lamp. Instinctively, I thought of the kids. But something in his eyes alerted me. I pulled the bedcovers up to my chin. Was he naked under that thing?

'Sssh.' He put his finger to his lips. 'I just want a quiet word with you.'

Quiet word? In my bedroom? Was he crazy? Mathilde would go completely bonkers.

He sat down on the edge of the bed. The dressing-gown gaped open to reveal his dark, hairy legs. I'd seen them before, of course, when we'd all been down on the beach, but here in my room . . . I felt sick.

'You're doing such a fantastic job here, Thea,' he whispered. 'I'm very pleased with you.'

My flesh crawled. I couldn't speak. I could barely look at him. His moist lips, the dark stubble on his jaw, his hair already beginning to recede. How had I ever thought him handsome?

'I realise things can be difficult.' He nodded towards the wall.

On the other side of it Mathilde would be – hopefully, at any rate – fast asleep. 'And I think you know she's not well.'

Wide-eyed, all I could do was stare at him and nod.

'But between us, I'm confident that we can manage things.'

Between us? Manage things? He was hardly ever here. Two days a month at the most, and when he was here, he made things worse, not better.

He reached out and stroked my cheek. I could hardly breathe. He lifted my chin and rubbed his thumb against my mouth until my lips parted. 'Thea,' he breathed, and then he was on me, his face on mine, his mouth on my lips, his wet tongue forcing a pathway to mine. I was practically choking, and his whole weight seemed to be on me now, pressing against my ribs, almost suffocating me.

I pushed with all my strength. I knew I probably only had once chance. I pushed and as I pushed and his weight momentarily shifted, I moved quickly to one side so that I was no longer pinned down by him. 'Get out,' I told him. 'Get out of my room now.' Though thankfully I had enough presence of mind to keep my voice down.

He made a face as if I was simply being a bit of a bad sport. 'Why not?' he asked. 'What's the matter?' He bent closer again, his hot breath repugnant on my skin. 'She'd never know.'

'Non, Léo.' It was a whisper, but I put everything I could into it.

He sat up and regarded me coolly. 'No woman says "Non, Léo",' he informed me. 'I'm your employer. You must do as I say.' And he smiled that wolfish grin of his. It's all a game for him – I can tell. But I wasn't playing.

'If you force me, I'll tell the police. I'll tell Mathilde. I'll tell the children. I'll leave this house. I'll—' Despite my good intentions, the volume of my voice was rising.

'All right, eh bien, *I get the picture.' He got to his feet. 'Pity,'* he said. *'*Quel dommage. *It's boring here. It could have been fun.' And he gave me one last appraising look before he walked out of the room.*

I'm still shaking. I'm furious too. How dare he! It's going to be impossible now to get to sleep. And did I say enough to put him off – or will he try it on again? Will I have to worry every time he looks at me, every time he comes back for the weekend, every time I'm left alone in a room with him?

Oh, God. What am I going to do?

'You bastard . . .' Mathilde let the diary fall back into her lap. She knew exactly when this had happened. She'd had no idea at the time, only that the next morning, before Léo left, he had gone up to Thea, chucked her under the chin, whispered: 'Thanks for last night, *chérie.*' That's all she'd known.

Had he intended her to hear, to suspect? Reading Thea's account of that time in her diary, Mathilde thought that he probably had. Just as he'd warned her, no one said *non* to Léo. He would not forgive Thea for doing so.

And then . . . Mathilde lifted the diary and turned her attention to the next passage. Though it was the end, and she knew only too well what was coming.

When he said that to me, Mathilde was looking daggers at us both. Shit, I thought, what now?

Later, she sprang it on me. 'You will have to leave,' she said. 'You've betrayed me and my trust in you. You'll have to go.'

'I can't!' I cried and I begged. 'How can I? Mathilde . . .' She knows.

'You give me no choice, Thea.' Her face was closed. I've

never seen her look that way before. It was as if she had forgotten
– everything.

'But you don't understand. I haven't done anything—'

But Mathilde stayed firm. 'I don't believe you,' she said. 'And remember that no one else will believe you either. So, you must get out and stay out.'

'The children . . .' I love them so.

'They are not yours, they are mine. And it's time you accepted that.'

Yes, they are hers. Of course, they are hers. Both of them are hers. I packed a suitcase. What else could I do? Where else could I go?

I stayed the night in Sauzon at Lise's, the flower lady I sometimes talk to when I'm in town. But I didn't sleep. I stayed awake, thinking. And I know one thing. I can't leave Belle-Île. It would be impossible even if Élodie and Jacques had not begged me to stay. I can't stay in the Old Lighthouse, obviously, but I can stay here. It will be painful, but . . . I have money. I can get a job, find a place to live. Damn it. I'll stay here and Mathilde can't stop me. No one can.

She was right, of course. Mathilde had not been able to stop her. She had been astonished that Thea had chosen to stay, that she had not run back to Cornwall, to England. That was what Mathilde had wanted, of course. She was deeply ashamed of it, but she had wanted Thea gone, so that she wouldn't have to think of her any more, wouldn't have to see her, so that she could put her and everything that had happened between them right out of her life. But no. It was not possible. Because Thea was going to stay on the island.

Mathilde had gone to see her one last time at Lise's house

339

in Sauzon. She had tried so hard to persuade her to leave Belle-Île. But Thea was stubborn and she remained firm. It was even possible that the more she tried to persuade her, the more intransigent Thea became.

'I am going nowhere,' she said. 'How can I? I am staying here. This is my home too.'

Mathilde went to the bathroom while she was there. She wasn't sure at first what she was looking for. She sneaked into Thea's bedroom, saw her diary lying on the bed and slipped it into her bag. It was evidence, an insurance policy if you like. She had no intention of reading it – not then. But Thea, she swore, would never be able to tell.

Thea had never come back to the Old Lighthouse to see the children, nor had she confronted Mathilde about stealing her diary. In time, she had bought the shop and the house where she still lived, opened a florist's with Lise, who had apparently taught her everything she would ever need to know about flowers. And she had bought that rather ridiculous motorbike. When Lise died, Thea had continued running the shop herself, then she had met Sébastien, married and finally had a daughter of her own. Mathilde thanked God for that at least.

It was done. There was one more section of the diary left but Mathilde could not bring herself to read it. So, she would go and see Thea and she would take the diary with her, to return it at last. She would beg for Thea's forgiveness, and together they would decide what they should do.

CHAPTER 46

Étienne

It was easier with Colette by his side.

Étienne led her over the gorse, the scratchy grass leached pale by the salt and the sun, over the rocks and right up to the edge of the cliff. He expected her to tense, pull back – after all, why should she trust him? – they barely knew one another. But she didn't. Which made him wonder – did she know what this was all about?

He stared out to sea. A black cormorant was diving, unaware. Étienne tracked its passage under the strands of slippery kelp, through the ravine. He took a deep breath, allowed his gaze to drift down to the place, down to where the water was sometimes clear, sometimes shadowy, down almost vertically to the savage rocks below. He was conscious of the girl at his side, so still. 'This was where it happened,' he said.

'And you haven't been able to come back since?' Her voice was soft, strangely understanding.

He tore his eyes away from the spot. Stared at her, at the dark eyes that sometimes seemed so wise. 'You remember?'

She shook her head. 'Not exactly. Not in any detail. I remember there was an accident, a tragedy.' Her voice tailed to a whisper. 'I know that a boy died.'

Yes, a boy had died. A boy had jumped. Some might say he had been pushed, even if no one had physically touched him. People called it thrill-seeking, tombstoning even, though Étienne wouldn't dwell on that image. Boys – and girls too, these days – did it for the rush of adrenalin, the pure thrill of the 'sport'. Jumping from a ledge or a cliff top into the ocean. Étienne let go of Colette's hand and took a step further forward, to the perfect grey ledge – perfect, that was, for jumping from.

'Étienne.'

He knew that she didn't want him to get any closer. It was dangerous, of course. There were brutal rocks lying under the surface of the water. People had suffered twisted ankles, broken legs, spinal injuries, paralysis. People had died. *A boy had died.*

He sensed that she hadn't taken her eyes from his face. 'Étienne?'

He took a deep breath and stepped right up on to the narrow ledge. It protruded from the cliff; it was flat, cold and unforgiving – exactly as he remembered it. 'It's OK,' he threw back at her, his voice catching in the breeze. 'Don't worry.' Though it wasn't OK – how could it be? 'I just want to . . .' Remember what it felt like.

'You're much too close.' Her voice had a fearful note to it now.

'This is how close we were,' he said. 'All of us.' He needed to recapture that feeling one more time. The sharpness of the wind on his face, the tug of it in his hair and nothing in front of him, just air and the sea down below. This was how it had been that first time he jumped – the only time he'd jumped.

So close that despite the terror, he had almost felt compelled to do it. So close that he almost couldn't help jumping. So close that the black sea, the dark lumpen mass of rocks, were pulling him and all his senses down towards them by pure force of gravity and it really took no effort to simply let himself go, to jump rather than fall.

'They were crazy times,' he said. Even as he stood there, his eyes half closed, he felt the rush as the tide surged into the ravine.

'Take a step back, Étienne.' She was right beside him again now, her voice urgent. 'Take a step back and tell me about it.' She reached out her hand.

The fear seemed to break over him and he felt himself crumble. He took her hand, stepped back, realised how close he had come.

Colette pulled him down on to a rock threaded with yellow lichen. They were still close to the cliff edge, but the pull, the vertigo, had gone.

'We met up every summer in the holidays,' he said into the wind. 'There was a group of us.' Étienne, Denis, Jules, Yann and Gabriel. 'I know Belle-Île's a great place' – he turned to shoot her an apologetic glance and once again saw the understanding in her eyes – 'but we were fourteen- and fif-teen-year-old boys, we got bored easily. We went cycling, hiking, swimming. All that sort of stuff.' He bent his head and watched an ant scurrying across the rock, followed by another, working as a team. He thought back to those summer weeks when he had come here with his mother; his father came over too at the weekends, for a week if the company could spare him in early August. But here . . . The weather always seemed fine, their mothers were glad for them to be off their hands all day. Their friendship was loose, easy, based on necessity. Back on the mainland in term-time they probably didn't give one another a second thought.

Again, Étienne looked towards the water swirling around the angry rocks, spraying white spume, submerging them. Sometimes you wouldn't even know they were there . . .

But they knew. 'There was one boy, Yann Chirac, he was always pushing us to do stupid things, you know, daredevil stuff.' He glanced back at her.

She nodded. She was still sitting with her legs curled up under her and she was still steadily watching him. He wondered if she remembered the gang of boys who used to cycle through Sauzon, whooping and shouting. Who used to wheel it as far as they could along the coastal path and then tug their bikes up to the top, race along the sparse path up to the Pointe. There were five of them, and the youngest, Gabriel, was only thirteen.

'Boy stuff,' she said. And he was sure she did remember. They must have been disruptive for the Bellîlois, the people who lived here all the time, the 'boring old islanders with no life' as they used to call them. They hadn't taken any notice of the kids on the island, either. He'd seen them around, but they were different; Étienne and the others had no interest in making friends with them; they knew they were outsiders and they behaved like it. *Merde*, but they were arrogant as well as stupid, he and those other boys.

'Let's liven the place up!' Yann used to shout. 'Let's show them what life's all about!'

What life's all about – as if any of them had the faintest idea.

'I was bullied at school in Locmariaquer,' Étienne said. He'd hated school, in fact; when he was young he couldn't wait to leave and go into the oysters like his father before him. But

344

that was before he met the crowd here on the island. Before Gabriel. After that, he didn't know what the hell to do and oysters were last on the list.

'Why?' she asked.

'I was a bit of a geek. A dreamer. Not as sporty as I pretended to be.' He pushed his hair back from his face. How close had he got to going over the edge today? But for this woman – would he have done it? Probably not, he thought. He probably still wouldn't have had the guts. 'That's no excuse for what I did,' he said quickly. 'But it was different here.'

'You could be different here.'

'Yes.' He was glad that she got that. You could reinvent yourself if you needed to; pretend that you didn't care, when you did; pretend that you were brave, when you really weren't; laugh when really you wanted to cry. Peer pressure, he supposed it was. No wonder it took such a bloody long time for men to grow up. He still didn't think he'd got there.

'And you still can,' she said.

'Maybe.' Again, he looked out to sea. In the distance he could see two yachts heading for Sauzon harbour. She was right – he still could. Because he could write a different story too, a story about the boy he once was, about the other members of the Summer Gang, about Gabriel. Though Étienne knew it wasn't quite like that – it was more a case of having to write that story and at the same time being scared to. He was getting there, though. And now he had got here too.

'Whose idea was it?' Colette asked. 'To jump off the cliff? To play dare?'

He shrugged. 'Yann's. Everything we did was his idea. He was a bit crazy but he could be a laugh, you know. He was definitely leader of the pack.' He laughed bitterly. Yann liked to

345

jump – you could see it on his face; his grin when he surfaced, pure bloody triumph. But what he liked doing even more was taunting the rest of them – especially anyone he thought might be scared. 'We all looked up to him, hung on to every word he said. God knows why, the guy was an idiot.'

She smiled. 'That's often the way. At that age . . .'

'Yes,' he said. 'At that age.' Again, no excuse. Étienne had been well brought up. His father was a hard worker; he'd earned his promotion to foreman in the company, he was reliable and the men trusted him. His mother was lovely; she adored his father, did her best to make everything right, loved this island as if she'd been born here. God, they must have been so ashamed.

'It sounds like Yann was the most to blame,' she remarked.

'That's because you weren't there.' The words came out sharper than he'd intended.

'So, it wasn't just Yann. You egged each other on?' she asked.

He nodded. Looked down into the abyss. They'd done it a few days before. They'd all jumped – all bar Gabriel, that is. Yann and Denis had done it a few times – there was no stopping those two. He could hear Yann even now. 'Come on then. Who's next? Who's chicken?' He looked around their faces, trying to winkle out the weakness. He knew who was scared.

When Étienne had jumped, it had almost killed him. The pull, the rush of the wind, the exhilaration and fear streaking though his body as he fell. Because it didn't feel like jumping, it felt like falling. The icy splash as he'd hit the water, the second of pain – only, was it pain? Had he escaped the rocks? – the submerging under water, all the breath sucked out of his body until his chest was so tight he thought he'd explode. The dropping and then the relief as you came up, as you broke the

346

surface. To their cheers. He felt something of the triumph then himself, but more an unadulterated determination – this would be the first and the last time. Étienne had never experienced anything like it before. And he never wanted to again.

Now, there was only time for one more.

He waited and he knew what was coming.

'Étienne,' Yann said. 'It's your turn, *n'est-ce pas?*'

'*Non*, I'm done.' He had looked away – too quickly, he knew.

'Why?' Yann came nearer. He was sturdy although not tall, and he looked up to Étienne – physically at least. That was probably part of the reason why he disliked him so. 'Are you scared?' His face was close and cruel.

'Get lost.' Étienne tried to laugh as he said it but the words emerged higher-pitched and less assured than he'd intended. 'Come on, let's—'

'One more.' There was a definite change in Yann's tone now. It was the bully in him and Étienne knew he wouldn't let it go.

Étienne had to get out of it. And he couldn't afford loss of face. 'Gabriel,' he said. Clutching at straws. He never seriously considered . . . It was a diversion, that's all. 'What about it? Is it your turn or what?'

Everyone turned to look at Gabriel. They'd almost forgotten he was there. He was a bit smaller and skinnier than the rest of them, but he always tagged along, watching.

'Gabriel?' Even Yann hesitated.

Gabriel was watching Étienne, not quite realising what was happening. 'Huh?' He blinked, licked his lips nervously. He wasn't used to so much attention.

'You up for it, Gabe?' And yes, those words had come out of Étienne's mouth. He could hardly believe it. It was sheer self-preservation, he supposed. Pathetic self-preservation, he thought now. He still didn't think it might happen. He was the one who knew Gabriel the best. Gabriel stayed all summer down the road towards Le Palais and before the others had come along they'd hung around together, gone swimming in the bay and cycling along the inland paths. Étienne had liked that time much better, though he'd never dream of admitting it back then. Gabriel didn't bully him – on the contrary, he looked up to him because he was older and cleverer and yet just as unsporty as he was. He was a quiet, gentle boy and most likely he too was bullied at his school back in Vannes, just like Étienne. They had a lot in common. Étienne also knew that Gabriel would be scared shitless right now. But he could hardly take it back.

'What did Gabriel say?' The only indication that she was affected by the story was the way Colette was hugging her knees even more tightly.

'He said he didn't want to.' Quite rightly. They all should have said no. In many ways, Gabriel had been the bravest. He couldn't control his fear. He was shaking, his skinny knees trembling.

Yann had found this hilarious. 'Hey, look at him, he's pissing himself.'

The rest of them laughed, but uncertainly. They all seemed to have grasped that things had gone too far. 'Let's call it a day,' said Denis. He was as good at jumping as Yann and was agile as a cat, but he was kinder. Étienne remembered how he'd been when they'd run into each other in Sauzon a few weeks ago – kind enough not to mention the past, but it had clearly affected him; Étienne could see it in his eyes, the sense of discomfort, the way he was with his boy.

348

Yann's eyes were gleaming in that way he had, like he smelt blood. 'One more,' he said again. 'One more before we go.' And again, he turned to Étienne.

In that second, Étienne had a choice. In that second, he knew he couldn't do it. He couldn't do it again. That paralysis, that fear. He would shit himself. He would die from sheer terror. He wasn't even a strong swimmer. He couldn't do it again.

'Gabe?' His voice was jeering now. He could hear it as if it was coming from someone else's mouth. 'You're not scared, are you?'

'Yes.'

Again, they all laughed. Again, Gabriel was the only one brave enough to admit his fear.

'But you see if you play with the big boys,' Étienne told him, 'you have to play the same games, you know.' At the time he'd imagined this to be quite clever.

But Gabriel had shot him a look so beseeching that he almost crumpled.

Somehow though, this made him even more cruel. 'Or go home,' he'd snapped. 'In fact, let's all go home.' Because it had only been meant as a diversionary tactic; he had no intention of seeing it through.

And that's when it happened. One second they were all standing on the top of the cliff debating, the next minute Gabriel ran.

Colette's eyes widened. 'You mean he ran . . .'

'I had the chance to stop him.' He'd been so surprised. But he was standing closer to the cliff edge. He had the chance to stop him. 'I tried to grab his arm.' *No, Gabe, wait, it's not the right time* . . . But he couldn't get hold of him, he felt Gabriel's skinny body brush against his hand for a brief moment. But

349

Gabriel was going too fast, he'd made up his mind, he propelled himself to the edge of the cliff. And over.

'Over the cliff. He just plunged over the cliff.' Étienne's voice was choked with tears. He'd had nightmares – many nightmares where he awoke panting and soaked with sweat. And he'd never cried for Gabriel. But now the tears were rising thick through his body and Étienne could do nothing about it. He seemed to fold and crumple right there on the cliff edge. He sobbed and sobbed and then he was aware of Colette, beside him, holding him, murmuring to him, stroking his hair.

'The timing was wrong,' he stuttered. 'We all knew you had to get the tide right, otherwise the rocks . . .' His voice cracked. 'We'd talked about it.' Even now, they could both see the rocks lurking below the surface of the ocean, black, shadowy and treacherous. 'He didn't jump out far enough from the cliff face, he didn't wait for the waves, he didn't . . .' My God, but they had been such idiots. He could hardly believe it now.

'He shouldn't have jumped at all,' she murmured.

'And he wouldn't have.' Étienne hung his head. 'He wouldn't have, if not for me.' He couldn't deny that to anyone, let alone to himself. He'd said it to his mother, many times, but she'd told him to hush, not to think about it. 'He made his own decision,' she'd said, 'poor boy.' But he hadn't, that was the thing. Étienne was older. Étienne had made the decision for him.

'He'd already said no.' Colette seemed to be thinking about it. 'So, why . . .?'

'To be accepted. To be one of us – one of the big boys. Sometimes that's what you have to do.' Étienne had put him in that position. Étienne had made him feel that it was something he had to do. Christ, perhaps he had even done it for Étienne

– he would never know. But the guilt would always hang heavy on his soul. There were some things you could never forgive.

'But to run like that . . .' Colette shook her head. He could see tears in her eyes too as if she was imagining how it had been, as if she was imagining poor Gabriel . . .

'He didn't even think about it.' That was the crazy thing, the unexplainable thing. He hadn't spent any time protesting, he hadn't wavered, he hadn't stood shivering at the edge like the rest of them, trying to pluck up the courage to do it, waiting for the right moment, taking care to launch himself right out to sea away from the cliff face and beyond those rocks. He hadn't done any of that. If he had, they wouldn't have let him jump. But he hadn't. He had run, and so his poor body had fallen and smashed right into those rocks. Étienne could even remember the sound. It had been ghastly – the thump of impact.

'Did he die instantly?' Her voice was hollow – just like he felt. Why had he chosen Colette to tell? he wondered. Why had he needed her to come with him, to help him do this? Probably because she was the one person here he felt drawn to; he wanted her to understand. And now she *would* understand – and she would hate him, just as he hated himself.

Étienne gave a small shake of the head. 'We got down there, tried to rescue him.' Not by jumping, by scrambling down the cliff face. 'One of the gang cycled off to get help, to phone for an ambulance. But he died from his injuries, quite soon, before he could even be moved'.

They sat for a few minutes longer, Colette holding him, still stroking his hair. She was only being kind, of course, she was that sort of person. Nevertheless, it felt good. After the accident, Étienne had gone into a complete decline. He wouldn't go

351

out, he didn't want to see any of the other boys, he stayed away from the cliffs. The next year he refused to return to Belle-Île.

'You blamed yourself?' Colette murmured.

'Of course.' His mother had done her best. She had told him it wasn't his fault. She'd told him that everyone had forgiven anything there was to forgive. But that made no difference. Étienne was unable to forgive himself.

'And his parents?'

'I never talked to them about it.' His own parents had protected him from any repercussions, he supposed, and Gabriel's had left soon afterwards. They never returned to Belle-Île – at least as far as he knew. He should imagine they couldn't bear to. 'But they must have been devastated.'

'And you never came back to the island?'

He shook his head. 'The first time I came back was when my mother died. I came back to sort out the house – as you know.' He eased himself away from her, though he also thought that it would be good to stay there for ever. Not facing the world, not admitting what he had done, not taking the blame.

'But you didn't have to come back, Étienne,' she said.

He blinked at her.

'You could have employed someone to clear the house so that you didn't have to come back here.'

'I suppose.' What was she saying?

She clasped his hand. 'You came back because you knew you had to face up to what happened.' Her eyes were searching his. He wasn't sure he had ever experienced this sort of closeness before. 'That's what I think, anyway.'

He shrugged. Part of him didn't want that closeness. Whenever anyone had tried to get close in the past – that was when

Étienne had run. His mother had told him before she died that he must face up to the shadows of the past. Perhaps that was why she had stayed here, not selling the house on Belle-Île but choosing instead to spend most of her time here.

'That's why you started writing the story too.'

'The story?'

'Oh, Étienne,' she said. 'You need to write it all down because that's how you can face up to it. It's your way.'

'Right.' What made her such an expert in psychology anyway? But he couldn't help but listen.

'It's a kind of release,' she said. 'It's closure.'

He stared at her. She made it sound so simple.

'And then you need to forgive yourself, you know.'

'How can I?' The words stuck in his throat. She had no idea how bad he felt, how bad he'd always felt.

She patted his hand. 'Because you were just a boy. Because you were terrified yourself. Because you didn't mean it to happen.'

All these things were true. But how could that be enough?

'I feel so sorry for you.'

And she did look sorry for him; her eyes were brimming with pity. He looked away. 'I don't want your pity,' he muttered. 'I don't bloody deserve it for a start.'

She put her arm around his shoulders. 'I think you do,' she said. 'And I think you should begin to forgive yourself too. It's time.'

They walked slowly back into Sauzon. Étienne knew that Colette would be wanting to get back, cook supper, see to her mother. It would be hard to let her go. It was early evening now, there was still plenty of light and he could still feel the

353

sun warm on the back of his neck. Sauzon was mostly in shade, even the sea was growing inky.

'I think we should come back another day with some flowers to lay on the rocks where he died,' Colette said.

Étienne turned to look at her. Did she think that flowers were the answer to everything? They hadn't spoken for a while but he was still feeling very close to her. He was glad that he'd told her about Gabriel. Étienne was feeling – not better, exactly, but as if he could see something in the distance, some thread of hope that he might catch on to, that he might use to make something a bit better of his life. He shook his head. He'd longed for so many years for some way of deleting the past. It was impossible. But '*D'accord*,' he said. 'OK.'

'It's a simple mark of respect,' she said quietly. 'And it will show Gabriel that you're still thinking of him too.'

'Every day,' he said.

She smiled. 'Finish writing the story, Étienne,' she said. 'It's the right thing to do.'

He felt rather than saw her stiffen as they walked around the bend of Cours des Quais. He followed the direction of her gaze. A woman – in her late sixties, he guessed – was standing on the corner of Rue Rampe des Glycines wearing a slightly bemused expression. She seemed to be looking for someone. Her fair hair was touched with silver, she was thin, slightly bent and had an air of elegant fragility about her. When she saw them walking towards her, she brightened.

'Mathilde,' Colette said when they were still a few metres away.

The woman nodded and smiled. '*Bonsoir*, my dear,' she said. 'How nice to see you.'

But Étienne could feel Colette's resistance. She seemed very defensive. 'Were you looking for me?' she enquired politely.

'Indeed I am.'

'What can I do for you?' She gestured towards the house on Rue Saint-Nicolas. 'The shop's not open till tomorrow morning, obviously. Though I suppose I could go in and—'

'It's not the shop I've come to visit,' the woman said. 'And sorry that it's rather late. But I've come to talk to your mother. If she will see me, that is.'

CHAPTER 47

Élodie

Élodie hadn't yet finished making her driftwood puppets – a couple had become a family, because didn't that tend to be the way? But now, she had turned her attention to creating a stage for them. Perhaps she'd got a bit carried away, but she could envisage the puppet theatre as a complete piece; almost see it in a children's nursery somewhere, hear the cries of delight as some kind parent manipulated the puppets to make them sing and dance. She smiled to herself. Perhaps she was living in some sort of cloud cuckoo land – no doubt Jacques would say so. She had, after all, envisaged the piece as a Victorian puppet theatre and they were not living in Victorian times, in case she hadn't noticed.

During the past few days, Jacques had been a wonderful distraction, but this morning she had told him to stay away. 'I need to work.' She was firm. 'I need to catch up.' There were the animals she had put aside, those she still had to deliver, the wood that she had collected that needed sorting. And her puppets, *bien sûr*.

'No problem.' He held up his hands – Jacques, forever the innocent, never to be blamed – but also pulled his sad face until she had to laugh. He was like a whirlwind – he had spun back into their lives and everything he touched had gone flying. It wasn't disruptive, though; more as if he were a catalyst of some sort. Through Jacques – and the taste of the world outside that he had brought with him – Élodie was waking up. She was in a rut; they all were. She could see that now.

Since Jacques's return their mother had a new spark about her; they all had. She had cleared out the Old Lighthouse and done a heap of spring-cleaning. She was still in that reflective mood she'd been in of late but she seemed more cheerful; there was more of a sense of purpose about her. Élodie was pleased that she didn't seem sad about her father leaving. But could it last? How would she be when Jacques was gone? And how would Élodie be?

Because he would leave again. Élodie sanded down a rough edge of the wood, smoothing it with her fingertips until they were covered with dust. She loved that, the feel of wood, getting to the core of it, the sawdust; the rich sweet smell that was part-wood and part-sea. It was surely unique. Wherever possible she preferred to work by hand, to use only a few basic tools, to let her hands and the shapes and textures guide her. Her attention was caught by an interesting knot in the wood – that would be a good place to start a theatrical mask, perhaps something ornate and Venetian. She should look up the images. But Jacques – he would leave again because his life wasn't here on this sleepy island; his life was on the mainland – possibly with his wife, but certainly with his children.

She'd heard some of the phone calls. Jacques had a habit of coming over to her studio 'for a bit of peace and quiet' as he called it, before proceeding to disrupt hers. 'I have a few calls to make,' he'd say. 'Do you mind, *chérie*? I don't want Maman to hear. You know what she's like.'

And Élodie would try to work, all the time half-listening to his tempestuous conversations with Karine: 'Yes, I'm coming back, of course I'm coming back. Not this weekend, but soon. I can't say. Damn the bloody schedule. These are my children . . .' There were equally emotive conversations with the children themselves, Jacques trying to deal with the repeated question: 'Daddy, when are you coming home?' Nicole and Raphaël had the biggest claim on her brother – and that was how it should be.

Other times when he came over, he would wander around her studio, restless and unable to settle. 'What are you up to?' he'd say. Then, 'Have you thought about putting this bit here and maybe changing this, so that . . .'

'Jacques,' she'd say. 'Please.'

'Sorry.' Then he'd grin, pull that face and persuade her to go out walking, go down to the beach to collect driftwood, shells and sea glass. And that would be work finished for the day. They would wander for hours around the bays and coves, and talk, and yes, collect a few bits and pieces of sea treasure. It was lovely, but Élodie did need to get on. These snatches of time with him were like snapshots of the past. But they were gone; this was now. And after Jacques left, her work would be her lifeline again. She paused for a moment, gazing almost unseeing at the pieces she had chosen for her proscenium arch.

During their walks and talks Jacques had opened up to her about his marriage, as she'd known he would. It hadn't been all bad. Reading between the lines, Élodie thought, mostly they had been happy, mostly Jacques had been content to let Karine have her way in matters such as the style in which they did up their house, the manner in which the children were schooled and brought up, even where they went on holiday – and how often they came to Belle-Île, Élodie found herself thinking. This had freed him to get on with his own life: his work, his sporting activities, meeting with friends – women too, Élodie was quite sure there had been other women, though he hadn't admitted it yet.

But perhaps Jacques was seriously unhappy, perhaps Karine had found herself a lover; certainly, she did not respond to him in the same way – neither physically nor emotionally. Jacques felt that he had not given his wife enough and that as a result he had lost her. Élodie understood. Perhaps, as he had told their mother, the absence of real depth in their relationship had meant they had drifted apart. Perhaps he had always been too selfish – yes, and spoilt, she had to admit – to give Karine what she wanted. But how could Élodie give him any answers? Whatever the causes, Jacques had reached a turning point in his life and seemed to want to stay here with them on Belle-Île until he decided which direction to take.

Élodie moved away from her puppet theatre and blew the dust from the wood she was working on, brushing her hands clean on her overalls. She opened her laptop and waited for it to boot up. She clicked on her email inbox. She didn't bother to check it every day, which was remiss of her, she knew. She was running a business, so that should include admin such as keeping her website up to date (at least she had a website, she thought, thanks to Jacques who had set it up for her on one of his early visits with Karine when the children were very young). But that side of things didn't interest her. She supposed that Jacques was more like their father – a businessman, good with figures and also with people – and that she took after her mother. Not in looks so much, although they were both tall, slender and fair, but in preferring a life of solitude, their favoured companion the coastal landscape of Belle-Île-en-Mer.

She deleted the junk and dealt with a couple of emails from galleries on the island. They usually emailed as a back-up; they were mostly aware that it was easier to contact Élodie by phone; at least that way they could leave a message, and if she was busy she would come back to them in a day or two.

Élodie opened the oldest email – sent almost a week ago. Had it been that long? She skimmed the text. *I saw your work in Sauzon . . . I left a card . . . I am interested in seeing more . . . an exhibition next spring.* She frowned. Ah, yes. The Modus Gallery. She remembered the blue and green business card. Colette had brought it round the day she visited the studio. Élodie checked the name on the email: Armand Dubois. There was a phone number. If she was an aspiring artist and sculptor in the proper sense of the words, if she had one iota of ambition, if she valued her work and wanted it to reach a wider audience . . . she would call him. That at any rate, was what Jacques would say.

Élodie knew that her brother didn't entirely understand her choices. Sometimes she didn't understand her choices either. But . . .

On impulse, she picked up the phone and tapped in the number. One conversation, she thought. That was all it need be. At any moment, she could end the call. She wasn't committing herself to anything.

'*Bonjour,*' said a male voice, the type of voice which might not want to be diverted from work in hand.

'*Bonjour,*' she said briskly. 'This is Élodie Blaise from

360

Belle-Île-en-Mer. Could I speak to Armand Dubois if he is free?'

'Speaking, and yes, I am free.' His voice was smooth, low and more welcoming now. Élodie tried to imagine what he might look like. Medium height, she guessed. Dark hair. Well-cut suit. After all, he wasn't an artist, he was a gallery owner. Like her and Jacques, they were different species. 'It's great to hear from you,' he said.

Thankfully he didn't add 'at last' and Élodie decided against apologising for her tardy response. She didn't have to explain herself to anyone. '*Merci*. And thank you for leaving your card at the flower shop.'

'Oh, you're very welcome. I've looked on your website since then, obviously. I love your work.'

'You do?' Élodie couldn't help a note of surprise creeping into her voice. Her work sold, yes, but she wasn't used to hearing such lavish compliments. 'But I'm afraid the images on the website are rather out of date.' She couldn't remember the last time she had even looked at it. 'I'm doing some other work which I haven't quite got around to . . .' Her voice trailed. Yes, for about the last ten years.

'I don't blame you.' He sounded both friendly and understanding. Élodie felt herself warming to him a bit more. 'Artists like you don't want to be distracted by that sort of thing, I imagine. They want to be in their studios, creating, that's what it's all about, hmm?'

'Yes,' said Élodie, 'that is what it's all about.'

He cleared his throat. 'May I ask – have you exhibited your work on the mainland?'

'No.'

'That astonishes me.'

'I haven't approached anyone,' Élodie said. She didn't want him to think that no one wanted her. Maybe they didn't, but . . .

'Ah, I see.' He chuckled. 'You really are a solitary artist, is that it?'

'Yes.' She didn't seem to be good at one-to-one conversations either. Jacques was right. She needed to get out more.

'Could I persuade you to come and visit my gallery?' He didn't seem to mind, though.

Élodie checked the address at the bottom of the email. 'In Auray?' She felt a flutter of nervous anticipation. No, she told herself, naturally you do not have to go.

'Yes. It's by the river. We have a good and regular customer base. We are well thought of, I believe. People come here specifically to see our exhibitions. We even sell internationally. Plus, we have a lot of drop-in customers obviously. Tourists.' He said the word with only the slightest hint of disapproval.

Élodie found that she was smiling. 'Should I bring some of my work for you to see? It's rather difficult; most of it is—'

'Too big, yes, I can imagine from the horse.' Once again, he chuckled. 'Photos would be ideal.'

'Oh, yes, photos.' God, she was such an idiot. Obviously, she would take photos – that was what people did. If she went. 'Yes, of course.'

'You are sculpting more animals? This is what interests you?'

'And other things too.' Élodie looked at her puppet theatre. Before now she had made miniature façades for little driftwood houses, driftwood planes and boats with driftwood sails, which felt as if she was sending the wood back to the sea again. But lately she had preferred the challenge of muscle and movement, the draw of reality. Even the puppet theatre seemed almost alive to Élodie.

'Good, good. May I ask what sort of things?'

'Currently a puppet theatre.' Which sounded ridiculous.

'How interesting.'

'I do miniatures too,' she said, in case he was unnerved by the prospect of transporting large sculptures. Though she had to say, he didn't sound unnerved in the least.

'Fantastic,' he said. 'I like variety.'

'Then I'll come over.' Élodie had made the decision.

'Excellent. And if you like our gallery,' he said, 'would you perhaps consider being part of our exhibition?'

Would she consider . . .? Élodie took a deep breath. 'Yes,' she said. 'I would.'

'I don't wish to make too many assumptions, Mademoiselle Blaise.'

'Élodie, please.'

'Élodie. But that being the case, and even if it were not the case, I should love to visit your studio, to see your work in progress, in the flesh as it were – and, *bien sûr*, also to consider how it will fit into the exhibition.'

'Oh.' This was going rather too fast. But of course, he'd want to see her work if it was to be part of his exhibition. And she had said she'd consider it. She glanced at the email again. The exhibition was entitled: *From the Earth, from the Sea: Locally Crafted Sculpture and Made Objects*. It sounded perfect. 'Yes,' she said. 'That would be fine.' She'd really done it now. Her palms were damp and her heart was thudding. But the opportunity sounded too good to miss.

'*Eh bien*.' She could almost see him rubbing his hands together. 'When are you next coming over to the mainland, may I ask?'

If only he knew the truth. Élodie hadn't visited the mainland for four years, and before that she'd only gone to Quiberon on an errand for her mother. She had been to Auray, but not since she was about twenty. She remembered the river, an old bridge, some historic houses. She thought of Jacques. But she must be brave. He had done it. He lived in a different world. She wasn't being fair to herself – or her work – if she didn't at least try. The first step outside the comfort zone would probably be the hardest. 'I could come over the day after tomorrow,' she said in her best casual voice. Because she should do it quickly, before nerves had the chance to build and stop her altogether.

'*Parfait.*' He paused and she heard a rustle as if he were consulting a diary. 'And would you allow me to take you out to lunch?'

Élodie stared at the phone, took a deep breath. She was an artist, and about to be exhibited on the mainland in a gallery with international clients. Of course, she could go out to lunch. 'That would be lovely,' she said.

Jacques burst into the studio less than twenty minutes later. He was grinning.

'You look happy.'

'I've made a decision.'

'Oh, yes?' Would he leave again? – was that it? Would he leave Élodie to deal with the fall-out that his departure was guaranteed to cause – again. But of course he would. She knew that he would. Jacques would always do what he wanted to do.

'I'm not going back to work in a stuffy old office.' And as if to demonstrate his desire for fresh air, Jacques flung open the window of the studio.

The sea breeze nipped in and Élodie moved some of the more delicate limbs from her puppets, which had been airing on the windowsill. She didn't want the family to blow away. 'What are you going to do then?' The sound of the sea was like an echo in her heart.

'I'll go freelance. It's the obvious solution.' He spread his hands. 'I've got plenty of contacts, you know. I can work from anywhere. That's the beauty.'

But where, Élodie wondered, was anywhere?

'I can rent somewhere,' he said breezily. 'Any place. I can travel. I can spend time with the children. And time with you and Maman, of course.'

'Sounds perfect.' As in almost too good to be true.

He bent to drop a kiss on her head and she smelt the citrus of that new aftershave. 'It is,' he said. 'And how about you? Are you having a good day?'

'Not bad.' Élodie tried to hide her triumph. 'As a matter of fact, I've been asked to exhibit at a gallery in Auray.'

'Auray?' He whistled. 'Very up-market. Well done you.'

'And I'm going over there to check the place out,' Élodie continued. 'The day after tomorrow.'

'Are you indeed?' Jacques swung her chair around and stared her out. He always could. She tried to stay serious but after about ten seconds they both burst out laughing. 'My sister, the sculptor,' he said. 'The professional.'

'Yes.'

'Well done, Élodie,' he said. 'I'm proud of you.'

'*Merci*.' She smiled. Took a deep breath. Because she hadn't done it yet.

'It's a day of changes, all right.' He glanced around the studio, a wistful look on his face.

'It seems so.' Because of him, thought Élodie. He was the whirlwind, the trigger.

'And it's not only us,' Jacques folded his arms and continued to survey her.

'Oh?'

'Because Maman has just left the house – she's gone to visit Thea.'

'Really?' Élodie had been hoping and she had been waiting. And that was so typical of Mathilde, to do it when she least expected it.

'So this evening I suggest that you come over for supper and I will cook *moules et frites* and we will cross-question her in order to find out the truth.' He wagged a finger and raised an eyebrow.

The truth. Élodie had always assumed she knew it. But she also knew now that this wasn't the case. 'Colette wants to know too,' she mused. In fact, she had promised to try to find out. But since then, Jacques had bounded back into their lives and she had almost forgotten that promise.

'Does she indeed? That means they've both kept quiet on the matter.' Jacques frowned. 'So why the big falling-out? It sounds as if Thea saved Maman's bacon in more ways than one. She should have been eternally grateful to her, if you ask me.'

'Exactly.'

'And what about you, my dearest?' That look of tenderness appeared in Jacques's dark velvet eyes. He reached out and gently brushed her hair from her face. 'Are you ready to face the world, my Élodie?'

Oh, Jacques, she thought. Was she ready indeed? If she went over to Auray, if she saw the gallery, if she met Armand Dubois and let him take her out for lunch. After all these years, her life would most certainly change.

'Yes, Jacques,' she said. 'I'm ready.'

CHAPTER 48

Colette

'I'm not sure.' Mathilde's appearance had taken Colette completely by surprise. 'I'll have to . . .' She gestured towards the house.

'We were close once.' Mathilde was holding something in a carrier bag tightly to her chest.

'I know.' Which was exactly the point.

Colette glanced at Étienne who had moved closer to her side, not interfering but ready to be protective, she sensed, clearly sensitive to the situation, despite what he'd just been through.

'I should have phoned first. *Je suis désolée.* I'm sorry.' Mathilde did look rather distraught, her usually neatly styled hair in disarray, her lipstick slightly smudged – and she was still hugging the carrier bag close to her as if it held something precious, something she couldn't bear to be parted from.

'My mother is very frail,' Colette said. 'I'll go inside first and see if she's awake, and if she wants to see you.' But immediately she'd said this, the words sounded too harsh. 'I'm sorry,' she said, 'but . . .'

'I understand.' Mathilde nodded. 'It's been a long time.'

Colette turned to Étienne. 'See you later?' Even before he had begun his story, she had guessed that it concerned the tragedy up on the cliff that summer. She had been young at the time – barely a teenager herself – but she remembered the publicity, the gossip, the sadness it had brought to their small community. She'd had no idea though about Étienne's involvement.

'*À bientôt,*' he agreed. 'I hope your mother . . .'

'*Merci.*' Colette knew that it had been painful for him up there on the cliff top, but she felt that his mother had been right – facing up to things was difficult but also necessary at some point in everyone's life. It had taken Étienne years before he'd been able to revisit that place, that day, and now that he had . . . Colette hoped that with the chance to write about it, in time he could move on from the tragedy, from the sense of blame and guilt so deeply instilled in him. Another bond between them, she thought. They'd both left the island and not wanted to come back, not wanted to confront the past. And yet here they both were.

'And thank you.' He bent to kiss her lightly on both cheeks, just a brush of his lips, a touch on her shoulder, but she felt it. A frisson, a spark.

Perhaps she had imagined it. Even so, she smiled as she watched him walk away.

'One of our summer visitors?' Mathilde enquired, also watching him.

'Sort of.' Colette knew that she sounded unfriendly. She felt unfriendly. They walked in silence up the hill, past the shock of white jasmine on the corner, the scent of which hung sweet and heavy in the air.

When they reached the house and the flower shop Colette turned to face her. 'Would you mind waiting here for a moment, Madame?'

'Of course not.'

The house was quiet and dim as Colette let herself in. Already, she thought, it was beginning to feel like death. She shivered. She should be here, all the time, sitting with her mother, but . . . Francine had seemed determined she go out with Étienne. And she wondered – did Francine know who he was? Could she somehow know what he had experienced and what he could now be going through? She wouldn't be at all surprised.

Colette opened the door of her mother's room. She was still asleep. Francine had given her something to eat; Colette saw a plate on the bedside table and the water glass refilled. The nurse had been here too, she could see the signs, new notes written up on the clipboard at the end of the bed. They had given her mother a little hand-bell to ring if she needed anything; no doubt Francine would hear it, even from next door.

Colette glanced at the nurse's notes. Temperature rather high, pulse weak. She was aware that in the latter stages of the illness, she was likely to suffer from high temperatures, confusion, perhaps an inability to speak or move her limbs. Colette understood how leukaemia worked – she had read up on it. At first her mother's body had started producing more white blood cells than it needed. She might not even have noticed any changes in her health at that early stage. But as these cells multiplied, they would have begun to interfere with her vital functions – including the production of healthy red cells needed to supply oxygen. The production of healthy white cells would be limited too by these other white monsters, as

Colette found herself thinking of them, so that gradually her mother would become unable to fight infection. She couldn't fight back. Colette let out a small sigh.

She would let her sleep. Sleep was healing, too. At least it was a time when her mother could be at peace. She crept out of the room and returned to the front door. 'I'm sorry, Madame Blaise,' she told Mathilde. 'She's sleeping. I don't want to wake her.'

'No, it's fine, I understand.' Though Mathilde's face fell. She thrust the carrier bag towards Colette. 'Please, when she wakes, would you give her this?'

'What is it?'

Mathilde looked away, into the distance. 'It doesn't matter,' she said. 'Thea knows.'

'And what should I tell her?'

'Tell her that if she will see me, I would like to come back,' Mathilde said. 'Any time. Just let me know. This is my number.' She pulled a notepad and pen from her bag and scribbled a number on it.

'Very well.' Colette took it. 'I'll tell her.'

Mathilde straightened. 'Please also tell Thea that what happens next is entirely up to her,' she said.

Colette frowned. What happens next?

'She'll know what I mean.' Mathilde nodded. 'It can all come out if she wishes.' She spread her hands. 'Everything. If that's what Thea wants, if that's what she thinks is right.'

'I see.' Though she didn't. 'Very well.' Colette turned back towards the house.

'And please also tell her . . .' Mathilde reached out and touched Colette's arm. 'Please also tell her that I'm sorry.'

CHAPTER 49

Colette

Back in the house, Colette resisted the temptation to look in the carrier bag – Mathilde had given it to her mother not to her, and being ill didn't mean she had also lost her right to privacy. She cooked a light supper for herself, paced the house and stared out into the evening as it darkened into night. There was so much to think about – her mother and how little time might be left, Étienne and his revelations on the cliff top, and now Mathilde.

She sat with her mother for the rest of the evening while she slept, holding her hand; her skin so papery and light that her hand felt almost weightless in Colette's. Her breathing was shallow; Colette watched the faint rise and fall of her chest under the white cotton nightdress.

Colette must have fallen asleep herself because when she awoke, with a start, the room was dark except for the soft glow of the night-light. For a moment, she was disorientated. Her back was stiff, and her arm – still flung over the bed – ached. She adjusted her position and leaned forward. Her mother's breathing was still shallow, but her eyelids were fluttering.

'Maman,' she whispered. What was she dreaming about? Colette's eyes filled. She should have come back before. She had wasted so much time.

Colette woke again as dawn was breaking and the room was filled with a misty light. She smoothed her mother's hair from her brow. Her skin was moist. Colette got up and stretched, went over to the window and eased open the shutters a little. The harbour was waking: people were drifting along the promenade, Berthe Le Bris, the owner of the café next door, was sweeping up outside, a fishing boat was coming into harbour, and she saw Henri standing on the quay to greet it.

'*Chérie*.'

Colette turned. Her mother was awake, her eyes brighter than they had been for a while.

'Good morning, Maman.' Colette bent to kiss her cheek. 'Would you like something to drink – some water or mint tea?' Later, she'd go down into the garden and pick a few sprigs of rosemary. Rosemary was energising; made into tea, she'd read that it could ease aching muscles and bring down temperatures. She put a hand to her forehead. She was hot now, almost burning.

'Water, please. And could you help me sit up, *chérie*?' Her voice was faint but unwavering.

'Of course.' Apart from the high temperature, she seemed better this morning. Colette helped her into a sitting position, put more pillows behind her head and back for support, fetched the water and a warm flannel and a towel to wipe her face. She held the glass as her mother took a few delicate sips of water, like a bird.

'You had a visitor yesterday evening,' Colette told her. 'Mathilde Blaise came to see you.'

'Mathilde . . .'

'She brought you this.' Colette fetched the carrier bag from the small coffee table in the corner of the room and placed it on the bedcovers in front of her.

'Will you open it for me?' Her white hands lay perfectly still.

'Of course.' Colette opened the bag to reveal a package wrapped in green tissue paper. Carefully, she unwrapped it. It was a battered red leather book. She handed it to her mother.

A small sad smile appeared on her mother's face. She touched the cover, opened the red book, ran her fingers delicately over the script on the first pages. 'So, she has brought it back to me at last,' she said.

It was a diary, Colette realised. Her mother's diary? It must be. She recognised her handwriting. Was this the diary she had been referring to when she'd said: *I wrote it all down . . . But now it is lost*? Colette supposed that it must be. But why would Mathilde Blaise have her mother's diary? Had she left it there at the Old Lighthouse when she moved out? It seemed unlikely. A diary was so personal, so private. Why hadn't her mother ever reclaimed it?

'I can't blame her,' her mother whispered, as if she knew where Colette's thoughts were running.

'Mathilde?'

She nodded. 'She was so scared of losing her, you see.' She looked at the diary and, softly, her fingers fluttered over the open pages, but Colette could see that she was not reading the words. It was as if she was watching the girl she once was.

'Losing her?'

'We do strange things.' She reached out her hand for Colette's. 'When we think we are about to lose those we love.'

Colette took a deep breath. It might be now or never. 'Will

you tell me the truth, Maman?' she asked. 'Will you tell me what happened between you and Mathilde? Will you tell me what my father meant when he talked about your secret?'

'So, you heard it all that night?' Her mother let out a small sigh. 'I thought perhaps you had.'

'And will you tell me?'

'This will tell you the truth.' She tapped the diary with her forefinger. 'This will tell you what I did.' She looked as if she might cry.

Colette reached out for her. 'It doesn't matter what you did,' she said fiercely, feeling her mother's body, so small and vulnerable, against hers. 'I don't care any more.'

'Thank you, *chérie*.' She rested her head against Colette's shoulder and very gently she eased her back on to the pillows. She mustn't tire her, mustn't excite her. Perhaps she shouldn't have given her the diary at all. Most of all, her mother needed to rest and gather strength.

'I thought I would take our secret to the grave.' Her voice was so soft that Colette had to lean forward to hear her. 'But now . . . What is she saying? Is she saying that she wants everyone to know?'

Colette frowned. She wasn't making much sense. On the one hand, she seemed more lucid than she had been for days; on the other, this thread was hard to follow. Was this the period of confusion she had read about, associated with her illness? Or was it a brief time of lucidity and energy before the end?

'When I came here to the island I wanted to get as far away from home as I could.' She smiled wistfully and she looked so young at that moment, like a child. Colette knew what that felt like; she'd felt the same. And she wished she'd known her then, when her mother was a young girl in Porthleven, when she first came over here to Belle-Île.

'"I'll show them," I thought. And then I'd go home. I always assumed I'd go home after that summer.' She fixed her gaze on Colette's face. 'But that summer changed everything.'

Colette held the straw again to her mother's dry lips and she took a small sip of water. 'How, Maman? How did it change everything?' This was what her grandmother had longed to know before she died – why had her daughter never come home?

She took a rasping breath. 'Read this and you will see.'

Colette looked down at the diary, still open on the bed. She'd been given permission. From these pages, she'd find out everything she wanted to know. 'Léo Blaise?' Was that it after all?

Her mother seemed to sink back further into the pillows. 'Not Léo.'

'Then what?' Colette couldn't imagine. She had been the au pair. What had she done – stolen the family silver?

'I thought of leaving the island so many times after that summer, you know,' she whispered, each word clearly requiring an effort. Colette wanted her to go on, but at the same time she wanted her to stop. This might be too much for her. 'Maman . . .'

Her mother put out a hand, took another rattling breath. 'I thought of going home.' Her eyes were far away now, perhaps back in that time, that summer. 'But they both begged me to stay close by.'

'Élodie and Jacques?' Colette guessed.

She nodded. 'I still thought that I might be needed . . .' Her voice trailed. She stopped speaking, breathed again, seemed to muster more strength from somewhere. 'And then I met your father.' She squeezed Colette's hand. 'And I thought I could start again. With him. With you.'

'Oh, Maman, don't tire yourself, please.' Colette guessed that she was telling her this part of the story because it wasn't in her diary and she wanted Colette to know. But she wondered what time the nurse would be coming this morning. She was worried. Shouldn't her mother be resting? Should she be talking like this, worrying so much about the past?

'But I lost you both.'

Colette reached out to stroke her hair. 'You haven't lost me,' she soothed.

'And Mathilde. Did she . . .?'

'She wants to come and see you,' Colette told her. 'Would you like that, Maman?'

'Yes.' There was no hesitation.

'And she said she was sorry.'

But her mother's grip on her hand had loosened. Her breathing had altered.

'Do you want to rest, Maman?' Colette rearranged the pillows so that she was comfortable. Her eyelids were closing, she was drifting back to sleep again.

Colette took hold of her hand once more. 'I love you, Maman,' she said. Had she heard her? She needed her mother to have heard her. 'Whatever it is that happened before.' And then she felt the faintest squeeze on her hand. She had heard her. She knew.

CHAPTER 50

Élodie

Élodie took a deep breath of the fresh, salty air as she stood on deck, gripping the hand-rail, watching the island recede into the distance. The Fort, the little terrace of houses up on the hill, the colourful harbour of Le Palais. Her island; her distance. Her life. But she shouldn't be melodramatic, Élodie told herself. She wasn't leaving her life. It was all still there back at the Pointe – the Old Lighthouse, the studio, the beach and the treasures it gave – and it would all be waiting for her when she returned. She was simply stretching her wings, taking a leaf out of Jacques's book and seeing what the rest of the world might have to offer. Nothing had to change. She wasn't actually flying away.

It hadn't been easy to decide what to wear. Élodie had discovered she had few choices. She bought almost all her clothes from a small independent boutique in Le Palais. She preferred loose smock tops which were easy to work in, and natural fabrics like linen and hemp which felt good next to her skin. Leather boots had to be strong enough for winter trudging along the beach; and in the summer, espadrilles or flip-flops were the easier and most comfortable options. She rarely went out in the evening. There was nothing suitable in her wardrobe for a day trip to Auray (and lunch, she reminded herself), so a plain linen shift dress with deep pockets, leather sandals and a casual, loose-fitting jacket it would have to be.

It was a straightforward journey by train to Auray and the gallery was easy to find. Élodie walked past slowly. She wanted to take it in first as an outsider, get a feel of the territory. Auray was pretty much as she remembered. An old stone bridge spanned the wide river and the harbour of St Goustain, medieval timbered buildings had become upmarket cafés and restaurants, and steep cobbled steps wound up towards the church. The Modus Gallery had a prime position in the centre and on the riverside. So far, so good. It was spacious, its frontage open and inviting. It definitely had impact. She paused for a moment. Currently, there was a painting exhibition called simply *Waves* – massive canvases of blue ocean covered the walls. Élodie smiled. It seemed like her kind of place.

She had a cup of coffee in a café three doors down and visited the bathroom to re-apply lipstick – normally she didn't bother; her make-up routine consisted of cleansing and moisturising, and she only looked in the mirror to make sure she didn't have any charcoal smudges on her nose. Then she retraced her steps to Modus. She took another deep breath and walked in with confidence, as though she had every right to be there.

'*Bonjour*,' she said to the man behind the desk, who must be Armand Dubois's assistant since he wasn't terribly smart and didn't look a bit like her impression of the man she'd talked to. 'I'm here to see Monsieur Dubois. My name is Élodie Blaise.'

'Mademoiselle Blaise.' He jumped to his feet and she

immediately realised her error; there was no mistaking that voice. 'Allow me to introduce myself. Armand Dubois at your service.'

'Élodie, please,' she said again. He was an attractive man, but somewhat rough around the edges – unshaven, crinkly brown-eyed, slightly unkempt dark wavy hair. He was wearing blue jeans and a loose shirt and Élodie realised she hadn't needed to worry about what to wear. He looked very different from his voice. But actually, now she came to think about it, his voice suited him.

'Thanks so much for coming.' He took her hand and clasped it warmly. 'I am delighted to meet you.'

'*Merci, Monsieur.*' Élodie was slightly overwhelmed by his enthusiasm. He had, after all, seen only her driftwood horse.

'Armand, please.' He beamed. 'I was looking at your website again this morning. I love the concept of working with materials found in the natural world, in the landscape in which you live.'

'*Merci beaucoup.*'

'You achieve a great sense of life and movement in your work – and from driftwood alone.' He shook his head. 'It is quite remarkable.'

Goodness. '*Merci,*' she said again. What a welcome. 'Although driftwood does tend to have a life of its own. The shapes, the way it has been re-formed by the ocean, its history.'

'Ah, but you make us see that.'

'Thank you.' Élodie realised that she'd already thanked him four times and she'd barely been here four minutes.

'So, this is the gallery. We are pleased to welcome you.' He gestured.

Élodie looked around. The space was high, open and roomy,

379

the exhibition of paintings magnificent. All around her, giant pictures of rolling waves filled the white walls, seemed to be flowing towards her. There were turquoise waves, green waves, indigo waves and every shade between. They curled, rolled and spun, in sunlight and in shadow, sending glittering drops of water spinning into the air above and trails of foam in their wake. Occasionally there was a figure, a surfer, caught in the opaque tunnel within the wave or riding its crest, arms akimbo. Sometimes a swimmer plunging head first into the approaching wave or a diver kicking with his flippers under water. Mostly, it was simply water and sky. 'Who is the artist?' she asked Armand. 'These pictures are breathtaking.'

'Aren't they?' He smiled. 'Louis Thoraval. He lives in Rennes, he is Breton, but born on Finistère; you can almost tell, do you not think?'

'Perhaps, yes.' Élodie considered this. She had been there a few times when she was young, in the days when her father had come over and taken his family on a trip 'to catch a glimpse of the wide, wide world', as he used to say. She had relished the drama and wildness of Finistère, its many moods, the brooding atmosphere of Brittany's west coast which in many ways was so like home.

'We are fortunate here at Modus,' Armand continued, 'to have such a wealth of talent in the area.'

And now she was part of that talent he was referring to, Élodie thought with a small shiver. Was she up to it? Jacques thought so. He had urged her to do this, to come here. She straightened. 'Is this your gallery?' she asked Armand. Was he a painter himself perhaps? She had envisaged him as a businessman, but now that she'd met him, now that she'd heard the passion in his voice and seen the work in his gallery, she realised that he could be an artist too. He certainly had an eye.

'Yes, it is.' The phone rang and he pulled an apologetic face. 'Please, do take a look around. Dominique will be here soon and I will be free.'

'Of course.' Élodie was more than happy to do that. She wandered round the exhibition, taking in the rich colours of the paintings and their deceptive simplicity – she had always been fascinated by the purity and yet complexity of the sea, and in her view, the artist had captured this perfectly. Armand had mentioned movement, and Louis Thoraval had achieved that too through the roll and curl of his waves, the compelling rush of the tide as it surged forward. The scale of the exhibition was ambitious, but perfectly suited the sense of space in the gallery; the clean lines and strong, unrelenting whiteness that showed off the paintings so well. What would her work look like in this space? She tried to imagine. There was room for a few larger pieces. The design of the gallery was basically open plan; it had an upper floor too, a mezzanine, and there was another room at the back.

'I am planning to host three artists for your exhibition.' Armand was at her side again.

'My exhibition?' The words sounded strange and unfamiliar to Élodie.

'If you agree to show your work, that is. We could discuss which part of the gallery you would use when we have more idea of the pieces we plan to show.'

'Thank you, yes.' *We.* This was the other side of branching out, of making her work more public, Élodie realised. It would no longer be solely her property and it would no longer be just her making the decisions. They would be collaborating – obviously – on which pieces to feature, and this would depend on what Armand wanted for the exhibition as a whole. Élodie

381

felt the hairs on the back of her neck prickle with anticipation. It was all so adult, so professional, so different from what she was used to. She was surrounded by seascapes, not exactly floundering, but trying not to get out of her depth.

'What do you think?'

She smiled. 'It seems like a perfect way of drowning to me.'

He chuckled. 'Indeed. An excellent way of putting it.'

'Have you sold many of the paintings?' If she didn't already have the ocean right on her doorstep, Élodie would love to hang one of these works of art on her wall in the studio, to contemplate and adore. Armand hadn't shown her the catalogue but she guessed them to be pricey – this was no run-of-the-mill set-up selling average art. It was a collector's heaven.

'Almost half sold already,' he said. 'And the exhibition has only been open for three weeks.'

'*Très bien*.' Élodie nodded. 'That's very good.'

'We think so.'

'And do you exhibit artists who are already popular?' Élodie had not heard of Louis Thoraval. But then again she wasn't an authority on contemporary art. Coming here had made her contemplate just how insular she had become.

Armand considered. 'We prefer to show artists and makers who have not yet made a name for themselves. I don't want to sound too pompous, but a show here has been known to alter the direction of an artist's career.' He was watching her carefully. 'And that is something that is not the ambition of every artist.'

Élodie felt herself flush under his scrutiny. Already she felt that he knew her rather well. 'I agree,' she said. 'It's something I'd have to think about.' Because it was best to be honest. *You'd be mad not to*, Jacques had said. But she hadn't completely made up her mind; she was still considering Armand's offer.

382

'Fair enough.' He took her arm. 'Come and see the permanent exhibition.' He led her to the back room of the gallery. This space had less impact, but Élodie could see immediately that there were some interesting abstracts as well as landscapes of the local area. 'We organise four special exhibitions a year, running one into the other so that there's always something extra for our visitors to see.'

'And what are your terms for selling artists' work?' Élodie felt she ought to be businesslike.

'We keep thirty-five per cent of the selling price,' he said. 'That's non-negotiable. As you can see, we provide a good platform here and we need to cover all our expenses and outgoings.'

'Of course.' Élodie was already paying twenty-five per cent to the small craft shops and galleries on the island. Armand's figure seemed more than fair.

'And we would discuss the selling price.' Again, he gave her a keen look. 'I think you would find that you may need to put up your prices to something that reflects their real worth.'

Élodie raised her eyebrows. So, he thought she was too cheap. She didn't know whether to be offended or flattered.

'It would be great to have some original pieces.' He looked at her enquiringly. 'If you were to agree to my proposition, would you be able to make some special works for us by next summer?'

'I don't do anything twice,' Élodie told him, aware of the slight edge to her voice. Did she want to do this? Did she want to be dictated to? Part of the joy of her work was that it was hers alone, to do with as she chose. 'Each piece is unique.'

'That's good.' He beamed at her. 'I was sort of hoping you would say that, you know.' He put his head to one side. 'Did you bring those images you mentioned?'

'Yes, I did.' She pulled her phone out of her bag and he beckoned her back to the front desk. There was someone else holding the fort now, a fine-featured, dark-haired woman wearing a close-fitting and elegant lilac dress which merged perfectly with the wave paintings. She shot Armand an intimate smile.

'This is Dominique,' he said in introduction.

'Armand's partner.' She held out a slim and manicured hand.

'Dominique, meet Élodie Blaise,' Armand said. 'The sculptor I was telling you about.'

'Pleased to meet you.' Élodie took Dominique's hand. She kept her own nails short because it was easier for working, and no amount of hand cream could stop them from feeling dry and dusty to the touch. That was what came of working with wood for a living, she thought ruefully. Although she often wore gloves for collecting, she'd never work in them and she'd had way more than her share of splinters and torn cuticles. She probably smelt of wood too. And the sea, of course.

'And you.' But in contrast, the smile Dominique sent Élodie's way seemed brittle.

'Shall we?' Armand glanced encouragingly at Élodie.

She tapped on the gallery icon on her phone. 'These are some of the pieces currently in my studio.' She held out her mobile to show him.

'Hold on.' Armand took a connector out of the desk drawer. 'May I?'

She nodded and he connected her mobile to the large screen on the desk. 'Let's see now . . .'

Élodie blinked to see her work so big and close up all of a sudden. Almost larger than life. 'This is the puppet theatre I'm working on currently.'

He zoomed in. 'How perfect. And all made from drift-wood?'

'With a bit of sea glass thrown in.'

'It is charming.' Considering she was his partner, Dominique didn't sound impressed. Was that 'partner' as in business partner in the gallery, Élodie found herself wondering, or as in partner in life? From the intimate smile, she guessed the latter.

'You can use it and yet it is also beautiful,' Armand said, and Élodie was relieved to hear the thrill in his voice. 'That is a rare thing, is it not?'

'I suppose it is.'

'That was what struck me with your driftwood horse. To recycle the wood is to be applauded, for sure. But also to have panniers for herbs, trailing flowers . . .'

'That was the florist's idea.'

'Even so.' He regarded her seriously. 'I like that you consult in this way with clients, I like this working practice. A piece of art is not there only to delight the senses, it can also live side by side with the practical, the useful.'

'I like to think so, yes.' Élodie flipped the images along to show him the various puppets she had made.

'And yet they are almost too good to play with,' he mused.

'I wouldn't say that.'

She could tell that he liked this from his slow smile. His hair was just long enough to curl around the collar of his shirt and there were traces of white and grey at his temples. How old was Armand Dubois? Mid-forties, she guessed, and still an attractive man. Élodie sensed Dominique's sharp glance across at her and she looked away, back to the screen.

'You are not precious about your work,' Armand said, as he swiped through the photographs. Élodie guessed that he was referring to the goat and the curly-woolled sheep – quite clearly still works in progress and both with more than a hint of humour about them, she hoped. 'I am glad about that.'

'It's art,' she said with a light shrug, 'not life, death or rocket science.'

He nodded. 'But so often, artists take their work too seriously. Believe me, I know.' He rolled his dark eyes and gave a little laugh.

Élodie smiled. She could well imagine.

'They do not understand that art is a commodity. It is worth what anyone might pay for it, you know? Some artists have such a superior view of their work, they imagine it is worth all their hours of toil, but sadly this is not necessarily the case.'

'I'm not like that,' said Élodie, just in case he hadn't got that yet.

'I can see that you are not.' He looked intently at the last photograph of a kingfisher on a branch, poised as if to dive, streaked dark wood making up the separate strands of his tail. Again, he smiled. 'And now I think it is time for lunch, *non*?'

He took her to a small restaurant up the hill. Auray's river was wide and green and lacked the drama of the sea Élodie was used to, but she had to admit that the town was charming in other ways. An old hand-rail led the way up the cobbled steps, the timbered buildings seemed to lean into narrow streets more like alleyways, and ancient black lanterns and sculptures decorated the stone walls. Dominique had not seemed too enamoured of the fact that they were going out to lunch together but Armand was apparently oblivious. Perhaps he took too much time off having lunch with his artists and clients, Élodie thought. Perhaps Dominique mistrusted him. Who knew?

386

Over a delicious lunch of gilthead bream and lentils, they chatted about art and he told her how he had come to own a gallery. He was an artist as she had half-guessed, but in his own words, he didn't have the talent to make much of it. Instead, he took a degree in business studies and when his parents passed away, he used his inheritance to set up the Modus Gallery.

'Have you ever shown your own work?' Élodie asked him. She hoped it wasn't just the good food and laid-back atmosphere, but she was beginning to feel very relaxed with him. Better still, she felt that already she trusted him. And that was vital, if she was going to say yes to his proposition.

Armand laughed. '*Merde, non*,' he said. 'I am a realist more than I am a dreamer.'

'And yet you have a great vision,' she said shyly. 'Your exhibition, your plans, the gallery itself . . .'

'*Merci*.' He took a sip of his wine. 'You are kind. But it has been quite the learning curve.'

'You've made mistakes?'

'Who doesn't?' He shrugged. 'But now, I have more experience. Now, I know what I want.'

She had certainly noticed that. Élodie hesitated. 'What made you choose me?' she asked.

'I fell in love with your driftwood horse. Standing outside the florist's like that, I couldn't decide if he wanted to canter inside the shop and cover himself with flowers or simply gallop away.'

Élodie threw back her head and laughed. The image was so glorious – and yet she had considered this as she was making him. That was the thing about movement – one also had to decide in which direction a creation was going. She stopped laughing when she realised how closely he was observing her.

'You should laugh more often,' he said. 'It suits you.'

And it was true, she realised. The man hardly knew her and yet he was bang on. She enjoyed her work, her solitary walks along the cliffs searching for sea treasure on the beach, her quiet evenings with her mother at the Old Lighthouse and her meetings with Thea. But how often did she laugh? She repressed a small sigh. She laughed with Jacques, of course. Perhaps in some ways her relationship with her brother had been so close and so rewarding that it had spoiled her for the rest of the world, for the future.

Armand refilled their glasses with the last of the grape-fruit-scented white wine and ordered coffee and dessert. 'We must indulge,' he said. 'It is not often we get to celebrate a new partnership, and besides, it is strawberry tart.'

This was all so new to Élodie – the food, the wine, the company. But she was beginning to think she could get used to it.

'And I should like to ask you,' said Armand as their desserts arrived, 'how it is possible for such a wealth of material to come from the beaches of one small island?'

'We have some strong tides and currents.' She took a spoonful of strawberries. The dessert was perfectly balanced in sweetness. 'And many storms in the winter.' What was washed up on the beach certainly produced enough for her creative needs.

'Do you pick up everything the sea brings you?'

She wondered if he was teasing her. 'Not everything,' she said sternly. '*Naturellement*, there is a selective process.'

'But of course.'

'Not every piece of wood lends itself to the natural form.'

'I should think not.' He laughed. 'I did not suppose for a moment that you used any old plank.'

She laughed with him. Thought of all the wood she collected, sorted, cleaned. 'Though you'd be surprised.'

He put his elbows on the table and leaned closer. 'And after that, when you have the pieces you need – how do you begin?'

'I study the subject. Take photographs. Make drawings.' Élodie felt herself flush. No doubt it was the wine. 'I decide on the framework, decide how to stabilise the piece, create a plan.'

'Do you make a maquette for the larger pieces?'

Élodie was surprised at his knowledge. She could see the advantages of making a miniature, but – 'Very rarely. I tend to go with the flow.'

'And does it not worry you?' Armand paused his conversation to take a last spoonful of his dessert. 'The impermanent nature of your work? That you will lose it eventually?'

'Yes, it does.' This was something Élodie often thought about. No matter how much you cared for driftwood, no matter how much you protected it from the elements, if a sculpture were left outside it would last no more than ten years at best. 'But so much in life is transitory.' She met his gaze with some difficulty this time. She could explain how she felt about the nature of her work, about the island and the landscape, the visitors who came and went with the ebb and flow of the tide. But was it appropriate? After all – she hardly knew the man.

'I think I understand. But I wonder . . .' He eyed her intently. 'Have you never considered preserving your work by casting in bronze?'

She shook her head. 'Never.' But even as she said it, she was pondering the possibility. Could she do that? Could she bring that kind of permanence into her work, her life?

The waitress brought their coffee and although they

continued to chat on lighter subjects, the strong bitter coffee signalled the end of their meal.

'*Eh bien*,' Armand said at last, as he lazily pushed his cup to one side. 'I suppose I should get back to the gallery to relieve Dominique before she shuts up shop and comes looking for me.'

And although he said this with humour, Élodie sensed that it implied a possible scenario. 'Does Dominique have a share in the gallery too?' Armand had treated her more like an employee and yet she had called herself a partner. If she was a partner in the gallery, Élodie would like to know.

'We met at college,' Armand told her. 'We started the venture together and so I do not correct her when she calls herself a partner. But in truth . . .'

Élodie waited.

'We are not partners, *non*. Not in any sense of the word.' He glanced across at her. 'You would be dealing directly with me.'

Élodie wondered what she should say to that. She was, she had to admit, rather relieved. Dominique had not seemed like the friendliest person, and this experience would be hard enough for her as it was. 'That's fine,' she said. 'And thank you so much for lunch and for showing me the gallery. But now, I must be getting back to Belle-Île.'

'Before we part . . .' Once again, he was looking at her intently. 'May I ask if you have come to a decision? I do not intend to push you if you need more time, but you understand that if you say *non*, I will have to ask someone else.'

'Well . . .' Élodie was wavering. She should talk to Jacques, she thought. She needed someone else's input on this and he was the person who had always helped her find her way – even when he was so far from her.

'I think you know how much I would love to show your sculptures, Élodie,' Armand continued. 'And I am sure we would work well together.'

She nodded. She felt that this was true. Armand was waiting. He had taken her out to lunch and gone to a great deal of trouble. Any other artist would jump at the chance, she knew that. She took a deep breath. She could make the decision alone – she had to. She had forged an independent life for herself after Jacques left and she didn't need his advice now. She closed her eyes for a half-second. She knew what she had to do. 'The answer is yes, please,' she said.

'Wonderful.' Armand raised his glass and grinned from ear to ear. 'To the start of a mutually beneficial relationship,' he said. 'I am looking forward to working with you, Élodie. It is the start of something very exciting – you will see.'

Something very exciting . . . On the ferry travelling back to the island, as the jagged mass of green and grey that was Belle-Île drew closer and clearer with every blink of the eye, Élodie could hardly believe the leap that she had made. But she didn't regret it. In the cool of the evening air, the smells of salt and engine oil mingled in her nostrils. She had sobered up now but she could still feel the adrenalin pumping through her veins. She felt proud that she'd done it, excited that she'd been able to. She had fallen into a trap living and working on the island as she did; it was too easy to live that life and for nothing to change. But now . . . Perhaps after all, something *should* change.

Élodie liked Armand Dubois – maybe she had even flirted with him a little over lunch, and for Élodie it had been a long time . . . Working towards this exhibition, and the exhibition itself, would add to her life, she thought, rather than take anything away. Like this water that flowed between Belle-Île and the Gulf of Morbihan. It wasn't just a separation, a division that made the island what it was — a solitary piece of land. It was also a bridge, a connection to a different life. Armand Dubois was right — it was new and it was going to be exciting too.

CHAPTER 51

Colette

Colette was in the flower shop adding the last touches to a small bouquet ordered by Anneliese for her sister's birthday.

'We are fortunate that we have the music festival this week,' she said as she counted out the coins from her purse. '*Ma soeur*, she imagines they are playing for her alone.' She chuckled.

'Oh, is it this week? How lovely.' Colette remembered those festivals so well. She hoped that the music would drift up to the first floor above the shop and that her mother would hear and enjoy it. She had always loved the Fest Noz, when live bands played in the harbour and on the beach: traditional Breton folksongs, sometimes classical guitar, something more pop- or rock-orientated for the younger contingent perhaps. The music never seemed to puncture the peace of sleepy Sauzon, but it did inject some life and vitality; it was a time when the whole village – Bellîlois and tourists alike – could come out of their houses and join in the fun.

'Here you are, it's finished.' Colette handed Anneliese the

bouquet, made up of white roses, pink oriental lilies, carna-
tions and box.

'*Merci beaucoup*, my dear. She will love it.' Anneliese took
them, inhaled their scent.

'And have a lovely time.'

'You are not going?' Annaliese was aghast. 'But Colette, the
whole village will be there.'

Colette shrugged. 'My mother . . .'

'I understand.' Anneliese put a hand on her arm. 'Take care,
Colette, thank you for the flowers. And give my love to your
mother.' She crossed herself.

'*Merci*, Anneliese, *au revoir*.'

Colette was thinking about closing up for the day when
Étienne strolled in. 'Hey.'

As always when she saw him, Colette's heart seemed to grow
a bit lighter. 'Hello,' she said. 'How are you feeling today?'
She examined his face. Did he look a little less burdened? She
hoped so.

'Ready for a break,' he said. 'How about you?'

Colette hesitated. Francine was with her mother this afternoon
and although there were things to do in the shop . . . She decided
not to make the same mistake her mother had made. Life was
short – and it wasn't even her shop. 'Why not?' She washed her
hands at the sink. 'Did you have something special in mind?'

'Music,' he said. 'There's a bit of a *plage musicale* going on
tonight – in fact it's already started.'

'The Fest Noz.' A traditional festival of the night. 'Has it
begun already?' Colette strained to hear, and sure enough she
could catch strains of an accordion and a violin.

'We could go a bit later,' he suggested. 'Wait till it's warmed
up?'

'Perfect,' she said. That way, she could make her mother some tea and spend some time sitting with her before leaving her to sleep. She felt a little leap of anticipation. 'Just for an hour or so,' she warned him. These festivals were important in Brittany and in her experience could go on well into the night. They were meaningful too – an expression of individual identity within their community. Colette could picture in her mind her parents dancing on the beach, the sea dark and heaving behind them, the moon shining above. 'I'll have a word with Francine.'

Francine urged her to go. '*Mais oui*,' she said. 'You shouldn't stay cooped up here the whole time. It is Fest Noz.'

'Are you sure? I feel I want to stay—'

'With your mother, I know you do. But she's tired and I'm here. You are young. It is summertime. It is a warm and romantic evening. Go and listen to some music on the beach, why don't you?'

The band of folk musicians were on the sandy shingle beyond the harbour. They were a motley crew playing a variety of instruments – one on mandolin, one playing the *bombarde*, another on the little bagpipe, plus the fiddle player and the man on the accordion. They wore the usual white shirts and black waistcoats and trousers, and Colette was sure she recognised a couple of them from the old days.

As well as the musicians there was a barbecue, the heat from the smoking coals spiralling into the night air. Colette spotted Henri and his son manning it, busy grilling fish and shellfish. '*Ça va, ma petite?*' he called, and waved.

'*Ça va*, Henri!' she called back.

Groups of tourists were listening to the music, cliques of Sauzon old-timers sitting on the beach and the harbour wall, on blankets and beach chairs, clapping and tapping their feet. Colette saw Berthe, Claude Macon and some of the other shopkeepers, and Anneliese and her family sitting together, a white lace tablecloth laid out in the centre of the little group, Colette's flowers to one side. She smiled. They were such a community, these people of Sauzon. They had taken her mother into their midst and looked after her. Since Colette had arrived, there had been so many small gifts left at the door – chocolates and tasty patisserie from Madame Riou at the boulangerie, choice cuts of meat from the butcher, the occasional goodies from Berthe and Anneliese, even fresh fish from Henri and his son. Colette had been overwhelmed by the love and the care.

Étienne, though, was steering her away from the Bellîlois towards a secluded spot by the harbour wall. 'I look around,' he muttered, 'and I imagine what they are thinking, what they are saying.' He tore his hands through his hair in the way that Colette had grown accustomed to. Writer's imagination, she found herself thinking. 'Étienne . . .' She grabbed his hand. 'They weren't there. They don't know what happened.'

He stopped, took hold of her hands in both of his. Colette felt her heart miss a beat. It was only friendship, she reminded herself, that was all. 'They do talk though. They talk to me, some of them. It's been brought up, the whole episode, the tragedy.'

'Small-town chat.' She'd experienced it for herself.

'Exactly.' Étienne shuddered.

'Don't let it get to you.' They were still standing facing one another, the music playing behind them. She almost didn't dare look into his face. 'It's you who have to move on. They don't matter. It's you who have to forgive yourself.'

For a long moment he was still. Then he seemed to shake himself like a dog exiting water and came to. 'You're right.' He spoke almost briskly. 'I'm sorry, Colette. I should have asked you straight away – is everything all right at home?'

They carried on walking down the beach. The tide was out and a half-full moon glimmered on to the sleek oily water. There was a pause in the music and she caught the soft pulse of the tide in the breeze. 'Mathilde, you mean?'

'Ah, so that was Mathilde Blaise.' He looked thoughtful. Everyone talked, Colette reminded herself.

They sat down beside the harbour wall, some way from the musicians but able still to enjoy the music as it wafted towards them. Colette leaned back and exhaled. 'She brought round a diary,' she said.

'*Merde*.'

'My mother's diary,' she clarified.

'Jesus.' He picked up some gravelly sand and let it sift between his fingers. 'Have you—?'

She shook her head. She'd hardly had a moment, but besides that, it didn't seem right. It would be disrespectful. Yes, she wanted to know her mother's secret, but not like that, not by reading her diary when she was still alive. And besides, if she waited . . . Her mother might tell her herself.

'So, how was it between them? Did they speak to one another?'

Colette shook her head. 'Maman was asleep.' She looked out into the distance towards the ocean. Which in some ways had been a blessing. 'But Mathilde will be back.'

'And then perhaps you'll find out what happened between them, eh?' Étienne was watching her thoughtfully.

'Yes.' She gave a rueful smile. 'Maybe I will.'

'How has she been, your mother?' Étienne's voice was gentle, almost caressing. Colette found herself wishing she could simply close her eyes and that he might stroke her hair, her cheek, her brow.

'It's almost as if she's waiting.' Colette hadn't voiced this thought before – not even to herself.

'What is she waiting for?' Étienne frowned. She was glad he didn't find this thought too morbid. 'For death, do you think?' He placed his hand over hers, as if he could soften the words, take some of the pain away.

'Perhaps.' Colette considered this. It was a depressing illness, degenerative and terminal. 'Or perhaps she's waiting for Mathilde.' And whatever Mathilde had to tell her. So, if it wasn't Léo Blaise who her father had been referring to when they had that quarrel, then who was he, this man her mother had loved? Could this be the secret that her diary would reveal?

Étienne fetched them a *bolée* of cider each from the café on the waterfront and they drank this with a plateful of langoustines cooked in garlic and chilli on Henri's barbecue, the juices soaked through the papery skins. The music played on. Colette recognised the traditional echoes, harmonies and refrains of the *kaner* and *diskaner*, the responsive singing where one singer began and the next responded. These songs, this music, were part of her past, but still remained in her mind, in her heart. The roots of Breton culture ran deep.

Berthe danced with Claude, and Henri with his wife, then with Anneliese, clapping and twirling in the traditional twos and fours. Soon, nearly all the villagers were dancing their *gavotte bretonne*, in a line, taking small skipping steps in four-four time and swinging their arms. The pace quickened, the line swayed, curving into a circle, re-forming, fluid as a river.

Colette watched with a sense of contentment; she knew that each individual was just one element within the whole, as in the Breton community, that this dance represented the culture into which she'd been born. There was laughter, clapping, the trumpeting of the *bombarde*, the rise and fall of the fiddle urging the dancers on, faster and faster.

'Shall we?' said Étienne, when they had finished their supper and wiped their greasy hands on the paper napkins Henri had provided.

Colette swigged her cider. 'You're joking.'

'Why not?' He jumped to his feet, pulling her with him. 'Have you forgotten how?'

'No,' she laughed. 'I haven't forgotten how.' And together they linked arms and joined the circle. To Colette it was as if she had never been away.

Later, they made their way from the harbour back to the house. Colette would have liked to stay longer, but she knew she'd regret it. Her mother probably wouldn't be awake, but she still needed to be there.

'How's the story going?' she asked him, as they climbed the steps to the waterfront.

'Which one?' He gave her a lopsided grin.

'The one from the heart.' It was darker now and lights were twinkling along the promenade outside the little cafés and bars. Colette felt energised by the dancing, no longer surprised that her feet had remembered every step.

'It's almost done.'

'Good.' Colette took his arm as they started to climb the hill. But she couldn't help being a bit sad as well. He had been such a support to her and she dreaded him leaving, knew that it would happen soon. He'd only stayed so long to face up to those past ghosts, to sell the house, to write his story . . . But friends like Étienne didn't come along every day of the week.

And he was just a friend. Étienne had made no move towards her, and there had been opportunities enough since she'd split up with Mark, not least tonight when they'd danced so close together, arms entwined, fuelled by cider and the romance of the night. So clearly, she'd been wrong to think there could be more between them. She reminded herself of how reluctant he was to let people in. And perhaps he was right. Perhaps in the end, friendship was more valuable than love.

'And it is thanks to you, Colette.' They reached the flower shop and for a moment Colette thought she saw the twitch of Francine's lace curtains as they stood at the gate. Like the old days, she thought – but not.

'You did it yourself.' Now, as she looked into his face, she wanted to trace his eyebrows with her fingertip, she longed to stroke her thumb against his unshaven cheek and feel the touch of his skin, she ached to touch his mouth, run her fingers through his hair.

'This may not be the right time,' he said. 'What with your mother and—'

'It is.'

'Colette.'

'I'm here.'

When he kissed her, she felt the warmth of his lips contrast with the lightest of breezes playing on her neck, turning her skin to goosebumps. She felt his arms tighten around her, the press of his mouth, the sweetest, most golden feeling. And she knew it wasn't only friendship. There had to be more. Because he was a perfect fit.

CHAPTER 52

Colette

For the third morning in a row, Colette awoke in the chair feeling cramped, her arms and back aching. Her mother seemed to be sleeping peacefully – her breathing weak but steady. Colette reached over and gently put a hand on her brow. She got up and stretched, went to the window, thought of that kiss. It was just a kiss, but . . .

Her glance fell on to her mother's diary, still sitting unread on the bedside table. That diary might tell her everything she wanted and needed to know. But she wouldn't read it, not yet. As she'd already told Étienne, it didn't seem like the right time. Her mother was still aware, still alive, still here in this room. And Colette wanted to be in the present moment with her, while she still could. There would be plenty of time later – to read about the past, to fill in the gaps, to understand.

Her gaze drifted to the photograph of the boy – Jez – taken in Loe Bar. The perfect day. Why had her mother hidden it away? Because it reminded her of those old times in Cornwall when she was a girl of seventeen? Because of the boy? Or did it remind her too much of that girl she once was?

Mathilde Blaise was coming to visit this morning. Colette drew the blinds to let in a glimmer of morning light, though not enough to disturb her mother or strain her eyes. She wanted light, but she could no longer take it. Colette would have a shower, make some coffee, bring some more fresh flowers into the room to disguise the stale and metallic medicinal smell. She knew that her mother was waiting for Mathilde to come.

The nurse popped in at the start of her shift and made the usual checks.

'How is she?' Colette asked. Her mother's eyes were closed and the nurse looked more serious than usual.

'It won't be long.' She put her hand on Colette's arm. 'I'm sorry, my dear, but you should be prepared.'

Colette nodded. She'd known this, but it was still heart-breaking to hear. 'How long?' she whispered.

'A day or two, hours perhaps.' The nurse was still for a moment before she started packing away her things. 'It may be longer, but she's on her way.' She moved to the door and Colette went out with her and down the hall. 'Thank you,' she said.

'Will you be all right?' The nurse looked concerned. 'You should tell Francine.'

'I will.' Though Francine was already aware.

'The doctor will call in later. You have my number.' The nurse became brisk. After all, she had so many patients, so many others to see.

'*Au revoir.*' Colette shut the door behind her. Days or hours? After all this, how long did they have?

Mathilde arrived half an hour later.

402

'Come in.' Colette took her through. 'She's very weak,' she whispered before she opened the door of her mother's room. She hoped she didn't need to say more, that Mathilde would understand.

'Oh, my dear.' Mathilde almost crumpled as she took in the sight of the frail figure in the bed. 'Oh, my poor dear.' Tentatively, she stepped towards her.

'Mathilde,' she whispered. She struggled to sit up but Mathilde put out a hand to stop her.

'Just rest,' she said. 'Rest now, my dear.'

It seemed to be all right, but Colette decided to stick around. She didn't want to pry but neither did she want her mother getting upset on what could be her last day on this earth. She and Mathilde clearly had something to resolve and if Colette was right, this visit could be what her mother was waiting for. Hopefully, this would give her a chance of finding some peace at last.

Mathilde sat on the chair that Colette had vacated and gently took her mother's hand. So far so good. Colette made a tactful withdrawal to the kitchen, leaving the door ajar.

'Thea, I have come to beg for your forgiveness.' Mathilde's voice was soft. 'I have done so many things that were very unfair and very wrong.'

Oh, dear, thought Colette. Though this wasn't exactly what she'd been expecting.

'I shouldn't have slept with him,' Mathilde went on. 'I know that. It was an unforgivable thing to do. And I certainly should never have told him our secret.'

For a moment, Colette felt that she was losing her balance. *What?* She held on to the kitchen counter and stared back towards the room she had just left.

'You see, I was angry and bitter about Léo. I felt betrayed. You of all people . . .'

Léo again, thought Colette. But who . . .?

'There was nothing between me and Léo,' Colette heard her mother say in her rasping whisper. 'Nothing.'

'I know that now.'

'Sébastien,' she whispered. 'Why did you . . .?'

'I intended to drive you away. Right away. But you were so stubborn, you wouldn't go. And Sébastien . . .' Mathilde's voice broke.

Colette frowned. What did her father have to do with this?

'Sébastien didn't want me. He never wanted me. He loved you, Thea, not me. I hope you know that now.'

Colette leaned on the counter. Her father had betrayed her mother. Her father had slept with Mathilde Blaise. But . . . Her mind spun back to the night he died, to the argument she'd overheard, trying to make sense of it all.

You don't have to pretend any more, he had said to her mother. *At least, you don't have to pretend with me.*

Mathilde had slept with him. Mathilde had told him Thea's secret.

'Yes, I seduced him.' Mathilde was whispering now, but Colette's ears were tuned in to her words. She shuddered, but still moved closer to the door in order to hear more clearly. 'He was cross with you for working all hours and not being around when he wanted you to be. He was flattered, no doubt, by my attention, he was a man, *n'est-ce pas*?' Her voice hardened. 'But I only did it because I thought that you and Léo had once done the same.'

'I understand.' Her mother's voice was so quiet, Colette had to strain to hear.

'It was a crazy time for me.' Mathilde's voice went on, gentle but determined. 'I thought that she was Léo's, Thea. I was so sure. And it was such a blow. I can't tell you.'

She? Who was Mathilde talking about now? Colette hovered, ready to rush in. She could see through the gap in the doorway – her mother and Mathilde, hands clasped, Mathilde openly weeping, her mother's eyes so achingly sad.

'When I realised that Sébastien didn't want our liaison to continue,' Mathilde went on, 'when I knew he was going back to you, that he had never left you, never wanted me, that he regretted it all . . . That's when I truly lost my reason. That's when I told him what had happened between you and me. Our secret.'

Their secret. A silence seemed to pervade the room, stretch out to where Colette stood in the doorway. She could piece most of it together now even though she still didn't know what the secret could be. That was why her parents had argued. Colette's father had challenged her mother about it: *It's not a secret*, he had said. *Not any more.* And Thea must have known there was only one person who could have told him. Mathilde. Her mother hadn't had an affair all those years ago, but her father had. Colette realised that she was shaking. And yet he had asked, hadn't he? He had demanded that her mother tell him the man's name. So, who were they talking about, for God's sake? Léo? Jez?

Colette wanted to race headlong into the room, yell at Mathilde Blaise for trying to break up her parents' marriage all those years ago when she, Colette, was thirteen, for seducing her father, for making them argue, even for the fact that her father had gone out fishing that awful night . . . But she stayed where she was, her shoulders slumped. What was the point?

What would it achieve? She stared over at the two women. This was her mother's business, her battle. And it looked as if the fighting was over.

'We were wrong.' Mathilde spoke softly. 'What we did was wrong.'

'Yes,' said Colette's mother, feebly but quite clearly. 'It was wrong.'

'But now we can do something right.' Mathilde paused. 'Do I have your permission to tell her?'

There was another deep, impenetrable silence, broken only by Mathilde's weeping.

Colette edged back into the room. She saw her mother gently touch Mathilde's hand. Ever so imperceptibly, she nodded.

'Goodbye, Thea.' Mathilde must have seen it too. She leaned over and kissed her brow. 'I am so sorry,' she whispered. Still weeping, she made her way past Colette and slowly out of the room.

Colette glanced towards her mother. She was staring ahead, lost once again in one of those old dreams of hers. All those years Colette had blamed her . . . She turned and followed Mathilde into the hallway.

Mathilde turned to face her. She had wiped her eyes dry now. 'Thank you for letting me see her,' she said.

'I did it for my mother.' Colette knew that she sounded harsh. She felt harsh. Especially now that she knew the truth.

'Have you read your mother's diary?' Mathilde asked her.

Colette shook her head.

'When you do, you might understand, *chérie*.'

Colette wasn't so sure. She watched Mathilde walk away and she was glad to see her go.

CHAPTER 53

Mathilde

Mathilde stood at the French windows and watched Élodie heading towards the Old Lighthouse. Mathilde had asked her to come over; she had told Jacques to make himself scarce for a couple of hours. *I have things I have to say to Élodie.* Things she should have said a long time ago.

She smiled as Élodie drew closer. She had such an ethereal look about her, a sweet kind of fragility that made one think she was insubstantial – weak, even. But in fact, Élodie was strong. Look at her now. She had stood up to Léo when many – including Mathilde – hadn't dared, she had continued to see Thea against Mathilde's wishes, she had been loyal enough to stay here on the island to stay close to Mathilde, and yet now she had found the strength to branch out in her work, to agree to this exhibition in Auray, to develop her business and go out into the world. Mathilde was proud of her. She had always known it. Élodie was special.

Mathilde went over to the stove to make coffee the way Élodie liked it – strong and yet mellow. Many of her dearest memories of Thea were of Thea and herself sitting in this kitchen long after the children had gone to bed, drinking coffee or wine, exchanging confidences and dreams. That was what friendship was all about, and theirs had been one of the best. Now, though . . .

It had been a shock to see her like that, dying, and at such a relatively young age. But Mathilde was glad she had gone there, glad she had returned Thea's diary and said her piece. And now – this was one last thing she could do for her before she died; the only thing. Had her old friend forgiven her? She hoped so. Thea hadn't said so, but Mathilde would have to live with that and it was no more than she deserved. It was only right that Mathilde had asked Thea's permission to tell the truth, that Thea's diary was back where it belonged. Mathilde should never have taken it. But then again, there was so much she should not have done.

'Mama?' Élodie drifted into the room in that way she had. 'Mmm, I smell coffee. How lovely.' And she settled herself at the pitted oak table that had experienced and witnessed so much in their household. 'What did you want to talk to me about?'

Mathilde poured the coffee and brought it over. 'I saw Thea.' She put the cups on the table along with a small jug of milk. And what about Élodie? Would she be able to find it in her heart to forgive?

'I'm glad.' Élodie's smile was wistful. 'How was she, Mama?'

'Very frail.' Mathilde reached out to pat her hand. She couldn't bear it if Élodie did not forgive her. How could she live without Élodie nearby? She had always been so scared of losing her. 'I'm sorry, *chérie*, but I do not think she will be with us for much longer.'

Élodie's eyes filled.

'Which is why I must talk to you.'

Élodie looked up, surprised. 'About Thea?'

Mathilde nodded. 'You always wondered why we argued. Why I asked her to leave?'

'Yes.' Élodie was watching Mathilde rather warily, as if she wasn't sure she would like what she was about to hear.

And you won't, thought Mathilde. *You really won't.* She took a deep breath. 'When Thea first came to live with us, Élodie, I was pregnant.'

'Yes, I know.' Élodie smiled. 'That was why you needed her help.'

'It was.' Though it was so much more than that. With Léo away so often, Mathilde had needed a companion other than Jacques. Truth was, she had needed a friend. 'But what I didn't know,' she paused, 'was that Thea was pregnant too.'

'Really?' Élodie frowned.

Mathilde knew what she was thinking. 'She hid it for a long time,' she told Élodie. 'Thea was such a slight young thing, she hardly showed, and we were always so isolated here.' Élodie knew that better than most.

Mathilde remembered the day she'd noticed. It was some weeks after that terrible incident on the beach when Jacques could have drowned and Thea had saved his life. She and Thea had been clearing out one of the bathroom closets, looking for cot sheets for Mathilde's new arrival.

'You know, being on Belle-Île really suits you, Thea,' Mathilde had said, surveying her. There had been nothing of her when she first arrived on the island. 'You're looking so well. Almost . . .' *Blooming,* she had been about to say.

At that moment, Thea had reached up to the top shelf of

the closet, her shirt rising – and Mathilde had let out a small gasp. 'Blooming,' she said.

Thea had stood there holding a pile of sheets. Her eyes were wide, her face pale. She looked terrified.

'Thea?' Mathilde stared at her. 'Are you pregnant?'

'She was so scared,' Mathilde told Élodie. 'This was 1969. Of course, it happened, girls got into trouble, but it was very frowned upon back then, as you can imagine.'

'Of course.' Élodie let out a small sigh. 'Poor Thea. But what . . .?'

'I will tell you.'

Thea had burst into tears, and admitted that it was true. *I'm so sorry*, she kept muttering. *I should have told you, Mathilde. But . . .*

'She didn't know what to do,' Mathilde went on. 'She was so far from home. She had told no one.'

'Your parents?' Mathilde had said to her. 'What about your parents?' Surely, they would help the poor girl?

Thea had shaken her head. 'I was going to write to them. I even started the letter. But I can't tell them. They wouldn't understand. I know exactly how it would be. They'd die of shame. And they'd make me get rid of it somehow—' She was almost hysterical by now.

Mathilde gathered that her parents were very conventional, very rigid in their thinking, and that they lived in a small, tightly knit community within which such shameful things as unplanned teenage pregnancies were swept under the carpet and never spoken of. Anyway, it was almost too late for Thea to go back to England, to be whisked away to the home of some maiden aunt where she could stay until after the baby had been born and given away for adoption.

'They would never let me keep it,' Thea had moaned. And Mathilde had understood as only another pregnant woman could understand. Their pregnancies had united them more than ever.

'What did she do?' Élodie's voice was so low, Mathilde could hardly catch the words. 'What did you do, Mama? What happened to the baby?'

What could she do? She was hardly going to tell her to leave. Thea had saved Mathilde's son's life. She owed her everything. 'I comforted her. We talked about it. Discussed the options.'

'We're in this situation together,' Mathilde had told her. 'I'll help you all I can.' Though even at the time she had no idea how it could possibly work out. Would Léo consent to Thea keeping her baby at the house while she was still working for them? She guessed not. Léo wanted his own family; he wouldn't want to be responsible for anyone else's. She could hear him already. *What do you think we're doing here, Mathilde? Running a home for unmarried mothers?*

She shrugged. 'I told her that I would think of something.'

Élodie stared at her. 'But babies don't just go away.'

'Some do.' Mathilde felt the old grief creep into her. 'Some do, my darling.'

'But didn't Papa notice – about Thea?' Élodie was still frowning.

'He was away quite a lot at that time.' She didn't say it, but Élodie would know. A heavily pregnant wife didn't interest Léo; he had other fish to fry. He had come back that weekend after Mathilde had found out about his mistress, but he'd had plenty of other things on his mind and it had been a flying visit. It had been easy for Thea to wear a loose dress, to keep out of his way.

411

'But what did you think would happen when Thea's baby was born?' Élodie had hardly touched her coffee but now she picked up the cup and slowly sipped. 'How could you hide a baby?'

'We didn't really plan anything.' Amazing though it seemed, this was true. Their friendship had grown stronger with every day that passed. Mathilde knew that Thea was becoming increasingly desperate as her time got closer. She kept out of sight when anyone from the village came to the Old Lighthouse and Jacques was too young to take much notice. But they still had no idea what to do. It was almost as if they had both decided to let events take their course, to deal with it only when they were forced to. They were living in a different, almost unreal world, the three of them: Mathilde, Thea and Jacques. As for the rest . . . 'I couldn't imagine Thea ever leaving us,' Mathilde said.

'But she did.'

'Yes, she did.' Though that, of course, was much later. How had they ever thought that they could get away with it? How had Mathilde imagined that she could live with this lie? She had been deluded – they had both been deluded. One of them grieving and scared, the other one desperate, not knowing where to turn.

Mathilde sighed. Now she was coming to the hardest part of the story. 'I was further on than Thea,' she said. 'But not by much.' She gazed out, beyond her darling Élodie, to the ocean she'd always loved. 'I was looking for some of Jacques's old baby clothes. I knew exactly where they were – in the top of the wardrobe in my bedroom. I called to Thea to give me a hand, but she was looking after Jacques and . . .' Her voice trailed. She remembered her own impatience. 'I'll get them myself,' she'd muttered, and she'd grabbed a chair and

412

climbed up. 'They were right at the back of the top shelf,' she told Élodie. 'I thought I could reach. I stretched out. I lost my balance. I slipped.'

'Oh, Mama.' Élodie's expression was concerned. 'Were you all right? What happened?'

'I went into labour prematurely. The midwife was in Le Palais attending another birth. Thea looked after me, but . . .' Her voice broke. Thea had wanted to telephone Léo but Mathilde had been terrified. What if he guessed that this was her fault? She remembered his fingers pressing into her neck. She had promised to be careful. 'Don't phone him,' she had begged Thea, 'not yet.'

Élodie reached over the table and took her hand. 'I don't understand, Mama,' she said. 'It was all right in the end, was it not? I'm here, aren't I – and so are you?' She smiled.

She was breaking Mathilde's heart. 'I lost my baby,' she said. She remembered only too well that feeling of grief, of loss, of pure devastation. And underlining this was that overwhelming fear – what would Léo say? How angry would he be? He wanted this baby. He had a boy and now he wanted a girl; his perfect family. He had already threatened her. He would blame her for the loss. He would never forgive her. And besides, she could feel him losing interest, she needed to draw him back into their family again. 'My baby was stillborn, Élodie,' she said.

'Oh.' Élodie was clearly trying to compute this. 'You mean this was before I was born? You mean I had a sister or a brother, who didn't survive?'

Mathilde shook her head. This was so hard. But how could all the certainties of so many years be wiped away in one stroke? 'It was before you were born, Élodie, yes,' she said. 'Because you are Thea's daughter, not mine.'

413

CHAPTER 54

Élodie

Walking back to her studio, Élodie paused for a moment, as she often did, to watch the sea. It had been a calm morning with a soft haze lying over the ocean, but now the weather was drawing in. It reminded her of that day with Jacques in the bivouac in the pine forest. The sea was changing – Élodie was so attuned to the moods of the ocean that she sensed it before she saw it, before she heard it. Now, the waves were faster and more determined, the tide was higher, the rush was louder. The breeze had picked up and was catching her hair and whipping it away from her scalp, into her face as she turned. There would be a summer storm.

Everything is different now, she thought. She was different now – a different person – and nothing would ever feel the same again. In the past hour, her whole world had spun on its axis. Things that she had always assumed to be true were no longer true. Her mother – Mathilde – was not her mother at all. Élodie's very identity had been snatched from her, like the tide snatched the sand, drawing it back into the depths of the ocean.

She turned around to look at the Old Lighthouse. The light was layered on the horizon above the house; a dark cloud hanging heavy in a brooding sky, pinpricks of brightness from a half-hidden sun. And yet it explained so much. The relationship between Thea and Mathilde, for one. The way she herself thought. Mathilde's irrational fears. Élodie looked away. She turned from the lighthouse and from the sea and opened the studio door. She had planned to work this afternoon, to think about her upcoming exhibition, about new pieces she might create and show to Armand Dubois. She wanted his approval; she respected his opinion and she didn't want to let him – or herself – down. But now . . . She couldn't think about work. She could only think about this bombshell.

'I don't understand,' she had said to Mathilde. Thea? *How* . . .? But even as she asked the question, even as the woman she had always thought of as her mother started to explain, it was already falling into place. Mathilde had lost Léo's baby. He would be angry, she was grief-stricken. Thea was expecting a child and she didn't know what to do about it. As a single woman back then this was a very different prospect from how it would be in this day and age – Élodie must remember that. Thea would have been terrified. And yet this baby could solve both their problems. Because apart from Thea and Mathilde – no one else knew.

'It sounds crazy.' Mathilde had tried to reach out to her but Élodie was unable to respond. Not yet, at least, until she understood the truth of what had happened.

'It *was* crazy.' Her voice was high, almost hysterical, and she saw Mathilde flinch. *Get a grip, Élodie*, she told herself. She lowered her voice. 'Whose idea was it?' Whose mad idea?

'Mine.' Mathilde seemed unrepentant. But as she pushed

her coffee cup to one side, Élodie saw that her hands were trembling. 'It seemed so obvious.'

'Obvious?' Élodie echoed. But, yes, she could see that she had been the answer to Mathilde's prayers.

'It was the only way I could think of for us – Thea and me – to take control of the situation,' she said. 'There was the probability of public shame, humiliation, separation. I was scared of what your father – Léo – might do . . . If he had even found out that Thea was pregnant . . .'

'Yes.' Élodie could see that of course. He would have sent Thea back to Cornwall immediately – pregnant or not, single parent or not. He'd never been known for his compassion.

Mathilde leaned forward across the table. 'Don't think for one moment that Thea wanted to give you away, Élodie,' she said. 'That was the last thing she wanted to do.'

Élodie felt sick. She didn't want to think about that. She wanted to feel angry with Thea, not sorry for her; she didn't want to imagine her heavily pregnant and alone, about to give birth in a strange country, not knowing where to go or who to turn to. 'So why did she?' she muttered, even though she knew.

'She was thinking of you, Élodie,' Mathilde said. She leaned back but Élodie knew she was still watching her closely. 'I could offer you, her child, what she could not. You would want for nothing. You would be looked after and loved. Thea understood that. She made an unselfish choice – for your sake.'

'But to give up her daughter . . .' Although Élodie had never given birth, she could imagine how it would feel, the strength of the bond between mother and baby, the need to be together.

'I told her she could continue working at the house,' Mathilde said. 'I told her that this way, she wouldn't lose you, not really. She could be with you just as much as she wanted.'

And Élodie realised that this was what had happened – at first.

'I made Thea see that this could be the perfect solution for both of us,' Mathilde said. 'What else was she going to do? At least this way she wouldn't have to give you away to some stranger for adoption and never see you again. She could stay close to you – even though you wouldn't know who she really was.'

My mother, thought Élodie. 'But weren't you worried that Thea would have second thoughts?' she asked. 'What guarantee did you have that she wouldn't just turn round one day and tell me the truth, whisk me off somewhere? Especially when . . .' When my father made my life such a misery, she finished in her head. That must have been hard for Thea to witness, surely?

'I *was* worried.' Mathilde wrung her hands and Élodie could see that worry, that anxiety, the same anxiety in her that she had always been aware of, growing up. What a fear to have to live with. 'But we'd made an agreement. I had told Thea that no one must ever know, that she would never be able to claim you as her child.'

Even so, Élodie thought. That wouldn't have stopped her worrying.

'And then—' Mathilde's voice broke.

'And then?'

'And then things changed.' Mathilde was clearly finding this ever more difficult and despite everything, Élodie's heart went out to her. 'As time went by, I became jealous of the two of you,' she admitted. 'You got on so well. You adored her. She was more like a mother than I was.'

Élodie was silent. It was true. She had been devastated when Thea left. 'So you told her to leave.' Mathilde had been the

417

one to break their agreement, then. She had promised Thea she could stay with Élodie but then she told her to go.

'Yes.' Mathilde hung her head. 'I saw something between Thea and your father and I thought . . .'

'You thought they were having an affair. You thought they'd been having an affair for years.' Élodie realised that it went further than that. Another piece of the puzzle slotted into place. 'You thought that I was his child.'

'Yes.' Mathilde put out a hand and rested her palm on Élodie's wrist. 'The dates . . . It was just possible, you see.'

This time Élodie didn't pull away. She thought of how that must have been for Mathilde, the betrayal she must have felt. 'But I wasn't his child.'

'No.'

'So, who is my father?' Though perhaps she should be asking Thea that question. Thea, who was in fact her mother. And in a way, she saw now, she had always felt it. Mathilde had been right to be jealous. When Thea was their au pair, Élodie had certainly loved her like a mother.

'A boy in Cornwall.' Mathilde looked out of the window towards the sea. 'A boy Thea met before she even came here. That's what she always said. He's your father, Élodie.'

A boy in Cornwall. Élodie let this sink in. She wasn't even French. She'd been born in France but of two British parents. 'Why didn't you ever tell me, Mama?' she whispered. Because Mathilde was still her mother in one very real sense of the word; she had still loved her and brought her up in her family. That couldn't be wiped out and of course Élodie didn't want it to be − whatever else Mathilde had done, whatever the morality behind it all.

'I should have told you before, you're right.' Mathilde let

out a deep sigh. 'I know that. I was so terrified of losing you – especially when Thea decided to stay in Sauzon and she was always here, always around. But your father—'

'Léo.' Élodie's voice sounded harsh to her own ears. That man had blighted her life, and to find out that he wasn't even her father . . .

Mathilde eyed her sadly. 'I can't imagine what he would have done,' she said. 'And as for me – what would I have done without you, Élodie?'

'Oh, Mama.'

'After he left,' Mathilde went on, 'I started thinking about so many things. How badly I had treated Thea, what I had put her through, how you deserved to know the truth, *chérie*.'

'And so now you decide to come clean.' Élodie shook her head. 'Now, when she's so ill, when she's dying, when I can't even have a relationship with her even if I wanted to.' She let out a sob. 'Why didn't Thea tell me herself?' she asked. 'Later, after she left, after I had grown up?'

A guilty look crept over Mathilde's face. 'That was my fault too, *chérie*,' she said. 'I had broken our pact. I was so scared that she would now break her promise not to tell. So I went to see her. I stole her diary. I told her that I would deny it. That no one would believe her. That all she would do was upset you, and for no reason. I told her that she could not be so selfish as to take you away from the family that you were now part of, the family you loved.' She lowered her head and stared down at the table. 'I said a lot of terrible things. A lot of things I bitterly regret. I was in a bad place, Élodie, you must know that. I was so deluded I almost believed you were truly mine.'

'I see.' Élodie tried to compute this. Mathilde had been cruel, even though that cruelty had first been inspired by love.

419

She had been possessive too and insecure – but that was hardly surprising given the man she had married.

'And so you threw her out with nothing.' Élodie got to her feet. 'You denied her even the right to see her child.'

'Not nothing.' Mathilde hesitated. 'I had money inherited from my parents.'

Élodie stared at her. 'You gave Thea money?'

'Only to help her out when I told her to leave,' Mathilde said quickly. 'She didn't want to take it, but—'

'You paid her off?' Élodie was finding this the worst part of the story, the hardest to hear. 'Thea sold me to you, for what? For the price of a flower shop?' She was crying now, hot tears coming from somewhere so deep inside her that she didn't think she could stop.

'It wasn't like that, Élodie.' Mathilde tried to catch hold of her arm. 'We were her family. She had nothing. I paid it into her bank account. I forced her to take it.'

'In return for her silence,' Élodie muttered. She must leave. She had to let it sink in. There was so much to think about and she needed to talk to someone – not Mathilde or Thea but someone else, someone who could be more objective about all this. Jacques, she thought.

'Will you see her, Élodie?' Mathilde's eyes were pleading. 'Will you go and see Thea? She's always loved you. She regrets her decision, I know she does. Like me, she has lived with the guilt. But at the time . . . We couldn't see any other way—'

'I don't know.' Élodie was already walking towards the door.

'Can you forgive us?'

Élodie looked back at the woman she had always thought of as her mother. It was wrong to keep the truth about someone's birth from them – once they were adult enough to understand.

It had been wrong of Mathilde to break her agreement with Thea too. So many things seemed wrong and she didn't know what she felt about any of it – not yet. She only knew that she felt lied to and betrayed by two of the people she loved best in the world. And Jacques? Her beloved Jacques was not even her brother.

In the studio, Élodie wandered around, picking up random pieces of driftwood, staring out of the window, looking into space. On the table in the corner sat her puppet family with their friendly but rather surprised faces, their wedge noses and O-shaped eyes and mouths. She heard the rain come, just as it had come that day when she and Jacques had run for the pine forest. It lashed against her windowpanes, it pounded on the roof. Élodie listened to it and didn't know what to do. She was angry, she was confused, she was at a loss.

She needed to come to terms with all this – somehow. But she also needed more answers. She must go and see Thea, she realised. She didn't have much time.

CHAPTER 55

Thea

Thea awoke from a sleep that wasn't like a sleep at all. Perhaps that was how it was near the end: one drifted in and out of different levels of consciousness, sometimes surfacing and clinging on, sometimes slipping deeper and deeper into some murky place that was neither past nor future. It was tranquil, though, in that place and Thea was almost ready to stay there. But not yet. She was still holding on, still waiting.

She had been surprised that Mathilde had returned her diary. Why now? Because she, Thea, was too weak to take action? Or because the guilt had finally become too much for her? Whatever the reason, Mathilde had now declared her hand; she had decided that the truth should be revealed.

Thea studied the light squeezing through the shutters and tried to decide what time of day it might be. Late afternoon, she thought. The quality of the light was mellow. If she wanted to, she could ring this little hand-bell and someone would come – Colette or Francine. She was not alone.

★

Thea had been in denial at first. She and Jez had been careful. She couldn't be pregnant. She wouldn't be pregnant. She told herself it wasn't happening and for the first few months it was easy to pretend. She was more than four months gone when she finally accepted the truth. She panicked. She even went to the library at Le Palais to find out how she might get rid of it. One night after Mathilde went to bed, she drank half a bottle of gin and climbed into the hottest bath she could manage. But it just made her sick and gave her a stinking headache the next morning. Not to mention the guilt.

Time passed. She was almost seven months when Mathilde found out – fortunately, she'd always been slim and her bump wasn't too difficult to hide – and it was even later when she was pegging washing out on the line one morning that she saw Francine in the distance, walking towards the Old Lighthouse. Thea never found out what she was doing there – she just ran back inside and hid until she was gone. Francine had guessed, though.

Now, Thea heard a voice coming from outside, by the front gate, and she recognised it as Francine's. '*Merci beaucoup*. Yes, I will give them to her. I will tell her. *Merci.*' Well-wishers. They had turned out to be a supportive community here in Sauzon.

Francine had never mentioned anything of this when Thea moved in next door to her, even after Sébastien died, though Thea wondered how much she had heard that night, how much she knew. It was only after Colette had left the island, when Thea was at her lowest – lower even than she had been when she left the Old Lighthouse – that Francine had asked her: 'Did you have a baby? What happened?' And Thea had told her, relieved at last to share her secret.

None of it would have happened if Léo hadn't been the way

he was, if Mathilde hadn't lost her baby, if she hadn't been half crazy with grief from that loss; fragile, so fearful of her husband.

'When are you going to tell him?' Thea had asked her. 'It'll have to be soon. What happens if he suddenly turns up here and there's no baby?'

Mathilde had cried and cried. Thea had never known such grief and Mathilde wasn't strong.

'I can't,' she wailed. 'You don't know what he's like. He'll kill me.'

'He wouldn't do that. I won't let him do that.' Thea had tried to comfort her. Mathilde must be exaggerating, but better to have no husband at all, she thought, than to have one who made your life a misery.

'How are you going to stop him?' Mathilde stared at her then – Thea was unable to hide her pregnancy any longer – and the naked envy in her eyes made Thea take a step away. 'And what do you think he'll say when he sees you?'

And then, Mathilde had come up with her plan. She was feverish with the excitement of it. 'It's the only way, Thea,' she kept saying. 'Can't you see? It's the only way.'

'No. It's a ridiculous idea. What are you thinking?' It must be the grief that was making her talk this way. 'You must tell him what's happened and we must have a proper burial—'

But when Thea went into labour and Mathilde still hadn't told Léo that she'd lost the baby, when she thought of the situation she was in . . .

'What are you going to do?' Mathilde demanded the first time Thea put her daughter to her breast. She had helped her give birth, just as Thea had helped her give birth to her own stillborn daughter. They were in this together. 'Go home? Leave her on a doorstep somewhere?'

'No. I don't know.' She couldn't bear the thought of being parted from her. It wasn't the social stigma – Thea could put up with anything. But if she went back to the UK she'd be forced to have her baby adopted. And if she stayed here . . .

'Think, Thea,' Mathilde had urged over and over. There was a kind of wildness to her that scared Thea. 'It's the obvious solution. The only option for both of us. Léo will be here soon. What then?'

'It could never work.' But Thea too was running out of ideas. 'You're mad.' Perhaps they were both a little mad. It was certainly a plan born of desperation, fear and grief.

Thea trusted Mathilde. She had become her closest friend and already they had been through so much together. This was the only way Thea could keep her baby near her, she saw that. And to lose her would break her heart. This way, her daughter would have a better life, and in the meantime Thea could watch over her. She trusted Mathilde to look after her child. There was no one else. Already, Jacques seemed to think that this new baby was his sister; that Thea had simply been sick and was now recovered.

Together, Mathilde and Thea held a simple and secret burial for Mathilde's daughter, laying her to rest in a wicker Moses basket one evening after Jacques had gone to bed, and burying her under the magnolia tree where Mathilde often liked to sit and watch the sea.

Later that day, Thea had cradled her daughter and gazed into the blue eyes so like Jez's. 'Can I name her?'

Mathilde stared back at her. She looked haunted and scared. 'Yes.'

Thea kissed her baby's head. A tear fell on the soft down, the fontanelle. 'Élodie,' she said. 'I will call her Élodie.'

★

425

'Maman, you have a visitor.'

With difficulty, Thea brought herself back into the present. And there they were: her two daughters, the one she had pushed away but who – thanks to Francine – had returned, and the one she had given away. Colette and Élodie.

CHAPTER 56

Colette

And then to simply slip away . . .

But that was how it happened in the end. Her mother had seemed to be clinging on to the last vestiges of life by some fragile thread, apparently unwilling to entirely let go. The last hours and days had merged into a trance-like time. Colette had spent most of it in that room, sitting beside her, reading poetry to her that she might not even hear, putting water or warm herbal tea to her parched lips. Watching her slowly fade.

The doctor had come by a couple of times and shown mild surprise that her mother was still with them. Étienne had been in too; he had made soup and told Colette that she must eat, that she must keep up her strength, that he would put a 'Temporarily Closed' sign on the door of the flower shop and that she mustn't worry – he was here if she needed anything, anything at all. 'You're not alone,' he told her. Colette was grateful for this, and to Francine who had often come in to keep her company. Élodie had spent time here too, holding

427

Thea's hand, spending these last hours with the mother that they shared.

Had she known she was about to die? Colette suspected so. It was as if she was waiting, and Colette realised now that the person she had been waiting for was Élodie.

Colette wandered across the room to the window, stared out at the harbour. They had taken her away yesterday afternoon. She turned, picked up the diary, still lying on the bedside table. Élodie had told her the story of her birth, her mother's secret, while Colette had stared at her, holding on to every word, half-mesmerised. She had a sister. She was almost unable to take it in, but it did make sense. At last, it all made sense and she was glad.

She still wanted to read the diary, though, longed to capture her mother as the girl she had been. She'd lost so much of her, after all – they both had. Colette hadn't wept when they took her away. She and Élodie had held her mother's hand for the last time, whispered their final goodbyes.

Colette picked up the pillow from the bed and held it close to her, but already there was little of her mother that remained – all she could smell was sickness and pain. And parting, she thought. She flung open the windows. What was needed in here was fresh air. And more flowers. She pulled the sheets from the bed, threw them into a corner of the room, took away the water jug and glass, tipped the water down the kitchen sink. She replaced the volume of Emily Dickinson's poetry she'd been reading to her, next to *Sons and Lovers* in the bookcase in the corner of the room. She'd never known her mother even liked poetry, she knew her so little. Colette held back a tear. There were so many versions of her that were not her mother, after all. The outside world knew a different Thea . . . That was how it was – for daughters, for mothers; different generations, restricted by family roles.

And now the awful practicalities lay ahead – arranging the funeral service, sorting out her mother's things, deciding what to do about the shop – about her own life too. What would she do? Where would she go? For the first time, she understood how Thea had felt when her father died. No wonder she had wanted to throw out his things – *he* was not his things, his things wouldn't bring him back, they would only remind her of what she had lost. She also understood why her mother had gone back to retrieve those few special possessions – at least then she'd have something, and anything was better than nothing at all.

'Colette?'

She looked up. Étienne had come into the house and was standing in the doorway.

'Oh, Étienne.'

He quickly crossed the room, held her in his arms and Colette rested her head against his shoulder and closed her eyes. She didn't think she'd ever been so grateful for human contact.

'I'm so sorry, Colette,' he whispered into her hair.

At last, she drew away. 'You know she's gone?'

He nodded. 'I wanted to come earlier, but I saw Élodie and Francine and . . .'

Colette understood. He wasn't sure. She wasn't sure. They didn't know each other well enough, and yet there was something. She remembered that kiss – it seemed like months ago now. Bad timing, she thought. But he was here.

'Have you eaten?'

'I couldn't.' But even as she said this, Colette knew that she

429

had to get out of this house – if only for a short time. She felt as if it were closing in on her.

Étienne seemed to realise this too. 'We could go to the café round the corner.' He gestured. 'You need a break.'

'OK.'

Étienne led the way outside. Colette grabbed her bag and followed him. As soon as the fresh air hit her she felt hungry. When had she last eaten? Not today.

In the café, Étienne handed her the menu. 'Or there's a special.' He pointed at the blackboard. *Filets de rougets de l'île.* Fresh mullet from the island. Colette nodded. It was a popular catch. Her father had often had a good haul of mullet and her mother had cooked it in a tomato sauce with black olives and *pommes miettes*. She had lost her father so long ago, but now she had lost her mother too. For the first time she felt truly alone. Colette put her head in her hands. Étienne grasped her wrist and she looked up, blinked. 'Sorry.' Though she knew from the expression in those green eyes that he understood, that she didn't need to apologise. He understood more about loss than most.

Étienne ordered the food and they talked quietly. Colette found herself telling him about the old days with her father when she was a girl, about his boat *L'Étoile*, about how she had so often run down to the quay to help him with his catch. She didn't think about what she had found out later, nor how her feelings about him might no longer be quite what they were.

'You two were very close,' he observed. 'When we lose a parent, it shifts us into a different role, and that's hard.'

That was it exactly. 'We grow up,' she said. 'There's no one left we can be a child with.'

The waitress brought their bill and Étienne took hold of her

430

wrist again as she went to pick up her bag to get her purse. 'Please let me.' He went to the counter and she watched as he pulled his wallet from the back pocket of his jeans.

'Thank you.' She couldn't express how grateful she was that he was here. But she guessed that he knew.

They walked out of the café side by side. On the corner, by the bush of white jasmine, Colette turned to him. 'I didn't want to tell you in there,' she said. 'You know what they're like around here for gossiping. Hearts of gold, but . . .' She smiled.

He nodded. 'So, you found out your mother's secret? You don't have to tell me, you know.'

But Colette looked at him and knew that she wanted to. Somehow, he had become the person she wanted to confide in, the person she felt close to. 'Listen,' she said. And she told him how it had been.

'I understand now,' she said. 'When something you love is taken away from you, you hold back in the future, you keep an emotional distance.' And by doing that, her mother had almost lost Colette too. She understood both her mother's loss and her shame. And maybe, back in Colette's childhood when her mother had seemed so far away, that's where she'd been – with the daughter she'd given away all those years ago.

'I know about emotional distance.' Étienne shot her a look she simply couldn't fathom. 'I've always been very good at that.'

They walked down the road until they were standing by the front door of the pink- and lavender-painted house. In a moment, she would have to go back inside and get on with it all.

'So, the two of them pretended your mother's baby was Mathilde's?' Étienne whistled low, almost under his breath. 'And that was why your mother never left Belle-Île.'

'Probably.' Thea had given up her child. But at least she

431

could still see her, even if Élodie never knew the truth. At least she could look out for her, always be around if Élodie should ever need her . . . It was that something-being-better-than-nothing thing again. 'And my father . . .' Her voice broke.

'Let's go inside for a moment.' Étienne looked concerned.

Colette found her key, opened the door and once again they were in the dim hallway of her childhood. The place where she had last laid eyes on her father before he went out, that night of the storm. She shivered. She tensed.

'It's all right, Colette.' Étienne was standing behind her. His hands were on her shoulders. He began to massage them in sure, strong strokes.

Heaven. Colette closed her eyes. She could feel the tension seeping out of her with his touch.

'*Merde*,' he murmured. 'What a revelation.' Étienne's hands had moved to her neck now and were sending all sorts of untimely but delicious feelings to every part of her body.

'My father found out just before he died.' Colette turned around to face him at last and told him the rest. She could only imagine that her father's loyalty was tested to the limits with her mother working all hours, with her holding her secret tightly to her and being unable to open up to him in the way he wanted. That didn't excuse what he did. But it helped Colette to understand. No doubt he quickly realised that his liaison with Mathilde was a terrible mistake. No doubt, he regretted it. But when Mathilde told him the truth . . . He was a traditional man in so many ways, his family true Bellîlois – he must have thought that Thea didn't trust him enough to tell him herself. He must have thought that she'd only married him to stay near Élodie, that Élodie's father was Thea's only true love. And that's what he had been asking her that night, Colette realised. He too must have thought that Élodie's father was Léo Blaise.

'It was hard for them both,' Étienne said. 'You talked to me about forgiveness up on the cliff top. It must have been so difficult for them to forgive themselves.'

'Yes.' Colette was grateful to him for his understanding.

'And, you know . . .' He stroked a hank of hair away from her face, but kept his hand there, warm against her cheek. 'In time, they probably would have talked to each other and worked things out.'

'I think so, yes.' Her father had been angry that night, but he would have got over it, she was sure. They had a strong marriage underneath it all. They loved one another. It was just . . . Étienne was right. There had been too little communication, too many secrets.

Colette took a half-step closer and felt herself once again wrapped in his arms. It wasn't only for comfort or support, she knew that, although that was part of it too. There was more than a spark of longing, and if this had happened at any other time in her life she knew it could easily be fanned into a flame. But her mother had died and soon Étienne would be leaving Belle-Île. So, this was for now, she told herself, as he stroked her hair. Colette felt the tears wet on her face. It was just for now. And she wanted it. She lifted her face for his kiss. Because at this moment, she didn't want him to ever let her go.

CHAPTER 57

Élodie

Élodie and Jacques were walking along the beach. And she had told him everything. The sky was still silver-blue, but the ocean was a pale olive and she thought she could detect an autumn chill in the air. Élodie could sense the seasons shifting.

On the sand, under a curl of seaweed, something glittered. Élodie bent to retrieve the piece of pale-blue sea glass, pitted and mottled from its journey, its edges worn by the sea, curved to the touch.

'Nice one.' Jacques bent over her shoulder to look.

Élodie slipped the sea glass into her linen tote bag. Again, it was just like the old days – but not. So much had happened. Élodie was still trying to get her head around it. Telling Jacques, seeing his reactions, was part of her process of coming to terms with the whole thing. She and Jacques shared so much; she knew him so well, she could almost predict every lift of the eyebrow, every pause for reflection, every sigh.

'*Merde*, Élodie,' he had said when she'd finished. 'That's one hell of a shock.'

434

'I know.'

He took her arm. 'You must have been angry.'

'I was.' She had been angry with both of them. How irresponsible it seemed, how careless to make such a transaction, such a deal. Both of them had acted selfishly. Neither had spared much thought for the child who would grow up living a lie, not knowing the true identity of her parents. And that was so wrong.

'But then I thought about how they must have felt.' She sneaked a sideways look at him. It was so weird – to know that she wasn't related to Jacques at all. 'Who knows what any of us would do when we're placed in a position where we have so little control over our own destiny?'

'Very wise words.' He was teasing, but she sensed a grudging respect.

They sat down on a flat rock as they had done so often and gazed out to sea. She felt the breeze caress her skin, smelt the citrus of his aftershave cutting into the salty scent of rocks, of seaweed, of the ocean. 'A strange friendship when you think about it, between the two of them,' he said, 'Thea and Maman.'

'Yes.' Élodie thought of how little they'd had in common when Thea first arrived on Belle-Île – and how much they had ended up sharing: a friendship, a daughter, a secret.

'How do you feel about Thea?' Jacques asked.

Élodie shrugged. Where to begin? 'I always loved her. I always knew there was a special bond between us.' She sighed. 'I just wish I'd known earlier – when there was more time.' She picked up a piece of driftwood still loaded with moisture from the recent storm that had tucked itself half under the rock. It would dry out in the studio, though; she kept a cage

435

of wood near the log-burner that was destined for greater things than burning.

'And how do you feel about Maman?' Jacques asked her. 'It would break her heart to lose you.'

'She won't lose me.' It was so like Jacques to see Mathilde's point of view. Although he'd loved Thea, although she'd saved his life that time on this very beach, she'd never been the one he tried to impress, the one he adored. No doubt who his mother was, none at all. 'She's still Mama.' She had brought her up, loved her and nurtured her. Élodie was her daughter in every other sense. 'And maybe we'll have a better, more honest relationship now, who knows?'

Élodie dropped the wood into her plastic carrier and pulled the photograph out of her shoulder bag. Colette had given it to her.

'I thought this boy was familiar when Maman first showed it to me,' she'd told Élodie. 'And now I know why.'

Élodie had taken the photograph she handed to her, scrutinised the grainy print for clues. There was a beach and there was a boy – tall, fair, apparently without a care in the world.

'I think this is your father.' Colette looked over her shoulder. 'His name is Jez. I think he's the reason Maman left Cornwall and came here to Belle-Île.'

Élodie had stared at her wide-eyed, then returned her attention to the photograph. She traced the figure of the boy with her fingertip. 'My father,' she whispered. It hardly seemed possible.

'It was taken at Loe Bar in Porthleven,' Colette told her. 'That's where our mother grew up. Maman said that it was her perfect day.'

'Perfect day?' Élodie was trying to work it out.

Colette gave her a sad smile. 'When I was growing up, I always thought Maman was dreaming of someone else, some other place, some other person.'

Élodie put her head to one side, still confused.

'I understand now,' Colette told her. 'She was thinking of you.' And she showed Élodie a passage from their mother's diary.

I look at you and I imagine that I can see something of your father in your eyes. Something of Cornwall and everything else that is gone. I feel as if my heart is breaking. This is what that feels like – I never knew. I've given you up because it seemed like I had to. But whenever I can, I'll hold you. All the time, I'll love you. You'll always be my daughter, my Élodie.

Élodie stared at the words on the page and blinked back a tear. This was what it felt like, to be cherished, to feel special . . .

'Thank you, dear Colette.' She had been so generous. Élodie went to her new sister and took hold of her hands. They had always been strangers and suddenly they were not. It was, she realised, a new beginning in so many ways.

'Perhaps you might go to Cornwall one day,' Colette said. 'It's a lovely place.'

'Perhaps.' *Something of Cornwall and everything else that is gone . . .* There was a possibility he might still live there. Could Élodie dare to try and find him? She wanted to. Especially now that she had heard about Thea's perfect day and read these words in her diary. She so wanted to.

'This is my father.' She showed Jacques the photograph.

'*Merde.*' He whistled. 'You have two new parents.'

'Apparently so.' She leaned towards him. 'It turns out that I'm a different person than the one I thought I was.' And she looked back at the sea as if she might find out something there. 'It's so confusing. Who am I really?'

Jacques put his arm around her shoulders. 'The same person you've always been, silly.' He pulled her closer. 'This doesn't change who you are.'

'Mmm.' Once again, Élodie examined the picture. Her father looked a bit of a wild boy, and she liked that. Had Thea loved him? If it had been her perfect day, then she supposed that she had. What had happened? Why had she left him? And more to the point, did her father even know about Élodie, the daughter he had over on Belle-Île? Élodie hoped that when she read it in full, Thea's diary would help her find out so much more. Colette had promised that she could read it. They both needed as many answers as they could find, she'd said, and she was sure that now the secret was out, Thea would have wanted it that way.

'You look a bit like him,' Jacques said thoughtfully. 'Angles and cheekbones and a little bit drifty.'

Élodie laughed. What would Mathilde and Thea have done, she wondered, if Élodie had turned out to look like Thea? That would have made things hard to explain.

'So, what are you going to do?' Jacques asked as they got to their feet and continued beach-combing.

'What makes you think I'm going to do anything?' she countered.

'I can see it in your face – it's your decision-making look.'

Élodie laughed. 'I'm busy at the moment,' she said. Perhaps Jacques did know her as well as she knew him. Perhaps they would always be part of one another, despite everything.

'For the exhibition, you mean?'

Élodie spotted a red-billed chough, *un crave à bec rouge*, soaring above them, wings spread – identifiable from that long curved beak of his and the sonorous cry that woke her sometimes in the mornings. And there in front of them, *un pipit maritime* scampered over the golden lichen on the rocks at the foot of the cliff, its yellow, grey and brown streaked plumage making it almost invisible until it moved. Should she sculpt either of these for her exhibition? Armand Dubois had seemed rather taken with her driftwood heron.

'Yes.' Élodie thought of all these things she wanted to make, all her plans, the excitement she'd felt at meeting Armand over in Auray, talking with him, hearing his ideas for the exhibition. Thea's death, Mathilde's confession . . . All this had almost put her work in the shade. But not quite. That was important to her too; she wasn't about to let it go. 'I'll concentrate on that for a while,' she said.

'Which means you'll become a hermit,' he complained.

'Of necessity, yes.' She squeezed his arm. 'Though I might be persuaded to come out of hibernation for one of your omelettes or Mama's onion soup.'

He gave a mock bow. 'We exist only to serve you.'

'*Merci, mon frère.*' She laughed. 'But seriously, Jacques, I have to do this, it's important to me.'

'I know.' He clambered over the rock ahead and turned to give her a hand. 'And then?' he asked.

Élodie looked out towards the distant pale-grey horizon. 'And then I might go over to England for a while.' There, she'd said it. She was English through her birth parents after all. She might go alone – or she might even ask Colette to go with her. Élodie had always felt a strange pull towards the girl who reminded her so much of Thea and she felt sure that from all this . . . Well, at least a tentative friendship was already beginning.

'England. You?' He stared at her.

'Why not?'

'Because you hardly ever leave the island, that's why not.'

'All the more reason to do it now, then.' Élodie's voice was sharper than she intended. She softened. 'I won't be there for ever, Jacques,' she said. 'But would you look after Mama while I'm gone?'

'What do you expect me to do?' He sounded cross. She was clipping his wings, she realised. 'I've got my own life to live too, you know.'

Hadn't he always? 'You don't have to live here,' she said. Together they followed the rocky path back up to the cliff top. Élodie's bag was almost full and she needed to get back to work. She needed, she realised, to make plans, to organise her life, to move on.

'Very kind of you, I'm sure.'

Élodie ignored the sarcasm. Jacques belonged on the mainland. He needed to be able to see his children whenever he wanted to; he needed to be there for them. 'I just want you to be around for her while I'm gone. Phone her up, come over to visit once in a while, bring the kids. Otherwise . . .' Otherwise, she wouldn't be able to go.

They reached the top of the cliff. He was watching her intently. 'I suppose you want to find him?'

'I'd like to try.' Élodie started making her way along the sandy path that led back to the studio and the Old Lighthouse. Jacques fell into step beside her, though she had the feeling that he would have stayed on the beach, given the choice. They had come further than she'd realised — as always. Élodie looked at the Old Lighthouse, reassuringly solid in the distance. She knew nothing about her biological father. All she had was an old photo of a figure on a beach. But people had long memories and Cornwall was a relatively small place. Who knew? It was worth a try.

Jacques looked sulky. 'It seems as if you're moving away from us,' he said. 'It's rather selfish of you, Élodie. How will Maman manage without you?'

Élodie stopped walking. 'You moved away, Jacques,' she pointed out. 'You moved away and hardly came back and who looked after Mama? Who stuck around to make sure Papa didn't lose his temper too badly with her one day? Me, that's who.'

'I had good reason.' Jacques glared at her. 'She could have told him to leave years before she did.'

'He was her husband.' Élodie couldn't believe he still didn't get it. 'She loved him, Jacques. And you . . . You . . .' Above them, a gull shouted into the wind. She could hear the sea, the tide as it wheeled into shore, as it exploded against the rocks, as it hissed on to the sand. Inexorable, never-ending.

'What about me?' He grabbed her arm, twisting her round to face him. 'Now we're coming to it, eh? Now we'll find out what you really think.'

Élodie knew that Jacques was volatile. But when he was like this . . . He reminded her of Léo a bit too much for comfort. 'You're selfish, Jacques.' She remembered the desolation she had felt when her big brother had left Belle-Île. She remembered all the times she had wandered these beaches alone.

He stared at her.

'You do everything you do for yourself, not for me or Mama

or even Karine and the kids. You think you can take up with people and then drop them when it suits you. You visit and you rush around stirring everything up and then you leave and someone else has to pick up the pieces. You haven't grown up. You don't seem to have any sense of duty or responsibility . . .' Élodie realised that her breathing was shallow – that she'd said so much, and now she couldn't stop. She hardly even knew where it had all come from. 'You always just assumed I would stay here and look after Mama,' she threw into the wind. 'And I did. But now I want to do something for me for a change, that's all.'

Jacques carried on walking, fast, so that he was leaving her behind. 'So, when I was your brother you loved me and now that I'm not, you think you have the right to tell me how to lead my life, is that it?' he snapped.

'No, Jacques.' Élodie watched him walk away. She saw the anger in the set of his shoulders but she couldn't take any of it back, not now. God knows, she didn't have to explain to him how she'd always felt about her big brother, how she had worshipped him as a little girl, how she had followed him around, been grateful for every bit of attention he paid her. She didn't have to remind him of how inseparable they had become, the long walks they had taken over the cliffs and beaches, the art they had created together, the unhappiness they had shared as they both railed against Léo, as they escaped from a house that had become a place of misery and domination.

'I still love you,' she yelled into the wind. He was her brother and always would be.

Jacques turned around. He had heard her. 'And I love you,' he yelled back. 'Even though you've disowned me.'

Élodie laughed. Perhaps he wasn't so much like Léo after all.

'Come on then.' He beckoned her towards him. 'Race you back to the Old Lighthouse. Last one there makes dinner.'

'Unfair!' she shouted. 'I'm carrying this heavy bag.'

'Let me take it.' He met her halfway, grabbed the bag of treasure and hefted it over his shoulder. 'Let no one say I can't handle a bit of baggage.'

Élodie shook her head in mock despair. He had given her so much, sometimes without meaning to. Because of Jacques she had now found the strength to go out into the world, and take her art with her. The world was beckoning to Élodie; it held a promise that she wanted to hear. Because of Jacques, she would be able to go to Cornwall too. He would help her. She could break free.

CHAPTER 58

Colette

Colette began to dismantle the window display that she had arranged with such care when she'd first started looking after the flower shop. Everything was different now. She had got involved with the business, started making floral arrangements, explored new ideas about how she could grow and use flowers and plants for healing . . . But now, her mother was gone and this part of her life was over.

With Francine and Élodie's help, Colette had organised the funeral and said her final goodbyes. She had gone through her mother's possessions – many things she gave to Francine who wasn't well off and hopefully could make use of them, others she gave to a charity shop and the rest she reluctantly consigned to the bin. Francine and Colette hadn't begun well, but by now they'd forged a bond of mutual respect, and she knew how much Francine had cared about her mother. As for the rest, there wasn't much she would keep – Colette wanted to travel light. Two exceptions were her mother's gold watch and her father's compass. She would wear the watch, and she might need the compass to show her the way.

She had also once again gone through her mother's financial affairs. She knew how much money she'd had and what assets there were; the shop had provided a small income, enough for her to live on. The house and the shop were paid for long ago, and God knows, thought Colette, her mother had earned them. And she had read the diary.

It had been a moving journey, reading the words written by the seventeen-year-old Thea, putting herself in her shoes, getting to understand why she had first left Cornwall, what she had hoped to find. More upsetting was the story of how Élodie had come into the world and how her mother had let her go. Colette understood so much more now. It was as if she was getting to know her mother for the first time, as if she now had a brand-new version of the past.

She had also spent some time with Élodie, though Élodie had confided that she needed to be working towards her exhibition and that this was taking up most of her energies for the moment. Colette sensed that Élodie's work was helping her, too; providing a focal point for her attention, distracting her from other thoughts and feelings closer to home. Colette was pleased for her, glad to see a certain light in her blue eyes when she spoke of the Modus Gallery in Auray, the summer exhibition, Armand Dubois . . .

Colette fetched a broom from the cupboard and began to sweep away the debris of the window display. It made her feel sad, but this had been her mother's work, not hers. It was time to let it go.

Étienne sauntered through the door of the flower shop much as he had that first day. 'Hey, Colette,' he said.

'Hello. I thought you were writing this morning.' It had only been two weeks since that kiss in the hall on the day Colette had confided in him. Since then, they had seen each other every day. They had walked, talked and grown closer. They had kissed, oh many times they had kissed and Colette had ached to take it further, but something had stopped her and Étienne seemed to be following her lead. Colette knew what it was. She had strong feelings for him but she felt vulnerable. They were in the same place now but they wouldn't be here for long – and what then? He had said himself that he was good at emotional distance.

'I have been writing.' He frowned as he watched her clearing, winding things down. 'You're closing the shop?'

'I have to, Étienne.' Half the flower buckets were empty; she'd already given away most of the pot plants. Élodie's horse with the herbs in the panniers was still standing outside, but Élodie had agreed to take him back. It would be a nice reminder for her – of their mother, of the flower shop she'd loved. Colette shrugged.

'But you love it.' He was staring at her. What did he think – that she was going to stay here on the island and become her mother?

'Yes, I do.' She'd loved having flowers back in her life. For the first time something had felt so right. But . . .

'But you're going to sell it?' He still seemed confused.

'My life isn't here, Étienne.' And this was why, she thought. Why she hadn't let him get too close.

'But—'

'Besides, I've had an offer.' Colette lifted her head and looked at him. Philippe Lemaire had come to see her again last week. He had upped his offer and she couldn't see how

446

she could refuse. Who else would be interested in the flower shop? 'Some guy wants to turn the place into a music bar,' she told him.

'A music bar?' Étienne turned to look out of the open doorway. '*Merde*.'

Colette couldn't agree more. But Étienne wouldn't be here and neither would she. What did they care? Only . . . she could smell the scent of oregano and thyme drifting through the air from Élodie's horse and, truth be told, she could barely face the idea. 'He came to see me weeks ago,' she said.

'You didn't mention it.'

Now it was Colette's turn to be surprised. 'No.' Why would she?

'You thought it had nothing to do with me.' He said the words slowly.

She shrugged. 'I suppose. But it was more that I didn't think I'd accept his offer.'

'But now you will.'

'What else can I do?' Colette sighed. Even now, she still wasn't sure. 'He doesn't even live here. I've got no idea how he knew that my mother was . . .' Her voice tailed off. She'd had a thought.

'I thought you'd stay on the island.' Étienne turned away from her. His hands were stuck in his pockets. It was funny, she thought, but after all their walking and talking, all their getting to know one another, he seemed now to have changed back into the moody and enigmatic stranger who had first walked into this flower shop – and she had no idea what he was thinking.

'No.' She would always love Belle-Île and a part of her would always remain here, bound up with her childhood and her memories. But she didn't want to live here – not full time. 'I thought I might. But I've grown up. Grown away.' What was there for Colette here on the island? Her parents' ashes? A stormy past? She was a daughter of Belle-Île, but daughters leave, go back, leave again. She was glad that she'd returned, learnt about her mother's life, spent this time with her and got to know her all over again. She wouldn't have given that up for anything. But she wasn't trapped here like her mother had been trapped. She could leave Belle-Île.

He nodded. But Colette sensed his disappointment. Maybe that was why he wouldn't look at her. She moved closer until she was standing beside him and she tucked her hand into his arm. She had the feeling that despite his protestations to the contrary and despite everything that had happened here, Étienne had strong feelings for the place too. 'How about you?'

At last he smiled. 'I've finished what I needed to do.'

'You've written the story?' Colette pulled him round to face her. 'Why didn't you say?'

He shrugged. 'It's done.'

'And?' She searched his face. Had he found the forgiveness he was looking for?

'And so, I was wondering . . .' He bent slightly to kiss her on the mouth.

Oh, Étienne. The kiss tasted bitter-sweet to Colette. So much hope, but in the end, all she could see was their imminent parting.

'Will you come there with me one last time?' he asked her.

'Of course.' Colette pushed the thought away. There were a few more days, surely? But he had finished what he had come here to do, so perhaps this would be the last time after all? 'Shall we take those flowers?' With everything that had happened,

448

Colette had almost forgotten about that promise to lay flowers on the rocks for Gabriel.

They selected five of the brightest gerberas left in the shop.

'Give me ten minutes, will you?' she asked Étienne. 'There's something I have to do.'

'I'll wait for you down in the harbour,' he said.

Colette flipped through the paperwork by the till, looking for his business card. She found it at last and a piece of paper fluttered to the floor. She glanced at it. Béatrice Charron. She should phone that kind woman, let her know about her mother's death. Colette felt terrible suddenly – she should have told her before the funeral, of course.

After the phone call to Béatrice, she rang Philippe Lemaire. 'Could you tell me some more about what you intend to do with this place?' she asked. 'For example, is it to be a music bar? Or was it more of a night club that you had in mind?'

After the calls, she found Étienne down by the harbour and they made their way along to the path that led up the cliff. It was a familiar journey, although now there was a definite chill in the air. Fewer people sat in the harbour and outside the Hôtel du Phare, and those out walking along the promenade wore jackets and fleeces zipped up against the wind. Colette spotted Henri by the crêperie talking to Anneliese and she waved to them both.

The entire village had come to pay their respects to her mother; Colette had been moved. Everyone had asked her the same thing as Henri. 'What will you do now, *ma petite*? Will you stay? Will you go?'

'Nothing I can do will ever make it right,' Étienne said when they reached Pointe du Cardinal. It looked even bleaker at this

449

time of year; the wind was tearing at the sparse undergrowth and rough grass, the sea crashing on to the rocks with venom. But his voice was matter-of-fact, no longer angry, she noticed. He seemed lighter somehow, and she hoped that at last he was managing to come to terms with what had happened all those years ago. 'Nothing will bring Gabriel back or give him the life he should have had.'

'No, it won't.' Colette looked down. Almost against her will, she imagined running, jumping, falling . . . She felt the magnetic pull of vertigo, sensed the navy sea pulling closer, enveloping her in its tidal rush. She shuddered.

'Colette.' He spoke sharply as he pulled her back from the edge.

'Sorry.'

Étienne hung on to her arm. He took her hand in his and held it tight – as if she were precious, she thought. 'But writing about it was cathartic.' He gazed out to sea. 'It released me from what's been pressing into my head for as long as I can remember.'

The burden of guilt, Colette thought – the heaviest burden of all.

'I realised that everyone makes mistakes. It's just that mine was a bloody big one.'

'But not only *your* mistake.' Colette squeezed his hand in return. If Yann hadn't goaded them, if Gabriel hadn't run . . .

He blinked, and Colette looked up at him to see there were tears in his eyes. 'And I realised I have two choices.'

'Two choices?'

'I have to either move on with my life and put it in the past, or . . .'

'Or?'

'Or go crazy.' He grinned, but there was no humour in it.

'I hope you've decided to go for option one,' Colette said. 'Going crazy won't help anyone.'

He laughed. 'Practical Colette.'

She pulled a face.

'What?'

She shrugged. 'It's not exactly the best compliment.'

'But it's only part of your charm.' He said the words lightly but she felt herself flush.

'Shall we lay the flowers down?' she asked.

'Yes.' He knelt at the cliff edge. Very gently, he laid them on the ledge jutting out from the cliff face, the rock that she knew they had jumped from when they'd done their daredevil tombstoning. His lips moved in a silent apology or a prayer; his message to Gabriel.

Colette stood beside him. Like Étienne, she closed her eyes. Like him, she whispered a prayer – for her mother, for her father, for Gabriel, the young boy whose life had been snatched from him.

After several more minutes, Étienne got stiffly to his feet and they started back along the cliff path, walking in an easy rhythm, arms linked. 'So, if you're not staying here, Colette,' he said, 'where exactly are you going?'

'I haven't decided.' Perhaps she should stick a pin into a map and let Fate choose. Colette wondered who would visit her. Étienne? She glanced across at him but couldn't read his expression. Élodie? Would Élodie visit her wherever she decided to go? Colette thought that she would. She had the feeling that Élodie would be venturing on to the mainland much more after her summer show. She would go to Cornwall too – in fact, they had made tentative plans to make the journey together.

Colette was looking forward to that. They might not find Élodie's father, but it would certainly be a pilgrimage, a nod to their mother's early years, a nod to her first love and that perfect day of hers. Colette didn't think that Élodie would ever leave Belle-Île for good, but who knew? She did seem rather taken with Armand Dubois . . .

'And your mother's shop . . .' Étienne tailed off. He was watching her.

'. . . can never be a night club,' she said. How could it? Her mother would turn in her grave. It might not have been Mark who talked to Philippe Lemaire on the quay at Quiberon or even over morning coffee in Sauzon before Lemaire's first visit. But it would have been in his interests to do so. If it *was* Mark, no doubt it was a chance meeting, but he was an estate agent and he wanted his girlfriend back. Why not help things along? Why not advise Lemaire to avoid the words 'night club' so that Colette might look on his offer more kindly?

'What did he look like – this little bird that told you about the flower shop being for sale?' she'd asked him. 'He was English,' Lemaire had admitted at last. 'Tall, dark hair, a visitor not a resident.' So perhaps Mark had been trying to control her life even more than she'd given him credit for. Or had he seen her mother's illness as a potential business opportunity? It sickened Colette to the core.

'So, you'll say *non* to Monsieur Lemaire?' Étienne didn't seem too surprised.

'I will.' As her mother had always said, they needed to have a flower shop in Sauzon. She'd talked to Béatrice Charron who had promised to speak to her daughter's boyfriend, the horti-culturalist. Maybe there was someone else besides her mother whose dream was to open a flower shop on Belle-Île. Colette would wait for that person. She'd keep it on the market until they came along. She owed that much to her mother, at least.

'When I think of you, Colette . . .' Étienne said.

'Yes?' She tried not to feel hopeful.

'I think of you among flowers.'

'That's nice.' She sneaked a look at him. 'And that's one thing I do know. I want to carry on working with them.' She felt almost shy now as she explained a bit more about it. Flowers for healing, meadow flowers, growing wild flowers. 'It's my pathway. My mother was right.' Colette couldn't believe she hadn't realised earlier. She had fallen back in love with flowers. 'It's what I want to do.'

Halfway back, as the path wound towards the sea, where there was an unexpected viewpoint and the autumn sun seemed to spool like a ring of liquid gold into the water below, Étienne halted.

Colette turned to face him. Over the past weeks, he had become increasingly familiar and dear. Belle-Île had brought them together and it would be hard to lose him, she knew. But . . .

'I've never been good with romance,' he said. He tore his fingers through his hair.

Colette smiled as she looked into those green eyes. 'It's a whole new genre,' she said.

His lips twitched with laughter. 'Come here,' he growled.

Something about this kiss was different from the others they'd shared. It was stronger, more demanding, it made her ache inside. Colette knew that she wanted more. Who cared that tomorrow he might be leaving? Who cared that she was vulnerable? This man was here now and she wanted him.

'It's early days,' he said when they finally broke apart and stood staring at one another.

453

'It is.' But that kiss hadn't felt like early days. It had felt like a promise of much more to come. 'Étienne,' she whispered into the sea breeze. 'I think that you and I—'

'Let's get back.' He slung an arm around her shoulder and they continued along the cliff-top path, still side by side but even closer now.

'OK.' She liked the feeling. She liked it a lot.

He glanced across at her. 'You know, Colette, I almost thought that if you were going to stick around here, then I might give the place another try myself.'

'You *almost* thought . . .?' Her mind spun.

'But now I'm thinking . . .'

'Yes?' She couldn't help smiling as they passed by the cove where he had seen her skinny-dipping that day.

'Locmariaquer is a nice place,' he said conversationally.

'Mm.' She was noncommittal. What was he saying, exactly? Was this his way of telling her that he was leaving today?

'And it's close to Belle-Île,' he said. 'So, we could visit any time.'

She turned to look at him. His fair hair was greeny-gold in the yellow evening sun. 'We?'

He shrugged. 'You could give it a try,' he said. 'We could give it a try. If you want.'

The thought of this warmed Colette from the top of her head to the tips of her toes. Give it a try, she thought. Why not? She turned to him, and at the same second he turned too. 'What about that emotional distance you're so good at?' she asked.

'Ah.' He tilted her chin so that she was looking straight into those amazing eyes. 'It seems I'm not as good at it as I used to be.' He grinned. 'These things happen. *C'est la vie.*'

'Hopefully you'll survive.'

'Hmm.' He smoothed her hair away from her face, but the wind blew it straight back again and they both laughed.

'And guess what?' he said. 'In Locmariaquer, at this precise moment in time . . .'

'Yes?' She smiled. His hair was not only greeny-gold but also sticking up at all angles. It was a good look. She reached up and trailed her fingers through it.

'. . . we don't even have a flower shop. So . . .?'

'That's interesting,' she said. It made her want to kiss him again, and so she did. 'That's very interesting indeed.'

ACKNOWLEDGEMENTS

Massive thanks go to the lovely team at Quercus who once again have helped make it happen in so many varied and clever ways . . . My truly wonderful editor Stef Bierwerth – the most perceptive and supportive editor a writer could hope for, and all the rest of you gorgeous people at Quercus working so hard on my behalf and providing so much support: Jon Butler, Hannah Robinson-Cowie, Rachel Neely, Cassie Browne, Laura McKerrell, Jeska Lyons, Frances Doyle, Katie Day, David Murphy and Rebecca Bader.

Thanks to the team at MBA. I adore my agent Laura Longrigg more than I can say; thanks, Laura for working tirelessly on my behalf, for providing a listening ear whenever needed and for your equally sharp editing eye. Your tact and diplomacy are second to none. Thanks also to the great team at Midas PR who have helped me promote the books – especially Sophie Ransom who possesses endless enthusiasm and so many fabulous ideas (Sophie and I love our meetings in Salisbury) but also Rebekah Humphries and Alice Geary for the work they have put in during the past year. Each book is without doubt a team effort.

This novel came into being on my annual writing holiday in

Andalucia in 2016. I plotted it and planned it (in my time off!) and somehow it took shape in the sunshine under the carob tree at the stunning Finca el Cerrillo. So thanks go to Gordon, Sue, Alison, David, Christine and all the team there who help make these things happen. We have just visited for the seventh time and we're already looking forward to next year.

Belle-Île is a fascinating island to visit and I thoroughly recommend it. I also enjoyed my time exploring Locmariaquer in Southern Brittany and following in my character Étienne's footsteps. Porthleven too is dear to my heart. As usual I read lots of books to help me in my research for *Her Mother's Secret*. Of particular help to me were: *Porthleven in years gone by – shops and businesses* by Tony Treglown, *A Gift from Brittany* by Marjorie Price (Gotham Books), *The Oysters of Locmariaquer* by Eleanor Clark (Secker & Warburg) and *100 Edible & Healing Flowers* by Margaret Roberts (Struick Nature). The photographer Pierre Jamet took many stunning photographs of holidaymakers on Belle-Île between 1930 and 1960 and these (some of which were made into posters and had been pasted around the streets of Le Palais when we visited) were hugely inspirational. The book of the photographs (published by Hengoun Editions) is a fabulous souvenir.

I'd also like to thank Pauline and Alan Cory for inviting us to stay in their house in Brittany during our trip and for suggesting relevant itineraries and research books. I have done my best to remain faithful to Porthleven, Locmariaquer, Belle-Île-en-Mer and all their inhabitants – past and present; if I have failed in any way then I apologise unreservedly. All characters are totally fictitious and although the places are real enough, I have certainly used some artistic license to make them fit my story. Any mistakes are certainly my own.

I know all this thanks stuff can get a bit much but I also have to thank my incredibly supportive family and friends – especially Wendy Tomlins and June Tate who are quite simply the best, my mother Daphne Squires, my beautiful daughters Alexa and Ana and my son Luke, daughter-in-law Agata and my gorgeous fast-growing grandson Tristan. He's only two but maybe one day he'll read this book, who knows?

Writers are a wonderful and supportive bunch. Bloggers are also a wonderful and supportive bunch. There are too many to name but you are all special . . . Thank you.

Last but never least, my husband Grey – camper-van driver, photographer, sounding-board, fellow plot-stormer, and travelling and research companion extraordinaire.